DRAMATIC. CONTROVERSIAL. EXPLOSIVELY REAL.

Praise for
DAYS OF FIRE by John F. Mullins . . .

"As only a veteran operations man can, John Mullins knows and understands how the Special Forces and the Central Intelligence Agency came together in the controversial Phoenix Program during the Vietnam War. Articulate and forceful, Mullins gives the readers the facts."

—MARK BERENT, bestselling author of
ROLLING THUNDER, STEEL TIGER and
PHANTOM LEADER

"If you want to fully understand America's top secret war in Vietnam, read *DAYS OF FIRE*. Mullins writes with the authority and conviction that only someone who's been there can. The combat is real, the insider information probably still classified. Mullins brings the action to the reader, up close and personal."

—J.C. POLLOCK, author of *PAYBACK*
and *MISSION M.I.A.*

DAYS OF FIRE

John F. Mullins is a former U.S. Special Forces Major. His novel is a stunning work of military intrigue that blends fact and fiction in a breathtaking story that captures the reality of Vietnam.

DAYS OF FIRE

JOHN F. MULLINS

DIAMOND BOOKS, NEW YORK

DAYS OF FIRE

A Diamond Book / published by arrangement with
the author

PRINTING HISTORY
Diamond edition / September 1991

ISBN: 1-55773-621-9

Diamond Books are published by The Berkley Publishing
Group, 200 Madison Avenue, New York, New York 10016.
The name "DIAMOND" and its logo are trademarks
belonging to Charter Communications, Inc.

PRINTED IN THE UNITED STATES OF AMERICA

10 9 8 7 6 5 4 3 2 1

CHAPTER 1

SPECIAL Forces Lieutenant Jim Carmichael was moving through the elephant grass, getting cut to pieces. God, he hated the stuff. The leaves cut like tiny razors. Every exposed part of his body was covered by slashes. The individual cuts leaked only a little blood, but there were so many of them it looked as if he were sweating red. He wore sleeves rolled down and gloves stolen from an air force pilot. But still the stuff got through.

He was moving far faster than he liked. No time to scout an area for danger before moving the bulk of the company into it. The best he could do was keep a point ahead fifty meters. It was impossible to send out flankers in the dense grass; too much chance of loss of contact, and loss of contact carried with it the probability of getting into a firefight with your own people.

Still, he had little choice. The decision makers had decreed that his company be on the day's objective by a certain time, and the artillery had the nasty habit of shelling every place except where you were expected to be. He'd had the unpleasant experience of being on the receiving end of "friendly fire" before. Friendly fire isn't friendly.

The handset clipped to his harness hissed. "Skipjack one, this is Sharkfin six, over." Shit! he thought. What now? He answered the call.

"What's your situation, Skipjack?"

"Continuing to move on Objective Sigma. Expect to reach it in approximately three-zero, over."

"You were supposed to be there by now. You'd better move your ass if you expect to get there before dark. Out."

Carmichael wished helicopters had never been invented. Sure they were great for Medevacs; he'd been glad enough for them when he was wounded. Sometimes, when used properly, they provided good fire support. But they also allowed field grade officers who should have been sitting far in the rear to fly overhead and harass the troops. Most had never had to walk the terrain, had no idea how long it took to move tactically from one point to another, and so made arbitrary decisions and expected the troops to carry them out. This was the first war in which tactical decisions were not being made by the junior leaders on the ground, and the results showed.

He was damned if he'd try to move any faster. He cursed the fool who had dreamed up this operation in the first place. The lightly armed Montagnards, the hill people recruited, trained and led by the Special Forces, were no match for the numerically superior North Vietnamese forces who occupied the area. The only way to survive was to hide, beat the NVA at his own game, hit him when he wasn't expecting it. That couldn't be done if you constantly advertised your position with a chopper flying overhead.

The first night after insertion he'd heard over the radio the results of what happened when the NVA found you. The area the task force was supposedly surrounding had been divided into four equal sectors. Four companies had been inserted, his in the northwest sector. The company in the southeast had been hit shortly after insertion and within two hours had been effectively destroyed as a fighting force. Forty Montagnards and two Americans were killed and almost everyone else wounded. One of the Americans had been an old friend, one with whom he had served in the first tour. He listened on the radio as his friend died, bleeding to death as the High Command apologetically told the surviving American that they couldn't get anyone out, the L.Z. was just too hot.

His company, on the other hand, had been very lucky. Apparently most of the NVA had been concentrated in the southern sectors. They only came across trail watchers, whom they promptly killed, and the occasional courier. The couriers they attempted to capture, with a notable lack of success. The Montagnards really couldn't understand why the Americans were so eager to take a Vietnamese alive, and had a tendency to shoot them on sight. Northern Vietnamese, Southern, it didn't matter to them; but they got in trouble with the Americans for shooting the Southerners.

The documents taken from the dead couriers greatly troubled him. They indicated that the NVA was not suffering much from the almost incessant aerial and artillery bombardment. It was a big jungle and there were lots of places to hide. One report in particular worried him. It indicated that, while many of the Yellow Star battalions had already broken through the so-called cordon, there was still quite a large force somewhere to the north of his company.

He supposed the present situation was his own fault. He made the mistake of sharing the information with Major Walters, the ''B'' Team commander, who became quite excited at the prospect of his people finding the enemy and fixing them in place, supposedly the purpose of the operation. The major pushed the company to move ever faster, insisting that they catch the enemy before he got away. Never mind that at this speed they would probably stumble upon him. It was always easier to make decisions like that when you were flying overhead. You didn't have to move through the stuff.

Up ahead Jim saw one of the infrequent bare patches of ground upon which even the elephant grass refused to grow. He'd noticed several of them while flying over on the way to the insert, four days ago. The grass was smooth and green, rippling gently in the breeze. It gave no hint from above that it was ten or twelve feet high. Then holes like this one, looking like acne scars. The 'Yards thought such places were haunted because people had died there. He wasn't so superstitious. Probably patches of overly alkaline soil, he thought.

He moved to the edge of the open area and signaled the company to halt. Up ahead he could finally see the objective. It looked ominous, a long finger of land poked obscenely into the valley, its top swathed in the eternal mist of the jungle. The elephant grass covered it halfway up, then disappeared abruptly into a wall of green. The trees rose two hundred feet into the sky, their canopies so tightly interwoven that little light could penetrate. Inside, he knew, would be a second canopy a hundred feet off the ground, this one composed of vines and creepers needing little light to survive, drawing their sustenance from the living flesh of the trees which shielded them from the sun. At ground level would be the ferns and thorn vines growing in an eternal twilight, intertwined around the giant fungi that when disturbed gave off a graveyard stench.

He observed it for a few minutes, trying to figure a good way to approach. It didn't look promising. For all he knew, an entire battalion could be hiding up there. If he'd had a choice, he would have bypassed it, spending a couple of days working around it and coming up from the rear. He didn't have a choice.

He walked back to where Sergeant First Class Zack Osborne and the second platoon waited. Zack's homely face crinkled into a smile as he saw Jim approach.

" 'Bout fuckin' time you called a break, Trung Ui," Zack said. "I figgered you was runnin' a road race, fast as we was movin'. You sniff out a whorehouse up there?"

"Nah," Jim answered, dropping to the ground beside the burly sergeant. "A shitstorm, maybe, but no whorehouse. You know I can't smell as good as you anyway. I don't have the equipment."

Zack Osborne's outsized nose had been for years a matter of discussion in the Special Forces. Some said that it was larger than his male member. Others said it took the place of it. Of course, nobody wanted him to be self-conscious about it. So they called him Hosenose.

Zack rubbed his most outstanding appendage with care. "We don't get out of this fuckin' grass, this sonofabitch is gonna be cut clear off. I'm about ready for this Chinese clusterfuck to be over. We ain't lost, are we? I mean, you bein' a loo-tenant and all!"

All Special Forces NCOs believed it was foolish to trust any officer below the rank of captain with a map and compass. Even if that officer, as was presently the case, was a first lieutenant who had been a Special Forces NCO for several years.

"Glad you've got so much faith," Jim said sourly. "Now, if we can cut the bullshit, let's see what we can do about making this next move as painless as possible." He pulled a worn map from the side pocket of his tiger-stripe pants and spread it on the ground.

"The way I see it," he said, "is that this finger would make a hell of a good fortified position: fields of fire in three directions, an escape route to the rear. Too damned narrow for us to hit head-on; couldn't deploy most of the company. How about if you take second and third platoons around to the right and come up just about right here?'' He pointed to the spot with a twig. "If they're up there, and I think they are, it'll make them have to fight in two directions. What do you think?''

Zack judiciously studied the map, taking his time before replying. Jim waited patiently. Had this been a conventional outfit, he would simply have given the order and have expected it to be obeyed. Of course, Jim reflected, if it had been a conventional outfit, he could have had no confidence that the order would have been followed, or that the subordinate would have been able to find his way to the designated point, or that he would have attacked once he got there. In Special Forces the officer didn't as much lead as suggest. And the NCOs were perfectly justified in rejecting the suggestion if, in their professional opinion, it was a bad one.

Zack finally grunted. "Looks okay to me. Gonna take me about an hour to get around there. You gonna be able to hold off shithead-in-the-sky that long?''

Jim grinned, cracking the encrusted salty dirt on his cheeks. "I think I feel some radio problems coming on. Probably won't be able to hear a thing until you call to tell me you're in place.''

He got up, muscles complaining from the movement. Must be getting old, he thought. He was twenty-six.

At the front of the column the Montagnard company commander awaited him. Captain Buon was looking at the objective. "Beaucoup V.C.?'' he asked.

"Yes, I think maybe beaucoup V.C.,'' Jim said. "Better get your people ready.'' He explained his tactics.

The captain smiled widely, showing his prized gold teeth with colored porcelain inlays. "We kill V.C., number ten goddamn sumbitch.'' He chattered in Rhade to the runners, who set off down the column.

Jim thought that the captain's previous advisors had taught him well, both in tactics and in language. No one had to teach the little Montagnard bravery. It was his fifth operation with Captain Buon and he thought he was one of the finest soldiers he had ever known. Each year the captain survived, he added another gold tooth, achieving much status in his tribe. He loved fighting, the Americans and his tribe, in that order. Whom he fought made little difference. He would dearly have loved to kill some of the Vietnamese soldiers who had for so long oppressed his people. But the Americans insisted that he not do so, and out of respect for them he confined his killing to those of the North. They were Vietnamese too, and while they had a shorter history of killing his people, they had made up for lost time. His father and mother had been among those reduced to blackened husks in the village of Ban Tleng when the NVA, irritated because the villagers couldn't see the benefits of a socialist future, brought in flamethrowers.

Jim sat back-to-back with Captain Buon, checking his rifle. He liked the newly issued M-16, but paid heed to the old saying "Remember that your weapon was made by the lowest bidder." All along the column the indigenous soldiers, small in stature but great in heart, were doing the same. First they ejected the round carried in the chamber and inserted a fresh one. Blew all specks of dust from the action, gave it a little extra squirt of gun grease. They opened the front left magazine pouch, checked the strips of tape affixed to the magazine to provide a grasping point to make sure the moisture hadn't made them give way. They adjusted the red and green scarves, marking them as the 1st CIDG Company, Minh Long Strike Force, so that they could be clearly seen. The scarves were a source of pride as well as a means of quick identification in the heat of a firefight.

Jim called Sergeant First Class Lally to the front. Lally was the replacement for the former heavy-weapons man, who had been killed the month before. Another friend. This was Lally's first operation with the company.

"George, I need you to keep the fourth platoon behind us in reserve," Jim said. "Zack's taking second and third around to the right. I'm going to go with recon and first straight ahead. There's not room for more than that on line and we don't know what we're gonna run into up there, so I'll need some backup."

"How about me going with the assault and you following up, boss? After all, you being a highly trained officer and all,

I'd hate to see the taxpayers' money get wasted if you get whacked.''

"Sorry, buddy. 'Spirit of the Infantry, Follow Me!' and all that shit. Besides, I wouldn't be able to see a fucking thing if I stay back there. Sombody's got to and you're elected.''

Lally shrugged. "Your funeral." He moved off.

In truth, though the suggestion had been tactically sound, Jim wouldn't even consider not being in the front. Now that the time was near, he felt the old familiar prickling of excitement. His heart was beating faster, skin felt feverish. His senses were heightened, vision was clearer, sounds were more sharp, the tiredness from the long march had gone away. He had never felt more alive. He wondered if something was wrong with him. He should have been feeling fear, and to a certain extent was, but it was a familiar fear, almost an old friend, and he welcomed it and the adrenaline rush it brought.

It seemed forever before he heard the single code word spoken over the radio indicating that Osborne was in place. Mercifully, Major Walters had not bothered them in the interim. Perhaps he had been off irritating someone else.

He gave the crank-up signal to Captain Buon, who grinned again and started forward, and the soldiers fanned out in a ragged line to either side.

They had advanced almost two hundred meters when the first shots were fired. A Montagnard point man, sighting a figure in a khaki uniform through a break in the grass, loosed a full magazine at him. The man disappeared and the Montagnard advanced quickly, followed by several of his brethren.

Jim heard the firing to his left, identified it by sound as an M-2 carbine and thus friendly. He was about to ask Captain Buon what had happened when the whole world seemed to fall in on them. One second he was standing in a half-crouch with the only sound the wind sighing through the tallgrass. Then he was pressing his face into the ground as the hundreds of sharp cracks of bullets passing impossibly close sounded in his ears, followed by the roar of the gunfire. Bullets struck the ground in front of him, stinging his face with dust and gravel. He felt something jerking his pack, realized bullets were striking it.

To his right he heard a gurgling noise, saw the striker who

had been guarding his flank lying there with blood frothing from his mouth. Then two rounds struck the man in the top of his head, the sound like a sledgehammer hitting a pumpkin. They tore off a great chunk of skull and splattered brains and blood on the grass behind him, where they slowly dripped to the ground.

The noise was deafening. He wondered why he had not been killed. No one could live through this fire storm. Realized that he had not yet fired his rifle, cursed himself and let off a burst. He could see nothing at which to aim. No matter. The bucking of the little black gun was reassuring. He quickly ran through one magazine and dropped it, loaded another and fired.

Think, you asshole! he told himself furiously while loading the next magazine. This is doing absolutely no good. Got to do something. Okay. What?

The firing showed no signs of slackening. But to his right and left he heard the sounds of others returning fire, and this heartened him. At least everybody wasn't dead.

Looking closer at the pattern of bullet strikes around him, he saw that all were either hitting in front of him or passing just inches above his back. Through some great stroke of luck he had thrown himself into a slight depression, perhaps a ditch from some long-ago field. The enemy fire had chopped down enough grass that he could see thirty or forty feet. He picked out individuals and clumps of people scattered along the depression. Some of them were using their dead comrades as cover.

The radio! He wondered if it worked, hoped it had not been shot to pieces. He grasped the handset and put it to his ear. Tears of relief jumped to his eyes as he heard the familiar hiss.

"Sharkfin, this is Skipjack, over." Silence. "Sharkfin, this is Skipjack, come in, please." Again silence. "Goddamn asshole, when I don't want you, you're on the radio all the fucking time."

"What was that, Skipjack?" came the familiar voice.

"Sharkfin, this is Skipjack. We've got a bad situation down here. We are under heavy, repeat heavy, fire from the objective. We need help and need it bad, over."

"Roger, understand heavy fire. Do you have casualties? Over."

"That's affirmative. Do not know at this time how many. We are pinned down and cannot move. Can you get us some support? Over."

"Roger, what exactly is your position?"

"We are approximately one-zero-zero meters from the tree line. It appears that most of the fire is coming from that location. We need some relief, over."

"Roger, the FAC is calling in a fire mission. We have eight-inchers and one-seven-fives on call. Skipjack, as soon as we get the fire suppressed, I want you to move on that tree line. Do you understand me?"

"Roger, Sharkfin, I read you," Jim said, reflecting that he had little choice anyway. If he retreated, the enemy would shoot him in the back. If he stayed where he was, sooner or later a bullet would find him. If he assaulted, he would probably be shot too, but perhaps he could take a few of them with him. Once more into the tree line. Seemed like he had assaulted so many, all of them looking substantially the same. None of them, however, had been this bad.

He listened as the FAC in the tiny plane circling above called in the fire mission, hoping the artillerymen had the coordinates right, hoping the gunners had laid their pieces in properly, hoping that the 175, which was not really a precision weapon, erred on the side of being farther away rather than being too close. From the fire mission he understood that the first round was going to be willy peter—white phosphorus—used as a marking round. He heard the FAC say "Shot," repeating the transmission of the unheard artillery battery commander indicating the first round was on the way. He hunkered down, covering his head with his hands, knowing as he did how futile the action was.

Seconds later he heard the sound of an express train rushing overhead, heard, barely, the FAC saying "Splash" as the round impacted fifty yards into the tree line. A great umbrella of white smoke and fiercely burning pieces of phosphorus erupted. None of it penetrated even the first layer of canopy.

As the FAC called in a fire-for-effect, he inched his way to the nearest group of people to his left, hoping to find Captain Buon. The firing had scarcely slackened with the impact of the artillery round, and now resumed full force. Again and again the rounds plucked at his pack, struck the ground both in front and behind him, missing him almost as if he were in a protective bubble. The constant snap as they passed overhead sounded like the sharp pitched crackling of pine boughs in a bonfire, a hundred times amplified.

The first high-explosive rounds hit the tree line at about the same time he reached Captain Buon, who was smiling his gold-toothed smile at the sky. A fly was crawling in his exposed eyeball. Suddenly the ground shook and the high-pitched whine of metal fragments filled the air. He cautiously raised his head and watched as the dirty black explosions obscured the tree line, some hitting the trees, others impacting just in front. He thanked God this bunch of artillerymen seemed at least to be able to hit the target. To either side the surviving Montagnards were watching this display of power in awe, some even getting onto hands and knees for a better look. He shouted for them to get down, knowing as he did it they could not hear him.

When the first fire-for-effect ended, the enemy fire began again and chopped several of them to pieces. One fell next to him, the reflex action of his legs drumming the ground as nerve synapses fired in mad abandon in the final expenditure of energy.

The handset crackled. "What's your situation now, Skipjack?" it asked.

"Simple enough. God, Jesus Christ, Buddha, Mohammed and Mickey Mouse, along with at least half the fucking North Vietnamese Army, is shooting at me. What the fuck do you think my situation is!" he screamed. "Goddamn artillery didn't do a goddamn bit of good. They are obviously dug in. We need delay, I repeat delay, fuse. Most of the shit didn't even get through the trees, much less to them."

He heard the major direct the FAC to specify delay fuses for the next volley. The command net was jammed with demands for clarification of the situation. Walters ignored them. Soon the sky would be filled with helicopters, as every senior officer in the area came to get their two cents in. The longer he could hold that off, the more likely he would be able to put himself in for a decoration for controlling the action.

Jim heard the next rounds crash through the trees on their

way to the ground. The first encounter with a tree branch however small began the delay mechanism. It generally gave the shells time to bury themselves in the ground before exploding, though some went off scant inches aboveground. The effect was far more efficient than the point-detonating rounds they had used before. Great gouts of earth erupted all along the tree line.

"Six, this is Skipjack. Much, much better. Give me another twenty minutes of the same, then walk it back from the tree line a couple of hundred yards, over."

He received a curt "Roger" and since the enemy fire had slackened to a few stray rounds cracking overhead, decided to chance a rush along the dead space. His heart sank. After a quick tour he saw that little more than half the original force was able to function. The Montagnard soldiers he passed, those still alive, grinned almost apologetically at him, sorry they hadn't done more, encouraged that he was still well and able to lead them. They trusted in only two things: the Americans who helped them and the Buddha. When ready to assault, they took the medallions of Buddha hanging from leather thongs around their necks and clamped them firmly between their teeth, secure in the knowledge that should they die, they were assured of being reunited with the godhead.

Back at his original position he assessed the situation. The artillery was suppressing the enemy, but he held no illusions they had been destroyed. The best to be hoped for was that the enemy would pull out. He hoped so. It was a very long hundred meters to the tree line.

No use delaying. The artillery had started working its way back into the trees. Now or never, he thought. No guts, no glory. Fuck it. Nobody lives forever.

The psyching wasn't working. He was seized with lethargy. How easy it would be! Just to lie here and let someone else worry about it. Nobody could blame him. Nobody else would subject themselves or their troops to that killing zone. Major Walters would raise hell, maybe relieve him. But fuck him anyway! Let him come down here and do it, if he wants it done so badly. I'm tired. I've had enough. No mortal man should have to go through this. It's just too much.

He checked his rifle. Half a magazine left. He ejected it, inserted a fresh one, put the partly depleted one into the side pocket of his pants. Grenades, yes. None broken loose in the movement. He felt the blood rushing through his veins, knew he was going to do it. Couldn't, if asked, have explained why. He just had to, that was all. And perhaps that was good enough.

He jumped up, shooting into the tree line, running forward and hoping someone was following. In a ragged line they were, the well and the walking wounded, their shot-up comrades providing covering fire. Fleeting thoughts struck him as he ran forward. How easy it was to get through the elephant grass, since most of it had been neatly mowed by bullet scythes. How little noise there was except the blood rushing in his ears. How the specks of fire in front of him looked almost beautiful even though he knew them to be muzzle flashes. How his legs seemed to carry him impossible distances with each stride, and yet how far away the tree line continued to be. How could the Montagnards run faster than he? Yet here they were, surrounding him, firing as they ran, their faces contorted with effort. In front of him went two, grinning back at him when he shouted at them to get out of his way. One stumbled, coughed a great gout of bright red blood. The other took his place.

And what was this? A tree? It took a moment to realize that he was out of the open. All round him were scenes of carnage, pieces of corpses draped in abandon half in and half out of collapsed bunkers, steam rising from torsos ripped apart by the blasts. And people were still shooting at him, the artillery hadn't killed them all. Not nearly.

There! A foxhole he had run completely by. A rifle muzzle was protruding from it, firing at his people. He pulled an M-26 grenade from its keeper, yanked the pin and let the spoon fly. Training now took over. Let it cook off, count one one thousand, two one thousand. Pop it down the hole, take cover. In two seconds, not enough time for a man in the hole to find it and throw it out, it goes off, blowing the camouflage cover off the hole and filling the air with the black smoke of high explosive. Nobody can live through that, but better make sure. Jump up, point the M-16 down at the hole, look into the muzzle of an AK-47 being held by a very much alive, if somewhat explosion-addled NVA soldier. Jesus! Finger locks down on the trigger, twenty rounds of 5.56 into him, rendering a human into a pile of bloody rags.

Away, break away! Fire coming from a bunker farther up the hill. Shield behind the bole of a tree, machine-gun bullets kicking off bark on both sides. Toss a grenade at the bunker. It bounces off and rolls back toward him, explodes just to the front and fills his calf with tiny wire fragments. It is more painful than incapacitating. Another grenade at them, this one thrown with more force. It goes off behind them, temporarily stilling the fire. Two Montagnards assault, one cut in two from another bunker, the other making it to the first, where he very carefully shoots the occupants in the head.

It becomes a pattern, toss grenades at the bunkers until close enough to wound or daze the occupants, then assault. When he runs out of grenades, he uses those tossed to him by the 'Yards, who know they cannot throw them as far and as accurately as he can.

The bunkers are tied in with interlocking fields of fire. It is bloody work. He realizes that his assault force is getting smaller and smaller. The bodies of most are scattered down the hill behind them. Still, nobody falters.

He tosses a grenade, watches in pleasure as it hits behind a hole, then rolls neatly downhill into it. No worry about live ones here; the RPD machine gun that had been firing at them is blown completely out and comes to rest a couple of meters away. Pieces of flesh still cling to it.

His ears are ringing from the shooting and the explosions, but he begins to realize that the firing has died down to a few reports on the flank. He rushes forward to the last bunker, sees that it is placed just below the crest of the hill. He also sees that the hill he has just assaulted at such cost is only a bump on the finger, rather like a raised knuckle; and that after a small dip another hill rises to at least double the height of the one on which he is standing. He can see people moving around up there, many more.

He slumps down behind a tree, aware for the first time of his exhaustion. The trembling takes over, as he knew it would. The surviving tribesmen watch in silence as he shakes, most of them too tired to care.

After a moment he roused himself, aware that if he did not do something, the others would stay just as they were, and he very much feared a counterattack. He searched for a leader who was still alive, found the first platoon leader, ordered him in broken Rhade to position his people to defend themselves, then went to search for Lally and the reserve platoon.

The smell was overpowering as he stumbled back down the hill. An unholy mixture of blood, TNT, shit and smokeless powder. A sweet smell, full of rottenness. The tiger-striped bodies of his troops and the khaki-clad of their foes lie together in fraternal intimacy. Here and there the Montagnard medics move, attempting to save whom they can. Smoke and mist hang close to the ground, drifting gently around his ankles. The uncaring trees were already sealing their wounds off with congealing sap.

Just into the tree line he found Lally and the fourth platoon moving carefully forward. The sergeant's face blanched when he saw him.

"Jesus Christ, you're hit!"

Jim looked at him as if he were speaking in an unknown tongue, then, as the meaning soaked in, looked down at himself and realized he was covered in blood. Some of it, he knew, was not his. Part of it, especially that which was still leaking through his fatigues, obviously was. He didn't remember being hit, other than by the grenade fragments. Stretching his mind, he could remember being struck with a sledgehammer blow to the leg, but had dismissed it with the thought that he had run into something.

Lally insisted that he sit down, tore open his pants leg to expose a nasty-looking hole in his upper thigh. The edges were puffed out and blue. It leaked blood at a slow but steady rate. Obviously didn't hit an artery, he thought. I'd be dead by now.

"No time for that now," he said, grabbing the sergeant by the collar. "Get the platoon forward. The cocksuckers are gonna come back at us and we've got at the most fifteen effectives up there. They'll shove it right up our asses, you don't get somebody there. I don't know where the hell Zack is with the others. You're what we have right now. Now!" he screamed when Lally looked as if he were going to object. "Go! I can take care of this. I used to be a medic, remember?"

Lally shouted commands at the platoon and they moved

off at a trot. "At least let me help you put a bandage on it," he said.

"We fuck around here much longer and we're all going to be dead, and I won't need a bandage. Do us all a favor and get the hell up this hill!" Lally moved off to catch up with the platoon.

He tore his pants leg further, dreading what he would see on the back side. The bullet had passed through, and none too cleanly. The hole was much larger and more ragged. A large chunk of meat hung down, held to his leg only by the skin. Still, it didn't appear that anything vital had been hit, and there was still no real pain. He knew the pain would come later. He removed the field dressing from the pouch on his shoulder strap and opened it, placing the main pad on the worst part of the wound and winding the tails around his leg as tightly as he dared without cutting off blood circulation. Debated giving himself an ampoule of morphine, decided that at this point the pain would be preferable to the further addling of his brain. The grenade wounds he decided to ignore. The fragments would not be easy to dig out. He might not survive long enough to worry about that anyway.

After resting for a moment he became aware of a nagging voice at his shoulder. He grabbed the mike, answered with his call sign, listened for a moment as the voice on the other end shouted in his ear, keyed the mike to shut it off and waited until he figured the tirade might be over, then released the push-to-talk switch.

Satisfied, he again keyed the mike. "Sharkfin, this is Skipjack. Sitrep, over."

"Send the sitrep, over."

He was amused to hear the suppressed anger in the voice. Supposed that his next Officer Efficiency Report was going to look like dogshit. Couldn't bring himself to worry about it.

"Have taken the objective. Suffered heavy casualties in first and recon platoons. Approximately one-five effectives left. Fourth platoon moving forward to reinforce. Have negative contact with second and third. There are a hell of a lot of people on the hill above the objective and we are at this time getting ready for a counterattack, over."

"Roger, Skipjack. How many KIA? Over."

He grimaced. The all-important body count! Didn't matter how many people you lost. But you needed that body count to put up on the general's briefing charts. Otherwise how could you get your "attaboys"?

"Haven't had time to go around and count toes," he replied, "but I estimate three- to four-zero. Listen, we need some more heavy stuff on the hill above the objective. Estimate there is at least one reinforced company, possibly more, up there. We don't have the people to stand them off. Also need reinforcements, over."

"Affirmative on the heavy stuff, negative on the reinforcements at this time. We'll see what it looks like after the artillery gets through, over."

"God damn it, we were supposed to find and fix them, and if they ain't found I'll kiss your ass. I don't know how much longer the company can hold out. I need the cav in here, over."

There was a silence on the radio, and the answer, when it came, was almost apologetic. "There's a cav company in trouble on L.Z. Monkey and all available are going there. I don't even know how much arty we can give you, but we are attempting to get air. You're gonna have to hold out there, Skipjack, until we can get something to you, out."

It was a measure of how resigned he was to the status quo that he did not bother to object. Of course the cav company would get priority support. They were Americans. His company of indigenous troops would have to take the leavings.

He got up, almost fell back down. The leg had stiffened badly. As he stumbled up the hill it loosened up, but started bleeding again. It soaked through the bandage, trickled down into his boot. With each step it oozed out the vent holes in the instep.

When he reached the troops, he saw that Lally's people had spent the time well. They were digging in, clearing fields of fire, siting weapons to ensure interlocking fire.

He found the command group, such as it was. Lally was busy giving commands, looked at him as if to ask the lieutenant if he would like to take over. Jim wearily signaled him to go on, found a shell hole and hunkered down in it. Time to try to do something more for his leg. He wondered about the bombardment he had been promised, was ready to call about it, then heard the shells rushing in. Not nearly as many as before. Perhaps only one battery firing. There were long pauses between volleys and the pattern was skimpy. Not nearly enough.

Through the trees he saw them coming. Many times during his two tours in Vietnam he had been frustrated because he had not been able to see the enemy. Mostly you fired at muzzle flashes, at scarcely seen movements. It now seemed ironic, because at this one moment he could see more enemy soldiers than he had seen in almost two years of combat. When going through basic training, he had been fascinated by the tales of the human-wave attacks in Korea. He had never expected to see one. Now he was. And wished he wasn't.

The Montagnards, he was glad to see, were maintaining fire discipline. They waited until the front rank was less than fifty meters away, then opened very effective and accurate fire. The shooting from the enemy ranks was intense and, though wild and inaccurate, began to take its toll. To add to the problem, an RPG gunner located somewhere to the front started firing grenades into the hastily prepared company positions.

Ignoring the bullets striking around him, knowing that they were random rather than the deadly accurate fire of before, he crawled to the C.P. It was behind a felled teak tree and had been spared the worst of the fire.

"You see that fuckin' gunner?" he asked Lally.

"Thought I saw a backblast about a hundred meters up." Lally chanced a glimpse above the tree. "There the cocksucker is. I got the runner looking for an M-79. I'm gonna put a grenade right up his ass." A diminutive Montagnard made a sliding stop into the hole, triumphantly clutching the grenade launcher and a bandoleer of H.E. rounds. Lally broke it open, inserted the massive round. "Now watch this, boss," he said.

You could almost see the low-velocity round in flight. It was deadly accurate up to seventy-five meters; required only a slight elevation at one hundred. The round impacted just at the feet of the enemy gunner, reducing his feet and calves to hamburger and sending hundreds of tiny serrated wire fragments up into his groin, where they spun through intestines, liver and heart, killing him before he had a chance to realize he was dead.

Lally turned to Jim, opening his mouth to say something. His face dissolved in a spray of blood. A stunned look fogged his eyes. He dropped to the bottom of the hole, writhing in pain.

Carmichael grabbed him, held his head in his lap. The wound, he saw, was not fatal. The bullet had passed through the side of his face, narrowly missed his tongue and exited just under the chin. It appeared that the force of the impact had broken his jaw, since it wobbled when Jim tested it, but other than being extremely bloody, the wound was not that bad. He searched through dimly remembered medical training, finally settled upon packing Lally's mouth with gauze from the company first-aid kit and placing a pressure bandage on the outside wound, the tails of which he tied over his head. Lally now looked like a child with a very bad toothache. He was in obvious pain, but Jim hesitated to give him morphine. There was too much chance that he would pass out, and unconscious, he might aspirate seeping blood, drowning himself.

He turned his attention back to the battlefield. The enemy soldiers were still coming over the bodies of their comrades. He had to admire their courage. The surviving Montagnards were still pouring fire into their ranks, especially the little BAR gunner who was firing precise three-round bursts. Each time he fired, people dropped, most shot through the head. But it couldn't last. The firing from his side was growing more and more sporadic as the troops fell victim to enemy bullets or ran out of ammunition.

Time to die, he supposed. The thought didn't frighten him nearly as much as he had thought it would. There was regret that he had not lived as much as he would have wanted, would never go to the places he wanted to visit, would never love as many women as he would have wished. Mostly there was resignation. He loaded another magazine into the rifle, took careful aim at an oncoming soldier, dropped him, took aim at another and missed, cursed himself and got a third. He kept on firing, hitting more than missing, but it seemed to make no difference. He loaded another magazine, took the .45 from the holster at his hip and jacked a round into the chamber. He could not, would not, be taken alive, and it was much easier to blow his brains out with the pistol than with the M-16. He laid it to one side and continued to fire into their ranks. They were within grenade range now and he could see the stick grenades arcing overhead, smoke trailing as they flipped end over end. Had their grenades not been notoriously unreliable, it would have been all over. Only a small percentage went off, but the damage they did further reduced his effectives. Not too long now. He moved the .45 closer.

Suddenly from the flank came a great burst of fire. It scythed the enemy ranks, cutting them down like so many stalks of wheat. Within seconds the lead rank had been annihilated, throwing the second into confusion. As they milled uncertainly the fire was shifted, as if some precise machine were controlling it. Most of them did not survive the first few seconds. Those who did were cut down by the suddenly revitalized survivors on their former objective. The third wave wisely decided to retreat in haste.

His mind uncomprehending, he did not at first realize whence his deliverance had come. He stared, dazed, at the masses of khaki-clad bodies before him. Some, he saw, had come within just a few feet of the defensive line. Some still moved, but not many. Those who did were being picked off by the surviving Montagnards. He wondered if he should stop them; after all, the rear-echelon commandoes always wanted prisoners. Decided that it would do little good to try. And he was just too tired.

He heard a familiar voice calling his name, felt Lally tugging at his pants leg to get his attention. Turned and saw Zack Osborne coming through the smoke and fog. Opened his mouth to tell him to get down, didn't the damned fool realize they were under fire? And felt himself slipping from consciousness. Fought, couldn't surrender, not now, too much to do. They'd be coming back.

He came to with the sharp smell of ammonia in his nose. Brushed the evil-smelling thing away and saw Zack smiling down at him.

"Glad you're back with us, Trung Ui. Don't move your arm! Got some serum albumin going in you. You lost a lot of blood. Lay back down! We got everything under control right now and you need the rest. We ain't out of this yet, I'm afraid.''

Jim tried to talk, found his mouth so dry he could barely croak. Zack gave him a sip from his canteen.

Finally he asked, ''Any help coming?''

'' 'Fraid not. I called Sharkfin just a couple of minutes ago with a sitrep. Cav's got themselves in a real shitstorm up on Monkey. Looks like we're it right now. Don't look too bad at the moment. Charlie's up there lickin' his wounds. Gave a real quick count; looks like we dropped close to a hundred out front. It'll take them a little while to come at us again. Meantime, I've got the 'Yards taking the most seriously wounded back down the hill to the edge of the tree line. Cocksuckers did at least promise us some Medevac choppers. You want to get on one? Don't know how long the dressing on your leg is gonna keep the bleeding stopped, and you're leakin' from a bunch more small places.''

Jim shook his head. ''How about you, George?'' Zack asked.

Lally was sitting looking at them, his lower face horribly swollen. The bruising had already crept up to his eyes, almost closing them. He signaled his intentions by switching his M-16 from safe to rock and roll.

Zack shrugged his shoulders. ''Didn't think so.''

''Not that I'm not grateful for you showing up when you did,'' said Jim, who was feeling somewhat better from the blood expander flowing into his veins, ''but where in the fuck were you all this time?''

Zack looked offended. ''You should have seen the shit you sent us through, Trung Ui,'' he said. ''Goddamnedest thicket I ever saw. We were about halfway through when we heard the firing cut loose. Tried to get to you, but there was just no way. We finally got through and were getting ready to join you when we saw the guys uphill massing and coming down. Figured we could do you more good on the flank than trying to get to you.''

''You hadn't done that, I guess I wouldn't be here asking you where the fuck you had been. You sweet motherfucker, we get out of this alive, I'm gonna buy you the best blowjob in Qui Nhon.''

''Yeah, well, we got to get out of this one first. Now the

bad news. Second and third platoons weren't hit bad, we got about thirty people there. But the rest of the company is chewed up.''

''How many?''

''Near as I can figure, there's nobody that's not wounded. Probably twenty of 'em can still fight.''

''How many for Medevac?''

''Another eighteen.''

Which meant, he thought, that he had lost thirty-two KIA. Counting the seriously wounded, exactly half the company was out of action. Zack had been guilty of a gross understatement when he called it bad news.

He looked at his watch, tapped it to see if it was still running. It was hard to believe that scarcely an hour had passed since the first engagement. He felt immeasurably older. ''Think they'll hit us again before dark?''

Zack nodded. ''They don't know we're not gonna get help. They'll want to knock us off here as soon as they can, then get set up to kick ass on the cav as soon as they copper in down below. They get back down to the tree line, they'll eat those boys' asses up while they're trying to land.''

''You got everybody getting ready, I guess?''

''They're setting up what claymores we've got right now. Everybody else is digging in. Actually, as positions go, this one isn't too bad. Trees are too thick to let 'em use mortars. They're on higher ground than here, but too far away for it to do them any good. So they've got to come down the slope, into the saddle and back up again to get at us. There just weren't so many of them, we might have a chance.''

Jim got on the radio. ''Sharkfin, this is Skipjack, over.''

''This is Sharkfin. Skipjack Two says that you have been hit. Get yourself on the first Medevac, over.''

''Negative, negative. We need everybody we can get down here. Listen, can we get any support at all? Over.''

''We've got some fast-movers that got weathered out over the Trail and are looking to expend ordnance. They will be on station in approximately one-zero. Can you use them?''

''What are they carrying? Over.''

''Five-hundred pounders and twenty mike-mike, over.''

The hill where the enemy was forming up was dangerously close for the bombs. Still, it was better than nothing. ''Roger.

When they come in, have them drop the five-hundreds up toward the crest of the hill. I figure that's where the C.P. must be. Then have them come in and strafe with the twenties. I'll mark our front line with a flare. They're going to have to get in close.''

"Roger, understand. Am having the Dustoffs bring in some ammo to you. Understand you are low. God damn, Skipjack, I want you to know you're doing a hell of a job down there. I'm asking for a Silver Star for you.''

And what about the thirty-two dead 'Yards? he thought sourly. What are they going to get? A death gratuity for the dependents, he knew. A few thousand piasters, which the Vietnamese would cheat them out of.

"Get everybody dug in deeper," he instructed Osborne. "We're gonna get a lot of shrapnel down here when the jets drop their stuff.'' He turned to survey the front. "Ah, fuck, here they come again.''

The North Vietnamese, having seen how ineffective the mass attacks had been, started using fire-and-maneuver. It looked like a company-sized unit was moving up on them. They were maneuvering by squad, one unit setting down a base of fire from covered positions while another made a short zigzag rush forward. Again the bullets snapped by his head. Again people jerked, lay forever still. It seemed it would never stop. He wondered if he was already dead and this was hell and he was forever condemned to fight this battle. He fired until the barrel grew so hot the smoke from the lubricating oil obscured his vision, grabbed a carbine from the dead man beside him and continued to shoot. The enemy was so close that a person didn't have to aim, just point and shoot. One he hadn't seen ran in from the flank, firing wildly down into his hole. Bullets jerked the dead man beside him, tore gouts of earth, sent spumes of dirt into the air. He swung his weapon, shot the man in the chest once, twice, three times. The underpowered carbine bullets seemed to have no effect on him, hopped up as he was on combat euphoria and drugs and God knows what else. He pulled the trigger again and again, watching in horror as the bullets tore holes in the khaki, blood spurting, smoke rising from smoldering fabric. What nightmare was this? The enemy soldier, young, probably no more than eighteen, had his lips drawn back so far the teeth looked like tombstones. His eyes were blank and staring. He moved toward Jim, the triangular bayonet affixed to the end of his AK-47 in the thrust position.

Lally, successful at last in freeing himself from the soldier who had fallen on him, fired a burst from his M-16 up into the man's armpit. The powerful little bullets exploded from his face and head, effectively terminating him from the neck up. He fell forward, blood from carotid arteries spraying across Jim's legs.

Jim threw down the carbine and retrieved his M-16. He'd thank Lally later, if either one of them survived. More were coming. At least two points on the line had been breached, the NVA occupying the holes and shooting into the flanks of his troops. Only a matter of time now. Take as many of them as you can with you, then stick the .45 into your mouth and pull the trigger. Can't get taken alive; there are things worse than dying. He rose to a crouch, barely aware he was screaming. Gun on full auto now, no need to worry about conserving ammo. Shrapnel from a bullet impacted the tree beside him, slashing his cheek. Blood ran warm and smooth down his neck. Claymores were going off all down the line, mowing down flesh in a hail of explosive-driven ball bearings. Grenades were tossed so close that friend and enemy alike suffered from their effect.

All semblance of control was gone, the battle crazily joined. People ran by him, he didn't know if they were friend or foe anymore. Butt-stoke one, shoot another, grab another and throw him to the ground with fingers wrapped around his throat. Feel the trachea collapse beneath his thumbs as the man claws ineffectually at his eyes. Legs drum the ground, pelvis thrusting up in obscene travesty.

The shock wave of a massive explosion struck him, heat like an oven. Heavy pieces of metal set up a low-pitched hum through the trees, shearing off heavy branches as if they were twigs. With what conscious mind he had left he realized that the bombs were much closer than he had planned.

"Get down," he screams, knowing as he does so it is useless. Nobody can hear over the jets rushing in, the rattle of gunfire, the heavy explosions. He huddles, covering his head with his hands. Fetal position, return to the womb of mother earth. Only she can protect him now. As if she hears, dirt from a nearby hit covers him, the rich smell filling his lungs. Can hardly breathe, feels the shock of the heavy bombs transmitted directly to him. Wonder if his lungs will collapse from overpressure; eardrums are already gone.

He waits for the shocks to end. Gives it a count of one minute when they do, then cautiously raises his head.

The very face of the earth has changed. Trees are gone, uprooted, sheared off at the ground. Great craters pockmark the once-smooth slope. The attack has been broken. Anyone who was not under cover when the bombardment started has disappeared. Here and there are pieces of clothed flesh, the only sign anyone had ever been here.

The jets came in again, the roaring of their 20mm cannon filling the air. The enemy hill was obscured by the smoke of their impact.

Intense calm settled over him. He shook the dirt from his rifle and worked the action to make sure it was clear, then checked ammo pouches, finding that he still had four full magazines. He felt no real emotion, only that there was a job to be done. They all had to die, every one. No mercy. Mercy was for the civilized world, the world that had sent him here, and that world didn't exist anymore. Nothing existed outside of now. Only this existed, only this was truth, and truth was that you killed them before they had the chance to kill you.

He got up and hobbled down the line, methodically pumping a round into the head of any enemy soldier who still moved. The blast blew their heads apart, spattering him with blood and brains. He ignored the pleading looks, the hands thrown up in futile attempt to ward off the bullet. When none were left living; he shot the dead. After a while he ran out of ammunition, kept futilely squeezing the trigger, hands working convulsively, killing them over and over again in his mind in the hope that they would never again rise, never come at him with fire and flame and thunder.

Zack Osborne pulled an ampoule of morphine from his pack, caught the lieutenant in a bear hug and injected it into his hip. He held him close, felt the trembling of his body, the great shuddering breaths, the anguish which came from him like a palpable force. It took a long time for the drug to take effect.

• • •

HE woke as they were loading him onto the chopper. The troop-carrying birds of the 1st Cav were disgorging their loads as quickly as they could land. What was left of his company was marshaled off to the side of the L.Z. waiting to be taken out. They were pitifully few.

The helicopter rose into the air, banked and flew over the valley. Below him the elephant grass had been felled in great fan-shaped swaths, corresponding to the fields of fire of the enemy gunners. The Valley of the Fan. Hiding the face of death, its ribs watered by blood. If the world were right, if there were such a thing as justice, nothing would ever again grow from such a bitter flood. But it would, even more rank than before. The earth had limitless ability to soak up man's insanity and make itself whole again. He turned away.

CHAPTER 2

HE made the long circuit of hospitals: Qui Nhon for stabilization, Cam Ranh Bay for initial debridement of the wounds, a very short stopover in Japan, finally back to the States. Several times the attending doctors wondered if they would be able to save him; to the wounds was added the complication of falciparum malaria running rampant through his weakened system. The days passed in pain-filled haze.

His first clear memory was of waking up in a strange bed. There was something odd. He puzzled over it for a few moments, then realized that he wasn't surrounded by the familiar olive-green cloud of mosquito netting.

The sun through the window struck dust motes, sending them in lazy patterns through the air. He could hear no jets, no artillery, little more than the sound of the door opening. A pretty face, small, framed in dark hair, peered in at him and, seeing him awake, retreated before he could speak.

Too bad. He had wanted to ask her where he was. Ah, well, someone was bound to come by soon. In the meantime he would relax and enjoy these few moments that were magically free from pain. Agony had filled his existence so long it felt strange to be without it, as if he were a husk that only pain could fill.

The door opened again and a khaki-clad man with an eagle on his collar came in, followed by the face Jim had seen before.

"Well, Captain Carmichael, I'm glad you decided to join us at last. We thought you didn't like our hospitality." The colonel laughed heartily at his own joke. "I'm Dr. Cable, and this is Spec 4 Lisa Brown. She's been keeping an eye on you."

Jim tried to speak, could not. His throat was parched. He

mouthed "water" and the specialist was at his side in an instant. She poured liquid from a carafe on the bedside table and held his head up as he sipped it. It was wonderful, clean and clear and held not a hint of the acrid taste of iodine tablets.

"Feel better now, Captain?" the doctor asked.

Jim nodded, asked "Where am I?" He was horrified to hear how weak his voice sounded.

"Letterman Army Hospital," the doctor replied.

"In San Francisco? Christ, how did I get here?"

"Nobody wanted you except us. Thought you were too complicated. Afraid of what it would look like on their records if they lost you." The doctor snorted. "Cut-crazy bastards wanted to amputate your leg at the last stop. Lucky for you they didn't get to it before you were shipped here. Don't know where the army is getting its doctors these days. Sears Roebuck, apparently. Anyway, you're in good hands now. Notice how well you can hear? We sewed your eardrums back together. Figured we might as well while you were out of it. I know how disorienting it can be to wake up and not be able to hear anything. Happened to me once, during the Korean War. Chinese mortar shell."

"Am I all still here, Doc?"

"Most of you." Seeing the look of panic fleeting across his patient's face, the doctor hastened to add, "Nothing major gone. We had to debride the gunshot wound and take out a lot of fragments from your lower body. Anybody ever call you magnet-ass, by the way? You attracted a hell of a lot of metal. That's what they called me back in Korea after the mortar shell. Doctors took pieces of it out of me for six months. Some of yours we couldn't get out. Would have done more damage than leaving it in place. As it is, you look like a baseball with all the stitches." The doctor laughed at his own humor again. "So what else do you want to know, Captain?"

"Why do you keep calling me Captain? Last I heard I was a first lieutenant."

"Not according to your records. You were promoted to O-3 two weeks ago. Congratulations. I guess the promotion party can wait awhile."

"What date?"

"Date? Ah, you mean today's date. August 18, 1967. You've been here for six days. Most of that time we've kept you pretty hopped up. Figured it was about time for you to come out and join the world, so we started weaning you a couple of days ago."

"What now?"

"Now we've got to get rid of the malaria. The leg is still infected. But the malaria worries me the most. Falciparum has a nasty habit of turning into blackwater fever and shutting the kidneys down. Then you die. And we don't want that to happen. The Army Medical Corps has spent entirely too much money on you to let you croak now." The doctor laughed again.

Jim decided he liked this doctor despite his irritating laugh. At least he hadn't tried to bullshit him.

"I think it's time for you to get a little more rest," the doctor said. "A little consciousness at a time is enough for anyone." He injected a hypodermic needle into the tube dripping a clear solution into Jim's arm."

"Lisa here will take good are of you, won't you, Lisa?" The young corpsman nodded and smiled.

Jim was enchanted. Lisa was the first Caucasian female he had seen in almost a year. The lack of oriental features was soothing. Through the haze of the rapidly-taking-effect painkiller he thought her quite beautiful.

"I think the captain likes you, Lisa," said the doctor. "Better be careful and stay out of his reach when he gets his strength back. These Green Berets are notorious. Probably carry you off to his lair and feed you rats and snakes. Make you jump out of perfectly good airplanes and other such silly pastimes."

Was that a speculative look Jim thought he caught in her eyes? Surely not. Probably just the effect of the drugs flooding so pleasantly through his body. Wishful thinking. Still, when he got better . . . He drifted off to sleep.

THE next weeks were filled with pain. To avoid addiction to the painkillers, they were slowly withdrawn, ones of lesser strength being substituted. Unfortunately they were also of lesser effectiveness.

The hole in his leg constantly suppurated. Another debridement was performed. This involved the scraping away of dead muscle tissue in hopes of removing the focus of infection. It was a procedure he remembered from his days as a medic; he had performed it on lab animals during training, and later on wounded Cambodian soldiers. The theory was that this, combined with heavy doses of antibiotics, would speed the healing process. But the Southeast Asian bacterium proved stubborn.

Occasionally a piece of metal would work its way to the surface. He could always tell when one was ready to come out. The spot would turn red and tender, then swell, then a boil-like pustule would form. If he caught it early enough, Doc Cable lanced it. More often it broke on its own as he tossed in the bed, the tiny piece of metal hard to find in the pus and blood.

By far the worst were the malaria attacks. They came in predictable patterns. For a day he felt fine. Then the chills came and shaking racked his body. It was so violent Lisa had trouble keeping him in the bed. He felt cold, so cold, wondered if he would ever be warm again. He was covered from head to toe with heavy wool blankets but they had no effect on this internal frost.

The chills lasted from eight to ten hours, then his temperature began its inexorable rise. Soon the covers were thrown off and even the feel of Lisa's cool hand on his brow was unbearable. Within a couple of hours he was delirious. He had horrible dreams of burning: inside a crashed helicopter, in a blazing building, being roasted slowly on a spit over hot coals.

As the process completed itself, the fever broke. This was signaled by the sweats, his body pouring out fluid in an unending flow, soaking the sheets three or four times a day. Then the cycle began again.

The combination of chloroquine, primaquine and pyrimethamine seemed to be having little effect on the disease. A tropical-medicine specialist was called in for consultation. To the other drugs he added quinine dapsone. The dapsone caused diarrhea. In his lucid moments he was ashamed to smell the stench as his bowels evacuated themselves onto the bed. The two times he had attempted to get up and go to the bathroom he ended up flat on his face on the floor, earning a furious scolding from Lisa. Thereafter he endured it as she patiently cleaned up after him, never showing the least expression of disgust or embarrassment. No need for her to, he was disgusted enough for them both. But the dapsone finally killed the bug.

He had been in the hospital just over two months when one evening Doc Cable showed up in his room after rounds. Jim looked at him in surprise; after-hours visits were not usual.

The doctor closed the door behind him, came over to the bed and opened his medical bag. Christ, Jim thought, what now? It was bound to be painful, and he was heartily tired of pain.

From the bag came a full bottle of Bourbon.

"Thought you might be in need of this by now," said the doctor. He poured a healthy shot into each of two glasses, handed Jim one and raised his own in silent toast.

The liquor flowed hot and smooth down his throat, sending smoky tendrils of pure pleasure flooding throughout his body.

"Not bad, is it? Still think the medical profession screwed up when they got away from the therapeutic value of medicinal alcohol. Of course, most of the medical profession thinks I'm a dinosaur, but fuck 'em."

"Fuck 'em indeed," Jim agreed, holding his glass out for a refill. "So, Doc, what's next?"

"You're doing pretty good. Lots better than anyone would have ever expected when you came in here. Including me. Looks like we beat the malaria, even though you may have recurrences. The infection in your leg is largely licked and the wound is starting to close. You've still got some metal in you, but nothing that's going to cause any real problems. What I'm leading up to is, after some physical therapy to strengthen that leg, you're going to be pronounced fit for duty. I plan to profile you, give you a piece of paper that will keep you to limited duty for a while, but that's not going to last forever. You see what I'm saying?"

Jim shook his head. "I don't want a profile," he said.

Doc Cable looked at him with exasperation written all over his face. "God damn it," he exploded, "what I'm trying to tell you is that they're likely to send you right back to Vietnam! And you may not be so lucky next time. If you can call what you've gone through lucky. We damned near lost you.

Hadn't been for the grace of God and a strong constitution, we would have.''

Jim was silent, allowing the doctor to play out his anger. He took another sip of the Bourbon.

Cable looked at him speculatively. ''That's what you want, isn't it?''

Jim nodded.

''Why?''

He shrugged. ''Hell if I know,'' he said. ''I could tell you that I thought what I was doing was important, but that would be a lie. Or I could spout some patriotic bullshit, but you know it would be just that. I've given a lot of thought to it. Best I can come up with is that I've left too many friends back there. If they're there, I should be.''

Cable took a measured sip of Bourbon. ''Guess I understand,'' he said. ''Felt pretty close to the same way myself after I got hit in Korea. But I was luckier than you. That war ended before I got the chance to go back. This one doesn't look like it will ever end no matter what our wonderful politicians tell us about light at the end of the tunnel. Really, you don't think you've done enough? I read your 201 file. This was your second trip over there. You went as an enlisted man the first time?''

Jim smiled. ''Yeah, '63 as an S.F. medic. Hell of a lot different war then.''

''How so?''

''No big-unit actions. Just a lot of little skirmishes with local-force V.C. units. No conventional U.S. troops, so you didn't get nearly as much support. But I liked it a lot better. At least then you felt like you were doing something and weren't just a tiny cog in some vast military machine.''

''Take a lot of casualties?''

''Not at first. For some reason the V.C. let us build our camp without a lot of interference. Guess they figured we were going to be like the French, build this fortified complex and stay inside it, let them have a free hand outside. They were pretty surprised when, after getting our Strike Force trained, we started patrolling all over the area. Caught 'em with their pants down more than once.''

''Then what happened?''

''Then it got serious. They started seeing us as a threat,

pulled in a Main Force V.C. battalion, attacked the camp. Hell of a battle.'' Jim was silent for a moment, eyes distant. In his mind he was replaying that night of terror and confusion. "They came in from the south side, through the rubber trees. For some reason, the people in Saigon had picked a spot for the camp right in the middle of a rubber plantation. We were down in a valley, hills on two sides. And the trees came almost right up to the wire. We'd asked permission to cut them back. Saigon came back and said no. Said the French plantation owners, who they didn't want to anger, had refused permission. So we had no fields of fire, no observation.

"Sappers came first, blew holes in the wire, got inside the camp and raised hell. Then the assault troops came. Breached the perimeter in two places. We poured the fire into them from the flanks, broke the assault, started trying to mop up the ones who were still in camp. I was in the dispensary by this time, trying to take care of the wounded. We'd made the mistake of only sandbagging the buildings halfway up, so the bullets were flying through the tin from waist level up. Had to work squatted over. Hell of a mess. Floor was covered with broken glass, blood, shit, everything. Kept slipping as I tried to move around. Stood up just once, that's when I got the scar on my shoulder. Carbine bullet went through one of the posts, hit me, embedded itself. Lucky it was almost spent, would have broken the bone otherwise.'' He fell silent. How could he describe how he had felt that night? How could you tell someone about the beautiful terror?

"Anyway we fought 'em off, killed a lot of them. And that's when it really got serious. They started terrorizing the villages, going in and killing anyone suspected of collaborating with us. We'd been doing village sick call all the way along, taking a patrol out and treating all kinds of weird diseases. First time any of these people had ever seen anything like modern medicine, even though what we were doing was pretty primitive by U.S. standards. Treated everything from goiter to tuberculosis. Did a lot of dental work. Ever try to pull a tooth from someone who's been chewing betel nut all their lives, Doc? Not too much fun. The stuff is abrasive, wears their teeth off right down to the gum line. Then the roots get infected, they get these horrible abscesses. Can't use extractors, can't get enough of a hold. So you use elevators, slowly pry the thing out. We gave 'em novocaine, but the abscesses blocked a lot of the effect. So they just had to suffer through it. But you should have seen how grateful they were, to finally get rid of the pain of the tooth!

"Anyway once we'd get these people treated, we'd get 'em to come to the camp for follow-ups. The intelligence sergeant would talk to them, find out who'd been visiting their villages, names of the local V.C., who was cooperating with them, who they'd seen moving through the area when they were out in the fields. Pretty damned effective. They were grateful for the treatment, so they'd tell us just about anything. We had three to four hundred people showing up every day.

"The V.C. couldn't let that go on. First they started spreading the story that the Americans were poisoning the people who came in. Any patient we couldn't cure, they were used as examples. See what the Americans are doing to you? That didn't work too well because for every patient we lost there were fifty who showed obvious improvement. The V.C. lost face.

"So they let it be known that anybody who showed up for treatment at the camp would be regarded as a 'counterrevolutionary enemy of the people.' Started selectively killing people, especially those they suspected of giving us information. They'd go into a village, pick up a few people to use as examples, make the rest of the village watch as they cut off their heads. They'd carry the heads around to other villages to show what happened to people who cooperated with the My Lo, long-noses, they called us.'

"Murdering bastards," swore Doc Cable.

"Yeah. And it didn't really matter to them who they killed. Men, women, even little kids on a couple of occasions. But you look at it their way, it was something they had to do to stop us. Right and wrong have a way of getting mixed up over there.

"Anyway, although it cut down on the number of people who cooperated with us, there were still plenty who did. Enough for us to get some pretty detailed info on the agitation and propaganda, agit-prop, squads who were doing all this. We figured out the pattern, came up with a pretty good idea of where they might be next, started sending out ambush patrols. Caught enough of them to make it costly. Killed some, captured a few.

"Now, we'd captured V.C. before. Usually turned out to be some young kid who'd been forced into joining, or occasionally somebody who'd joined up of his own free will. Once you showed them you weren't monsters, weren't going to rip their hearts out and eat them as they'd been told, they saw they'd been lied to by the V.C. and would often cooperate.

"But the agit-prop guys, they were a different breed. They were absolutely convinced of the rightness of what they were doing. True believers, Hoffer would say. Anything to further the cause, all acts were justified. They scared the hell out of me, I can tell you that. It was as if their humanity had been squeezed out of them by their convictions. No room for both. They had absolutely no doubts. Certainly willing, even eager, to die for their cause. More important, they didn't care who they had to kill."

"So once you got these guys, did that solve your problems?" asked the doctor, pouring Jim another shot. "Sounds like you had a pretty good handle on it."

"Shit, Doc, you ought to know better than that. If there's one thing I've learned in that war, it's that whatever one side comes up with the other will go it one better.

"By this time my team's tour was almost up. A replacement team from Bragg came in and was getting briefed on the operation, orienting themselves to the area. Everything looked good, V.C. activity in our area of operations was way down. We were regarded as one of the success stories of the war.

"A couple of days before we were due to leave, the replacement team leader, Captain James Mosely, decided he wanted to observe a village sick call. One was scheduled in a nearby village. He, my team leader, team sergeant and myself hopped in a jeep and took off. Sounds pretty stupid in retrospect, but hell, we'd shut down the V.C. in the local area and this place was only a couple of miles away, so where was the danger?

"What we didn't know was the V.C. High Command had decided something had to be done about us. They sent in a special unit, their best assassins. These guys avoided all contact with the villages, stayed back in the jungle, so we never got any information about them. Apparently they'd been setting up ambushes at random around the camp for a week or two. That day they got lucky."

Jim was aware that he was talking too much. The liquor had loosened the ordinarily firm hold he had on such memories. They were too close, hurt too much. But he was gripped by the need to let this out, perhaps in the hope that someone would understand, would know what motivated him and why. Then perhaps they could explain it to him.

"There were two jeeploads of us. Four bodyguards in the first, then us. A mile outside camp we went through this little village. Nobody in the streets, no sign of people. That should have tipped us off, but by that time it was too late anyway.

"You ever been ambushed, Doc? No? It's a hell of a feeling. One second complete silence and the next everything happens. Total surprise. It stuns you, makes it difficult to move, your body doesn't seem to want to obey what your mind is saying. Only takes microseconds to get moving, but it seems like an eternity. Lots of people never make it past that point.

"They hit the first jeep with a grenade. Landed right on the gas tank. Killed everybody in it instantly.

"My team sergeant, Master Sergeant Goodly, was sitting beside me in the back of the other jeep. Took a round through the back of the head, exited under his eye. My team leader, Captain Hackier, was driving. He got three rounds through the hip and fell out of the jeep on his side. Mosely got hit in the chest and fell out on the other side.

"There I was, still sitting there wondering what the fuck had happened, bullets flying all around, and I hadn't been touched. Couldn't have sat there more than a couple of seconds before I came to my senses and fell out backward. I crawled round to the side where Hackier had dragged himself to cover, behind some railroad tracks.

"He knew he was going to die, I think. Bleeding pretty bad, in a lot of pain. Told me he couldn't move, that I should save myself, get out, get back to the camp, get help. I didn't want to go. Stupid. I would've died there had I stayed. Hackier realized that, ordered me to go. I crawled down a ditch, had gotten maybe twenty-five yards when I heard an explosion. They'd thrown a grenade on him, blew his guts out.

"Guess I went a little crazy then. I jumped up, ran to the nearest hut I could find, I guess figuring to work my way from hut to hut until I was clear of the village.

"One place I ran to I could hear shooting from the inside. I peeked in the door, saw a guy still shooting out into the bodies on the road. I shot him in the back, must have got the spine because he just folded up backward. God, it felt good!

"I stopped there for a few minutes trying to decide what to do next. The shooting died down. I looked out the window. They were scavenging the bodies. Captain Mosely had come over with his personal pistol, a chrome-plated .357 Magnum. One of the V.C., a big guy for a Viet, pulled it out of the holster, looked at it for a second, then pumped a round into Mosely's head. Then the bastard laughed.

"Then I did something stupid. I wanted more than anything else in the world to kill these bastards. More, even, than to live. So I opened up on them. Got a couple, I think. But not the bastard I wanted. He looked right at where I was, didn't even take cover. I'll never forget the expression on his face. Arrogant, almost as if he were daring me to hit him.

"Guess that's when I came to my senses. Realized I was the only live friendly still in the village. Very lonesome feeling. I ran like a scared rabbit."

He was sweating profusely and shivering. Christ, he thought, I hope it's not the malaria coming back. Deep down he knew it wasn't. It was instead the release of feelings he had kept bottled inside for so long. The fears, the shame of running away, the guilt at having been the only one to survive, the struck-dumb terror looking his enemy in the eye and seeing the implacable threat written there—all consumed him. And all drove him.

"I guess what I'm trying to say with all this, Doc," he said, his tongue thick with the Bourbon, "is that I don't have a hell of a lot of choice about going back. It's what I do. I'm a soldier. I know nothing else. I don't choose to know anything else. There's a saying in Special Forces that sums it up just about as well as anything else can. It's a shitty war, but it's the only war we've got."

"You know, don't you, that there are a lot of shrinks who'd just love to get their hands on you?"

Jim smiled. "You know better than that, Doc. Even the

shrinks admit they can only help someone who wants to be helped. Way I see it, I don't need any help. I'm doing what I want."

"Even if it means you probably won't survive it?"

"That's not a major consideration. Live hard, die young and leave a beautiful corpse. Nah, I'm sorry, that's too glib. I don't want to die. I don't think anybody does. Certainly I wouldn't want to soldier with anyone who did. People like that have a tendency to get other people killed along with them. But I do accept the possibility, even the probability, of that happening. It scares me, sure. But not enough to stop me. But enough of that morbid shit. Let's talk about something important. Like when you're going to let me get out of this goddamned bed."

"Anytime you think you're ready."

"Obviously not tonight. I've drunk so much already that I'd fall flat on my ass even if I didn't have a hole in my leg."

"Actually, you're scheduled for physical therapy starting tomorrow. That's really the reason I came by tonight. Figured it was cause enough to celebrate. Now I don't know. Seems sort of futile somehow. But not much choice, I suppose." Doc Cable smiled at the irony. "It's what I do. I'm a doctor. I patch up soldiers so they can go out and fight again." Cable rose to leave, stumbled slightly and put a hand on the bed to steady himself. Jim's hand found his and clasped it.

"Thanks for everything, Doc," he said.

"We're a strange breed, we soldiers," the doctor said, freeing his hand and patting Jim on the shoulder. "Only we can understand one another. I wish you luck, Captain Carmichael. You've picked a hard road. I'm afraid you're in for some surprises once you get out of here. Not too many people around here have any use for soldiers."

"I read the papers, Doc. And watch the TV. Looks like there are a lot of people up in arms about the war. Protests on all the campuses, soldiers being spit upon, people burning their draft cards. But I appreciate the warning anyway."

"As long as you understand. Now, get a good night's sleep. The people in physical therapy are downright sadists. You'll probably like them."

Jim grinned. "Gotta be hard, Doc. You ain't hard, you ain't shit."

"Fucking Green Beanies, you're all the same. Have a good time and I'll check in on you from time to time."

LATER, as he was drifting off to sleep, Lisa came in. He heard her sniff the air, come closer to him, sniff his breath. He reached up, pulled her face down to his. She did not resist.

Her lips were soft and warm, breath spicy. He thought that he had never felt anything quite so good. He wanted it to go on forever, but all too soon she pulled away, fussed for a moment with his covers, then with a deep breath and a setting of shoulders as if she were making her mind up about something, turned and left.

That night instead of the usual nightmares he dreamed of Lisa's soft body lying in the bed beside him. They made love over and over again. In the morning when he woke he thought he could smell the faint scent of her upon his pillow.

WHEN Lisa came to work the next day, Jim observed her closely, hoping to determine by any change in her manner whether the last evening had been a dream or reality. But she was her usual self, cheerfully berating him for transgressions real or imagined, laughing at his jokes, groaning over his bad puns. Regretfully he came to the conclusion that he had been dreaming, the dream undoubtedly spurred by a great deal of wishful thinking.

But he was not able to dwell upon it for long. Dr. Cable, true to his word, had scheduled the first session of physical therapy.

He named them Boris and Natasha. Boris was a very large, gray-haired, hard-faced female. Natasha was a rather wimpy male corpsman who seemed to take joy in the pain he caused.

At first the exercises were all done in bed. Raise your leg, no? Here, let us help you. Oh, that hurts? Well, a certain amount of pain is inevitable. Here, let's try it this way.

They left him gray-faced and sweating. It hadn't hurt this much being hit. If it was going to be this bad, let the damned thing stay stiff. But he knew he wouldn't. He even tried some of the exercises again after the pain subsided.

Each day they came. Each day he cursed them. Boris remained impassive, Natasha got even for the curses by giving the leg a little extra flexion whenever Boris wasn't watching. Within four days they had him out of the bed, and in just over a week he was slowly, painfully shuffling around with the aid of a walker. In two weeks he had graduated to crutches. In three he felt confident enough to ask Dr. Cable for a pass.

"C'mon, Doc," he begged. "Give me a break. Send Boris and Natasha back to the Lubyanka for a refresher course. I've been stuck in this ward forever, it seems like."

"You'd be better off staying in here, you know, until you get well enough to go home on convalescent leave. It isn't the San Francisco you remember out there."

"Home? That's a joke. My home is Fort Bragg, North Carolina, and I'll be back there soon enough."

"What about your family? Your records indicate that your father is still around."

Jim's face darkened. "That would be the last place I'd go," he said.

"No girlfriends, fiancées, wives?"

"A little hard to keep any long-term relationships going when you're around as little as I've been over the last seven years. Since I joined the Army, the longest time I've spent in one place has been Vietnam. So no, nothing serious. Nobody I'd try and go back to visit anyway. Come on, Doc! I'll even go out in civilian clothes. Don't have a uniform anyway."

The doctor relented. "Hell, I suppose a few hours out won't kill you. Friday and Saturday nights only for right now, back in bed by zero two hundred. You do okay with that, we'll negotiate for longer periods. Fair enough?"

"Great, Doc. Appreciate it. I won't fuck up."

It was more than he had dared hope. Now, he thought, for the next stage of the plan. It would come when he saw Lisa again.

Before he could get his courage high enough to broach the subject, she mentioned it. "Understand you're going to be able to get away from here for a little while this weekend?" she said.

"Yeah," he said, hoping to sound nonchalant. "No big thing, just a few hours away. You know any good places close by?"

"A couple," she replied.

"Any chance of you showing them to me?" he asked, braced for the rejection he was sure would come.

She looked at him for a moment, an unfathomable expression on her face. Finally she said, "Sure. Why not? I'll pick you up at six. Gotta go. See you then. Oh, and wear something casual." She left.

Something casual. Clothes. Now, where in the hell am I going to get some clothes? First step is to get some money.

He hobbled to the elevator, took it to the administration floor. He knew there was a finance office there, hoped he could get some of his back pay. An hour later he stood outside the office with nearly two thousand dollars in his hand, representing three months' accumulated pay. It was the most money he'd ever seen at one time.

The next stop was at the small P.X. in the basement. The selection of clothes was not great, and he had no idea of current fashion. He hadn't had to worry about it for a long time. He finally settled for a pair of double-knit gray pants and a white shirt, T-shirt, shorts and, of course, white socks.

He was dressed and ready long before six. What did it mean, he wondered, that Lisa had agreed to go out with him? Anything? Probably not. Just a friendly gesture. After all, they had spent a lot of time together over the last months. Nothing to this, just being nice and showing him places where he could go.

Promptly at six a battered V.W. Bug pulled up to where he was standing. "Get in," she said. "The M.P.s raise hell if you park here too long."

He stuck his crutches in the back and with some difficulty folded his six-foot frame into the seat. As he did so, he found several new pains in his leg, but tried to ignore them.

"Good Lord, girl, didn't anybody ever tell you that you oughta wear clothes?" he said as he got a good look at her. Her tiny denim skirt covered, barely, the upper two inches of her thighs. She wore a tie-dyed T-shirt. It was obvious that there was no bra underneath. Her hair was fluffed out to twice its normal size. It was quite a difference from the white-uniformed girl to whom he had grown so accustomed.

"Gotta blend in with the natives," she said. "The G.I. look doesn't go over too well in this neighborhood."

"It's that bad?"

"And worse. Doesn't do any good to explain you're a medic. Then they hate you because you're supporting the war machine by taking care of the baby killers. Should let them die, they say."

"And I'm not going to blend in too well."

"Not too well," she admitted. "Short hair, G.I. shoes, crutches. You might as well be wearing a neon sign."

"Sounds like we're going to have an interesting evening," he said. "Oh, well, can't be any worse than the NVA. Lead on!"

The first place wasn't too bad. Very quiet, lots of older people. They were stared at as they entered, but except for a couple of whispered asides about his injury, he heard nothing bad.

It was also very boring. "Okay, Lisa," he said after a couple of drinks, "I appreciate your concern, but if I'd wanted to go to sleep, I could have stayed back in the ward. Isn't there someplace around here with some music? I'm not so much of a redneck warmonger that I don't like rock and roll."

"You sure you're up for this?"

"Try me."

Now, this is more like it, he thought as they entered the next place. A blast of music hit them as they opened the door, a group called Jefferson Airplane, she told him. He vaguely remembered having heard them on the jukebox in a club back in Vietnam. Hadn't liked them. Here with everyone talking and laughing and dancing, the music seemed right in place.

They squeezed into a booth and ordered drinks. "Much better," he said. "And nobody seems to be paying much attention to us one way or another."

"So far, so good," Lisa agreed. "Now, Captain . . ."

"Jim," he interrupted.

"Okay, Jim. What I was going to ask may sound stupid. And you can tell me so and I won't feel bad." She lowered her eyes. Her lashes fell long and beautiful across her cheeks. Finally she said, "I overheard you talking to the doctor today about not having a place to go and all. And what I thought was, if you wanted to, you could stay for a while at my place. It's not much, can't afford much on a Spec 4's pay. You don't have to answer now, it'll be a couple of weeks before you're out of the hospital. But think about it."

For a moment he was speechless. Long enough that she looked up quickly, afraid she had somehow offended him. "No strings attached," she assured him.

"No, no, it's not that," he said. "I'm just amazed. I never expected this."

"You didn't know how I felt about you?"

He shook his head slowly. "I'd hoped, of course. But I told myself that you were just being nice. Why?"

Now it was her turn to shake her head. "I don't really know," she answered. "Maybe it was all the hours I spent listening to you when you were out of your head. You talked a lot, some of it comprehensible, some not. There's a lot of rage bottled up inside you. And pain, and most of all loneliness. I know what it's like to be lonely. It eats at you, makes you do things you wouldn't ordinarily dream of doing, just to ease the pain for a little while."

"Someone like you, I wouldn't have thought you'd ever have to be lonely."

"You mean my looks?" When she laughed, there was a tinge of bitterness. "No, I'd never have to worry about company, male or female. This is the City of Love, haven't you read that in the papers? Free love, casual sex, group gropes, whatever you want. It's not hard to come by even if you aren't attractive, and I suppose I am. But I don't need that. I need someone I can talk to, someone who'll at least try to understand what's going on inside my head. That's what I like about you. You try to come across as such a hard-ass. But there's something else there. A tenderness that I can feel whenever you touch me. A capacity for more than war and hate and killing. That's the Jim Carmichael I want to get to know. And I don't have much time to do it. I know you'll be leaving at the end of your convalescent leave, and that I might never see you again after that. But we can have a little time together."

"I can't promise you anything past that," he said.

"Promises are bullshit! I told you, I know I'll probably never see you again after you leave. I can live with that. That's why I said no strings attached. I won't ask you to write, unless you want to. I won't be looking for vows of undying love, and promises to come back to me once this thing is over. It won't ever be over for you, will it?''

"I guess not."

"Ever ask yourself why?"

"More times than you can count. Doc Cable and I had a long discussion on the same subject."

"I know. I listened." She laughed. "It wasn't hard. By the time you two had killed that bottle you were so loud the whole ward could have heard."

"You little shit." He joined in her laughter. "And here I thought we were being so cool. What did you learn?"

"That you really have no idea what motivates you."

"True enough at that point. I've had some time to think about it since then, though. All the reasons I gave the Doc, they're only part of it. There's another reason, one that I'm not sure is entirely rational. But it's there. There's a feeling you get when you're living on the edge, a feeling like no other in the world. Combat high, some people call it. Hard to describe to someone who has never felt it. It's something you don't have to describe to someone who has. You get shot at, the first time, you're terrified. Your diaphragm contracts, tries to pull everything in your chest up into your neck. Heartbeat shoots up, you can hear your pulse inside your head. Feel like you can't move, try to talk and all that comes out is a squeak. Then the adrenaline rush hits you, can't take more than a fraction of a second. It floods you, gives you tremendous energy. You're still scared, but euphoric. Seems like everything becomes sharper, you hear better, see better. Reactions get speeded up, feel twenty feet tall. All you've got to do is suppress your desire to get the hell away from there and let your reactions take over.

"When it's over, there's the letdown. Like coming down off morphine. So you want that high again. You get addicted to it, bad as any junkie sticking a needle in his arm. And the next time you get shot at there's not quite as much fear and so not quite as much of a high. But then something else will happen, something more dangerous, like a grenade coming in, or a mortar barrage, or an ambush and, bingo, there it is again.

"Some people, they never get over the fear, continue to find it hard to suppress the urge to flee. A perfectly healthy reaction, but one that doesn't get them too far as soldiers. So they do only one tour, drop out, get as far away from the military as they can. Count themselves lucky they survived, have no desire to go back to it.

"Others, they're like me. Continue to go from one bad situation to a worse one. Get pissed if they get assigned to a company that isn't seeing much action. Volunteer for the Mobile Strike Force; what we call the Mike Force. Units that are sent where it's hot. Or for the Delta Project, or SOG. Casualties get pretty high. Lots of my friends are dead. I don't know anybody who hasn't been wounded at least once. Sounds stupid when I talk about it. Not much survival value in it. Nobody I know really expects to live through it."

He took her by the hand and looked into her eyes. "So do you still want me to stay with you, realizing that I'm a weirdo?"

"More than ever," she said, squeezing his hand. "I've known other men, civilians mostly. Boring. They don't know how to live. They're tied up with petty shit: how much money they're going to make, what kind of car to drive, how they look. And the dropouts, the hippies, are no better. They're worse conformists than the straights. You look at them, it's almost like a uniform. Long hair, beads, scruffiness; it's like someone decreed that, if you're going to be a hippie, this is what you wear. And not an original idea among them. Knee-jerk reactions to the straight life, to the war, to the so-called establishment. Phony, most of it. Once they grow out of it, they'll be more straight than the ones they're supposedly rebelling against. Most of them come from middle-to-upper-class backgrounds, poor little rich kids, and that's what will tell in the end. Not hypocritical ideas of brotherhood and peace and loving your fellowman. The only men I've known who know how to cut through the bullshit are like yourself. People who have been there, who have nothing to prove to anyone. Who live for today, because they know damned well there is no tomorrow."

"How do you know so much about it?"

"Once upon a time I knew a guy very much like you. He was a sergeant in Special Forces. I met him at Fort Sam Houston when I was going through training. He was wonder-

ful, funny, tender and strong. Sometimes all at once. I loved
him a lot.''

"Where is he now?''

"He was killed in the Ashau Valley. On his second trip.''

"I'm sorry.''

"Don't be. He wasn't. I can't be. I had him for a little
while, and that little while was more than most people have
in their lives. And don't worry. I'm not looking for someone
to take his place. No strings, remember? When you get ready
to leave, you just walk out. Unless I kick you out first!''

"Fair enough. You said it would be a couple of weeks
before they spring me? Where did you get that info?''

"I asked the good doctor. He tells me just about anything
I ask.''

"Then let's celebrate. Waitress!''

His voice drew the attention of the next table. Four men
sat there. All wore hair that was long and greasy, had muscles
showing plainly under dirty T-shirts. They stared at him. He
stared back, causing them to shift their eyes. They muttered
among themselves. He turned back to Lisa.

At the feel of a hand on his shoulder he tried to turn, hit
his bum leg on the table support, blanched with pain.

"Hey, man, easy,'' said the owner of the hand. "Didn't
mean to spook yuh. You hurt yourself?''

Jim identified the man as one of those who had been sitting
at the table. "No harm done,'' he said. "What can I do for
you?''

"You just back from the Nam, man?''

"Yeah, I'm just back from *Viet*nam,'' Jim said. In his experience only those who had never been there called it the
Nam.

"What's it like over there? I mean, I wanted to go but my
old man insisted I go to school or he was gonna cut my
money off, and nobody wants that, huh?'' He gave Jim's
shoulder what was meant to be a playful nudge. "How'd they
catch you, party too hard and lose your deferment?'' He
laughed at his own joke.

"Something like that,'' Jim said thinly.

"Yeah, well, that happens. You got a good-lookin' lady
here anyhow. Mind if I join you?''

"Yeah, we mind, shithead,'' said Lisa. "Now, why don't

you take your filthy ass back over to your own table and have a little circle jerk with your buddies before I kick your nuts up into your throat, you dumb fuck.''

"Hey, lady, don't get so upset," the man said, throwing up his hands in mock surrender. "I was just tryin' to be friendly." To Jim he said in a lower voice, "Tough bitch, man." He flashed a V . . . "Peace, brother."

"Pees on you too," Jim replied pleasantly. The man left. Lisa smiled innocently at him, her big dark eyes sparkling.

"Christ," he said, "where did you learn to cuss like that?"

"I told you I went out with an S.F. sergeant. And one thing I forgot to mention, my dad was in the Marine Corps."

"I might have known," he groaned. "A military brat."

"Best kind of brat. Besides, that asshole would have had all his buddies over here and they would have been trying to put the make on me, and I just wasn't up for that shit tonight. Now, where were we?"

They talked, laughed and drank until it finally occurred to Jim to check his watch. "Holy shit," he said, "it's twelve-thirty. I've got to get back or Doc Cable's going to turn me into a pumpkin." He retrieved his crutches from beneath the table. Getting up was painful. His leg had stiffened from sitting so long.

"Tell you what," Lisa said as they got to the entrance, "I'll go get the car and come back for you. That way you won't have to walk all the way across the parking lot."

He did not object. The distance to the car seemed impossibly long. Besides, the night air was pleasant after the smoky heat of the bar. He closed his eyes and let the breeze waft over his face.

"What happened, man, your watchdog leave?" He looked over his shoulder, saw the man from the bar flanked by his three buddies.

"This is the big badass soldier boy who was hiding behind that little cunt," the man sneered. "Don't look so big and badass to me, does he to you?"

Jim shifted his grip slightly on the crutch, placing most of his weight on his good leg.

"I think we ought to take his sticks away from him, see if he'll crawl around like a worm," said one of the others.

"What about it, maggot, you want to squirm around a little bit?" asked the first, moving toward him.

The crutch described a short upper arc, acting as an extension of his stiffened arm. Its tip caught the man in the crotch. A howl of anguish escaped his lips as he folded to the pavement. As he was dropping, Jim let go of that crutch, caught the other by its lower and swung it with both hands. When it impacted on the second man's head, it splintered. He dropped beside his companion and didn't move. The other two moved toward him, cursing. He held them at bay with the jagged ends of the crutch, thrusting at them when they got too close; backing awkwardly away. Okay, Jim, he thought to himself, any more bright ideas? This is going to hurt. A lot.

Bright lights flashed along with a screeching of brakes and blowing of horn. A battered V.W. was barreling directly toward the two men. They barely escaped its path, throwing themselves out of the way. As they were getting up, it came round again, scattering them. Twice more it came back, chasing one behind a group of cars and the other back into the building. It was like a bullfight, except that this bull looked like an enraged rat.

The V.W. screeched to a halt beside him. "Will you get your ass in here instead of standing there and laughing like an idiot?" Lisa shouted. "The cops will be here before long."

"Who cares?" he said as he folded himself painfully into the seat. "We weren't causing any trouble, they were."

"This is San Francisco and you and I are G.I.s," she said, speeding out of the parking lot. "Welcome to the world, love."

At the entrance to the hospital he finally got up enough nerve to ask a question that had been tormenting him.

"Did you, one night a few weeks ago, by any chance, come back to the ward after hours?"

"Now, that would be against regulations, wouldn't it?" She was half turned to face him, her eyes glistening with—what was it?—amusement? "And you know that good little soldiers don't break regulations, do they? Regulations like those against fraternization between officers and enlisted people?" She pulled his head down to hers.

Too soon she broke the kiss. "Now, Captain, the way I

see it is you've got about five minutes before bed check, no crutches and a long limping walk back to the ward. Good night.''

He ate up several of his precious moments by staring after her departing car. He couldn't wait for the next two weeks to pass. Or for that matter, tomorrow.

THE next day he waited for her to show up for work. By the time she was two hours late he remembered that she had weekends off. When he was sick, she had been there almost every day, and he had gotten used to it.

The day was long and boring. The idea of going out alone had no appeal, so he resigned himself to more boredom that night. He went to the hospital library and searched for something he had not already read. It was a difficult task. He'd always been an avid reader. While confined to bed he had done little else, going through the little library's meager offerings quite thoroughly.

After some persuasion he got the supply sergeant to issue him a cane to replace the two lost crutches. The sergeant assured him there would be a Report of Survey on the crutches, and that he would have to pay for them. Typical, he thought. He disliked supply sergeants in general; they all seemed to think the items under their care were their personal property and hated to release anything. After all, if you gave something out to someone who needed it, you wouldn't have it anymore. Then what did you do if someone came asking for it?

By four o'clock he was going thoroughly crazy and beginning to reconsider his decision not to go out. There was a small Officers Club on the grounds of the hospital and, while he didn't particularly feel like sitting around drinking, he was beginning to think it would be better than dying of boredom.

A corpsman came to the door. ''Hey, Cap'n,'' the man said, ''you've got a phone call at the nurses' station.''

''I figured you might need rest after your big night last night,'' came her voice over the receiver. ''That's why I didn't call sooner. How are you feeling?''

''Great. No, that's a lie. Physically great. But I'm bored to tears.''

She laughed. ''We can cure that. Do you want to come

over to my place for a while? I've spent most of the day cleaning, so it should be fairly presentable. We could drink a little wine, maybe send out for a pizza. I'm no cook, so I won't subject you to any of my culinary masterpieces. Sound okay?''

''Sounds wonderful. Can I bring anything?''

''Yeah, yourself. I'll pick you up at the same time as last night.''

Her apartment was only a few blocks from the hospital. Luckily it was on the ground floor; there was no elevator and he didn't feel up to climbing a lot of stairs.

The place was tiny, essentially one room with a small bathroom off to the side and a kitchenette. But it was clean and bright and decorated as well as her tiny salary would allow. It reflected her personality, feminine but not excessively so.

''Sit,'' she commanded. She poured him a glass of white wine. ''I got you something today. I hope you won't mind.'' She gave him a sack with a department store logo.

Inside were a pair of jeans, a bright red shirt and a pair of sandals. ''I had to guess your size,'' she said. ''I hope they fit. I thought you might want to get out of your midwestern mufti and join the local population.''

He laughed. ''And avoid any more bar fights?''

''That too. Don't know what we're going to do about the haircut, though. I don't suppose you'd consider a wig?''

''Kiss my ass,'' he said. ''Mind if I try these on?''

''I wish you would. You look like an IBM repairman. All you need is a plastic pocket and a bunch of pens.''

''Kiss my ass a lot,'' he growled, grabbing the sack and going to the bathroom.

''Promises, promises,'' she said as he closed the door.

The jeans were a tight fit. First he tried to put them on over his boxer shorts, got a lot of material wedged in the crotch for his trouble. He finally decided the shorts had to go. The pants fit much better. The shirt was of a very soft material and was also form-fitting. It clung to him, accentuating his chest and flat stomach. Good God, he thought, looking at himself in the mirror, I've lost a lot of weight.

She looked at him up and down as he emerged from the bathroom, smiled in approval. ''Nice,'' she said. ''You've got a great ass. Those baggy double-knits didn't do a thing for it.''

"You don't mince many words, do you?"

She shrugged. "I say what I think. And I do what I want. Does that bother you?"

"No. I'm just not used to it. Most of the American girls I've known wouldn't say shit if they had a mouthful. Of course, I haven't known any American girls for a long time. This is the first time I've been back to the States since '63."

"You didn't come back here after your first tour?"

"No, I went to 1st Special Forces Group in Okinawa. Was going to come back to go to Officers Candidate School, but the group commander talked me into applying for a direct commission instead."

"I didn't realize that. So things have changed for you more than I knew."

"It's an entirely different world. The TV shows are different, people are different, obviously the women are different. When I left, the biggest worry of the girls I went out with was getting pregnant. Now with the pill I guess that's gone away. They tell me there's a sexual revolution going on, and it looks like I've been left out."

"You haven't missed much," she murmured.

"You speak from experience, I take it. Tell me about it."

"Not now. Maybe later. For sure later. There are things you need to know about me, but I'm not sure I trust you enough to tell you right now."

"Not trust me enough?" His feelings were hurt. "Why, do you think I'm going to spread it all over the hospital?"

"Maybe. Men talk, brag. It's happened to me before."

"Then you went out with the wrong men. But I understand. Can't force you to talk. I guess you'll do it when and if you get ready."

"Don't sit there so stiff! Christ, your face looks as if it's made from rock. I'm not saying anything against you personally; please don't take it so. It just takes a little time, that's all." She shifted toward him. Her full breast brushed his arm. "Now, shall I call for the pizza, or are you going to kiss me first?"

THE pizza never got ordered.

"Think you'll be able to live for a whole week without me?" she teased him as they dressed.

"In great agony," he replied. "I'm going to want you all the time. Christ, I won't be able to keep my hands off you."

"Horny little devil, aren't you? You'll just have to suffer. They catch us doing anything at the hospital and I'll get an Article 15, probably get restricted to barracks, and then where will you be?"

"Up shit creek without the proverbial paddle, I guess. Okay, you convinced me. But every time you see me, just know that I'll be thinking about next Friday. And what we'll do then. And you'll think about it too."

"You *are* a bastard. Thank heavens I won't be seeing you all that much during the week."

"How come?"

"I have a job, remember? There are other patients, and you're almost well. I don't think the ward nurse is going to put up with me spending as much time with you as I have over the last couple of months. Too bad. It was nice taking care of you. Made me feel needed."

"You're still needed," he told her seriously. "If not to take care of me, at least to be there. And not just sexually either. I like you a lot, Lisa Brown."

"Yeah, well, before we start blubbering, let's get you back to the ward. Having trouble walking?" she asked, grinning wickedly. "I know I am."

"Those guys were right, you know."

"Oh?" Her eyebrows arched.

"Yeah. You are one tough little bitch. And," he said, blocking the blow she threw at his stomach, "I say that in the nicest possible way."

THE next week was, as he had known it would be, difficult. Each time he saw her she gave him a knowing little smile and he was instantly aroused. He had to force himself to stay in his room, buried in a book, watching but not watching the inane TV programming, just to keep from following her around.

From the news he saw that opposition to the war was growing. Just across the bay at Berkeley the students seemed to spend more time marching and protesting than they did in class. He wondered when they studied. Probably didn't. Must be nice, he thought. Wish I had the money to do that.

Boris and Natasha continued to torture him, but were privately amazed at his progress. Something, they didn't know what, caused him to push himself to the limit. He could have told them what it was, but didn't.

The fruit of his labor came on Friday when Dr. Cable told him he could have the entire weekend off, Friday afternoon to Sunday midnight. "I guess you can find a place to stay all that time," he said, a broad smile splitting his face. "Must be a nice girl. You were in a hell of a lot better mood last week. I don't know her, do I?"

"I doubt it, Doc," he lied. "Just somebody who takes pity on a poor soldier boy."

"Sure. Well, don't let her break anything. If you continue to progress, you can be sprung from this place in another week. Then it's back to Fort Bragg for you?"

"Don't think so. I might take a little time off. Maybe see this part of the States. Haven't really spent a lot of time on the West Coast."

"Yeah. I understand. By the way, this doesn't have any relation to the fact that Specialist Brown just put in for a thirty-day leave, does it? No? I thought it was just a coincidence. That's what I told the charge nurse anyway. Have a good weekend."

"THE DOC is onto us," he told her that night in the lull after the whirlwind of their first lovemaking.

She snuggled closer, threw a leg over his. "I know," she said. "He told me to be careful. I think he feels like he's my dad. He sat me down for a long father-daughter talk today. Warned me not to get too attached to you." She giggled. "I'm afraid I shocked him. Told him all I was after was a good fuck."

"And am I?"

"Yeah."

"Is that all?"

"Yeah," she said again, enjoying the expression on his face. He looked so forlorn! She relented. "You're more than that and you know it. Maybe that's what I thought it would be at first. And I did need it. You're my first man in a long time. I told myself you'd be safe, that you and I could spend some time together and enjoy ourselves and then you would go away and forget about me. And I could forget about you. And maybe that's what will still happen. But to paraphrase something I heard last weekend, I've grown to like you an awful lot, Captain James No Middle Initial Carmichael. Why don't you have a middle name, by the way?''

"We were too poor. Couldn't afford it. I got the first name, my brother got the middle. Wasn't too bad a deal for me. His name is Ferdinand.''

"You're such a liar!''

"Yeah. And you are a sexy little wench. And if you don't stop what you're doing, we're not going to get any pizza tonight either.''

HE slept lightly, as usual. The slightest noise, or even an absence of noise, would bring him instantly alert. He was surprised at how comforting it was to have her beside him on the bed. Her soft breathing was soothing to his soul, her warmth a balm. It was a very long time since he had slept with anyone, hadn't realized how much he missed it. Why did he feel so safe with her? He found it much easier to drop back off to sleep after one of his alerts. And his dreams were far less threatening. At times they were almost pleasant.

The weekend ended all too quickly. Every moment had been filled with joy. He found her wickedly funny, ever ready to point out the foibles of the human race, including herself. They talked of nothing serious; the war didn't exist, there were no political problems in the world, the United States was not tearing itself apart like some giant beast caught in a trap from which it could not be extricated. Nothing existed outside the little bubble they made for themselves. They pointedly refused to discuss the future. Perhaps it was because they realized that the future would go on in its inexorable way, ignoring puny man's efforts to influence it.

It intruded upon him the next week when he received a call from the assignment officer in Infantry Branch back in Washington. "We understand that you'll be back to full duty before long," the major said. "Given any thought to where you'd like to be assigned? And before you tell me back to Special Forces, I hope you realize that you'd be doing your career some real harm. You haven't had an assignment out of

Group since you were commissioned. You badly need some regular-army time, command time especially.''

Jim was nice enough not to laugh openly over the phone. Career! What career? It was difficult to think about what would be good for your career when you had serious doubts you would live long enough to have to worry about it.

The major, mistaking his silence for assent, went on. ''Now, what I'd recommend is a basic training company commander slot. We have lots of them open: Fort Polk, Fort Leonard Wood, Fort Hood. Where would you like to go?''

''Major, I can save you a whole lot of trouble, make your assignment job much easier and get what I want too, if you'll go along with it. You're short on captains. A hell of a lot of the shake-'n'-bake first lieutenants you're sending to USARV are ending up in 0-3 slots, simply because there isn't anybody else to assign. And they can't handle it, most of them. Hell, the way you're promoting them it only takes a year to make first john.''

''So don't tell me. Out of the goodness of your heart you want to sacrifice yourself for one of them. Give you one of their slots, let that lieutenant get some more experience here in the States, am I right?''

''Wouldn't exactly call it out of the goodness of my heart but, yeah, that's the scenario.''

''You going to be in good enough shape to hump the hills?''

''If I'm not, I can always get a staff job until I am. Come on, let's not dick around with this. We both know I'm going to end up back over there anyway. I just don't particularly want to sit around in the States waiting to get orders.''

''Your funeral, Carmichael. What kind of convalescent leave are they giving you?''

Same thing Lally said, he thought, suppressing a shiver. ''Thirty days,'' he replied.

''You have an address where we can send the orders?''

''Send them here to the hospital Admin Company. I appreciate this, Major. I'll return the favor if I ever get the chance.''

''No sweat. Sort of expected it. Spent some time in Group myself, before they stuck me up here. May end up seeing you back over there. I'm sure the war won't be over before this assignment is. Take care.''

One hurdle through. Jim was elated. Now to get discharged from the hospital on time. Boris and Natasha had been horrified to hear that they might lose him so soon. He thought it was because they were having so much fun contorting his leg into positions that were not remotely possible for a human.

Doc Cable came by to do his final examination on Friday. He was unusually serious. His face was drawn and haggard. He was almost curt to Jim's repeated attempts at conversation.

"What happened, Doc?" Jim finally asked. "You look like shit. Anything I can help with?"

Horrified, he watched tears form in the older man's eyes.

Cable wiped them away quickly. "You're fit," he said. "As fit as you need to be. You can check out of here this afternoon. I suppose I'll see you before you leave the country. Check in occasionally. Maybe we can talk."

"You're sure there's nothing I can do?"

For a second there was fury in the doctor's eyes. "Sure," he said. "How are you at neurosurgery? Can you repair a severed lower spine? No? Well then, I don't guess you can help me very much." The doctor sat down heavily, covered his face. "Sorry, I didn't mean to take it out on you. It's not your fault."

"What happened?" Jim asked, dreading the answer.

"I guess I'll get to see my son a little sooner than I expected. He'll be on a Medevac flight next week. God damn it! What kind of war is it that you get shot by your own troops? He was shot in the back, Jim, by somebody with an M-16."

"You sure it wasn't an accident?" Jim asked. "That can happen in the heat of a firefight. You know that."

Cable laughed bitterly. "That's what I would like to believe. He was afraid something like this would happen. Told me about the discipline problems they were having. Last month somebody threw a grenade in the C.O.'s hut. They'd threatened him too, but he thought he could stay alert enough. Must have dropped his guard."

"Jesus, Doc, I'm sorry."

"Yeah, me too. Now I wish I'd never let him join the army, never have talked about the 'good old days.' This is my fault.

How am I ever going to be able to face him?'' Cable walked out.

My God, thought Jim. What kind of an army indeed? He'd heard stories about fraggings, but had never had to deal with it. Such incidents he had dismissed with the thought that they had to be due to bad leadership. But if it was growing this widespread, there must be something else seriously wrong. The war was bad enough; no front, no idea from where the enemy might come next. If you couldn't trust your own troops, whom could you trust? And D.A. wanted him to go to a conventional outfit for his ''career.'' What kind of career was that when you risked getting killed or maimed by your own troops? No thanks.

It was in those late afternoon hours as he was waiting to be discharged that he began to wonder if the war was lost. It did not shake his resolve to go back, but infused him with the sense of melancholy that all supporters of lost causes must have. But a lost cause was better than no cause at all. If there was nothing worth dying for, it followed that there was nothing much worth living for either.

CHAPTER 3

CABLE'S sorrow and his own apprehensions were soon forgotten in the joy of being with Lisa. They made love immediately after arriving at her apartment, going at it as if they were starving. This set a pattern which was followed for the next several days; seldom did they go outside except to get food. They were content with one another's company, needed nothing from the outside world, tried to keep that world from intruding on them. But intrude it would.

One day Lisa answered the phone, spoke for a moment, then handed the receiver to him. There was a peculiar look on her face. "It's for you," she said. "It's the first sergeant of Admin Company."

"Captain Carmichael? We need you to come in here, sir. There's a ceremony you need to attend on Friday."

"What kind of ceremony?" Jim couldn't imagine why they had called.

"I'll explain that when you get in here. You get fixed up with uniforms yet? No? Then you'll need to get over to Oakland Army Depot and get a set of Class As. Full awards and decorations and 'I been there' badges, sir. The colonel requests it. Come in around fourteen hundred. Be on time, please, sir." The first sergeant hung up before he could ask any more questions.

Lisa asked a question with her eyes. He shrugged. "Damned if I know. More army bullshit, I expect. Command Retreat or something. Need some Class As. Isn't Friday the first one in February?"

"Yeah," she said. "But we've never had one before. Which doesn't mean much. Well, Captain, shall we go out to Oakland tomorrow and get you fixed up in all your finery? You should look real pretty."

"Fuck you very much, Lisa. God hates a wiseass, you know. I really do."

OAKLAND was humming with activity. it was the outprocessing center for Vietnam returnees and the intermediate stop for those going the other way. It was easy to tell the difference between the two: the returnees were deeply tanned and, though they were in most cases only a year or two older than their counterparts, were immeasurably aged in looks. They stood around in loose groups, looked in contempt at the fresh young faces of the new men.

The recruits, for their part, regarded the returnees as having somehow failed. The war had been going on for eight years now. For the last four there had been full-scale U.S. involvement. That was as long as World War II, but this one seemed no closer to ending now than it had two or three years ago. Surely part of the blame for that had to lie with those who had been fighting it. Just give us a chance, the recruits said among themselves, we'll show old Charlie a trick or two.

At the Quartermaster Sales store Jim bought a set of Class A greens, two sets of tropical worsted Class Bs and a couple of sets of fatigues. He added captain's bars and infantry crossed rifles. Threw in some ribbons to which he vaguely remembered he was authorized. Upon checking the chart he found that he was authorized three more campaign stars on the Vietnam service ribbon. Be getting a little crowded on it soon, he thought.

At the P.X. he bought a set of Corcoran jump boots. Though technically he was not now assigned to an airborne unit, he was damned if he was going to go anywhere in straight-leg low-quarters. Neither place had berets, so he supposed he would have to wear his old one, tattered from years of use.

The next morning, as he was assembling his ribbons and pinning them and his badges on the uniform, the reality of the situation hit him. It had been easy to forget over the last couple of weeks that he was still in the army. Now the smell of the heavy green wool reminded him forcefully that, whatever happiness and joy he was experiencing right now, all of it would soon end. He would be back to doing his job, would be away from Lisa, might never again know the carefree pleasures of this simple interlude. With the thought came more sadness than he would have thought possible. He was a soldier! He couldn't let things like this bother him. But bother him it did. As he polished the boots he cursed himself for being such an asshole.

Finally he was ready. He dressed carefully, making sure there were no wrinkles in the trousers, that they bagged properly over the tops of his boots, that the tie was knotted just so, that the green blouse draped correctly, that all his ribbons and badges were straight. Finally he took the old beret, replaced the single bar affixed to the flash with the double tracks of a captain and, placing the flash directly over his left eye, pulled it down until it achieved just the right degree of go-to-hell rakishness.

He emerged from the bathroom. Lisa's eyes widened. "God damn," she exclaimed. "You look just like a Christmas tree."

"And thank you so much for that wonderful reinforcement to my masculine ego. Somewhat of an overstated effect, you think?"

"I think the people in hospital company are going to be jealous as hell. You look splendid. Come on, let's go. I can't wait until they see you."

"You're going to the ceremony?" he asked, surprised.

"And give up my precious day of leave? Not hardly. But I will be watching from a distance. This will be the first chance I've had to see you play soldier. If I was in ranks, I might have to giggle. Can't have that, with you looking so serious and all. But while you're standing up there in a rigid position of attention I want you to give just one small thought to what I'm going to do to you tonight after I get that war suit off you."

"You really are an asshole, you know."

"Yeah." She smiled wickedly. "Don't you just love it?"

He entered the orderly room, found the first sergeant, who popped to attention. It took a confusing moment until Jim remembered that the proper command was "As you were."

"Formation is in ten minutes, so I guess you won't have

time to get a haircut,'' said the first shirt in mock severity. ''You trying to look like a hippie, sir?''

Jim had already seen the Special Forces combat patch on the man's right shoulder. He relaxed and laughed. ''Not quite a hippie,'' he said, ''but I'll admit that when I put the beret on and my hair curled up over the sweatband, I thought, Don't I look sweet! How did you get stuck here, Sergeant Saunders? Don't we know each other from Bragg?''

''I looked at your records. We were there at the same time, so maybe so.'' A look of distaste came over Saunders' face. ''Got stuck here baby-sitting after I came back with a hole in my belly. Had to wear a colostomy bag for a while. Now the bag is gone but they still need a first sergeant. You want a cup of coffee?''

Jim accepted a cup. ''You call up Mrs. Alexander in D.A.?'' he asked.

''Fuckin' nearly every week. I think I'm about to piss Billie off. Maybe after I piss her off enough, she'll get me the hell out of here.'' Mrs. Billie Alexander was in charge of Special Forces NCO assignments and as such was either loved or hated and feared, depending on which assignment she had given you last and which you were hoping for next.

''So what's the story on this ceremony?'' Jim asked. ''Another army sideshow?''

''Yeah,'' Saunders said. ''With you as the main attraction. Might as well go out and face the music.''

Jim cursed under his breath as he stood in front of the massed company. Before him was Colonel Cable, smiling slightly as both listened to the droning voice of the adjutant.

''Attention to Orders!'' he said. ''By direction of the President, the Silver Star Medal is presented to Captain James NMI Carmichael, 05324976, Infantry, United States Army, for gallantry in action while engaged in military operations involving conflict with a hostile armed force in the Republic of Vietnam.'' The adjutant went on to describe his actions on that day. Much of what was said he did not recognize; events only half remembered were described in full and glowing detail in the citation. It was as if they were talking about someone else, someone who was brave, but also exceptionally foolhardy.

Exceptionally valorous actions? I was just trying to stay alive. My gallantry in action was in keeping with the highest traditions of the military service and reflects great credit upon myself, my unit, and the United States Army? What about the actions that shamed me and everyone else? What about throwing a company into a fight with a battalion? What about losing at least half of that company, maybe more? Was there nobody to speak for them?

As Colonel Cable pinned the medal to his pocket flap, Jim recognized that the reality of any situation was only what people wanted to recognize as the reality. With the stroke of a pen he had become a hero; it could as easily have gone the other way. Thus, because of the arbitrary decision of some anonymous staff officer, it was so. A battle that had been like so many others, with no clear-cut winner, was now being represented as a brilliant action and a vindication of the policy of letting indigenous troops do the fighting. Though with good American leadership, of course.

When the ceremony was over, the officers crowded around to shake his hand, congratulate him, bask in his reflected glory. All he wanted was to get away. The whole situation seemed so phony. He turned down invitations to join them at the club, pleading prior engagements. To get away he approached Colonel Cable, who had been standing off to the side.

"How is your son, sir?" he asked. "I'm sorry I haven't been in touch."

"He has his good and bad days. Like everyone else. We've taken care of the injuries. The physical ones anyway. The mental are harder to deal with. Part of the time he's suicidal, the rest he's angry. It's that anger that will make him survive, I think. He has a very strong will."

"Was the wound caused by what you thought?"

The doctor nodded. "A man in his company who he had just busted from E-5 back down to private. For smoking pot. Wouldn't have been so bad if he had just been smoking in the rear, Neil said. He would have had to bust half of the company if that was the case. This guy was smoking all the time, on the perimeter, on patrol, just before air assaults."

"What are they going to do to him?"

"Court-martial, Leavenworth, the usual. We've come to a

hell of a pass, haven't we? Still as eager as you were to get back over there?''

"Probably not as eager. But that doesn't matter too much. I should have orders in a few days, and eager or not, away I go.''

"Well, take care of yourself.'' The doctor touched the medal dangling from Jim's chest. "These are nice. I used to think I'd have done just about anything to have one. But they aren't that great as casket decorations. Keep your head down. Tell Lisa we miss her at work. I'll see you before you leave?''

Jim promised it, then went off in search of Lisa, returning so many salutes his arm got tired. Finally he gave up and went to the car to wait for her, only to find her already there.

"Listen to this,'' she said, turning the car radio up. The newscaster was describing a major offensive just then taking place in Vietnam. The Viet Cong, taking advantage of the usual Chinese New Year's truce, had attacked cities all over the country. The reports were confusing and contradictory, but it seemed that major victories had been scored by the enemy. Further details would follow as they came in. The newscaster's voice was followed, appropriately enough, by the song "Eve of Destruction.''

"Chinese New Year's?'' Lisa asked.

"They call it Tet,'' he replied. "Biggest holiday on their calendar. Anyone who can get away goes home to spend it with their families. Both sides usually declare a truce. So much for truces. Let's go home, maybe we can catch more news on the TV.''

OVER the next few days he stayed glued to the television. There was an air of hysteria in the news. The enemy, it seemed, had taken all or a part of many of the cities. Pleiku, Qui Nhon, Hue, Saigon, Can Tho; the names rolled by in a litany. It was described by pundits as clear proof that the war was being lost. These same pundits had only a few days before been extolling the progress of the conflict.

To Jim's soldier's eye, reading behind the headlines and the hysteria, it seemed far less bad. True, the V.C. had scored successes in the cities, but except in Hue they had very quickly been thrown out again, suffering horrendous casualties in the process. In no place had the conventional units of the U.S.

forces been hit except for harassing rocket and mortar fire and probes. The Main Force North Vietnamese units seemed to be staying completely out of the fray, hiding in their jungle redoubts and letting the Viet Cong take the brunt of the fighting. From his experience, Jim knew that body-count figures were often inflated, but if only a portion of this were true, the V.C. were suffering casualties from which it would take a very long time to recover. It seemed to him that instead of a disaster, there was a very great opportunity presenting itself. He hoped the generals at USARV were smart enough to exploit it.

But at the same time he saw how the event had mobilized people in the United States in opposition to the war. Not a day went by without a demonstration, angry protesters marching against anything even remotely military. It would have been unsafe to walk down the streets of San Francisco in uniform. And he felt a grudging admiration for the strategists in Hanoi. Unable to win a battle in Vietnam, they would take the fight to the streets of America. And there they would triumph.

He got his orders during this time. He was to report to Travis Air Force Base for shipment to Vietnam on 15 February 1968. He was assigned to the Replacement Detachment, Long Binh, for further assignment as befitted the needs of the army. It was only a week away.

He showed Lisa the orders. "Well, it's what you expected, wasn't it?" she asked, rather coldly, he thought. He dropped the subject.

The next couple of days he could feel her withdrawing from him. It was not an unexpected reaction, but it saddened him. They had always found it easy to share everything, but now were always most careful not to mention his departure.

There was a pulling away which manifested itself in long uncomfortable silences, an inability to joke about life, a marked decrease in the tender little touches they had so often shared. In sex it was the opposite. It became more intense, almost frenzied. It left them exhausted, barely able to move.

It was in this state that he finally asked her why she was pulling away.

"Simple," she said. "Damage control."

"Damage control?"

"Yes, damage control. Limiting the hurt that is going to come. I'm tired of being hurt. I hate it. And it's going to be very painful when you go away. So I shut off the hurt. And by shutting off the hurt I shut off part of what I feel for you."

"I understand, I guess. I wish it didn't have to be this way."

"No, you don't," she said tonelessly. "Not really. You're doing what you think you have to do, and not I or anybody else is going to get in your way. I was foolish enough to think that you needed me, once. And perhaps you did. But not anymore. All you need, all you want to depend upon, is yourself. You'll always go through life not needing anyone, following that inner compass that only you can read. So am I shutting myself off? You bet I am, because you've shut me out. I won't stop caring for you. I couldn't do that. But don't ask me to do more, because I can't. I can't sit here day after day, loving you and not knowing what is happening to you, not knowing if you're alive or dead. I did that once, and it almost destroyed me." There were tears standing in her eyes. She angrily wiped them away.

"So what do we do now?"

"We enjoy these last few days together, and then you'll go away. And we remain friends. I'll write, you'll write, and when you come back, as I know you will because whatever other quality you have, you're a survivor, maybe we can see each other. I'd like that. But I can't be thinking about you all the time and you won't be thinking about me, because you'll be spending most of your time just staying alive. Now go to sleep. I'll promise to try to limit my damage-control efforts if you'll promise to quit looking like a whipped puppy every time I snap at you."

"A whipped puppy? I thought I was handling this very well."

"That's what you get for thinking without qualification. Bad habit. Now go to sleep."

He thought that war was much easier to understand than was a woman.

HE arrived at Travis Air Force Base north of San Francisco, checked in, showed the Passenger Service NCO his orders and was given a flight number and time to report.

He asked for and was given directions to the Officers Club. He had no desire to sit in the terminal and think about Lisa. He already missed her. They had tried to appear unemotional when they parted. Casual. Yes I'll write, Take care of yourself, Goodbye. Hiding the pain. Perhaps a couple of drinks would make it easier to bear. Perhaps a lot of drinks would cause it to go away altogether. He doubted it, but in any case had no intention of getting on the plane sober. It would be a long, dry trip.

He sat at the bar, ordered a drink, took one long and satisfying gulp, then turned away from the bar and surveyed the room. In a corner table he saw a face he thought looked familiar. He walked over.

"Mark Petrillo!" he said. "Last time I saw you, we were leaving country in '63."

"How are you doing, Jim? Why don't you come join us?" "Gentlemen," he said, introducing Jim, "this used to be one of the finest medics in Group. Before he got tired of working for a living and got commissioned. You on the twenty-one-hundred flight?"

"Yes, sir," Jim said, belatedly noticing the gold leaf Mark was wearing on his collar.

"Shit, you never called me sir when I was an L.T. and you were a buck sergeant, so why are you starting now? Besides, I'm not used to this yet. Just got it yesterday. Reward for good and faithful service, and all that shit. You know these guys here?"

"Only Al," Jim said, smiling at Al Dougherty, the stocky fellow captain. "You going back to Project Delta, Al?"

"I don't think so. Mark sounds like he has a better deal. I heard you got hit. You okay now? Didn't try to shoot your dick off again, did they?"

Jim winced. "I hoped that story would go away. Guess not, huh?"

"In Group? You know better than that. Especially when people like me are around to tell a couple of young lieutenants like these that the captain used to have the name of Piccolo due to the fact he took three claymore pellets through the pecker. Had to play his dick like he was a symphony soloist so he could take a piss. You got an assignment, Jim?"

"Long Binh, unassigned." Jim replied. "D.A. said I

should try to get some command time, so I guess I'll end up as a company commander. Probably in the fucking Americal Division, with my luck.'' The Americal, having been patched together out of three independent brigades, was widely regarded as being the worst unit in Vietnam.

"Sounds like fun. You want that?''

"Like I want the bubonic plague. Seems a little strange that I can lead a battalion of 'Yards in combat and it doesn't count, but if I serve six months in a conventional outfit, I'm okay. But they never said the army was fair.''

"You might want to ask Mark about PRU then. How about it, Major Mark? You got room for another captain? Even if he does have the bad habit of getting his ass shot off with astounding regularity.''

"Oh, hell yes. There's always room for more. You heard of the PRU, Jim?''

"Provincial Reconnaissance Units? Sure. Used to be called Counter-Terror Teams. But I thought it was an Agency operation.''

"It is,'' Mark explained. "But officially you get assigned to the Civil Operations and Revolutionary Development Support branch of MACV. CORDS, for short. The Agency has always used military types to do the actual work. You interested?''

"Maybe. How much 'advising' do you actually do?''

"About as much as on an 'A' Detachment. You're officially assigned as an advisor, but since you have complete control over all the money, you can use it as a lever to get what you want. I think you'd like it. These boys are doing some pretty good work. Can't tell you much about it here, it's classified as hell and the tender ears of these lieutenants might not be able to stand it. Or we could go ahead and tell them, but then we'd have to shoot them. If you're interested, I can get you into Saigon for a briefing. Then you can make up your mind.''

"Fair enough. How long have you been with them?''

"A year. Extended for another six months. I'm just going back to RVN after a greatly enjoyed extension leave. Shows you how much I like it, that I didn't just stay home. So how did you get hit anyway?''

For the next two hours they swapped stories, each better

than the last. By the time they had to leave to catch the plane,
all were thoroughly drunk and the L.T.s were having serious
second thoughts as to the wisdom of associating themselves
with such a crazy bunch. Perhaps Canada wouldn't have been
such a bad idea after all, they thought.

"You gonna go with PRU?" Al asked, somewhere
over the Pacific.

Jim pulled himself away from the window. He had been
watching the tops of the clouds, their fluffy white surface
exerting a hypnotic influence as they slid beneath. It appeared
so clean up here. He envied the pilots who so often would
slip the bonds of earth and escape to this ethereal realm where
man was a puny and infrequent interloper.

"Don't know. How about you?"

"Sounds like a pretty good program. Absolute freedom
of action. You're the only American assigned to a province
team. The closest supervision would be from the regional
office, and they aren't going to bug you as long as you do
your job."

"Isn't this the same thing they're calling the Phoenix program? How do they put it, in their wonderful euphemistic
way: 'Neutralization and Elimination of the Viet Cong Infrastructure'?"

"Not so loud," Dave cautioned. "Yeah, the whole thing
is called Phoenix. And PRU is the action arm of the program.
The way it works is you get a blacklist of confirmed V.C.
agents. You go out and try to capture them. If possible. If
not, get rid of them. Same shit the V.C. do against the government's people out in the villages. About time we used
some of their own tactics against them, don't you think?"

Jim agreed. It made eminent good sense, and it seemed
nothing more than a logical extension of what they had been
doing against the Viet Cong military units. Ambushes, snip-
ing operations, mines and booby traps; nobody cared when
you used such tools against a V.C. squad. Why should this
be any different? Besides, there were a lot of people out there
who needed to be stopped: the tacticians behind the scenes
who sent out those squads to assassinate government officials
and Americans, to burn down Montagnard villages, directing
flamethrowers down into the pitiful bunkers where the women

and children tried to take refuge; the ones who buried alive the families of Vietnamese soldiers in the sand dunes outside Hue. For too long they had been able to do these things with relative impunity, hiding in their jungle redoubts or right under the noses of those who searched for them by acting as harmless villagers or even as government officials.

"How good are the actual lists?" he asked. "Do they really identify people or is it some more of the nebulous bullshit we used to get from MACV J-2?"

"Some places better than others, from what I hear. Depends on the quality of the people working on it. I hear that I Corps has the best. That's where I'm going to try to go. Mark says the regional officer in charge in Danang is an old operational type from the Agency, Clandestine Services branch, and runs a tight ship. Not like some of the others, who were desk officers for the Soviet bureau and God knows what else before the Agency decided it would be 'career-enhancing' for them to serve a tour in Vietnam."

"Sounds interesting. I'll listen to what they have to say. You leave anything behind in the States, Al?"

"You mean besides bad debts, traffic tickets and an ex-wife who gets half my paycheck every month? Not much. You were lucky you didn't have to go back to Fort Bragg. You'd be pissed if you saw the way they're flushing the young troops through Smoke Bomb Hill now. Seventh Special Forces Group is just a replacement detachment. Only people there are the ones who just came back and the ones getting ready to go. Hardly any training done at all, so the average guy who joins Group gets MOS qualified and goes through Qualification Course and little else before shipping out. How would you have liked that before your first tour?"

"Probably wouldn't have survived."

"And neither do a lot of them. Those that do, most of them, become pretty good soldiers. Some don't. The selection process has gone to shit, so some real losers get through. Christ, we had an image problem before this, now it's getting worse. We've actually got people coming back and becoming criminals, robbing banks and the like, for Christ's sake! And of course every newspaper in the country picks up on it: 'Crazed Green Beret Holds Up Bank,' that kind of shit. How come we never hear about crazed plumbers holding up banks?

I tell you, it's bad enough I wouldn't wear a uniform even when I was on leave in Tennessee, and you know how redneck that place is.''

"I know the feeling. You don't even have to wear a uniform.'' Jim told the story of his encounter in the bar in San Francisco.

"Shit, I'd love to have seen that. This Lisa must be quite a girl.''

"That she is.'' Jim smiled for a moment, thinking of her for the first time since boarding the aircraft. The pang of missing her tightened his chest.

"Pretty serious about her, are you?''

Jim's shrug was eloquent. "How serious can one of us be?'' he asked. "That doesn't work. You of all people should know that.''

"Yeah, I do.'' Al smiled. "My ex did the most foolish of all things. Said I had a choice between her and what I was doing.''

"Ever feel sorry for yourself?''

"Fucking nearly every day. You?''

"Yeah. Ain't it great?'' Jim was silent for a few moments. "You ever think about what you're going to do when you grow up?''

"You seriously think we're ever going to have to worry about it?''

"Probably not. Scary thought if we're wrong, though.''

"Ah, hell, if that ever happens, there's bound to be someplace in the world that can use us. Africa, Latin America, someplace else in Southeast Asia. Any luck at all we can live to a ripe old age and never have to grow up at all. Fuck it anyway. Suppose they'll let us get off this thing in Honolulu so's we can get a drink?''

To their great good fortune the aircraft developed mechanical problems in Honolulu. They were informed that it would be at least twenty-four hours before it would be fixed. The cheers were deafening.

"How about it, Mark?'' Jim bantered. "How much did you have to pay the pilot?''

"Don't be so crude. Do you think I'd do such a thing? An

officer and gentleman and scion of a fine old Mafia family? Besides, you don't pay the pilot, you pay the crew chief.''

"So what's the plan?"

"I thought you'd never ask. My family maintains a place in the city; it's empty except for the staff right now. We go there, get changed out of our war suits, I make a couple phone calls, get a party started, then you assholes are on your own. Face it, if you can't get laid here, you can't get laid.''

"Yee-hah,'' said Al. "Show us the way, O fearless leader. We who are your humble disciples will follow your example, yea, even unto the very jaws of hell itself.''

"This is what I get for consorting with a redneck failed Baptist,'' Mark said, shaking his head in mock sorrow. "You guys ready to go?''

JIM was amazed at the sumptuous "winter home'' of the Petrillos, and overwhelmed by the party which, seemingly on a moment's notice, sprang up. Everyone, it seemed, had been waiting for Mark's arrival; had been preparing for this big blowout for weeks. The pungent smell of good Maui wafted here and there. Within just a few seconds after arriving both he and Al had been offered tokes. As graciously as possible Jim refused. There was plenty of booze, and that was his drug of choice.

It did not take long to get into the spirit of things. He found out very quickly that this was a happy group, and nonjudgmental. Just as he would have expected out of Mark's friends. His haircut caused no untoward comments, nor did his clothes. Slowly he relaxed and let his guard down. He wished Lisa were there. He got a drink, drained it, then another. Shit, he thought. This stuff has about as much effect as Kool-Aid tonight. Wonder what she's doing? Wonder if she's with someone else? Probably, he thought. Not the kind to spend very much time by herself. Not that I blame her. Right now I don't feel too much like being by myself either.

"You look sad,'' she said. "This is a party, or hadn't you noticed? You're supposed to be happy at a party.''

He looked up quickly, aware that he had been staring at the floor for some time. He was awed by the girl standing there. Cinnamon. All he could think of was cinnamon. Skin of that shade, breath sweet and spicy, hair shining and burnished with shades of red. Forgive me, Lisa, he thought.

The evening passed in a series of flashes. At one point he remembered watching as Al performed mock baptisms on three very well endowed young ladies. At another point he was sitting on a bench in the garden with his cinnamon-colored friend, discussing philosophy and the possibility of eternal life and the fact that he didn't really care if it existed or not. Later they were in a cab going to a restaurant that stayed open all night; still later in a spare bedroom in Mark's house.

He woke the next morning wondering how much he actually remembered and how much had been a dream. Realized as he passed the boundary between sleep and consciousness that his arm was around someone. Moved slightly and felt her stir, turn around, look at him through beautiful brown eyes, and smile.

Much later they got up and showered together. Later yet they wandered downstairs, saw Mark, Dave and several unidentified people fortifying themselves with Bloody Marys.

"Damn," said Mark. "Thought there for a minute we were going to have to send in a Spike team after you. Told you you'd like my friends, didn't I?" he asked the girl. "Better than those wimp asshole lawyers your dad is always trying to fix you up with."

She made a face at him. "You started out as a lawyer," she pointed out.

Mark clutched his chest in mock pain. "Christ, did you have to tell them that? They all thought I was a piano player in a whorehouse. Now nobody will trust me."

"Don't worry about it, Mark," Jim said. "We didn't trust you in the first place. Any word on the aircraft?"

"Unfortunately it seems that they are going to have to fly the part out here from the States. We won't get out of here before tomorrow at the earliest." He took a bow, acknowledging the spontaneous burst of cheers and applause. "Now, shall we get down to some serious partying? Last night was a good prep, but now it's time for some industrial-strength debauchery."

LATER that evening Jim was talking with a serious-looking young woman. His friend from the evening before was at that moment away dancing with someone else.

"Do you believe in life after death?" she asked.

Jesus, he thought, where did that one come from? "I'm not even sure I believe in life before death," he said.

She thought for a moment. "That's very profound," she finally replied.

It is? he wondered. He had intended to be flippant.

"What you're saying," she continued, "is that this may all be an illusion, that we may not be living at all, may only be the products of the imagination of some cosmic force."

"But can an imagination, which is an arbitrary image, have creatures within it who are aware of their own existence?" he asked, deciding to get into the spirit of things. "Or does this cosmic being have to imagine itself being one of those creatures so that it can have an awareness of itself? And in so doing, doesn't that creature become an extension of itself and thus have an existence, since the cosmic force exists?"

"I think, therefore I am?"

"I think, therefore I think," he answered. "And what I think is that it really doesn't matter what I think. So I avoid thinking at almost any cost."

"That's very fatalistic," she said. She bit her full lower lip, waiting for his response. Her teeth were white, small and even. The effect was extremely erotic. He felt ashamed of himself for thinking such thoughts. You leave one woman behind, the next day you're in bed with another, and now you're thinking lustful thoughts about a third. You have about as much morals as a billy goat. Her eyes behind the thick glasses were a bright cornflower blue.

Back to the conversation, he decided. This was getting entirely too intense. He resisted the glib answer. "The only 'istic' I try to be is realistic. Are we tired of Philosophy 101 now? Didn't you come with someone, and won't he be looking for you?"

"Only a friend," she said. "He's off somewhere trying to get laid. Are you trying to get rid of me?"

"Not at all," he said. "Would you like to dance?"

"I'd far prefer to sit here and talk. You're interesting. Far more intelligent than you let on. Does it bother you to be perceived as such?"

"Only inasmuch as you'd rather have my brain than my body."

"Doesn't Eileen have first claims to the body?"

"Eileen? Oh, you mean Cin."

"Sin? As in mortal?"

"No, Cin. As in cinnamon. And no, she doesn't have first claim. Actually, at present I think she's laying claim to a friend of mine. Probably laying him too."

"Are you always this flippant?"

"Flippant? This is my serious side. Ladies in glasses always bring that out."

"You object to glasses?"

"No way. I object to clothes. Let's take ours off."

"Why?"

"Because I think it would be funny as hell to sit here discussing the meaning of life in the nude. And what is the meaning of life in the nude? she asks. Easy, he replies, making a small smile which indicates his superior wisdom. The meaning of life in the nude is the same as the meaning of life in clothes, except that eye-to-eye contact is more difficult."

She grasped his hand and turned it palm-up. Her touch as she traced the lines was feather-light, teasing. "Strong character line," she said. "But I already knew that. A very long life line."

"Tell that to the V.C."

"The hand doesn't lie. I'm a witch, and we know these things."

"I've known a few of those, but they spelled it differently."

"You really do find it most difficult to be serious, don't you? Do you want me to tell you your future?"

"Think you can do that? I don't. The future is a perhaps, a plethora of possibilities. *Et, je m'en vais chercher un grand peut-être.* I'm going to search for a great perhaps."

"Rabelais," she said approvingly. "And are you a true Rabelaisian?"

"I'm not much of a true anything. Except a soldier. And you didn't answer my question. Do you think you can predict the future?"

"Only the immediate one. The one in which a woman in glasses shows you that all those repressed librarian jokes aren't necessarily untrue. If you'd like." She smiled a long, lazy, sensuous smile.

"I'd like that very much."

"Then shall we get out of here and leave these lovely people to their revels?"

"On one condition. Tell me your name. I can't very well go around referring to you as the librarian."

"Why not? The people with whom I work do."

"And with whom do you work?"

"The government."

"U.S.?"

"Yes. And my name is Moira Culpepper. And I already know yours. Mark told me."

"You're a friend of Mark's?"

"Not exactly a friend. More of an associate. I've known him for a year or so. Now, have I satisfied your insatiable curiosity? Or would you prefer to sit around here and wait for Cin, as you so quaintly call her?"

"I'd prefer to go sin. And if it's mortal, so be it."

Mark watched them go, a speculative look in his eye. That worked out well enough, he thought. Too bad all operations didn't go that way. Perhaps they would have, had all her compatriots been as good as the librarian.

IN the early morning hours Moira again wanted to talk. Jim was feeling particularly mellow—a function of complete sexual satisfaction and the brandy he had been sipping.

"I'm curious," she started. "Are you ever afraid of dying?"

"Ce qu'il fait noter tout d'abord, c'est le caractere absurd de la mort."

"What one must realize first is the absurd character of death," she translated. "Amazing. A man who can quote Rabelais and Sartre, to all appearances an intelligent fellow, and yet you follow the profession of arms. What makes you stay in it? Surely you can't believe in what they make you do?"

"Sorry to disappoint you," he replied. "But I do. I believe in freedom, and resisting aggression, and fighting against those people who, because of their elitist attitudes, think they know the answer to all problems and are willing by force of arms to impose those solutions on others."

"And you think that's what's happening in Vietnam?"

"Absolutely. You have a group of people whose aim is to establish an entirely new social order; an imported product, a revolution from the outside, an insurgency in which the grievances are artificially created, in which the goal of liberation is a deception," he quoted from memory something he had read and admired.

"And do you think you're doing any good?"

"Very little," he admitted. "But that doesn't stop me. Let's face it, the biggest problem we have as a nation right now is that people such as I have been so brainwashed that we're ashamed to admit in public that we have feelings of patriotism. It's like admitting to some dirty secret. You're immediately labeled a political naif, or a crazed warmonger, or worse. And wars are won or lost with words; the ideas that words express. And we've already lost the war of words. The bad guys have taken the high ground, and John Wayne and the cavalry aren't going to show up. There isn't going to be a happy ending. End of story."

"So why do you keep it up? Some sort of Don Quixote complex? Tilt at windmills because they're there?"

"Perhaps partly," he admitted. "There's a sort of romance to lost causes."

"What about the fact that by fighting for that cause a lot more lives are lost? Including perhaps your own. Long life line or not."

"Lives are lost all the time, and for less reason than this. This is a war. People die in wars. To follow your logic, if there were any chance that you were going to lose a fight, you wouldn't get into it. You'd give it up, save all those lives which would have been lost, right?"

"Then there wouldn't be any wars at all. Is that so bad?"

"Aside from the fact that I'd have to find a real job, no. The problem is that your solution doesn't take into account human nature. There will always be aggressors. And you've got to stand up to them. If you don't, they won't stop. Unbridled aggression and individual freedom cannot coexist. So you end up in the long run by losing even more lives, because sooner or later someone *is* going to resist. And the wars will be bloodier and more pitiless because you have two completely antithetical forces. You have a war where no act, however inhuman, is foreign. A war where cruelty and atrocity are commonplace.''

''Isn't that pretty well what war is now? We read about the atrocities, see them on the evening news.''

''Not really,'' he said. ''They happen, of course. Rather inevitable that they do, but all in all I don't see that it happens. a lot more than in any other war I've studied. There are a hell of a lot more people in the news media covering this war, though, so it seems so. Everything that happens is studied under a microscope, and slanted to fit the particular bias of this or that reporter. But your average soldier is over there doing the best he can, being humane when possible, which is a hell of a lot more often than it could be, given the situation.''

''Then what is a war crime, if in war some things happen that you can't help?''

''What the hell happened here? Are you a news reporter? You don't have to answer that. I don't really much care if you are. I don't know what war crimes are. What I do know is that there are some things I won't do. I won't shoot unarmed people who represent no danger to me and my troops. I won't inflict pain for pain's sake. If I have a POW and the situation is such that I can get him out alive, I will. I won't kill him because he's too much trouble.'' He was silent for a moment, thinking of the wounded men in the Valley of the Fan. Had he compromised his principles there? Yes, he had. And he still didn't know why.

''Do you think assassination is a legitimate weapon?''

''Perfectly legitimate,'' he answered, glad for the slight change of subject. ''What I said about aggression and aggressors I very much believe. There are some people out there who very much deserve to die. I find no moral compunction against assisting them along. But I absolutely refuse to assassinate beautiful young women who have entirely too many questions. Unless they really just keep at it. You want to tell me what this is all about?''

''Just curious, I told you.'' Her hand moved up from where it had been resting on his thigh. ''And now my curiosity is satisfied. Let's talk about something else.''

"Not good enough." He grabbed her hand to stop what she was doing. "How long did you say you've known Mark?"

"A year or so," she answered, rubbing her wrist where he had squeezed it.

"To my knowledge Mark spent the last year in Vietnam. Tell me another lie."

"It's not a lie," she protested. "That's where I knew him from ."

"You were in Vietnam? Bullshit!"

"It's true! I work for USAID. I met Mark in Saigon, at the Duc Hotel. Ask him if you don't believe me." She swung out of bed and grabbed her panties. The slim line of her back and silhouette of one breast made a picture which was hard to resist.

"Hold it. Don't get pissed. I believe you. But that still doesn't explain why you asked all the questions. You'll forgive me for being a bit paranoid, won't you?"

She turned back to him. "And now it's you asking all the questions, isn't it? Don't. It's not important anyway. Give me a sip of your brandy." She leaned across him. Her full breasts pushed into his stomach.

HE woke, hours later, to a hand roughly shaking him. "C'mon, troop," said Al Dougherty. "Drop your cock and grab your socks. We've got a plane to catch."

Jim looked for Moira. She was gone, only the smell of her perfume on the sheets hinting that she had been there. "Was anybody in here with me when you came in?" he asked.

"Nobody but you. I saw you leave with the lady in glasses last night. So did Eileen. She was pissed, but consoled herself with me. Think I'll follow you around from now on and pick up your leftovers. Come on, man! You've got about thirty minutes to shit, shine, shower, shave and shampoo. That big-assed bird ain't going to wait for us."

THEY were the last two to board. As soon as they sat down, the door was closed and the engines started. Mark had saved seats for them in the rear.

"Sorry to run off and leave you guys this morning," he said. "But I needed to make a run for provisions." He un-zipped an AWOL bag. It was filled with bottles of vodka.

"That dry run from Travis was bad enough," he explained. "Didn't figure we'd want to go through it all the way across the Pacific. Now, if we can just find some O.J. . . . ."

Jim waited until Al was asleep before asking Mark about Moira. By this time he was feeling a pleasant glow from the vodka. Not that it was difficult to achieve a glow, with all the residual alcohol from the last two days in his body.

"She told me she knew you from Vietnam."

"That's true," Mark admitted. "I met her at the Duc Hotel."

"So far, so good. She said she worked for USAID?"

"Is that what she said? Then I guess that must be the truth. I don't really know her all that well."

"Then how did she end up at your house?"

"Don't know. Guess I must have given her the address at one time or another. I'm going to get some sacktime, okay?"

Jim found Mark's uncharacteristic evasiveness troubling. What did he mean when he said if she had said she worked for USAID it must be true? CORDS was a part of USAID, wasn't it? Did she have something to do with that? Was there a purpose in seeking him out? Or was he just being paranoid? Would he ever know, one way or the other? Would he ever stop asking questions? He went to sleep, a slight headache nagging at his brain.

CHAPTER 4

THE familiar smell of Vietnam struck him as soon as they opened the door of the plane: an amalgam of JP-4 jet fuel, unwashed bodies, the dank rottenness of decaying vegetation, and the sweet odor of burning shit. Pillars of smoke rose from hundreds of cut-off fuel drums used as field latrines. Early on in the war it had occurred to someone that they had a sanitation problem. There were so many troops clustered together, producing so much human waste, that the old methods of getting rid of it would not work. There was, obviously, no sewage system. Then some unsung hero devised an elegantly simple, if smelly, solution to the problem of disposal of the by-products of several thousand well-fed Americans. Fifty-five-gallon drums were cut in two and placed beneath the holes in field latrines. When half full they were pulled out, doused with diesel fuel, and set afire. One could always tell when you were getting close to an American base. The columns of smoke rose thousands of feet.

The noises too were familiar: the roar of fighters taking off, the whopping of helicopter blades, the distant boom of artillery.

"Home again," Al said. He smiled.

"Seems like we never left," Jim replied as they walked down the ramp and out onto the hot tarmac. They moved with a slow, energy-saving gait. Everybody sweated in the heat, but the new men kept trying to wipe it away. They let it soak them, knowing that the infrequent breezes would cool them better this way.

"FNGs think this is all a game, don't they?" said Al.

"And so did we. We were fucking new guys, once. Back when we were young kids. Five or six years ago. Remember how the old World War II and Korea vets used to give us hell? Where did Mark go? Sonofabitch disappears faster than anyone I've ever seen.''

"I saw him just a few minutes ago talking to someone in civvies. Let's get into the building. This concrete is cooking right through my fucking shoes.''

Inside they headed for a sign which said "Officers." A bored-looking NCO checked their names on a roster, told them that transportation would soon be there to take them to Long Binh, and pointed out a spot where they could wait. Al turned his body slightly so the NCO could see his combat patch. It irritated him to be treated in such a cavalier manner. Didn't seem fair somehow to be treated as a second-class citizen in the U.S. and then come here among one's own and get the same.

It didn't seem to matter to the NCO. He waved them on through and went back to his roster. His voice droned through the same litany for someone else as they walked away.

They waited for an hour, sweltering in the heat. Typical army bullshit, Jim thought. Hurry up and wait. He was now very glad for the Hawaii interlude. No one seemed to care that they were two days late. He assumed a Montagnard squat against the wall and let the crowd swirl around him. If someone had asked him what he was thinking, he couldn't have told them. His mind wandered, at points touching on Lisa, and snatches of combat, and wondering what the future would bring, all in a swirl of color and feeling and noise.

Al nudged him, breaking him out of the reverie. "Here comes Mark. Already changed into civvies. The guy with him looks familiar. You know him?''

"Take away the beard and a few years," answered Jim, "and he'd look like Sergeant Major Slim Feltrie. I heard he'd retired, but I didn't know he was working for these guys.''

The sergeant major was a legend in Special Forces, which contained more than its share of larger-than-life characters. He had been the most experienced warrior the organization had. He started his career with the Canadian-American 1st Special Service Force in World War II, was in the Dieppe raid and the Anzio Campaign, transferred to the Rangers and was at Pointe du Hoc at D-day. He was wounded there, shipped back to a hospital in England, went AWOL from the hospital and rejoined the unit, fighting his way across France,

Holland, Belgium and Germany. In Korea he served with the United Nations Partisan Command, conducting guerrilla raids in North Korean territory. He was on the White Star mission in Laos, then to Vietnam with one of the first teams deployed there. Like most Special Forces soldiers, he didn't look the part. He was tall and skinny, talked with the twang of his boyhood Tennessee and liked to let people think he wasn't too smart. His manner hid a first-class mind.

Jim nodded to he sergeant major, not knowing if he wanted their past association acknowledged. "You got changed fast," he said to Mark.

"Feltrie tells me you know one another," answered Mark.

"Slightly. The good sergeant major straightened me out when I was a young soldier. Young and dumb," he amended.

Feltrie smiled. "Still fighting with your fists, Jim?"

"Nope. Gave that up after our last 'counseling' session," he replied. He explained to the others that Feltrie was his company first sergeant, back when he first joined the army. Like most young airborne troops, he had thought he was a real badass. Liked to go to town and get into fights. After one such, when he had taken on a group of M.P.s, the sergeant major decided to teach him a lesson. Gave him a choice of nonjudicial punishment, Article 15, or the first sergeant's own punishment. He had thought he could do well against an old, skinny fart. It was a mistake. By the time Feltrie got through with him he was begging to go to the stockade. He hadn't gone out to look for a fight since.

"You weren't too bad, for a young kid," said Feltrie. "But not as good as I was. You're looking good. Guess they'll make anyone an officer now. Heard you had a little bad luck up-country. Ran into Zack Osborne last time I was in Nha Trang and he told me all about it. How you feelin' now?"

"I'm not going to win any footraces," answered Jim. "But I never won any before either. I imagine I can still hump a rucksack."

"Why don't we get out of here?" Mark interrupted. "You guys can talk over old times at the club later."

"We've been waiting for transportation to Long Binh," said Al. "Looks like they forgot us."

"Forget about Long Binh," said Feltrie. "Mark tells me

you guys are interested in working for us. I've got a truck outside. Throw your stuff in it and we'll head for Saigon."

"You sure about this?" Jim asked. "I'd hate like hell to be AWOL my first day back in country."

"You're already cleared," answered Mark. "You are now assigned to MACV CORDS. Orders to follow. Trust me, guys. If we wait until you get processed through Long Binh, we won't see you for a couple of weeks. And we need you right now."

Jim looked at Al, who shrugged as if to say, Why not? Stranger things had happened to both of them. They shouldered bags and followed Feltrie to the exit. The M.P. was shown a card. It was amusing to watch the man's face, his expression going from disbelieving suspicion to awed compliance. "My get-out-of-jail-free card," Feltrie explained when they were outside. "Works every time."

Their transportation was a new Ford Crew-Cab pickup with Vietnamese plates. Jim was impressed. "Nothing but the finest for the troops," quipped Mark. "Besides, this makes sure we don't look like everyone else. Wouldn't want the V.C. to assassinate the wrong guys."

"Glad to see logic still has a place in the world," said Jim.

On the four-lane highway going into Saigon he got his first look at the devastation of the Tet Offensive. There were few undamaged buildings. Most had been leveled in the attack or in the counteroffensive.

"Looks nice," said Al. "Urban renewal by B-52. They leave anything standing?"

"Shit, this is nothing," scoffed Feltrie. "Wait until we get into Saigon. Cholon is pretty well gone. The area around the Zoo you wouldn't recognize. We had a hell of a fight out by Tan Son Nhut; had to bring in the Delta Rangers to help out."

"My old outfit," said Al. "How did they do?"

"Damned good, after the first day. That first few hours wasn't too much fun. City fighting takes a little getting used to. The V.C. dug in at the bases of the buildings, which gave them good fields of fire down the roadways. Chopped us up pretty good until some bright boy from Delta decided that if we couldn't get them away from the building, we'd bring the buildings closer to them. Like right down on their heads. Got some 90mm recoilless rifles and a few truckloads of ammo, shot the supports out, buildings collapsed right on top of them. Was a lot easier going after that. News media gave us hell for it, of course. 'Destroying a village in order to save it,' that kind of shit. Kept asking us what about the civilians in those buildings. Civilians! Anybody who wasn't a V.C. had long since gotten their asses out of there. Most of them before the attack took place. Anyway, the V.C. got so chopped up they're having trouble mounting platoon-sized attacks.''

''I was going to ask abut that,'' said Jim. ''Last time I was down this road, a year ago, there were troops all over the place to keep it open. I haven't seen any since we left Bien Hoa.''

''It's the same way all over the place,'' replied Feltrie. ''Big patches of the countryside are up for grabs. Places you couldn't get into without a battalion and a B-52 strike, you could walk through now. Hell of an opportunity, but nobody seems to want to take advantage of it. Except us. That's why I'm glad you gentlemen want to volunteer. We need you.''

''Far as I know,'' Jim drawled, ''we haven't volunteered just yet. Thought we were going to Saigon for a briefing. See what happens after that.''

Feltrie shot a look at Mark, who felt compelled to say, ''Of course you haven't. What Slim meant to say was, we feel pretty certain you'll want to after you hear what we have to say.''

I wonder, thought Jim. Just too many coincidences piling up. Where had Mark called from to get Feltrie out from Saigon to meet them? There hadn't been time after they had arrived. And how had he gotten them assigned to CORDS? It look longer than thirty minutes to get orders cut. Especially from the personnel center at Long Binh, which was notoriously slow and inefficient. Everyone had heard the stories, apocryphal or not, of people who had been assigned to the replacement center, got lost and turned up a year later to rotate home.

He decided to wait and see what happened. Maybe he was just being paranoid. Though, he thought, being paranoid didn't preclude the fact that someone might be after you.

Saigon traffic was as bad or worse than he remembered.

Thousands of Lambrettas, cyclos, mopeds, bicycles, all mixed with military vehicles of all types, swirling and crowding through the narrow streets, jamming the traffic circles. Exhaust fumes clogged the throat even in the air-conditioned cab. Vietnamese police, "White Mice," blew their whistles and gestured frantically, having no noticeable effect on the chaos.

After much effort and thousands of curses they finally arrived at the Duc Hotel. "This is the Agency hotel, isn't it?" asked Al.

"We've got rooms already reserved for you," said Mark, increasing Jim's suspicions. On one level he was flattered. On another he was irritated. He was being manipulated, and intensely disliked losing control of his freedom of action.

"Too late to get anything done today," said Mark. "Why don't you guys grab a shower and get changed and we'll meet you in the bar later?"

"Want us to get out of uniform, do you?" asked Jim drily.

"You won't find too many of them around here," said Feltrie. "You might as well get used to it. The bar's on the top floor. There's a pool there too if you want to take a dip."

"Ain't war hell?" said Al. "Come on, Jim. I've got about three inches of trip crud to take off, and the bar is waiting."

Jim was impressed with the accommodations. The rooms were spacious, clean and cooled to bone-numbing chill by very large air conditioners. Better than most good commercial hotels I've been in, he thought.

When he got out of the shower he found that a houseboy traveling on soundless feet had unpacked his bags and ironed the wrinkles out of a shirt and slacks. Quiet as he was, he'd be good in a sapper battalion, thought Jim. Probably did that in his spare time. There was a radio on the bedside table. He turned it on, finding that it was already tuned to the Armed Forces Radio Network station. He got dressed to the sound of the Doors wailing about lighting fires. Obviously they had modernized the programming in his brief absence. When he had last listened to the station, all that could be heard was Perry Como and Frank Sinatra. And, of course, Lawrence Welk.

THE bar was well patronized, despite the fact that the workday was not officially over. Most of the patrons were fat and fiftyish—a far cry from the James Bonds the public would have expected in the CIA. There were a few younger, leaner, more fit individuals, but Jim's suspicion, later confirmed, was that these were military personnel seconded to the Agency. There were also a few females, most old and weather-beaten, but a very few were young and attractive. Jim's mind went back to Moira. He thought he would avoid them.

Mark and Slim Feltrie were at the center of a group of the younger men. Jim walked over to them.

"This is the guy I was telling you about," said Mark. "Thinking about joining our select group. We got in just at the right time, Jim. They're holding a countrywide conference of all PRU advisors. You'll get to meet just about everyone." He explained that they did it every quarter, getting together and sharing information. What worked, what new tactics people had thought up, any information that would be helpful. Then they sat around and bitched about how, if the bureaucrats in charge of the war would give them the support they needed, they could win the war.

Jim recognized many of the people to whom Mark introduced him. He had seen them in one place or another over the years: Fort Bragg, Okinawa, Nha Trang. "Looks like a Group reunion," he said. "Do all the advisors come out of Special Forces?"

Feltrie nodded. "Except in IV Corps," he explained. "Down there we use mostly SEALs. They like all that water."

"Yeah," chimed in another individual. "Fuckin' Squids got no brains anyhow. All they know how to do is lift heavy things and swim. We're thinking of replacing them with chimpanzees."

"Why, Jack?" demanded a short, powerful man, quite obviously one of the maligned SEALs. "You lookin' for a job?"

Jim got a drink from a waitress and talked over old times with some of the men he knew. The drink was followed by several more. Soon he was laughing and enjoying himself. It was easy to do among these men. There was none of the uneasiness or awkwardness he ordinarily felt in a crowd. These were people like himself, soldiers, sure of themselves and what they did. If you were one of them, you were accepted. If not, you would be made to feel in no uncertain terms that you were not welcome. None of the Agency types approached them.

It was explained that not many of the old Clandestine Services types served in Vietnam, doing their work in other places. They had been there in the early days of the war, before the war got popular. Before, like the army, it got to be a requirement to serve a tour there if one wished to be promoted. What was left was intell and admin types. Desk officers. People such as the man who'd been working on the Central European desk for ten years, spoke good Czech, knew the politics of the Bulgarian Communist Party better than most party officials, sent to Vietnam to run the Rural Development Program. Which he had not the foggiest notion of how to do. The very few who weren't careerists, who tried to go out and find things out, who tried to stay past one tour, realizing that there was no way one could learn all you need to know and do anything about it in a year, were told very politely but firmly that they were fucking up the program and themselves too. That it was time to move on and let someone else take his turn; after all, the war wasn't going to go on forever, and everyone had to have a chance. And the work you were doing on the Ukrainian wheat forecasts is much more important anyway. Time to get back to all that. This is all a sideshow, don't you realize? Our real enemy is the Soviet Union; doesn't really matter what's going on in the peripheries of the world. Got to keep an eye on Mother Russia, that's where the real action is.

"Glad you guys paint such a cheerful picture," said Jim. "How do we get anything done at all?"

"Mostly in spite of the system, and sometimes outside it. The only bright spot is that since they really don't know what we're doing, don't want to know in case they get called up in front of some congressional subcommittee, they pretty well leave us alone. Plausible deniability, they call it. They give us the money and resources and let us do things our own way."

"What about control? Surely somebody maintains oversight. Without that we could do anything we wanted out there. That's got to frighten someone."

"It does," said Feltrie. "They live in fear that there's going to be a big fuckup someday. But they don't know what to do about it. They set the system up, and so far it has run okay, and they don't know how to go about changing it. So they mostly depend on hiring the right people, people who have proven ability and who aren't likely to go off the deep end. No wild-eyed crazies. No homicidal maniacs, no matter what the media thinks. They vet them pretty thoroughly, reject the ones they're unsure about, send the others to the field and keep their fingers crossed. It's worked, so far.''

"What about the people they don't vet? Me, for instance. Yet it seems to be a foregone conclusion, the way you and Mark talk, that I'll be accepted.''

Feltrie shot a look at Mark, who said nothing. "Yeah, well, there are always exceptions,'' he said. "Anyway, all in all I wouldn't be doing anything else. How many times can a man truly say he's free to do what he's been trained to do? I'm sure you'll join us. Everything I know about you tells me you'll be perfect for the job.''

Within a week he was on his way to Hue. Still wondering what had convinced him to go. He knew that he was forever ruining any chance he might have had of a military career. This did not loom large in his calculations. The idea of taking a rifle company in a conventional outfit for six months did not appeal to him. And six months would have been all he was allowed. There were lots of captains who needed command time. In a way it was the same as the system described to him about the Agency. One had to get one's ticket punched, so captains were shifted in and out of the command slots regardless of operational needs.

He also knew that there was an excellent chance that the mission he would be called upon to perform would, if things went wrong, get him cashiered from the army and possibly jailed. The briefing in Saigon had left no doubt of that. Even though the mission was to capture members of the V.C. infrastructure, it was inevitable that some of them would die. Successful capture of a hostile was one of the most difficult missions you could undertake. And no doubt was left that the V.C. had to be neutralized. So if you couldn't capture them . . . And assassination, as such, was a crime under army regulations.

He'd be totally alone, the only American. He'd operated

before in small units, but there had always been at least one other round-eye with him. Someone on whom he knew he could depend when the shit hit the fan. In PRU there was only one U.S. type. And the PRUs were, for the most part, Vietnamese. He didn't trust the Vietnamese, regarded them at best as lazy and undermotivated. At worst cowardly and unreliable. Possible collaborators, some of them active V.C.

Despite the sometimes overly optimistic briefings he had received in Saigon, he had no illusions that this was the elusive solution to the war. But he was past worrying about solutions. Solutions were for those who thought up the grandiose plans, the high-level strategies. He was a cog in the machine, and knew it. But if he was to be a cog, he wanted to be an effective one.

As Feltrie had predicted, what he liked most was the freedom of action. He would be provided with a "blacklist" each month from the Province Intelligence Operations Coordinating Center (PIOCC). This list would contain the names of individuals who the PIOCC had determined to be members of the V.C. infrastructure of the province. The PIOCC was staffed by U.S. and Vietnamese intelligence officers, and supposedly knew what it was doing. Before a person's name went on the list there had to be at least three verifiable and independent reports certifying that he or she was a member of the Viet Cong. Vague suspicions, malicious slanders and witchhunt rumors were not supposed to be taken into account.

In fact, he already knew that some of the PIOCCs were less than reliable. The U.S. intelligence officers were second lieutenants fresh out of the intelligence school at Fort Holabird. They had no experience in the field, could not separate false reports from real ones and in most cases did not even speak Vietnamese. Thus they depended upon their Viet counterparts, who were a mixed lot. Some were smart, hardworking, reasonably honest men who were trying to do the best job they could. Others were miserable, grasping, venal sonsofbitches who operated solely in their own interest. If that interest involved taking a bribe to put someone's business opponent on the list, so be it. Thus the PIOCCs were at one and the same time the most important, most visible and weakest part of the Phoenix program.

The informal briefings he received from the other PRU advisors had been much more useful than the official ones given by Agency case officers. Most advisors set up their own intelligence nets and ran checks on blacklisted individuals before they targeted them. Funds for setting up these nets were easy to come by. The discretionary account provided to each advisor was more than adequate. The efficiency of the net depended solely on the advisor's ability to set it up and run it. The challenge appealed to him.

Too, he liked his province assignment. Thua Thien was supposed to be one of the worst provinces. The PRU detachment was stationed in the provincial capital of Hue. It was a major V.C. and NVA stronghold. They had been able to move about the province with impunity for a long time. What a challenge!

He looked forward to seeing Hue. The old imperial capital of Vietnam was supposed to be very beautiful, but flying over it, he saw that the beauty was gone. Some of the hardest fighting during Tet had occurred here. The enemy had taken over the old Citadel and had to be rooted out of it with massive firepower. He could only imagine how splendid it must once have been. The shattered walls attested to its size and intricacy. Here and there a piece of architecture which had not been destroyed hinted at its former grandeur. The rest of the city had not fared much better. There were great blackened areas where the wooden buildings once stood. The more permanent concrete structures were riddled with holes. He caught a glimpse of the fortified compound containing the Embassy House and was not impressed. The former PRU advisor had been killed there when it was overrun. It looked like it would not be hard to overrun again.

The main detachment of PRUs had fared a little better. They had been in their own compound and had fought off one attack after another, losing many but stacking up their enemy outside the wire in a jumble of limbs, shit and blood. He had been told that his first mission would be to recruit new members of the PRU to replace the losses, train them and lead them on an early operation to build up their morale. What had not been said was that he would have to reestablish contact and control over the shattered intelligence net. At least the former advisor had left fairly comprehensive files on it. Jim wondered how many of the informants were still alive. He knew that the V.C., after taking the city, had conducted a systematic search and had taken away anyone whom they suspected of collaborating with the government. They were later found in mass graves in the sand dunes outside the city. Many had been buried alive.

THERE was no one to meet him at the airfield when he landed in the Air America DC-3. He flagged down a marine jeep, threw his bags in the back and asked to be taken to the Embassy House. The driver, a lance corporal, eyed him in curiosity.

"You a spook?" he asked finally.

"Naw, man, I'm white," Jim answered, eliciting a chuckle from the driver, who was not.

"You don't look like the rest of them up there," he said.

"And what do they look like?"

"Lost, mostly. Like they woke up in the wrong place and don't know how the hell to get back. They stay in the compound, get a good suntan, wear their aviator shades and don't talk to anybody. Trying to act cool. Say boo to them and they jump out of their honky skin. You don't look like you'd do too much jumping. You look like a pro."

"Shows you how deceiving looks can be. I'm a supply clerk. Came up here to get inventory straight. You can't believe how bad the hand receipt records are."

"You lying like hell, but that's okay, I guess. Easy way not to tell me anything. How you like Hue so far?"

"What's not to like? Roads full of rubble, every other building burned down, people moving around like they're in a daze. Looks like everybody's favorite bad dream."

"Looks good now. You should have seen it a month ago."

"You here during the battle?"

The corporal nodded. "Fought our way into the Citadel," he said.

Jim remembered the news photographs of that struggle. He wouldn't have liked to be there. It appeared that there had been no good way to take the old imperial fortress. Not much choice but to go in and fight it out room by room. "That must have been nasty," he said.

"Lost a lot of brothers," the man said. "Don't know what for. Don't appear to me to have done much good."

"Never does," Jim agreed.

"You take care of yourself now, supply clerk spook," the corporal said as he dropped him at the front gate of the Embassy House. "Else the dinks are liable to cancel your hand receipt."

"Thanks, brother. You take care of yourself too. I ever see you around town, I'll buy you a beer."

He was even less impressed with the house up close. The wire around the perimeter had been patched poorly in the places where bangalore torpedoes had torn great gaping holes. The gate guard was lackadaisical, coming to him only after repeated calls, trailing his carbine by the barrel. He took a cursory look at Jim's I.D. card, then waved him on through and slowly returned to his post, where he promptly closed his eyes and fell asleep.

Jim left his bag in the courtyard and took a walk. No one challenged him as he poked his way around. The bunkers were all in disrepair, and even if they had been in good shape they would have been useless. None had adequate fields of fire out to any distance. On most the firing ports had been blocked with cardboard, to keep the mosquitoes out, he supposed. The interconnecting trenches, dug into the soft sand, had not been revetted and had collapsed. The few guards on duty paid no attention to him. Those who were awake, a minority, were playing cards or reading. He could see that the job was going to be even harder than he had thought. He retrieved his bag and made his way into the house.

CHAPTER 5

HE was stopped at the front door by a blond-haired young man. "And who might you be?" the man asked.

Jim took an instant dislike to him. He looked soft, untested. His skin was pale white, as if he had never been outside the confines of the house. And he spoke without moving his lower jaw, with the upper-class, Harvard-educated, effete rich-boy accent Jim found insufferable.

"Well," he drawled, "I might be Captain James NMI Carmichael, the new PRU advisor. But then again I might be a goddamned Russian soldier, the way security is around here. Now, are you going to get out of my way, or am I going to have to walk over you?"

"You don't have to be so angry, you know." The man blinked, looking alarmed. "I'm just doing my job. I'm the duty officer today. My name is Alfred Fitzwilliam." He offered his hand.

The handshake was soft. "If you were trying to do your job, you'd be out checking the guards. There's not a place on this perimeter that's properly covered. Who's in charge of the guard force?"

"At the moment, nobody," Fitzwilliam replied. "Your predecessor was, but after he got killed they fell apart. Won't listen to anybody, just do as they please. We're hoping you can do something with them. Do you want me to show you to your room?"

The man's manner had become almost fawning. He was obviously eager to please. For a moment Jim wondered if his own prejudices against the "upper class" caused him to be too hard on a man he had just met. Probably. Too bad. "Okay," he said. "Show me the way."

Fitzwilliam chattered all the way to the room. "You're in

the annex," he said. "We figured you'd like it better that way because of all the strange hours you people keep. Nobody to bother you, and you won't bother anyone else. I trust you'll find the accommodations suitable."

"I'm sure I will," Jim replied as pleasantly as possible. No reason to antagonize the little twit further. He probably couldn't help being an asshole. "You people have a tendency to do things up right."

As, indeed, they had. His quarters would have made an army general envious. He had two rooms, a bedroom with full-sized bed and real mattress, and a sitting room with a couch and chairs. A full bath was located just off the bedroom, with a shower, tub, bidet, and a real flush toilet. There were two large air conditioners, a small refrigerator, and even a TV set. Trust the Agency to think of everything.

"I'm sure you're bushed from the trip and want to get settled in, so I'll leave you now and get back to my post," said Fitzwilliam. "I believe the province officer in charge would like to see you first thing in the morning."

"And what time would that be?"

"Oh, right after breakfast. Say, nine o'clock. If that would be suitable for you."

Jim, who was used to much earlier hours, said that nine o'clock would be fine. He bade the duty officer goodbye, then proceeded to unpack. He placed his CAR-15 carbine on a chair in the sitting area, draping the heavy web gear full of magazines and other necessaries over the back. The Browning 9mm he slipped under a pillow. He had been issued four sets of tiger fatigues in Saigon, and these he hung up. They were sterile, had no insignia of any sort. From now on he wasn't a captain in the U.S. Army, he had been told. He was a "Mr.," a civilian advisor on assignment to the embassy. It was a cover which fooled no one, but the Agency insisted upon it. The tiger stripes, uniforms, and a couple of knit shirts and tan slacks were his only baggage. He had long ago learned to travel light. It was a pain in the ass to have to carry a lot of heavy baggage around in the heat of Vietnam. Besides, the houseboys would steal anything remotely valuable, so why bother?

He turned off the air conditioners and opened the windows, was glad to see they were screened. At least he wouldn't have to sleep under a mosquito net. There was no way he could hear suspicious sounds over the roar of the air conditioners, so he would have to sleep hot. He had little faith in the guard force. Time once again to depend upon his own senses and instincts. Not long until dark now. He pulled a packet of long-range-patrol rations out of his bag, reconstituted them with the hot water from the tap, ate them slowly and waited for the dark.

The next morning he woke, as usual, at five o'clock. He had little doubt that few other people would be up yet, so to kill time he exercised in the room. The leg was bothering him less and less. Shouldn't be too much trouble humping the jungle, he thought. After showering, shaving and donning clothes it was still not even seven o'clock. He decided to see if the mess hall was open. The Agency would be horrified to hear it referred to as a mess hall. They probably called it a dining facility. Just for a moment he wondered if he was being too hard on them. No, he decided, he wasn't.

He was the first one there. The attendant, obviously surprised to find one of the Americans there so early, made a big fuss over him. Coffee was brought, real brewed stuff, and good. The food was excellent, many choices, and all obviously prepared by a skilled chef. As he was eating, other Americans filtered in. None sat with him. From time to time he caught them looking at him, but nobody said anything. He had obviously been a subject of much discussion. Fitzwilliam did not show up.

He finished breakfast and, since it was still too early to see the POIC, took another turn around the perimeter. He was happy to see that the guards seemed to be taking more interest in their duties.

THE POIC looked at him from across a broad, paper-strewn desk. Disapproval was written across his face. "Fitz-william tells me that you were very rude to him last night. That you even threatened him. What do you have to say to that?"

Jim shrugged. "He irritated me," he said simply.

The gray-haired man stiffened. "I'm not sure I like your attitude," he said. "We have a tough enough time over here without having to deal with conflicts among ourselves."

Looks like you have a real tough time of it, Jim thought, noticing the basketball-sized belly that hung over the man's belt. He decided that it would not be good to antagonize the man further, however. Hard to tell whose ear he had, and Jim didn't need a lot of enemies in high places.

"I was probably a little too rough on him," he conceded. "But I hope you realize you've got a bad situation here."

"What do you mean?" the man demanded.

"Pretty simple. I took a look around the perimeter last night after all the lights were out. You want to know how many guards I found awake? Two. One on the front gate and one on the back. You've got ten firing bunkers around the perimeter. In eight of them everyone was asleep. The other two were empty. I suspect those guards went to visit their families through one of the two holes I found in the perimeter fence. For Christ's sake! This is the compound that was over-run a month ago. Your predecessor is either dead or spending his winters in an air-conditioned suite in Siberia because of it. As for Fitzwilliam, why wasn't he out making perimeter checks? Or isn't that part of the duty officer's job description? Let's face it, Mr. Copely, they could take this place with a platoon of Boy Scouts."

"Well, Mr. Carmichael, since you seem to know so much about it, you've just been appointed the compound defense officer."

"Accepted, and gladly. Free hand in what I want to do?"

"Within reason, yes."

"That include giving some training to the Americans, and being able to use them on the perimeter in an emergency?"

"I suppose so, though I think it will require quite a bit more than a little training." Copely grinned in a rather shamefaced manner. "These are not warriors, I'm afraid. You'll have your work cut out for you, trying to make them so."

"Leave that to me," Jim said. He rose to go. "I'm sure that things will work out just fine between us. I'll go and visit the PRUs now, if you don't mind."

"And there you'll find your work really cut out for you. They've been quite uncontrollable since we lost the last PRU advisor. Don't want to follow orders at all. Haven't run an operation for at least a month. Good luck."

• • •

THE PRU chief, Captain Vanh, refused to shake his hand. In perfect English, he said, "We do not need an advisor, Mr. Carmichael. We have been fighting this war for over ten years now, and each advisor they send us is worse than the last. They come here with their American ideas and their American squeamishness, and complain when we do the things we must do. Might I suggest to you, Captain, that you go to the Embassy House and stay there? Continue to provide us with our pay, and we will continue to find and kill the V.C. This way each side will be happy. Your superiors will commend you for doing such a fine job, and give you medals, and you will go home safely and be promoted and have a wonderful career. We will have the means to continue the fight and kill as many of the murderers as we can before we too fall in battle. It is a fair trade, *n'est ce pas*?"

Jim smiled amicably, recognizing the tactic. Make someone angry and find out more about them. He refused to rise to the bait.

"I understand your concerns, Captain, and believe me, I would like nothing better than to go away and let you fight your own war. But that's not the way it's going to be. Your government and mine have decided differently. They have decreed that we will work together. And as honorable men, we have to do the best we can with our orders. That doesn't mean that you'll have to like it, or me, or that I'll have to like you. But it does mean that we will have to put up with one another. And since it is my government which is putting up the money, it means that you will have to listen to me. Otherwise, I'll cut off your pay. For my part, I'll try to give advice only when necessary. As you so aptly stated, you've been fighting this war a lot longer than I." He thought that not too long ago he would have added in his mind, "and not too well either."

"I expect to learn from you," he continued. "But perhaps I can teach you a few things. After all, is it not an old Vietnamese saying that it is a truly stupid man who thinks he has nothing more to learn?"

Captain Vanh looked at the young American appraisingly. This one would not be so easy to fool, he thought. There was a hardness about him that belied his years. If he was competent as well as tough, he might be useful. He would see. Abruptly he said, "We have some new men going through training now. Would you care to observe them?"

THE men were being taught the painstaking art of silent movement. Jim could see that the training was good, as far as it went. They were instructed to lift the leg high, point the toe down, carefully feel for twigs and brush with the toes, moving them out of the way before putting down any weight, settle on that foot, then bring the other leg forward and continue the process. It was an extremely slow method of progress, sometimes measured in less than a hundred yards per hour. It also required good balance, something a man was not likely to have when he was tired, excited, or frightened. In enemy territory one was likely to be all three. He watched for over an hour as the recruits tried to learn the technique. Finally he got tired of watching them stumble and fall.

"With your permission, Dai Uy?" he asked Vanh.

The captain nodded, curious to see what the big, clumsy-looking American would do.

Jim took off his boots and socks and rolled his trousers up to the knees. He moved forward, keeping his feet close to the ground, stepping down on the outside edge of the sole, keeping his weight always on that edge. There was adequate sensitivity on the edge of the foot to feel for noise-making obstructions, and the exposed flesh of his lower legs would alert him to trip wires. Moving this way, his body was alternately shifted from side to side. Thus he was always in a fighting stance, and had less body exposed.

Vanh watched him move up behind the training NCO, one of his best men. He would not have believed, had he not been watching, that the American could move so quietly. It was obvious that the advisor's concentration was intense; sweat poured from him, dripping into his eyes, yet he seldom even blinked. Vanh had seen the same singleness of purpose in the stalk of the jungle tiger, the same concentration on its prey.

The NCO, concentrating on his troops, heard nothing but their stumbling. He was disgusted. Would they never learn? He missed his dead comrades. These clumsy fools would never be able to replace them.

Then he felt the hair at the back of his neck riffle in a warm breeze. He turned his head, found himself looking into a pair of blue eyes from two inches away. *"Choi oi!"* he yelled, jumping back. "American devil, where did you come from?"

"Very good, Captain Carmichael," said Vanh. "This is an American technique which we have not yet learned. Would you care to teach us?"

"Gladly," said Jim. "But it's not an American technique. It's Japanese, a ninja movement, one they used to approach their assassination targets. It's one of the reasons they got their reputation for being ghosts. I always believe one culture can learn from another, don't you?"

Vanh smiled. And what will you learn from us, young American? he wondered. Will you learn to lose your humanity, as I have? Will you learn to die inside, to become as hard and unfeeling as it is necessary to be to survive? Will it destroy you as it did so many of your predecessors? The ones who turned to drink, or drugs, or took so many risks they achieved the death and expiation for which they sought. Or will you become one of the dead-eyed ones, the killers, the stalkers of the night? Such as I am, such as I must be. It will be interesting to see.

JIM helped the recruits for the rest of the day. They caught on quickly. Many of the older PRUs came out to watch and soon were trying the new technique. He did not fool himself by thinking that he had won them over. But it was a start.

At dusk they broke off training. He was invited to share dinner with them, a courtesy they did not expect to be accepted. Most of the Americans preferred to dine with their own kind. He surprised them by saying yes, then by eating the simple fare with apparent gusto.

From them he confirmed that virtually no operations had been conducted since the Tet debacle.

"Because of the need to replace your losses?" he asked tactfully.

"No," Vanh replied scornfully. "We have enough experienced people to go out and do what we must. But the province chief will not let us. He says that we must wait, that the enemy is too strong and we are too weak. That we should let the Americans fight the enemy while we bide our time. We have done nothing since Tet except train, and perform guard duties.''

The training NCO chimed in. "We are soldiers, not guards! Each time we propose to go out, we are stalled with one excuse or another. The time is not propitious; the target has moved; there is no backup support if we get into trouble. As if the PRU needs backup! We want to be guards no more. We want to kill the V.C."

"Have you told this to the POIC?" Jim asked.

"We have, and it has done no good. He is afraid to cross the province chief. The chief is a powerful man, with many friends in Saigon. So the murderers go free, the ones who have killed so many of our people."

From their tales, it was not hard to understand why they were so eager to go out. It was blood vengeance, pure and simple. All had lost family members during Tet. Since the V.C. had been unsuccessful in getting to them, they had taken it out on the innocents. Captain Vanh had spent the days after Tet searching for his family in the sand dunes, finally digging them all up: wife, four children, mother and ancient grandfather. They had been herded there and shot, all except the children. They'd had their brains bashed out with rifle butts.

One of the younger PRU soldiers told him about his brother, who had witnessed the massacre. "They tied their hands behind their backs with string," he said. "He said it cut through his flesh, but he was so afraid that he didn't notice the blood dripping on his legs. They marched them out of Hue in a long column, the old and the young alike. Anyone who fell was kicked and beaten until they got up again. If they could not get up they were bayoneted, and an oxcart at the end of the column picked up their bodies.

"They got to the place and saw that a long trench had been dug. They were made to stand at the edge of the trench and look down into it. In it were the bodies of those who had dug it. Some of them were still twitching. The smell of blood was heavy in the air. Some started to wail, the women pleaded for their babies. They offered themselves to the soldiers: kill us if you will, they said, but take the children away. The soldiers laughed.

"It started at each end of the trench. Two men, two rifles. Each person was shot once. The wailing grew louder, people tried to escape. They were pushed back into place with bayonets. It was more cruel this way, waiting as the executioners worked their way down the line, seeing the others die and be pitched into the pit. Some begged the Communists to open fire all at once, kill them all so that they would not have to wait for death. It would have been easier to take. But the Communists are always careful to save bullets. So they had to wait their turn.

"Finally they came to my brother. He felt the bullet hit him in the back, and fell into the pit. He was stunned, but not dead. He felt the other bodies fall on top of him, cover him up. Their blood was mixing with his. He thought he would die then, but he didn't.

"Then he heard the roaring of an engine. The Communists, having no one left to cover the bodies, had taken a bulldozer from a nearby construction site. He could not see anything, but felt the earth shake, and the sand started pouring in on him. More and more, until the sky was blotted out. Then he knew that he must be dead.

"But still he was not. Buddha must have smiled on him. For he could still breathe, and after a while found that he could move, though the pain from his shattered ribs was great. He started digging, pulling the sand down, and just when he despaired of ever reaching the surface, he felt air. By then he did not care if the Communists were still there, let them shoot him. It would be better than slowly dying, buried there with the others. They were gone. He hid in the bushes for a long time and finally went back to the city. He was not even badly hurt. The bullet had broken two ribs and punctured his lung, but had hit nothing else. He is one of the recruits you were training today. Now you see, Captain, why we wish to fight? The blood of our families cries out. Blood must be answered by blood."

THAT night Jim lay awake for a long time. He was angry, very angry. The stories told him by the PRU had the ring of truth, and confirmed his resolve to do something about it. He'd heard stories about the province chief from a whole series of briefers. The man was regarded as one of the most venal and cowardly of all those in Vietnam. And that was saying a lot. He had to find a way to break the PRU loose from his grip. But no ideas came. Finally he got up and checked the perimeter. Already there was an increase in alertness. Apparently the night before, when he had woken sleeping guards with a blade at their throats, had its effect. He was even challenged a couple of times. He found no one asleep, although some of the bunkers were still not manned. One thing at a time, he reminded himself. If there was one thing one learned from the Asians, it was patience.

THE next day he left the compound in a jeep which had been assigned to the PRU. He was careful to check in the rearviews often, took a roundabout route and performed several switchbacks. By the time he reached the Perfume River he was reasonably sure there were no followers.

Still not completely satisfied, he parked well away from his destination and proceeded on foot. The street was crowded with Vietnamese, but there were enough Caucasians that he was not overly conspicuous.

He entered a small storefront beneath a sign which announced that herein one could find the finest tailor in Hue. A young Vietnamese greeted him. He asked to see the owner. The Viet asked the nature of his business. He replied that it was a matter of exchange. The Viet smiled knowingly. It was no secret that the Indian who owned the shop was the biggest black market money changer in the province. Many Americans came here. For greenback dollars one could get Military Pay Certificate (MPC) scrip at a rate of two for one. It was a good deal for both sides. The Indian sold the green to rich Vietnamese who wished to avoid the restrictions on currency transfers out of country. Most of them, being prudent, were salting away the profits they made from the war in foreign bank accounts. The MPC came from the many illegal businesses catering to the American troops, the two principal being prostitution and drugs.

For Jim it was the perfect cover. Nobody would be suspicious of one more American coming in to change money. Such transactions were illegal, of course, so nobody would think it strange that he had taken such precautions not to be followed.

He was admitted to the back room. The man who sat there was recognizable from the photo in the file.

"You wish to change money?" he asked. His voice was low and pleasant, tinged only slightly with a singsong Indian accent.

"Not exactly," Jim answered. "I'm a friend of Mike's."

If the man was surprised, he did not allow it to show. "Ah, the unfortunate Captain McGivern," he said. "So sad about him. He was a good friend and a valued business associate. Did he have a family? I have missed him."

"I'm sure you have," Jim said, trying to keep the sarcasm from his voice. "But there's no reason that you and I can't be friends too. Under the same basis. Mike left some very good reports on you. Said that you were the man to see if I really wanted to know what was going on in the province."

"The late captain was too kind." Too kind by far, the Indian thought furiously. "You must understand that things are not as they once were. Many of the people who talked to me are no longer alive. Those who are, no longer wish to take risks. Tet taught them that it can be very unhealthy to be suspected of collaboration with the government." He had hoped that all records of his cooperation with the Americans had died with the late captain. Had suspected that he would not be so lucky.

"But such things have happened before?" Jim said. "You have been here for a very long time. Before the Americans came you had French friends. Times were hard then too, were they not? Still, you always managed to succeed. There are those who say it is because you manage to please all sides: the French, the Viet Minh, the Polish members of the International Control Commission in the interregnum. Some say you even have links with the Chinese. I am sure that a resourceful man such as you can reestablish contact with people who will talk to you. Especially since the alternative is so unattractive. The tiger cages on Con Son Island are not a place you wish to be. That is where they put the black marketeers, I understand."

The Indian lifted his hands, palms up, and shrugged eloquently. "You are very convincing," he said. "I assume the terms will be the same as with the unfortunate Captain McGivern?"

"The same," Jim agreed. "I protect you from investigation. You continue to make money. All you have to do is tell me the things I want to know about the names I give you. Very little risk, and a great deal of benefit for you."

"Then it seems I have no choice. May I offer you some tea?"

Jim accepted. "The first thing I need to know," he said, "is anything you have on the province chief. Or anyone close to him. I need some leverage."

"You are dealing with a very powerful man. One who can make you disappear. It has happened before."

"Thanks for the warning. But this is not a subject for discussion. Tell me what you know."

As he had suspected, the Indian knew a great deal. The P.C. had his fingers in just about every illegal enterprise in the province, but that was no surprise. And there were few hooks on which to hang him. It was a small item, offered as an aside, that gave Jim an idea. The trip had so far been well worth it.

The next hour was spent in planning for communications. Dead-letter drops were the preferred method. Loading and servicing signals were agreed upon, as were locations.

"By the way," said Jim as he was preparing to leave, "the rumor going around has it that before Tet someone told the V.C. exactly where Captain McGivern slept. I don't know if that's true or not. What I do know is that you now have a very active interest in my well-being. Because if anything happens to me, you'll never be able to sleep again. You will know that when you do, someone will come to visit you in the night. And your sleep will never end. Know also that you are not the only one in the province with information. Each thing you tell me will be checked with someone else. If I ever find out that you have lied to me, I will be the one to come and visit you. I'll see you again, Mr. Chandragar."

The Indian's eyes widened as Jim called him by his real name. No one was supposed to know that. He hadn't used it for many years. This was a dangerous man. Still, it could have been worse. There were some things the young American obviously did not know. And it was useful to have a protector. He'd survived this long by playing the various factions against one another. As long as he continued to be useful, he would be safe. He smiled at the captain and watched him go, then called to his assistant and berated him for an hour for infractions real or imagined. Then, feeling somewhat more in control, he set about reestablishing contact with the members of his net.

JIM'S next stop was Provincial Headquarters. His request for an audience with the province chief was relayed through innumerable layers of bureaucracy. Jim sat in the waiting room, leafing through old magazines, intent on staying there as long as it took. When finally they decided they weren't going to get rid of him, he was ushered into a spacious office.

The cleats of his jungle boots squished slightly on the tile as he walked toward the desk placed at the far end of the room. The man behind the desk wore sunglasses even though the room was curtained into semidarkness. Jim had expected one of the corpulent mandarin types. He was disappointed. The province chief was thin, intense. His face was deeply carved from cheek to chin with lines that would seem to preclude him from ever breaking into a smile. His uniform was immaculate. Smoke curled from a cigarette held European style in manicured fingers.

"You are welcome, Captain," he said in French-accented English. "Please take a seat. May I offer you something to drink, a Scotch perhaps?"

"Thank you, but no. I'll not waste your time, Colonel. I know that you are a busy man. May I speak frankly, sir?"

"Of course. I prefer to speak frankly. Your predecessor also had that trait. A most charming man. We miss him."

That's the second time today I've heard that lie, thought Jim. "Then I'll get right to the point," he said. "I want to take the PRU out on operation. Soon. They need it. You know that our superiors want it. Do you have any objections?"

"You Americans are always so eager," the man said, sitting back in his chair. "Why should it be tomorrow, and not next week, or even next month? The war has been here for a long time. It is not going to go away."

"And neither are the Communists. Right now they are weak. But they are regrouping, and each day they grow stronger. Now is the time to act. Your daughter would understand that. She goes to a university in the United States. If someone were threatening her, as the Communists threaten your country, would you not take immediate action?''

The colonel sat very still. His face was even more rigid.

Jim continued, ''University of Oklahoma, isn't it? Good school. I have a couple of friends who go there. They might even know one another.''

''I have no objections to your conducting operations,'' the province chief said. ''What made you think I did? Of course you can go out. The men need it.''

''Then what they said about you was true, Colonel. That you are one of the most aggressive of field commanders, that you are a true Vietnamese patriot. I won't take up any more of your time.'' He was a little amazed at his capacity for hypocrisy.

After the American left, the colonel called his aide, who had been listening to the conversation from behind a panel. ''I want to know everything about this man,'' he said. ''Where he goes, who he talks to, what his patterns are. He may be dangerous.''

CHAPTER 6

If Captain Vanh was impressed with the speed in which Jim had secured permission to conduct operations, he did not show it. Matter-of-factly he started the planning.

The first target was the V.C. district chief for Phong Dien District. He was a notorious fellow, said to be responsible for many of the atrocities perpetuated during Tet. Jim picked him because of his notoriety, because there was little doubt that he was, in fact, V.C., and because the target was supposed to be so tough. Reports said he never traveled with fewer than twenty bodyguards, seldom slept in the same place twice, and at the least sign of danger retreated to the jungle, only to reemerge after the heat was off. He had been on the blacklist a very long time. The intelligence officers at the PIOCC routinely included him, but expressed little hope that he would ever be apprehended.

What the PIOCC did not know was that the impossible target had one flaw, as did most men, if you only took the trouble to look for it. His sources told Jim that the man had a weakness for the younger female V.C. cadre. He also had a wife who, when confronted with the evidence of her husband's infidelity, decided to take revenge. In exchange for protection, she agreed to let the source know the location of her philandering spouse.

He and Vanh planned the operation carefully. They could afford no mistakes. The mission was critical, not only because of the importance of the target but for the psychological boost it would give the PRU. A chance like this might never come again.

The PRUs infiltrated the area around the village singly and in pairs. To all outward appearances they looked just like everyone else: the same black pajamas and Ho Chi Minh sandals, the same conical bamboo hats, the same baskets filled with fruit from the market. Inside the baskets were Uzi submachine guns and M-26 fragmentation grenades. Tucked into their trousers were 9mm pistols and knives. If they were challenged by the V.C. in the area, they were to try to bluff their way through. If they could not, they would try to shoot their way out. If nothing else worked, they were to pull the pin on one of the grenades and blow themselves and everyone near them to bits. There was no worry about capture. Each PRU knew all too well what fate awaited him should he be taken alive. Long ago the PRU and the VC had sworn undying enmity, and no quarter was asked—or given.

Jim and the PRU captain waited until after dark to move. Jim's height made it impossible for him to try to infiltrate during the day. They rode in the rear of a covered vegetable truck to a prearranged drop-off point. As the driver slowed to go around a curve, they jumped out, rolling into the underbrush and waiting anxious moments to see if anyone had detected them.

As they set off through the jungle, Jim felt all his old skills return. It was nice to see that he had not gotten too rusty. The night enveloped them, the distant sound of insects and nightbirds their only companions. They moved silently and slowly. The only sound was the lack of sound as the denizens of the forest, sensing their presence, fell silent around them. They seemed to be moving in a bubble of quiet.

Travel was not difficult. This was not the tangled jungle to which he had grown so accustomed in II Corps. It was almost like a well-tended forest; wood gatherers had picked the floor clean. The trees were spaced widely enough that light from the full moon filtered through, allowing for fast movement. It was a perfect night. Jim was aware of a pleasant tightness in his chest, the stricture of compressed excitement. His skin tingled with anticipation. The trunks of the giant trees loomed whitely in the ghostly light. Their footsteps activated the luminescence of rotting vegetation. Was it strange, he wondered, that he was enjoying this, that he could appreciate the unearthly beauty of this hostile place? Why wasn't he like other men, who could be satisfied with their safe lives far from danger, who could savor the little victories won on the battlefields of corporate war? Instead he was on his way to almost certainly kill someone, and possibly be killed.

Captain Vanh's navigation was good. They reached the assembly point directly, without having to search. The squad leaders of the detachment were already there. After a few words from the captain they moved off soundlessly to rejoin their units. Jim checked his watch: five minutes to go. Perfect timing. So far he was impressed with the performance of the men. It had been his habit on previous trips to Vietnam to scoff at the fighting ability of the Vietnamese, as did most other Americans. Now he was not so sure he had been right. This group was as professional as any he had ever seen. The next few moments would tell whether or not his impression was correct.

The plan was brutally direct and simple. Two squads were to set up an ambush on the trail on the other side of the village. The remainder of the detachment was to infiltrate as closely as possible on the near side, then go in shooting as soon as they were detected.

The hope was that the V.C. would attempt to escape, whereupon the ambush would take them under fire. Jim had wanted to do it differently. Go in himself with perhaps one or two other people and attempt to capture the V.C. chief in his bed. He'd had to admit, after he had proposed it to Captain Vanh, that the chances of pulling off a movement of that type were slim. But it seemed to him to offer the best chance of taking the man alive. Vanh had wanted to go in shooting from the start. They had finally compromised: they would go in silently until detected, then he and Vanh would dash for the house in which they had been told the district chief would be spending the night. Perhaps they would be able to get to him before he ran away into the certain death of the ambush.

Each movement was excruciatingly slow. It was all very fine to practice this; in practice failure was met only by the jeers of your comrades. Here it meant the possibility not only of your death, which could be accepted, but also the death of people who depended upon you, which could not be. So you were extra careful, the foot slowly, gingerly touching the ground, moving twigs and leaves out of the way, inching forward, progress measured not in yards or feet, but in millimeters. A route had been picked which gave them the most concealment up until the last minute: along a scrubby stand of banana plants, past a pigsty at the edge of the huts, into the village itself. You had to remember, moving like this, that the full moon cast a shadow almost as distinct as the one in daylight. Stay to the shadows of the buildings, then, and when you had to cross an open area, stay low and move very slowly. Quick movement attracted the eye.

There! To the side a sentry, half asleep, filling the vision to the exclusion of all else. Movement carefully chosen to take him from the flank, in the blind zone where he cannot see you unless he turns his head; and even if he does, you move so slowly that he does not pick up the change from the ordinary that man depends upon to tell him that something is wrong.

Close enough now. In one movement clap your hand over his mouth, push his head sharply over to one side to constrict his airway, the knife thrusting upward into the solar plexus. The flesh is resistant, but not so much that the carefully honed blade cannot penetrate deeply. Push the haft quickly from one side to the other, the double edge severing arteries and veins, the suddenly loosened flow filling the stomach cavity through the torn diaphragm, the lungs awash in rich warmth. No outcry. No chance. What does he feel, you wonder, here in the last moments of his life? There cannot be much pain; it is over too quickly. Does he feel despair, knowing that it is ended? Is it, perhaps, even a relief? Lower him softly to the ground, feeling almost affectionate. You have shared the most intimate of embraces. Withdraw the knife, pulling hard to overcome resistance. The flesh is unwilling to give up its invader. Upon the blade remains only a thin film, looking black in the moonlight.

Perimeter breached. They should have had more sentries. Perhaps they have grown lax in the long rest. It is difficult not to. Man's natural tendency is to think that things will always remain the same.

Closer now to the target. Hearing preternaturally clear, the slight rustling of the feet as they touch the ground sounding like clarion bells. How can they not hear it? The crack of a small twig, unfelt at first by the foot, is like a rifle shot.

Vanh is beside him at the entrance to the hut. In the dim light his thin face looks like a skull. A skull grinning in triumph. He steps in, Jim following closely, and views the corpulent body of the district chief with glee. He motions to Jim—take the woman. Jim moves to the other side, stands ready to grab her to prevent the screams which could kill them all. Her breathing is soft and even, masked by the snores of the man.

Vanh takes a T-shaped piece of metal from his waistband, moves slightly closer to his target, and with a quick motion drives the sharpened end of a four-inch spike forcefully behind the ear.

There is a quiver, a quick and jerky drumming of the legs as nerve synapses fire wildly. Then nothing. The woman moans, stirs. Jim is poised to shut her off. Then she subsides, rolls over and petulantly pulls the covers from her dead companion. Her breathing again becomes regular.

Vanh offers his instrument to Jim, who pushes it away. Vanh shrugs, motions "outside." They go, as silently as they came.

Away from the village they summon the troops. It takes a long while for everyone to assemble. The ambush party is disgruntled. They have been cheated out of action. In rapid-fire Vietnamese Captain Vanh explains that this way is much better, that when the guards wake in the morning to find their leader dead, there will be much loss of face, and not a little fear. Who could have come so silently in the night? How could the man, sleeping in the middle of the village among many guards, have been killed? How could anyone feel safe when such things were possible? The story would spread, and would be embellished by many tellings, and no V.C. would be able to sleep well for a very long time.

It satisfied the troops. It satisfied Jim somewhat less. He held his peace until they returned, after arduous marching, his leg aching fiercely, to the camp. Then he requested private audience with the captain.

"You want to tell me why you did that?" he asked quietly.

The captain looked up at him through eyes fogged with fatigue. "I explained it to the men," he said. "You know enough Vietnamese to understand. Why do you bother me? I must sleep."

"Not good enough. I know and you know that we could have carried the plan through. We could have snatched this guy.'' Jim's voice rose in anger. ''Instead you don't even try! You snuff him out like a candle. God damn you, we could have gotten all kinds of information out of him. We could have rolled up his entire organization. Now all we've got is a dead body, and nothing else to show for it. Why?''

''What we had, Dai Uy, is a very high-ranking official of the Vietnamese Communist Party. A man who had dedicated his life to the cause.'' Vanh looked at the young American pityingly. This one was as naive as all the others. ''We have a law which states that the PRU can only hold someone for twenty-four hours. Do you think we could have made him talk in that time?''

Jim started to say something, was cut off by a wave of the hand.

''Would you? In twenty-four hours? No matter what was done to you? No? And neither would I, Captain Jim. And neither would he. And after that twenty-four hours, what would happen? He would be released to the District Interrogation Center. Which has your people closely supervising to make sure there is no torture. We cannot have torture, your press would make too much of it, again we would be painted as the barbarians.

''So he says nothing. And very quickly there is pressure from very high levels to release him. He has not confessed, they say. Perhaps we have the wrong man. The PRU was once again overzealous. There will be witnesses who come forward who will state that this is not the same man who was on the blacklist, that this is a terrible case of mistaken identity. Soon he will be released. It should be no secret to you that there are many in our government who are, as you Americans say, hedging their bets. They think that the war will be lost. They do not care to be labeled as 'enemies of the people' under the new government.''

The captain seemed to sag, to become smaller, as if he were pulling inside himself. ''So the only answer is to exterminate our enemies. I have no illusions. I also know that the war is lost. I know that our American friends will someday tire of the fight. I know that we shall perish. My fight, Captain Jim, is the fight of a trapped rat, biting anyone who comes close. Perhaps you can understand. Perhaps not. I know that I shall die. I know that I shall make many of them accompany me. I understand futility. Do you?

"Now I must sleep. Good night, Captain. If you wish to report this to the province chief, you should do so no later than ten hundred hours. He will be flying to the beaches at Vung Tau at eleven."

THE province chief called for him the next day. This time Jim did not have to wait so long to be ushered into his presence. The colonel still had his aviator glasses on. Jim wondered if he ever took them off. He noticed that the man's uniform was perfectly creased, the qualification badges and ribbons placed with excruciating care at precisely the proper places. Among the badges, Jim noticed, were U.S. Army parachutists wings and the unit crest of Fort Benning. He also had several awards of the Vietnamese Cross of Gallantry. This was handed out to senior officers, not on the basis of bravery, but on how important you were.

Upon seeing Jim the colonel smiled. There was no emotion in it. "Captain," he said, "please sit down. Would you like coffee? I apologize for the early hour, but I must go away later today. Tell me, Captain, how do you like your new job? Do you get on well with Captain Vanh? We have had problems with him in the past, you know. I hope that he is causing you no difficulties. Sometimes it is difficult to convince some of the people that the old methods are no longer acceptable."

Jim, who had been conducting an internal debate about what had happened, held his silence. He didn't know why. It would have been easy to have caused the replacement of the captain. Perhaps the next man would have been more amenable to his methods. He understood Vanh's point, but still, if one really wanted to do the job properly, these people would have to be brought in. Perhaps there would be some way to forestall the scenario Vanh had painted. But in the end he decided against it. The colonel was entirely too smooth, too pat, too perfect. He was the very model of a Western politician's idea of a perfect Vietnamese officer.

He became aware that the colonel was waiting for his response. Waiting with only faintly disguised eagerness. And an underlying amusement.

"Captain Vanh is a real pleasure to work with," he said,

putting on his best stupid-American act. "A very fine soldier. Rough around the edges, maybe, but who isn't?" He chuckled. "Of course, I'm just getting to know him."

The Vietnamese took another tack. "How went the operation last night?" he asked. "I have not yet received a written report." He was lying. Captain Vanh's report had been waiting for him when he arrived at the office.

"Fairly smoothly," Jim replied. How much did the man know? "We weren't able to capture the man. Too much danger. The decision was made to terminate him instead." Jim carefully avoided telling a lie. "Too bad it had to be that way. Always better if you can bring them in and talk to them."

"Indeed," said the Colonel. "Killing serves very little purpose. Still, sometimes it is unavoidable. Perhaps next time you will have more success. I am, however, glad that the PRU is back in action. They have been waiting for too long, as I had known. The President will be very happy to hear, when I talk to him later today, that one of the most brutal of our enemies is no more. We will speak again, Captain, but know for now that I am happy to have you working with us."

Jim, astounded at the depth of the man's hypocrisy, made his excuses and left. He found the nearest bar and had two stiff drinks of black-market whiskey.

The bar owner, pleased to have one of the free-spending Americans as a customer, started a tape on his stolen stereo. All the crazy Western music sounded the same to him, not like the delicate plucking and wailing of Vietnamese ballads. But they seemed to like it, and he was willing to endure the cacophony as long as it brought in money. He motioned for one of the girls to go over. Lazy sluts! They would sit around and play cards all day long if he let them. Surely the big American savage would at least buy a couple of Saigon Teas.

Jim, lost in his thoughts, felt someone tugging at his sleeve. A Vietnamese girl of indeterminate age with a face badly pocked by smallpox scars was trying to get his attention. Her short dress was impossibly tight, accentuating birdlike legs and fleshless ribs. She reminded him of a mongrel dog he had tried to adopt when he was seven. His father had shot it, claiming it was harassing the livestock.

"I love you too much, G.I.," she said. "You buy me Saigon Tea?" She rubbed her tiny pubis against his leg.

"Choi manh oi, Anh nhieu em nheu wa," he replied,
stressing the syllable which indicated that he loved her too
much too. "You buy your own Saigon Tea."

"Goddamn numbah ten cheap Charlie-fucking G.I.," she
spat, going back to her card game. She shot the bar owner a
look which said that she had tried, and couldn't be blamed if
the accursed American was stingy. Secretly she was relieved.
She didn't like going with the Americans. They scared her.

Jim watched her go, amused. Fuck it, he thought. The sun
was still shining, he was still alive, and things could be fixed.
He left money on the bar, enough for a tip for the girl, though
he suspected she would never see it, and went back to the
Embassy House.

THE POIC had left word that he wanted to see Jim
as quickly as possible. "I read your report," he said. "And
sent a copy to the regional officer in charge in Danang. He
wants to see you as soon as possible." The little man was
agitated. "I was afraid of this. The first operation of the
PRU, and the target is killed. Couldn't you have prevented
it? I don't know if you've heard of Roger McMurdock, the
ROIC, but he's a tough man. And he's very interested in
seeing that this program works. There's an Air America flight
out at two o'clock. Someone will meet you at Danang airfield. I suggest that you plan on staying at least overnight."

Shit! Jim thought. He had, of course, heard of Roger
McMurdock. Slim Feltrie had given him a thorough briefing
on the man while in Saigon. McMurdock was a well-known
Clandestine Services operative. He had performed hair-raising
missions all over the world, starting in the old Office of Stra-
tegic Services (OSS), the predecessor to the CIA, back in
World War II. He had been one of the officers parachuted
into Indochina during the last days of the war, and had met
Ho Chi Minh. Jim had looked forward to meeting him. But
not under these circumstances.

He packed more than enough to stay overnight. Slipped
the 9mm into the waistband of his trousers. Already it felt
natural there, like a comforting extra hand, cold at first,
then slowly warming to match his heat. He debated on the
CAR-15, then decided that no matter what happened, if he
was fired and shipped somewhere else, if he was sent back

to Saigon, whatever, he would need it. The rest of his gear could follow on afterward but he would go nowhere without weapons he trusted.

THERE was more than enough time to think on the ride to Danang. The patched-up DC-3 droned through the air, cooling wind whipping through the open pilot windows and cargo door. The ground slipped by underneath at a steady rate. They were flying just high enough to discourage ground fire. They paralleled Highway One, the "Street Without Joy" of the French-Indochina War. The French would not have recognized it now. No more did the jungle come right up to the roadway. Rome plows and Agent Orange had taken care of that. The ground was red, raw and ugly, a hundred-mile scar. No beauty here, but also less danger of ambush. The enemy was reduced to firing at convoys from hundreds of yards away, and except for the occasional sniper, seldom bothered. Trucks filled with supplies roared north, were passed by empties heading south. The war machine took up millions of tons of matériel. It was a case of the logistical tail wagging the tactical dog. Few people in the United States were aware that of the half million troops in Vietnam, only about fifty thousand were actually fighting. The rest were in support. It was a natural result of the tactic of dependence on massive firepower.

Away from the road the terrain was terribly scarred. He couldn't even guess how many tons of bombs, how many thousands of artillery shells, had been dropped in this area. In some places there were pockmarks scattered haphazardly across the terrain. In other areas the orderly march of craters spoke of B-52 raids. Little of this ordnance, he knew, had been expended at targets. Most had been fired or dropped on vague reports, or as so-called harassing and interdictory fire. Scaring the monkeys, he always thought derisively. From the ground he knew it would look different. Almost impossible to move through, the trees tossed around like toothpicks, the jungle vines intertwining throughout. You didn't walk through such areas, you crawled, snaking your way through the obstacles like playing in a jungle gym designed by a madman. The enemy would have taken the time to clear good fields of fire, and would be hidden so well you probably wouldn't see the muzzle flashes of the guns sending the bullets to crack around you. Advance would be suicidal. So you backed off and called in yet more fire, and hoped they went away.

He remembered his first ride in a DC-3 across terrain such as this, back in 1963. There had been no bomb craters then, no scarred earth. The jungle had stretched in smooth green as far as the eye could see, broken only occasionally by the orderly rows of rubber plantations. Here and there would be a town, few very large, just collections of tin-roofed huts. He had thought it very beautiful. But that had been when he was young, and much more innocent.

A Filipino driver in a new civilian Jeep met him at the airport. He was a cheerful man, chattering away about Danang, and the Philippines, and any other subject he could come up with on the thirty-minute drive to the Danang Embassy House. Jim nodded in the appropriate places, and smiled when he thought he should, and largely kept his thoughts to himself. He was miserable. He realized that he wanted this job, and the thought of losing it so soon filled him with anger and despair. He wondered what to tell the ROIC. Should he stick to the original story? That it had been simply too dangerous to try to capture the district chief? Should he embellish it by talking about the great number of bodyguards in the village? Or should he give up Captain Vanh and feel the sense of betrayal he knew would come?

In the end, Roger McMurdock saved him the trouble.

His voice fit the image of the man. No meek, self-effacing spy this. "Come in here, Jim," he boomed, after the young captain presented himself at his office. "Have a seat. No, here, close to the desk. I want to have a look at our newest star. Killed old Nguyen Van Thuong, did you? Ah, hell, I know you didn't actually do the deed," he said, waving off Jim's attempt at protest. "Vanh did it. But he sure as hell wouldn't have got that close if it hadn't been for you. Vanh is a high-diddle-diddle, straight-through-the-middle type. Only problem I have with him. Otherwise he's a helluva good man.

"You're surprised I know that much? Hell, boy, I was doing shit like this when you were a gleam in your daddy's eye. I know how to set up intelligence nets. Even better than the one you have with the Indian. Don't trust that cocksucker, by the way. Use him, don't blame him for that, he's good enough for the mission you have for him. When he stops being that, we'll see. Now, if you don't have any questions, as far as I can see, the sun is past the yardarm and I've got Al Dougherty up here, and I'm sure he already has a jump start on us in the bar. Come on! Let's shake up some of these old farts around here.''

Jim, quite overwhelmed by the nonstop monologue, and very glad that he was not going to be fired, followed the ROIC out of the office. He hadn't appreciated, until the man stood up, how big he was. He was Jim's height, but weighed at least fifty pounds more. Little of this looked to be fat. He walked quickly and surely, balancing each step on the ball of the foot. An old fighter's trick. He greeted people met along the way with a familiar growl, obviously enjoying himself. I like him, Jim thought.

Al was holding forth to the bartender when they arrived. His face broke into a broad smile. ''God damn, reinforcements,'' he said. ''I think I chased everybody else off. Bartender probably wants to go too, but I told him I'd shoot him if he even tries to take a piss. Rog tells me you got a good one, Jimmy. Barkeep!'' he yelled. ''Give the boss and Jimmy a drink. Quick. Elsewise they may cut your balls off.''

Jim, who was not yet to the stage where he felt he could refer to the ROIC as ''Rog,'' accepted his drink in silence from an obviously terrified bartender. No one else was in the club. Once again, the place testified to the Agency's ability to take care of itself. The furnishings were lush. The ubiquitous air conditioners kept it as cold as the tomb. Plush chairs were scattered about. The bar itself was of carved teak.

''Al, here, scored a good one too,'' the ROIC said. ''First PRU operation in Quang Nam Province since Tet, just like yours was the first one in Thua Thien. You guys have done good. Wouldn't have expected it that quick.''

''Which means,'' Al said, winking at Jim, ''that we could have fucked off for a while before getting started. We ain't too goddamn smart, are we?''

''Hell, buddy,'' Jim said, breaking his silence, ''nobody ever accused us of that.''

''Well, I'm damned pleased, boys,'' said Roger. ''Within a week we get a V.C. district chief and a sapper squad that's been giving us fits for years. Same folks, we figure," he said, addressing himself to Jim, "who captured the German medical team during Tet. Found most of 'em later. Wasn't pretty. They took special care with the women. Really fucked them up. And your guy, Nguyen Van Thuong, had a habit of disemboweling the people he caught, nailing their guts to a tree and leaving them. Sometimes it would take them days to die. So the world is marginally better off today than it was yesterday. How do you feel about it?"

"I came here afraid I was going to be fired. Since you obviously know everything that happened, and you haven't fired me yet, you must approve of it."

"And you don't?"

"Not as if I don't approve. Shit, I'm no fucking fool. What Captain Vanh said made a lot of sense. I'm sure as hell hoping he's got it wrong, though. He told me that there was a good possibility that if we'd turned in Thuong, he would have been released. Is that true?"

"All too true, I'm afraid. It's sure as hell happened before. Including with Thuong, back in '66. Makes no sense to you, does it? Not to me either. But that's what we have to deal with. That's why we pay you so fucking much money," he joked, knowing that with jump pay and demolitions pay and combat pay the captain made barely $900 per month, "to ride herd on these guys, and to take all that into account, and to try your goddamned best to take as many as you can alive. Don't expect it to be all of them. You guys are good, but you aren't miracle workers. How does it feel, by the way, to be working for the most misunderstood, one of the most feared and one of the most incompetent fucking organizations in the world? Only hope we've got is the KGB has even worse bureaucrats than we do. Used to be a good outfit, once. Al, tell him about your ambush!"

"Not all that big a deal," Dougherty said. "Found out where these cocksuckers were going to be. Province chief wouldn't let me take out the PRU. So the captain and I decided we'd go out ourselves. Carried a whole shitload of claymores. Set 'em up alongside a trail, hooked 'em up in series. Squad came along, just like they were supposed to, and we touched the mines off. Blew 'em to shit. Had a hell of a time getting documents off 'em, they were in pieces. They were on their way to hit the ARVN hospital again. One of their favorite targets, evidently.''

''Tell him what else you found,'' commanded McMurdock.

''Oh, yeah. Almost forgot. Jewelry. Couple of rings. One of 'em a wedding ring. One necklace. Gave 'em to the German medical mission. They belonged to the people who'd been killed. Neutrals. As if anyone could be neutral in this goddamned place.''

Roger stared deeply into Jim's eyes. As if to say, you see what we have to deal with? You still have compunctions against killing these assholes? These beasts who raped and murdered nurses who would treat the Communists as quickly as they would anyone else? Where do you stand, Captain James NMI Carmichael?

Jim raised his glass in slow salute. They drank together, a tacit understanding reached.

''Now,'' Roger said when glasses had been lowered, ''where the hell is everyone? We have some distinguished visitors from Saigon, and I think we should subject them to your presence. You wait here, I'll go stir them up.''

''So what do you think?'' Al asked after Roger departed.

''Looks like I'm not going to get fired, at least.''

''I'd say that would be the least of your worries. This guy is shit-hot.''

''As long as he lasts.''

''Hasn't done too bad so far. He's been over here four years now. And he likes us. So life isn't too goddamned bad. Never lived so high. Bunch better than being out with an infantry company, isn't it?''

Jim started to agree, then wasn't so sure. Roger was returning, Saigon visitors in tow. One of them was Moira.

CHAPTER 7

"THESE are my new young tigers," Roger introduced them. "A week in the field and already they've done more than anyone else has in the last four months. Gentlemen, this is Eliot Danforth and his able assistant, Moira Culpepper."

"The two captains and I have met," said Moira. "Jim, Al, how are you? Looks like you've acclimatized rather well."

"I'd say they have," said Danforth. He was a thin, aristocratic-looking man. Jim judged him to be another of the Eastern power establishment. "Congratulations. Our selection process is obviously working, if we get people like you."

Moira had the courtesy to lower her eyes at the mention of the selection process. Was it embarrassment, Jim wondered, or was she modestly receiving the accolades for a job well done?

"Mark sends his congratulations too," she said. "He'll give them himself, next time you get down to Saigon."

"Yes," said Jim, not trying to keep the edge of irony out of his voice. "I'll be glad to see Mark again. We've got a lot to talk about."

Al, sensing the tension in the air, and aware of the situation between Moira and Jim, decided to get things moving. "Give these people a drink!" he demanded of the bartender. "And get us one too. And don't stop bringing them. We've got some catching up to do. Roger, did I ever tell you about the time this asshole and I," referring to Jim, "were coming back from Saigon and I got shot in the leg?" He launched into a long and involved story which included him as the hero and Jim as an unfeeling bastard who had told him to shove his neck scarf in the hole in his thigh and shut the fuck up while Jim concentrated on driving out of the ambush.

Jim watched Moira as she listened to the story. Occasionally she glanced at him, but her look conveyed nothing more than general friendliness. A real pro, he thought. He had to admire her, even at the same time he was feeling resentment for being so well and thoroughly fooled. His own fault. It had always been a tendency of his to take people at face value. And, he had to admit, he had little experience with, and less understanding of, women. But when someone told you something, you believed them. Until events proved you wrong. He thought trust was a commodity he could no longer afford.

Other members of the mission began to drift in, aware of the visitors from Saigon and wishing to make themselves known. Gradually the place filled up. Moira was soon surrounded by a group of young staffers, each eager to vie for her attention. Roger and Eliot retired to a corner booth and engaged in whispered talk. Some deep spook shit, Jim supposed. He allowed himself to drink more than usual. Partly this was a result of feeling relatively safe in Danang. The Embassy House here had none of the defensive deficiencies of the one in Hue. He had noticed upon arrival that the guard force was sharp, alert and professional.

Partly the drinking was to relax. He realized how tightly wound he had become in the last week. And partly, he admitted to himself, it was because of the situation with Moira. He hated to be fooled. And she had done a very good job of it.

He became aware that Al was trying to get his attention. "Let it go, Jimmy," he said. "Not worth it. Come on! Let's get some attention. How about a rendition of 'Mary-Ann Barnes'?"

Jim joined him in song. It was an old Special Forces ballad, sung at virtually every gathering. They sang loud and clear, stopping conversation. The young men around Moira looked at them in distaste, whispering asides to her that Jim was sure included reference to the crudity of these soldier types. Fuck them, he thought, singing louder.

"Mary-Ann Barnes was the queen of all enlisted WACs,
She could do the tricks that would give the boys the shits,
Shoot green peas out her fundamental orifice,

Do a double somersault and catch them on her tits!
She's a great big sonofabitch, twice as big as me,
Hair on her ass like the branches on a tree.
She can shoot, ride, fart, fuck;
Fly a plane, drive a truck.
She is the girl that's gonna marry me,
Special Forces, Airborne, Ranger, Infantry,
Pathfinder tooooo.''

Roger, who had halted his conversation with Eliot Danforth to listen, applauded heartily. He was joined after a few
tentative moments by everyone else. Phony bastards! thought
Jim. The boss likes it, so you do too.

''You guys know 'Blood on the Risers'?'' asked the ROIC,
leaving Danforth to join them at the bar, making everyone
else wonder why these two crude soldiers had won the evident
approval of a man they all regarded in some fear. The bolder
among them drifted close, even attempted to join in some of
the songs. The others continued to attempt conversation, and
when that proved impossible because of the noise, drifted
away to their comfortable rooms. The PRU advisors would
be going back to the field soon, and good riddance. The club
was a much more pleasant place without them.

Moira stayed for a long time, listening and watching. She
thought about the times in bed with Jim. He had been a good
lover, considerate of her feelings and at the same time possessed of a passion which had overwhelmed her with its intensity. Making her forget her professionalism for just a little
while. A much better lover, in fact, than Eliot. Who, she
saw, was making the little head inclination which signaled
that he wanted them to leave. She sighed. Jim couldn't do
anything for her career. Eliot could. She left.

Jim didn't even notice that she had gone until much later.
He was having fun. The liquor flowed free and fast. As so
often happened, it seemed to energize him rather than infect
him with the lethargy it seemed to induce in so many people.
The group dredged up songs from memory, quickly running
out of military ballads, going to rock and roll from the fifties.
One of the older CIA men suggested ''Lili Marlene.'' The
high point of the evening came when Al, in a heartbreakingly

clear tenor, sang "Danny Boy." When he finished, all seemed
to tacitly agree that any more singing would be anticlimactic.

Things started breaking up around midnight. Roger, protesting that he had to work on the morrow, adamantly refused
the "just one more drink" and left. The other employees of
Embassy House departed soon after. Jim was left with Al at
the bar. They dismissed the bartender, telling him that if they
wanted another drink, they could get it themselves.

Jim felt a great wave of affection for his short, powerfully
built companion. Al's shock of black hair was down in his
eyes and he was trying to explain some profound truth, slur-
ring his words enough to be completely unintelligible. The
language, Jim decided, was a mixture of Bourbon and Greek.

"How long we been together, Al?" he asked. He was
aware that his speech was none too clear either.

"Long fuckin' time."

"Yeah," he agreed. "Long fuckin' time. Only friend I
got. Don't you ever get killed, you sweet motherfucker?"

"Me? Fuck that. Too permanent. I know people that was
killed back in 1963. And you know what? They're still dead!
Personally, I think dying is a highly overrated thrill."

"Me too. Think you can stand up? Not sure I can, and I
sure as hell don't feel like sleeping on the floor."

Supporting one another, they ricocheted down the long
hallway to the rooms they had been assigned. Al gave Jim a
big slobbery kiss on the ear, as Special Forces men are wont
to do, and gravely entered his room, where he fell across the
bed fully clothed, snoring loudly.

Jim, feeling for a moment very much in control of himself,
locked Al's door, opened his own, slowly and precisely took
off his clothes and hung them up, turned back the bedcovers
and crawled in. Got up after a couple of moments of shivering and turned the air conditioner down. Got back in bed.
The room started revolving around him. He put one foot on
the floor. It stopped. Got up after a few moments and went
to the bathroom, where he heaved up his guts. After the first
great wash of liquid there was little else. Still he retched, his
body attempting to rid itself of the poisons he had so happily
put in it.

When the retching finally stopped, he clung to the porcelain stool. It felt wonderfully cool on his face. Thought about

sleeping where he was, then reluctantly dragged himself off to bed.

IN her own room Moira tossed restlessly on the bed. Eliot had been particularly unsatisfying tonight. He always made love in such a cool and detached manner. As if this was a task which he thought to be beneath him. As she always was. He only liked the one position. For him it was a control thing. He could never let her forget that she was subservient to him—at work, in bed, when they talked of other things. She wondered if she hated him. Probably not, she thought. In a way she admired him. Aspired to be like him, always in control. And as much as he was using her, she was using him.

But at the moment there were other needs to be filled. And she thought she knew just where to go to satisfy them. At four o'clock she got up, put on a thin robe and went out into the hallway.

JIM heard the knocking as if from afar. It seemed to go on for a long time. He dragged himself from the bed, head still muzzy from drink, stumbled in the dark toward the banging, opened the door to see her standing there. She pushed her way inside without waiting for him to invite her, went to the bed and sat down, smiled invitingly.

"What the fuck do you think you're doing here?" he demanded.

"Now, is that any way to talk to an old friend? Come over here. Sit down beside me. I want to talk to you."

The light from outside streaming through the window was enough to illuminate the curve of a breast where her robe was falling open. She looked alluring, mysterious. Bitch! he thought. He flipped on the overhead lights.

She squinted nearsightedly in the sudden glare. "Do we really need that?" she asked, a little girl's plaintive quaver in her voice.

Oh, you are good, he thought. Despite himself, he was attracted. Mentally he scoffed. Just call me Mr. Gonad. What an asshole I am! She fucks me to get information, leads me around like some sort of tethered bull, gets what she wants and splits, and when she shows up again, all I can do is stand here with a hard-on.

"What do you want this time?" he asked, standing where he was. He did not trust himself to get too close to her. "You found out all you needed to know in Hawaii. Obviously I passed your little test. Otherwise I wouldn't be here."

"Oh, that," she said, dismissing it with a gesture. "I wondered why you were so unfriendly. Surely you can't think I went to bed with you just to get you to talk. If you'll just think back over that night, you'll realize I didn't have to. You were talking plenty without it. I went to bed with you because you attracted me, because you turned me on. You still do. Now, will you come over here and sit beside me? What on earth do you think I could want out of you now? We know everything you do."

That you probably do, he thought. Despite prior good intentions, he wanted more and more to go to her, hold her, make long and passionate love with her. The incipient hangover he'd woke up with had gone away. The residual alcohol still coursing through his body energized him. But still he stood his ground. God damn them anyway! They needed to know that they could not control him. And it had as well start with her.

Her eyes narrowed. She did not like rejection. She well knew the power of her body. With it she could get anything she wanted. She always had. She got up, walked over to the switch and turned out the lights. Went over to where he was still standing like some ridiculous statue, pressed herself to him and kissed him full on the mouth. At first he didn't react. It was like kissing a stone. Then as she worked at him his lips softened, responded. She felt him swelling against her belly. Grasped him, pulled him to the bed, pushed him down. She placed herself astride, pushed down on him. His body remained rigid and unmoving for a few moments. It was almost like she was raping him. It excited her.

Finally he began to move, slamming himself into her, an act of anger more than of love. She didn't care—anger, love, it was all the same. She used them, just as she was using him, to get what she wanted.

When finally she exhausted her desire, she fell forward onto his chest. He remained hard. I don't remember if he even came or not, she thought. Not that it mattered. She rested for a few moments, then got up and put her robe back on. Smiled at him where he still lay as she had left him. Blew him a mocking kiss and slipped out the door.

He lay awake for a long time. Feeling dirty. Feeling betrayed. By his own body. Slut! The word seemed appropriate, for himself as well as her. And he still desired her. If she came back in right now, he had to admit that he would probably do the same. The desire would, in time, he hoped, go away. He doubted that the shame ever would.

ROGER looked not a bit the worse for wear from the alcohol he had imbibed the night before. Jim wondered how he did it. He had a headache nagging behind the eyes that had not yet responded to the three aspirin he had taken upon finally getting out of bed. And Al looked like he was really suffering. His eyes were bloodred, body reeking from the chemicals it was throwing off.

It was Al who spoke first. "Can we go back to the field?" he asked. "I don't think my body can take much more of this."

Roger laughed. "Might have known the younger generation couldn't handle it," he said. Then he grew serious. "I want to tell you exactly what you can expect from me. Your mission is simple. As the people in Saigon say, 'Neutralize the V.C. infrastructure.' You do that, in whatever way you can,"—he fixed them with his eyes as he stressed the "whatever"—"and you'll find that I back you. One hundred percent. I'll keep the MACV brass, Agency honchos, press, everybody, off your backs. So far you've shown that you can handle it. You think you can go on doing that? Think about it before you answer."

Al looked at Jim, who nodded.

"You guys aren't stupid, but allow me for a moment to treat you as if you were. As if I wasn't quite sure you understood what I was saying, and so I broke it down into the simplest possible terms. No more bureaucratic euphemisms. You will be participating, indirectly and sometimes directly, in assassinations. And assassinations are forbidden by every military convention. You are still military men, even though you have been seconded to us. So if you got caught, if this thing were to come out, you could be subject to general courts-martial and charged with murder. And the penalty for murder, under the Uniform Code of Military Justice, is death. There is no statute of limitations on murder. So this could come back and bite you in the ass twenty, thirty years from now. Now, I don't think anything like that is going to happen. Hasn't so far, and there's no reason to think it will. The brass, all the way up and down the line, and that goes to the highest levels, know what happens here, and have been satisfied to be blind to it. But you can damned well bet that if anything ever happens, they aren't going to be the ones who take the blame. It will go right down to the lowest levels, and that means you. Now, do you still feel the same way?''

"Like you said, boss," Al said, "we ain't stupid. We just look that way sometimes. We pretty well figured all this stuff out before. But somebody's got to stop these cocksuckers. And if not us, who? And as for getting nailed for it, so what else is new? That's happened before, it'll happen again. If I remember my history right, the Brits did it to some poor Aussie asshole named Morant in the Boer War, and there are probably thousands of other examples that I don't know about. The guys at the bottom always get the shit. Sometimes you just can't bail it out fast enough.''

"Then I'll tell you one more thing. I'll back you to the hilt. You go down, and you can bet your ass, I'll be there with you. That's the way I work. But there might come a time when I'm not around anymore. These things happen. So cover your ass. Anytime you go out for a mission, make sure you have a signed arrest order. And find yourself a safe place, preferably out of this country, and make sure a copy of that order, or any other paperwork, goes there. Keep it forever. It's the old story of cover your ass with paper. People have much less of a tendency to point a finger when that finger points right back to them.

"Now, that said, let's get down to what the hell is really happening around here. I've got a map and a pointer, and frustrated intell agent that I am, I can't wait to show off what I know.''

For the next two hours he briefed them on the status of the war in I Corps. His knowledge was encyclopedic. He identified units, commanders, individuals; where people stayed, what their weaknesses were, whom they associated with. With such knowledge, Jim thought, how could you lose? Yet there was the nagging feeling they were. Why? he asked when the briefing was over.

"Because I can't get anybody to act on it," confessed McMurdock. "Doesn't do a goddamned bit of good to know all this stuff if you don't do anything about it. That's why you guys are so important. If I can get people like you in all my provinces, I think we can do some good. Hope so anyway. Hell of a thing, to think all this work has been wasted."

Yeah, hell of a thing, thought Jim. Wonder if it has. Not my place to worry about it. Time to go back to the field and make it happen.

"WHAT do you think, Jim?" asked Al. They had borrowed the ROIC's Jeep to go to Al's favorite restaurant in Danang. It was located on a houseboat on the river. Looking out from the windows, one could easily forget there was a war going on. The tables were covered with real cloth, they were sharing an adequate bottle of Algerian wine, the waiters hovered about catering to their every need. A cool breeze blew off the water. Even the roar of the combat jets taking off and landing at the air base was muted.

"I think that, no matter what Roger says, we had better be ready to cover our own asses."

"You don't trust him?"

"That's not the point. I think he can be trusted, yes. But even he admits that he may not be able to do everything. I think that not only had we better cover our asses with lots of paper but we have to realize that there may come a time when we have to run. And we had better make preparations for that now, before there's any need."

"Australia wouldn't be too bad," said Al, reflecting as he looked out across the river that things had come to a hell of a pass when you had to discuss desertion and flight as a possible result of trying to do your job.

"Yeah. Big place. Easy to get lost. And I liked the Aussies we worked with down in III Corps. Good soldiers. Does Australia have an extradition treaty with us?"

"Don't know. But I can find out. I'm planning to go there as soon as we get some R&R time. You ought to think about that too. Maybe we can go together. Good people, good beer, friendly women. What more can you ask?''

"Not much," Jim admitted. "Any ideas if we find out that the Aussies would ship us back?''

"Not good ones. Africa, maybe. I think that if Rhodesia got a couple of highly qualified counterinsurgency experts, they probably wouldn't check too thoroughly into backgrounds. We could probably get some false I.D. When I was stationed in Bad Tölz, I got to know some of the people who do such things. We could become Irishmen. My old man still gets a pension from the IRA, you know.''

"Life on the run. What a wonderful thought. Always looking over your shoulder, wondering if the next person you meet is really who he says he is, if the woman you're in bed with is waiting to put a set of handcuffs on you. Not too much different from right now. *En avant, la Légion!*" he toasted Al. The clink of their glasses sounded loud in the hushed confines of the restaurant.

"Enough of that serious shit," Al said. "The last time I was here they had this specialty, a big fucking fish cooked whole. Will you allow me to order for you, mon sewer?''

"But of course! You are so 'swave' and 'deboner,' mon chérie. I'd marry you, you weren't so fucking ugly. And if you didn't want to lead, every time we danced.''

"Ever think, when you were a kid, you'd be sitting in a place like this?''

"Shit, when I was a kid, I didn't even imagine there *were* places like this. I was raised on a farm in Oklahoma, remember? We didn't have too many world travelers there.''

"How'd you end up in the army?''

"Lack of choice, more than anything else. I knew I didn't want to stay in Oklahoma, be a farmer. There wasn't money for college, and I didn't know anything about scholarships. Guess I could have gotten one, if I had. My grades were always pretty good.

"Anyway, there was this guy who used to work for the old man, he was a paratrooper in World War II. Used to tell me about it. So I thought, what the hell, I'll join up for a while, jump out of airplanes, have a good time. Get out after my enlistment and decide what I want to do. This was 1960, remember, before anybody had even heard of Vietnam. So I joined up, went to the 101st at Fort ·Campbell, when they came around and started recruiting for some outfit called the Special Forces. Sounded like a good idea, so here I am. You?''

''Not much different,'' Al admitted. ''Except that the main reason I joined was a '57 Chevy.''

''Oh?''

''Yeah. One that didn't belong to me. I just sort of took it one night. I was gonna give it back! The judge gave me a choice, jail or the army. Never regretted it. Can't imagine what I'd be doin' now, if I wasn't here.''

''What you'd be doing now is getting drafted, and shipped over here as a poor fucking one-one-booger, infantry, probably in the 9th Division in the Delta. So everything works out. In one way or the other.''

''I guess so. Ever miss being a medic?''

''Sometimes. I enjoyed that a lot. You're about the only one I can admit it to. Somebody else might laugh and I'd have to beat the shit out of them. But I really liked treating people. Made me feel pretty good when I could help them.''

''Well, hell, we're still helping people. Just in a little bit different way. The way I see it, the guys we're working against are just like a disease. Bacteria. Only we're using lead instead of penicillin. Jesus, will you look at the size of that fish!''

COPELY was waiting for him when he got to Hue. Must be getting important, Jim thought. Last time I landed here I had to hitch a ride. Now the POIC himself meets me.

''Well,'' he demanded, once they had gotten into the jeep, ''what did the ROIC have to say?''

''He seemed to be pretty happy,'' Jim responded, enjoying the look of confusion written across the older man's features. ''Asked if I was getting the support I needed,'' he lied. ''I told him I was, of course.''

Copely shot him a look which he interpreted as gratitude. ''Well,'' he said, ''of course. We're all fighting the same war, why shouldn't you get all the support you need? You're an important member of the team here, Jim. And I want to take this opportunity to add my thanks to those of the ROIC for the job you're doing.''

You cynical old asshole, Jim thought. You were more than

willing to give me up when you thought the ROIC was pissed. Is there any such thing as being able to trust anyone? he wondered. Aloud he said, "Why, thank you, sir. I do appreciate that, coming from a man such as yourself." Let him read that as he pleases, he thought. "By the way, you don't mind if I start making those changes we talked about around the Embassy House, do you? Just to improve security a little bit. I'm sure we'd all sleep better if we felt a little bit more safe."

"What? Why, of course not. You're the expert. Just try to disrupt things as little as you can. After all, we still have our jobs to do in the meantime." If he felt uneasy at giving carte blanche to the man he privately regarded as a fanatic, he did not let it show on his face.

"Thank you, sir. We'll start right away. Tomorrow, if you don't mind. I'd like to get all the Americans together first. At five o'clock, before breakfast. That way we won't disrupt the duty day. We can do all our training before and after regular duty hours. Will that be all right?"

THE POIC was true to his word. All the Americans in the compound were there the next morning; grumbling, sleepy-eyed, but there.

He explained to them what he planned to do. There were murmurs of astonishment, some outright expressions of anger, but no one demurred openly. Good, he thought. They've obviously been briefed that they have no choice. The POIC probably told them that I had the blessing of McMurdock, and no one was eager to cross him.

In the next few days he thoroughly reorganized the defenses of the compound. Most of the bunkers had to be rebuilt. They had been emplaced more with an eye to facilitating traffic flow around the compound than for any tactical value. He tore them down, placed the new ones where they had good fields of fire in at least three directions, and where their fire would interlock with that of the ones on either side. He put screen wire over the firing ports. If the defenders had to shoot, the wire would not hinder their fire, and having the wire there to keep out the mosquitoes would keep them from blocking the ports with plywood.

He established good relations with supply sergeants from the nearby marine units. For some cases of steaks and ersatz

V.C. flags they were more than willing to give up surplus M-60 machine guns. He armed each bunker with three and stockpiled massive quantities of ammunition.

When the guards were off duty, he had them dig out the connecting trenches, revetting the walls with scrounged plywood. In front of the trench they stacked sandbags with small spaces left for firing ports. All a defender had to do was poke his gun through and sweep from side to side while firing. The resulting curtain of fire, deliberately no higher than twelve inches above the ground, would cut any attacker to pieces without exposing the defenders. Jim had found that it was easier to count on others' bravery when they did not have to face much danger.

He held alerts, measuring the time from the alarm until all defenders were in their places, and when it took too long, held them again and again. The guards came to realize that this drill might go on forever if they did not satisfy the crazy American, and started responding with a speed which finally pleased him.

The hardest part was to get the other Americans to realize the seriousness of the situation. He supposed it was a function of their training. A good agent handler or intelligence analyst had no need of infantry tactics. Still, it would have been nice if they'd had knowledge of any other weapon than the snub-nosed .38 special revolver they carried. He trained them from the very basics. Some of the younger ones took to it well, actually appearing to enjoy it. These he appointed posts on the perimeter to control the fire of a section of the guards. The ones who did not do well he used for communications and logistics duties.

It took a full month, but by the time he was finished he felt that they stood a chance of beating off all but the most determined of attacks. The guards were alert and sharp. He found none asleep during his random nocturnal visits. Weapons were kept clean, uniforms looked sharp, salutes were even thrown as he walked around the compound. He was satisfied.

WITH the PRU he was less satisfied. When first he had seen Captain Vanh after the trip to Danang, he told him that the ROIC had been complimentary. Vanh had been noncommittal. When Jim asked him when they were going to go out on another operation, he had stalled, saying it was important that they complete the training cycle of the new men before going any further. The purpose of the first operation had been served, he said. The men were not complaining anymore that they were doing nothing; they walked around with a sense of pride in their accomplishments.

Jim was not satisfied, but thought that it would not hurt to wait for a few days until he pressed the issue again. He used the time to check with the POICC and get an updated copy of the blacklist, then run it through the Indian to see how many of the names were valid. To his not very great surprise, few were.

He waited until after duty hours, then walked over to the PRU compound and knocked on Vanh's door. He threw the list on the table. The light from the unshaded bulb hanging from the ceiling shone on it like a spotlight. "Is this the real reason you don't want to go on operations, Captain?" he asked.

Vanh picked up the list, looked at the names that the American had checked in red. The young captain has been very thorough, he thought. He wondered whence the information had come.

"The names you checked off," he answered, "are political enemies of the province chief. People who don't agree with his policies. We have a choice, here in the PRU. Take the list and do what they say, or delay, get information to the people on the list so that they can take precautions. Make their peace with the colonel, or if they cannot do that, flee. I chose the latter. I do not know how much longer I can hold him off. Such are the things they would have us do."

"There is another choice," said Jim. He withdrew from his shirt pocket a sheaf of papers. "We can come up with a target of our own. Take a look at this."

The captain's eyes widened when he saw the name. He glanced up at the American, again wondered where he was getting his information. It was good. There was enough incriminating evidence here to justify the action.

"Would you care to help me plan the operation, Captain Carmichael?" he asked. "This may be a little complicated."

CHAPTER 8

"WE screw this one up, you and I will probably share a cell on Con Son," whispered Jim. Very slowly and carefully he brushed away the huge beetle crawling up his sleeve. The bug landed on its back, waved its legs in the air, then with a move that would have made a gymnast proud flipped over and landed on its feet, looking around combatively. Seeing nothing that it could fight, it moved off in another direction.

"If we live that long," whispered Vanh. They were emplaced alongside the road which led from Phu Loc to Van Xai. The road itself was little more than a dirt track. On it, and completely blocking it, was a bullock cart filled with sacks of rice. One of the wheels of the cart had come off, and two men struggled, not very effectively, to jack the cart up and replace it. Sacks of rice taken off to lighten the load were scattered about.

Two squads of PRU were lying in hide positions to Jim's right and left. Up the road, in the direction of Van Xai, was a two-man outpost with a radio. Jim had the handset of his radio close to his ear so that he would not miss the clicks, code that the target was on the way. One click every fifteen minutes to signal that all was okay, two clicks if they achieved positive target identification, three if someone else was coming down the road and four if there was trouble and the O.P. needed help. He had taught the PRU to use click code instead of talking over the radio. The enemy was adept at intercepting radio transmissions.

Back at the rally point another squad of PRU secured the area. It was extremely important for the purposes of this mission that no one follow them; that they have the maximum amount of time possible before anyone knew what had happened. This squad's mission was to allow them to pass through, then hold and delay any possible pursuers until they were well clear. Then the squad would exfiltrate by whatever means possible. Which meant in practice, Jim knew, that any survivors would break up into ones and twos, throw their weapons away, and go into hiding until it was safe to steal away.

There had been no arguments over tactics this time. Vanh had been happy to allow him to plan the entire operation, offering only suggestions on ways to facilitate what Jim was trying to do. In many ways it was a very easy target, far easier than stealing into an enemy village in the dark. The hard part would come after the target was taken.

How many times had he done this? Waiting for some poor unsuspecting target to come along. Spending hours in one position, afraid to move lest someone see. The body in a curious half-state between tension and rest. Ready to move on an instant's notice, yet settled in as well as possible to achieve whatever comfort terrain and conditions allowed. The mind chewing over the plan again and again, looking for weaknesses, hoping that nothing had been forgotten, becoming finally resigned that it was too late to change anything even if it was wrong.

Today was almost pleasant. The trees shielded them from most of the heat, the sunlight which made it through describing dappled patterns against the forest floor. Most of the time you weren't so lucky. It would be night, and you couldn't see a thing, and the imagination made every jungle sound the footfall of the enemy, encircling you just out of range, ready to fall upon and destroy you. Or it would be raining, and there would be no place to go, no way to shield yourself because of course you couldn't wear a poncho; the sound of raindrops hitting the rubberized material was unmistakable and would give you away. So you lay there and let it soak through, and no matter how warm it was, sooner or later the water took away your body heat and you tried not to shiver but couldn't stop it, and it seemed that you would never be warm again.

The only thing worse than lying in ambush was being on the receiving end. The nervous system was not built to handle that kind of surprise. The sudden roaring noise, the flashes of the explosions, the jolt as the body, attempting to respond, flooded with adrenaline, induced a kind of shock which was hard to overcome. Most people never did, because the ambush, if set up properly, was the most effective killing machine yet devised.

But today was different. The target was only one man, with perhaps as little as one bodyguard. He would be coming along in a jeep, suspecting nothing. Why should he have worried? No one wished him harm. He was too valuable to both sides. The American district advisors with whom he worked had inevitably commented on his bravery, traveling the roads as he did with so little protection. Just like one of us, they thought, as they emulated him. And if sometimes it didn't work for them, if a shot-up body was found at some out-of-the-way road junction, that just increased the mystique. And he achieved the reputation of being not only brave but extremely lucky.

Jim wondered what motivated him. Was he just an opportunist, playing both sides for his own advantage? Or did he believe in what he was doing, think that his actions were for the good of his country? Was he a long-term agent, or had he been recently turned? He knew as he turned these things over in his mind that it didn't really matter what the motivation. The actions were what counted, and the actions were causing this result. You pays your money and you takes your chances, Jim thought. And hopefully when the time came to settle debts, you would find that it had all been worth it.

Two clicks. He nodded to Vanh, who gave the signal to the others. They did not have long to wait. The jeep came careening around the corner, moving very fast. The driver had to stand on the brakes to keep from running into the bullock cart. He swung the vehicle to a stop, then stood up to yell curses. The man in the passenger seat sat there impassively, his polished brass gleaming in the sun. His little eyes peered from a fat face that seemed in danger of swallowing them. His lips were pursed in anger. He turned to say something to the driver.

The driver's tirade was stopped in mid-curse as his uncomprehending eyes took in the figures in black who stepped out onto the road. They were heavily armed, and all the guns seemed to be pointed directly at his head. He sat down and raised his hands as high as he could get them.

The target, Major Nguyen Quanh Binh of the Vietnamese Army, was perplexed. In Vietnamese he shouted, "What is the meaning of this! Who are you, and what do you want?"

Jim shouted the few Russian phrases he knew, as if he were giving orders to the unit. The black cloth tied around his face muffled his voice, but no matter. The PRU had no idea what he was saying anyway, as no one spoke Russian. They went about their tasks as if they did. They swiftly divested the driver of his pistol and wrapped his hands behind him with cloth tape. Over his mouth they slapped another piece. Into his ear one growled, "You saw nothing. Do you understand? If you tell anyone anything, we will come to your house and kill you and all your family, just as we did with the other traitors during Tet."

The terrified man nodded his understanding. He did not know what his chief had done to anger the V.C., but it had nothing to do with him. Already his mind was inventing stories to explain the disappearance of the man. Perhaps, if he phrased it right, he could even become the hero of the incident, fighting off scores of them before finally being knocked unconscious.

Major Binh was pulled from the jeep and, when he continued to protest, was knocked to the roadway by a blow to the back of his head. Rough hands pulled his chromed pistol from its holster. It was held to his head as his hands were pulled behind him and taped. He was so fat they had trouble getting his hands together, pulling until he thought they would disjoint his shoulders. His cries of pain were muffled by the tape they slapped across his mouth.

Another burst of the strange language from the big one and they picked him up and set him on his feet. The man came close and looked into his eyes. Blue-eyed foreign devil! Who are you? he wanted to ask. What language is that? Not English or French, both of which he spoke. For the first time he felt fear. There must be some mistake! Perhaps this was a unit new to the area, and they had not yet been told of his dual role. He could straighten that out soon enough. As long as nothing happened before he got the chance. He resolved to be very careful and do what they said to lessen the chance that there would be any more mistakes. He allowed himself a moment of amusement at the thought of how surprised they would be. He would demand that the men who had treated him so roughly be punished. Perhaps he would demand of the High Command that this entire unit be punished, to include the—what was he, Russian? East German?—who was giving the orders. He had heard that there were Soviet and Eastern European advisors with some of the special units but had never before encountered one.

At another command the unit formed up and marched into the jungle, with him in the center. Behind them the men with the cart abandoned it and melted away in another direction. The driver was left sitting in the jeep. They knew he would wait for a couple of hours before trying to get loose. He would not be sure that some of them were not watching him.

They moved at a punishing pace. He was unused to walking, and his bonds made it even more difficult. Soon he was panting and sweating, and within less than a mile he was stumbling and reeling. Whenever he tried to slow down, they pushed and pulled him forward, keeping the pace no matter what. They moved through the reserve squad at the rally point, stopping only briefly as the leaders conferred. It was difficult to breathe. He would have liked to gasp great lungfuls of air, but the tape over his mouth made that impossible. He wondered if it was possible to suffocate this way.

Heads would roll for this! Such a thing would have been unthinkable before Tet. The countryside had been so well organized and the communications and intelligence nets had functioned so efficiently that there would never have been the possibility of this kind of mistake. But so many of the cadre had been killed during the attack and its aftermath, killed needlessly to his way of thinking, that nothing functioned well anymore. His anger spilled over onto all those who had a part in it. If he had been running things, it would have been much different.

After what seemed like hours of marching, his anger was slowly sapped away. The fatigue stole it, replacing it with despair and depression. Would this walk never end? Did they plan to march all the way to Laos before they stopped? He could not make it, would die here alongside the trail, an ignominious end to a brilliant career. And all because someone had made a mistake. He had before felt impervious to the vicissitudes of fate, but now was possessed with a sense of his own vulnerability. What good had it done, all his plotting and maneuvering; the delicate balancing act that he had performed with such aplomb? It would all collapse with him on the jungle floor. Tears streamed down his face. His body screamed in agony, lungs burning, legs begging for rest.

THEY had come less than two miles. Not long now. He had been closely monitoring the collapse of Major Binh. He had been going through the stages even faster than Jim had hoped. He would soon reach dull-eyed resignation. Jim wanted him just on that edge.

A few minutes later he gave the sign to Vanh, who halted the column. They were at the edge of a small open area. Security was quickly placed, covering all avenues of approach. The prisoner was brought to the center of the clearing and shoved to his knees. Vanh stood before him. Binh stared up at him with dulled, hopeless eyes.

"Major Nguyen Quanh Binh," Vanh read from a sheet of paper, "Enemy of the People of Vietnam. You stand accused of crimes against the Party, against the Cadre, and against the Cause. The penalty for these crimes is death. The Peoples Tribunal of the Central Committee, of which this unit is an action arm, has decreed that this sentence be carried out. You will now be given the opportunity to make a statement which will admit your errors, serving as an example to others." Vanh nodded to one of the soldiers, who ripped the tape from the major's mouth and held a microphone to his face.

Binh's face was on fire where the tape had been ripped away, but it was as nothing to the flame in his soul. Who dared accuse him! There had been none more faithful than he. From the beginning he had played the double role, it was true, and sometimes that made it necessary to do things which made it look like he was a loyal servant of the government. But the High Command had always understood that need, and had even given him people to turn in. People who were no longer needed, or who were wavering in their commitment, who served no important roles. But had he not more than made up for that? Was it not he who had protected the secret party members in the district government? Had he not provided advance notice of planned attacks by government forces against V.C. units? It was he who had given the inside information on all the installations in Hue for use during the Tet offensive. Who made sure that the Phoenix blacklists always missed the important names, and included the names of neutralists and antigovernment nationalists. When mistakes were made and actual Communists were captured, he applied the appropriate pressure to get them released. All this, and more, he screamed into the microphone. He would not stand for this injustice! They must understand that they were making a mistake. He was an important man, probably the most important in the province. They could not do without him!

Jim understood perhaps a third of the rapid-fire soliloquy, but even that was enough to convince him that they had caught a very big fish. He made a gesture to Vanh, who met him to one side. "Hit him for details," he whispered. "Names, places, documents. He's smart enough to have kept materials to blackmail people. He's very scared. Tell him that you don't believe him, that his story is the attempt of a condemned man to save himself. Demand proof."

Vanh's eyes were very cold above the black mask. "It will be as you say, Captain," he agreed. "But I am sure you understood the part about his role at Tet."

Jim nodded. They understood one another.

For the next hour Major Binh talked. He named names, told them where they could find documents, told about future plans for the province. It did not take much prodding. He was so eager to clear himself he would have given up his nearest relative.

"I do not know what fool denounced me," he finally said, "but as you can see I am a true servant of the revolution. You should be spending your time finding out why I was denounced rather than treating me as such. I do not hold a grudge," he lied. "You are only doing your duty as you have been told. But your duty lies elsewhere, comrades. Now please release me. I will commend your revolutionary zeal to the Central Committee." And demand that you all be shot, he thought. To include your Russian friend. To hell with our fraternal Soviet comrades!

Vanh walked back over to Jim, the tape from the recorder

in his hand. "I think this is all we shall get from him," he said. "He is as dry as a rice ball that has been left in the sun. Now we must kill him."

"No," Jim replied. "You must not."

"Please, Captain, no more of this. We have no choice. If we bring him in, the province chief will know that we have run an unauthorized operation. If we let him go, it will not take him long to find out that there is no Peoples Tribunal of the Central Committee. And it will not be hard for them to figure out who could have run such an operation. He must die."

"I don't argue with that," said Jim, pulling his pistol from the holster. He flipped the safety off and shot Binh cleanly through the back of the head. "I only said that *you* must not kill him. This action will become known, sooner or later. Hopefully it will be later. You have to live in this country, I don't. And I think I'd stand a hell of a lot better chance in an American court than you would here. Call it a favor, Captain."

"Bury this piece of dung," Vanh shouted to the soldiers. "Dig it deep, so that the animals of the jungle do not poison themselves.

"Captain Jim," he said, "I think that I may have some rice balls in my rucksack. Would you care to join me? We have many things to talk about. Like what we are going to do next. What would you suggest?"

IT took Jim two weeks of work with the material he had gathered to be ready to go to the PIOCC. First he checked it with Chandragar. For further confirmation the PRU picked up one of the people named by Binh and interrogated him. The information had been good.

He dropped the folder on the desk of the first lieutenant who served as the senior advisor to the PIOCC. "A little interesting reading material for you, L.T.," he said, taking a chair. He noted the chromed .38 in a Saigon Cowboy holster, the K-bar knife strapped to the ankle, the M-2 pineapple grenade displayed prominently on the man's desk. Ain't you a badass? he thought.

The officer frowned importantly. "I don't think we've met," he said.

Jim, who was in civilian clothes, ignored him. The man damned well knew who he was. "I need some arrest orders," he said. "You'll get enough to issue them from what you have here."

"That's not the way it's done!" the lieutenant protested. "You know the rules. Verification from at least three sources, only hard-core V.C. targeted."

"Yeah, bullshit. Look, L.T., I don't know if you're crooked or just stupid. For your sake, I hope the latter. Every fucking list I get from you has nothing on it but people the province chief wants to get rid of. Most of them have nothing to do with the V.C., other than trying to stay alive when they come to visit them. I'm goddamned tired of it. You take a look through here, verify it any way you want—three, four, ten witnesses. But you fucking well take a look at it. And if you have any questions, you know where to find me. And if you have any complaints, you take them up with Roger McMurdock."

The lieutenant, who was neither crooked nor stupid, sat for a long time after he left. So that's the infamous Captain Carmichael, he thought. The stories had evidently been true. Strangely, he did not feel insulted. He knew that he was in far over his depth. He pulled the folder to him and started reading. Soon he informed the Vietnamese captain whom he advised, who was both crooked and stupid, that he wanted to see him. He looked forward to the meeting. For the first time since he had arrived in this godforsaken place he felt in control of a situation.

The first arrest orders arrived at the PRU compound a week later.

DURING the next three months people disappeared. Normal-seeming people, most of them. People whom no one would have suspected of any misdoings. And the Communists lost more eyes and ears, and didn't really know why. Fear possessed the cadre. The Chieu Hoi (Open Arms), an amnesty program, gained converts on a daily basis. Everyone knew that previously sacrosanct individuals were now suddenly vulnerable, and nobody knew why.

The province chief did. His informant in the PRU, though he had not been present during the interrogation, had gathered enough information to fill in what must have happened. Soon, he thought, soon they will use the information that they have gathered on me. He had to admire their technique. There was no evidence that anything had happened. Those who did not know of the former district chief's dual role thought that perhaps the Viet Cong had finally seized him. The Viet Cong themselves were in the dark, searching for a renegade squad led by a Russian. By the time they realized that this squad did not exist, it would be too late for most of them.

Perhaps he had misjudged the American. The young man seemed willing to do whatever was necessary. And he was so tactful. The meeting they'd had after the incident was totally innocuous. The American had denied that there had been an operation, he said, with a perfectly straight face, that he would never permit unauthorized operations to take place.

How much did they know? he wondered. In his mind he explored what the man could have told them. It was not much, not enough to affect the plans in any substantial way. They would think that his only motivation was corruption, making as much money as he could from his position. Just as the district chief had. Let them. They would find it of little use. Did they want to conduct operations? So be it. They would get as many operations as they could handle. Things happened on operations. Sometimes fatal things. Did they want different people on the arrest orders? It did not matter. Most of his enemies were already dead, and those who were not were sufficiently terrorized.

And if it did, for some reason, go wrong? He prided himself upon his ability to anticipate everything. He had his routes planned, knew when it would be time to go, had his accounts well established in European banks. No need to worry.

UPON return from the operation, Jim had copied the tape. He enclosed it, along with a letter, to Lisa. It was the first time he had written her.

"Dearest Lisa," he wrote, agonizing over the salutation. Should he have said "Lisa, my love"? He had confessed his love for her. He still felt it. Would she believe it? Probably not. Safer to say "Dearest." She was dear to him. Shit, would it always be such an agonizing thing, to decide how to address a letter?

"I'm sorry that I have not written before now." Why are you sorry? If you're sorry, why didn't you write? Cut out the bullshit, Jim.

"I am enclosing a tape. I would appreciate it if you would put it in a safe place. It will probably never be necessary to use it, but if it should come to that, it will be extremely important to me." Using her yet again, are you, Jim? What about the fact that someone could find out about your relationship to her? You could be putting her in danger.

"If you do not want to keep this, I will understand. Destroy it, do what you will. It could cause problems for you." There, discharge your guilt. You told her it could be a problem. If she still chooses to help, she knows the consequences.

"I think about you all the time. I miss you, and your presence, and the life that you have put into mine." Finally, you can speak without lying, Jim. This much, at least, is true. Will you tell her that you love her? Do you? Do you know what love is?

"I will understand if you want nothing else to do with me." Will I ever. "But you are the only one I can trust. Do what you think you must." More of an escape hatch for your conscience? "I miss you, and wish that I'd had more time with you. If this all works out, I would like to see you when I get back." On the off fucking chance that I'll get back.

ROGER McMURDOCK shifted through the sheaf of reports on his desk. Some were contradictory and conflicting, but taken together it was apparent that something very big was happening in Thua Thien Province. He had, of course, seen through the North Vietnamese with Russian advisor subterfuge at the outset. It had been an effective technique, he had to admit. It had thrown the opposition off for the critical period of time necessary for Carmichael and whoever was helping him to get a lot of them. And he felt no regret for the demise of the district chief. In fact, he reflected, if he had thought of it, he might have ordered the operation himself. Young Jim was a smart one, and would be very useful, if he did not go too far. In his experience that was always the problem with operations of this sort. When did you stop? Sooner or later the enemy would catch on to what was happening and would take countermeasures. And you would have to be very good, or very lucky, or both, to survive. The Communists had their assassins too, and they were good.

And perhaps the Communists would not get there first. Some of the people who were disappearing had relatives and friends in high places in the government. They would not take kindly to this renegade operation if it was found out.

Should he call Carmichael in, cancel the operation? Perhaps relieve him, send him someplace else in country for his own good?

No. He was in danger, but it was danger of his own making. And he was doing a great deal of good. The Viet Cong were hurting, and would hurt worse. More of them had been neutralized in a few months than had been the case in some years. Long-term agents, the ones hardest to replace, were going. Old-time cadre, well trained, highly motivated, were being replaced by newcomers who knew neither the area nor the people. So let the young captain run for a little while yet. There should be some warning before the blow fell. And if he was wrong, well, it was a war after all, and people did get killed in wars. He liked Jim Carmichael, but that did not get in the way of his sense of duty.

He fired off a cable to Saigon giving the bare facts of the case. He did not include his interpretation of the disappearance of the district chief, only that the man had last been seen in the company of a Communist squad accompanied by what appeared to be a Caucasian. Let the pencil pushers in the Embassy Annex figure out that one, if they could. He reported that the PRU in Thua Thien Province had suddenly become very efficient, adding that it was probably because of the inspiration they had received from the successful operations. Let it go at that.

THE aide read the night's cables, as was her custom, before taking them in. She placed the one from I Corps at the top of the pile, then sat ready to take comments. Generally her boss went through the pile in a hurry, dictating curt responses to some, forwarding a very few others to the chief of station and recommending that an occasional one be sent even higher. Today he was stopped, as she had known that he would be, by the first.

"This is extraordinary," he finally said, raising his patrician eyebrows. "By my count, ten, maybe more, high-level V.C. cadre have been eliminated in the last three months. That's more than in the preceding six months, if I'm not mistaken."

"Actually, longer than that, sir, if you count the time after Tet." They always addressed one another very formally in the office. After all, you could never tell who was listening.

"I wasn't counting that, actually," he said, irritated at the correction. "After all, they did have a long stand-down while they reorganized. I was counting only the operational time."

"Yes, sir," she replied, eyes lowered as she meekly took the unspoken rebuke. She thought what a pedantic ass he was. She would be glad when she no longer needed him.

Mollified, he said, "And what, in your analysis, is the cause of it?"

"I'm not sure that McMurdock's analysis is right," she said. "We've had successful operations in other areas, many times. In no case did they produce results such as this. There has to be something else. Perhaps it's the effect of the new advisor?"

"My thoughts exactly," he said, surprised that she had come up with it so quickly. "You vetted him, didn't you? What did you think of him? Anything extraordinary there?"

Indeed there was, she thought. But not in the way you think, you impotent old fool. "Nothing readily apparent," she said. "He was very intelligent, and quite well motivated, and seemed to have no problems with doing what had to be done. But we've had others like that, and they haven't achieved the same results. All that is in my report anyway. Would you like me to get you a copy?" I know you didn't read it in the first place. Not important enough for you to spend your precious time. Much more important for you to be at the Cercle Sportif playing tennis with your French friends.

"Nothing at all?" he persisted.

She thought about it. There had been something, something that was hard to put into words. Implacability, perhaps that was it. That once he had set his mind upon a purpose, it would be difficult if not impossible to change it. He would not be an enemy I would care to have, she thought. She realized with a start that she feared him. Perhaps that was the source of the sexual attraction. She could not remember the last time she had feared a man. She knew her power, and how easy it was to make men do as she wished. But she thought that past a certain point it would not be the same with him. She had felt the anger in him that night in Hue, and it had excited her to heights she had long forgotten. She stifled an involuntary shiver.

"No," she said, "nothing at all."

"I want to see all cables dealing with Thua Thien Province from now on," he said. "And any other correspondence from any source, Vietnamese, U.S. military, whatever. I like what I see so far, but these things can get out of hand too easily. We'll keep an eye on Captain Carmichael, a close eye. Since you vetted him, you'll be the action officer. Start a file, include everything we know about him. Send off for his records, for a start. He looks like one of those people who we'll be able to use a great deal, or who we will have to get rid of. The choice, I suspect, will depend entirely upon how lucky he is."

CHAPTER 9

"I think we ought to cool it for a while," Jim said. "We haven't really taken a rest since we got the district chief, three months ago. And I'm getting awfully fucking tired."

Vanh was looking at him quizzically. Fatigue was etched into the Vietnamese's face. He looked ill. Still, Jim knew he wanted to finish it. Only two targets remained on the list given them by the district chief. He said as much.

"Yeah, two," Jim replied. "And we've been chasing those two from one end of the province to the other. Hate to tell you, buddy, but I think they're onto us."

"But we know where they're going to be tonight. They made the mistake we were waiting for. Did you get the helicopters?"

"All laid on. They'll be hot on the pad at twenty hundred. Two slicks, one gun. Just like we planned. But I still think we should wait. We're tired, and people make mistakes when they're tired. There will be other chances to get those two."

"And if you're wrong? How many people will die because of it? No, I think we should go tonight."

It was the closest they had come to a disagreement since they first met, Jim reflected. He had come to like and respect the Vietnamese to an extent he would never have thought possible. He was a good soldier, an excellent tactician and a brave man. Hell, he thought, he's probably right. They'd planned this operation with the usual care, every eventuality had been foreseen, what could go wrong? Everyone was tired, but after this was over they could take a good long rest before deciding what to do next. Maybe he would even think about going on R&R. In all his trips to Vietnam he had not yet taken an R&R. There had never seemed to be time, and just when it looked like there would be, he had gotten wounded.

The things Al had told him about Australia intrigued him. Perhaps he would try to go there. Maybe he could talk Al into going with him.

"Okay," he said. "One more operation it is. And whether or not we get them tonight, we take a good, long break afterward. Agreed?"

"Agreed, Captain Jim." Vanh smiled. "I think that everyone could use it. Even the ones who have not been going out as often as you and I are showing the strain."

"Good. And I've got some good news for them. The ROIC has authorized a bonus for everyone, because of the success of the last few months."

"That is very good, my friend. It will please them. Not because of the money, but because it shows that what they have done has been appreciated. It has been a very good time, the best. I wish to thank you for it."

"No need to thank me. Everyone did their part."

"But if it had not been for you, we would not have known how to go about it. You brought new ideas, Captain Jim. And you have been there with us each step of the way, sharing the dangers and the hardships. For this we thank you. We will have a party after we get back. Drink much whiskey, eat good food, spend the time as soldiers should."

"Sounds good," Jim said, embarrassed by Vanh's uncustomary effusiveness. He liked it better when he was his usual taciturn self. "Now, shall we do the equipment check? Tired as we are, I'm sure someone has forgotten something."

THERE was nothing like the sound of a Huey. The sound of the twin blades whopping through the air seemed to become a part of your body, taking control, making the heart beat at the same speed. Your muscles vibrated with it. It filled the ears, the lungs, the very soul of you. Somehow you knew that years later, if you survived, this one sound would be the thing that would bring back the most vivid memories, the ones which would have you suddenly and terribly afraid once again. And that night you would wake up soaked with sweat, the menaces of the dark close and real.

The choppers were carrying them to the far end of the province, the border area where Thua Thien abutted Quang

Tri to the north and Laos to the west. Real bad-guy country, he reflected.

He rode with his legs hanging out the door, wind whipping his fatigues. His face was mottled with camouflage paint. A sweat rag made from a cravat bandage was tied around his head. No question of attempted deception on this trip. It was a time for stealth, then rapid and violent action, and a quick trip out. The wind whipping in the chopper was cool, drying the fear sweat which always soaked him before operations of this sort. Once he got on the ground, he knew, it would go away. The anticipation was the worst part.

They were flying very close to the treetops on the theory that by the time someone on the ground heard them they would be long gone before they could draw a bead. The pilots were good. They were used to this type of operation, being the same ones who flew the CCN teams from their base in Phu Bai on cross-border operations into Laos. Jim heard none of the usual radio chatter over the headset he wore, just occasional terse directions.

"L.Z. in sight," he heard. "Get ready." He signaled the others. They inched forward, almost hanging out of the doors. The chopper would spend little time on the L.Z. If you weren't out of it in seconds, you would be faced with the decision of whether or not to risk getting out as it was lifting off. And it lifted off very fast.

Jim took the headset off and tucked it under the pilot's seat, now watching the door gunner. The man was crouched over his M-60, watching the dark jungle for the telltale flashes of gunfire. His hand suddenly went up, then down.

Jim pushed away from the chopper and dropped to the ground. He ran toward the trees as with a great wash of wind the chopper took off, followed closely by the second. By the time he reached the tree line both had gone, the sound of their rotors a rapidly fading echo.

The team formed up inside the trees. A moment to verify that all were there, then they moved off. Jim took position three men behind point. They moved in single file. They wanted speed, and did not have time to put out flankers. The danger of ambush was alleviated by not walking on a trail. The jungle was not thick here, which made for easy movement.

Within an hour they reached their first reference point, a bend in a river. Their navigation was good. All the training had been worth it. They rested for ten minutes, then took up a new heading, followed it for another hour, rested again.

"Right on time," Jim whispered to Vanh. They were still over a kilometer from the target, but one never knew how well sound would carry, or if patrols were out. Best to be careful.

Vanh was still panting from the forced march. "We move slower now," he said. "Plenty of time to get there, hit them, and get to the pickup point before the choppers come back."

"You want to rest a little longer?" He was worried about Vanh. It was unlike him to take so long to recover.

"No! We go." He got up and motioned to the rest. Slowly they complied. Tired, very tired, thought Jim. The uneasiness he had been feeling was intensified.

It took another hour to cover the last kilometer. At the last they were moving very slow indeed. Which was a good thing, because the point man ran smack into the outpost.

Jim saw the two locked together. Shit! he thought. He ran forward to where they were struggling, tried in the dark to see who was what. They were so entangled it was hard to tell. Then he saw that one man's hand was jammed into the other one's mouth. On the assumption that only the man on his side would be worried about someone crying out, he stabbed the other man through the temple. He felt the bone crack as the blade entered the brain.

Furiously he motioned the others into place. This was coming unstuck fast. Best to get it over with and get out.

They fanned out to either side of the small group of huts. No question of trying to go in and do it silently this time. The machine gunner set up his weapon in the center, fed in a belt, took position.

The roar as they opened fire was deafening. The heavy 7.62mm bullets from the machine gun shredded the bamboo of the huts. The 40mm rounds from the grenade launchers landed among them, the fragments whirring through the air like scythes. The others fired a magazine of M-16, reloaded, and fired another.

The M-60 finished its two-hundred-round belt and fell silent. Jim, Vanh and two others ran to the huts. In the first all the occupants were dead. Two men with AK-47s, one woman. He shone a flashlight in their faces, what was left of them. Not the right people. He heard Vanh call, went to him at the second hut. There the two were, quite dead. Along with three children, the oldest no more than twelve. Also quite dead.

"Search them!" he ordered, his mind shying away from what he saw. Operate on a purely functional level, he told himself. Think about this later. There had been no indications in the intelligence that anyone other than the targets and guards would be here. Something had gone very wrong.

The men searched through the hut. No one touched the children, averting their eyes as they came close. A few documents were found, but nothing else. "Okay," he shouted, "out of here! Form up at the rally point and be ready to move. I don't like the feel of this at all."

He assumed the point. He knew the pace he was setting was punishing, but would not let up. He was furious. This operation was snakebit from the beginning. I know to trust my instincts. Why did I let them talk me out of it? His anger was directed primarily at himself. He was supposed to be the expert, the wonderful American advisor who knew so much. And he had acted like a raw recruit. Now he would have to live with the results.

The pickup point was at the same bend in the river they had used for a reference point. He had not wanted to use the same landing zone. Too much chance someone had seen them come in and would be staking it out. There was no clearing at the pickup point other than that the river afforded, so the plan was to be extracted on a string. It was a method he did not care for, but had seen no other option. The helicopter would hover just over the trees and drop ropes down to the ground. Attached to the end of the rope was a mountaineering snap link. The soldiers wore a special harness, known as a STABO rig, which had a matching snap link attached. The STABO rig looked like a parachute harness, with crotch straps that hooked into the front. The soldiers were to snap into the ropes, attach the crotch straps, and upon signal the chopper would lift them straight up until they were clear of the trees, then fly off with them dangling underneath.

They had walked for an hour before word passed up to him that they would have to stop, that Captain Vanh was very sick. Damn it! he thought. What else was going to go wrong before this night was over?

He walked back to Vanh, who was slumped under a tree. The little man was covered with sweat, and was shivering so hard that Jim could hear his teeth chatter. He tried to smile as Jim squatted beside him. It was a pitiful attempt.

"Time to take a break anyway," Jim said, trying to make light of it. "You'll be okay after a few minutes' rest."

"I do not think so, Jim," gasped Vanh, trying to control the shivering enough to talk.

"Quanh, Dinh," Jim ordered, naming two of the bigger PRUs, "give your weapons to someone else and rig up a poncho litter. We haven't that far to go, and we've got plenty of time. We'll give the captain a little ride."

He sat next to Vanh as the others cut a sapling for the litter. "Think you've got a touch of malaria?" he asked.

"Feels like it," Vanh admitted. "I've been taking quinine to try to hold it down, but I think it got the best of me."

"Probably because . . ." Jim started.

"I know," Vanh interrupted. "We are all too tired. You were right."

"Yeah, but we got those bastards. Now we get out of here, and get you to the hospital, and everyone can breathe easy for a while."

They placed Vanh in the poncho slung by its ends on a stout sapling. With a grunt the two bearers lifted him, settled the pole on their shoulders and indicated they were ready to go. Jim decided to walk just in front of them so he could be ready to help carry Vanh if necessary. The regular point man was nursing his hand were it had been bitten almost through, so Jim told one of the newer men to take the lead.

They set off again, at a much slower pace. Jim figured the pickup point to be less than thirty minutes away at this rate, and they had an hour before the choppers were scheduled to come back, so there should be no problem. He still had the gnawing feeling that more would go wrong before this night was over, but hoped that he was just overreacting. Perhaps it was the horror of seeing the children. Perhaps it was guilt, his subconscious telling him that he had done a terrible thing and that he should be punished. He knew that before now it was probable that his actions had caused the death of innocents. But he had never had to see it firsthand.

THE explosion filled the world. Blindingly brilliant light, a fraction of sound before the pressure overstressed otic nerves, then no noise at all. Things hit him just before the shock wave flattened him on the ground. He could not move, could not get his breath, could see nothing except the pinwheels of light that dazzled retinas sent to the brain. His head was propped up against the man behind him, and as his eyes began to clear, he saw that his body was covered with blood. His peripheral vision picked up muzzle flashes and movement, he knew not whose. Nor did he care. I must be dying, he thought. If I am, it's not too bad. I thought it would be much worse than this. I thought I would be in agony. I don't feel much at all. He closed his eyes and waited for the end to come.

After a little while he opened them again. He was starting to hurt. Damn it, he thought, you aren't supposed to be in pain when you're dead. Reluctantly he came to the conclusion that he wasn't quite there yet. He looked down at his body. Much of the blood had started to dry, though there was still some ooze on his legs and arms.

The pain got worse. Jim sat up, groaned, frightened the hell out of Captain Vanh, who had thought he was dead. He had crawled out of the litter where the bearers had dropped him when the explosion went off, retrieved a rifle from a dead man, and had been laying down a base of fire at the ambushers while some of his men flanked them. He crawled over to his friend. "Claymore mine," he said needlessly.

God damn, I can't hear a thing, Jim thought as he watched Vanh's mouth move. He assayed movement, found that, while it was quite painful, it was possible. Time to ignore the pain. He was still clutching the CAR-15. There were several shiny areas where the claymore pellets had struck it, but it appeared functional.

He pushed himself painfully to his feet, then advanced on the muzzle flashes, firing as he went. Vanh followed him. In this killing ground, to stand still was to die.

The fire slackened as the ambushers started to break off

the action. They knew better than to pursue. To do that would only invite another ambush.

Jim shook his head to clear it. He could still hear nothing. Vanh was saying something, motioning for him to come back. He followed to the original site, passing bodies along the way. Most were in North Vietnamese khaki. But the ones at the ambush site were not. The positioning of the bodies and the type of wounds made obvious what had happened. The enemy had set up a claymore mine on their route of advance and had detonated it when the point man got within range. The ball bearings, each the size of a double-ought buckshot pellet, propelled at a speed of over three thousand feet per second by the C-4 plastic explosive behind them, had reduced the point man to something that looked like chopped hamburger. By some freak accident, the mine had detonated when the column was marching one behind the other. Else the destruction would have been worse. As it was, the next two men in line were also dead, having received most of the projectiles that had missed or exited the first. Jim had been fourth, and had been hit by only a few, along with bone fragments from the others. He checked his wounds. For the most part they were superficial, though he could see that at least a few pellets had embedded themselves deeply in his thighs. Most of the blood and flesh he had taken for his own had been blown back from the men in front of him.

"How many more?" he asked Vanh. He could feel the resonance in his inner ear, but heard nothing more. He wondered if his eardrums were blown out. He knew that others could hear him from watching their responses. "I can't hear," he said. "Use signals."

Vanh held up three fingers, then drew his hand across his throat. Two fingers and a breaking motion Jim took to mean the number of wounded.

"Can they walk?"

Vanh nodded.

"Then let's get the choppers in here. Call them up, tell them where we are reference the original pickup point, and that we'll shoot a pen flare when we hear them. Tell them that it may be a hot L.Z., so prep everything outside twenty-five meters from the pen flare. Okay?"

Vanh nodded again. He gave him the handset of the radio

and watched as the Vietnamese spoke. Soon he gave the thumbs-up signal and held up five fingers. Jim took this to mean that they would be there in five minutes.

They pulled in the surviving members of the force and set up a small perimeter. The dead would be left in place. Jim didn't like the idea, but there was no way to get them out short of clearing jungle, and they had no time or equipment for that.

How had the NVA known where to set up the ambush? They must have tracked the team almost from the landing, known which direction they'd take coming back, set it up with that in mind. But if they'd known that much, why hadn't they warned the targets? He'd seen radios, both with the ambushers they had killed and in the camp they had attacked. Again the feeling that something was very wrong came over him. If the ambush had been set up just a little better, they would all be lying dead here now. No witnesses on either side.

No time to worry about it now. He sensed the vibration from the helicopters, their blades disturbing the heavy silence of the jungle. Vanh fired a pen flare. Jim knew that the pilots were confirming the color of flare before they came in. The gunship started working over the surrounding foliage with rockets and miniguns. He could not tell whether there was any return fire.

The rope deployment bags came crashing down right into the center of the perimeter. Vanh directed five of his men, including the two wounded, to hook up. The other rope he offered to Jim, who shook his head. He had never left before all his people were off the ground, no reason to start new habits now. Vanh said something to him, offered the rope again. He cupped his hand over his ear, said, "Can't hear you, buddy. Get one more man on that thing and quit wasting time. That chopper is exposed as hell sitting there like that."

Vanh ordered another man over, hooked him up. He spoke into the radio again. The slack was quickly pulled from the rope as the chopper ascended. The weight of the men slowed the ascent rate slightly, but it was evident that the pilot wanted to get out of there quickly, as he increased lift and raised them high. The trees were thirty to forty feet high in this area, and within moments the men were above them. Jim watched approvingly as the pilot took them even higher before he started forward movement. It was such a pleasure dealing with professionals. Perhaps this would be one time that he would not have to endure being skipped off the treetops.

Then the chopper was away, and the second in place. Only four of them to hook up this time. He snapped in, saw Vanh speak over the radio again, soon felt the tug as the slack was taken up.

The muzzle flashes and the roar of gunfire came again. Some were directed at them, some were obviously going for the helicopter. Oh, shit, he thought. Vanh was screaming over the radio. The soldier beside him jerked twice, then went limp. He returned fire, one magazine, then fumbled through his pouch for another. The harness being pulled tight by the rope made it difficult to get them out. Then he had one in his hand, started to insert it in the magazine well and watched it tumble to the ground below as with a great jerk the pilot applied lift and forward motion at the same time. He just had time to raise his hands in front of his face before hitting the first tree.

The gun went first, stripped from his hands by grasping branches. He hit one big limb, then another, knocking the breath out of him. They were banging into each other, trying to hold on, trying to turn so that their backs would take the brunt of the beating, but it did no good. The foliage bounced them about like puppets on an elastic string. One man's foot got caught in the V of a limb; the helicopter kept pulling, obviously lugging down with the load. Then with a tearing sound audible even over the roar of the gunfire the foot tore loose, bouncing them twenty feet as the nylon rope contracted.

He could only hope that they would gain enough altitude before someone got caught worse. It was standard procedure, should the people on the string get snagged badly, to cut them away. It was unlikely that any of them would survive the fall.

His shirt and pants were in shreds, exposing bare flesh to the tearing. I can't take much more of this, he thought despairingly. Maybe it would be better to be cut away. He thought about trying to get the knife out of his web gear, but was afraid he would lose it before he could do anything.

Then suddenly they were above it, bouncing once, twice

on taller trees before getting enough altitude to avoid them. The helicopter pilot obviously wanted to get as far from the ground fire as he could, was pulling pitch for all he was worth and trying to climb.

Jim looked up for the first time, saw oil and smoke streaming from the fuselage. My God, will it never end? It didn't seem that they were climbing, were far too close to the ground. The chopper had to be losing power. Too much weight.

He was still holding on to the man next to him. He felt no life there. Pushing him out to arm's length, he observed the man closely. The head lolled to the side, eyes wide open and staring. His one leg ended at the ankle, but it was obvious from the bullet wounds in his chest that he had not felt that final injury.

He very carefully removed the K-bar knife from its place on his shoulder harness, thankful that he always kept the blade honed. "Goodbye, my friend," he intoned, then slashed the rope. The body fell, tumbling, to the jungle below. It was swallowed up, not even a splash, not a sign that he was gone. Like a burial at sea.

The helicopter, freed from the weight, leaped upward. He could see the face of the crew chief peering down at him, perhaps assessing whether or not there was anything worth saving down there. He waved: I'm alive, god damn it! The radio was, of course, gone, stripped away like the rest of their gear.

The head disappeared. After a few moments, when he felt no sudden slack in the ropes, Jim figured that they were going to try to make it. The helicopter was still smoking, but seemed to be running okay. His vision was blurry, one eye puffing shut from a blow. He twisted to see the others. Vanh was hanging limp. "No!" he cried. Not that. He grabbed him, felt a slight movement. Like himself, Vanh had few clothes left. He looked terribly vulnerable. Jim hugged him close, trying to protect the frail flesh.

The chopper continued to climb, the air growing cold, the wind sucking away body warmth. He knew they wanted to get out of the range of the ground fire, which even now searched for them, but wondered if the cost would be that they would freeze to death. The other survivor, who through his cuts and bruises Jim recognized to be the training NCO, pulled in close and together they huddled.

They flew for no more than thirty minutes, but it seemed to be forever. He realized that they were not going in the direction of Phu Bai, supposed that they were trying to get to the nearest friendly location. His mind was fogging from the cold, but at least it had the effect of killing the pain.

He saw the cleared area approaching, far ahead. Roughly in the shape of a star, a "new model" Special Forces "A" Camp. Barbed wire surrounding it, the jungle cleared away to provide for the interlocking fields of fire he knew they would have planned. When they got closer he could see vehicles, then people running toward the X shape marking the helicopter pad. Would they make it? The helicopter seemed to be descending far faster than necessary.

Then they were over the pad and being lowered gently to the ground. Jim tried to stand up. His legs would not cooperate. Hands pulled at them, unsnapping them from the ropes, drawing them quickly out of the way, placing them on stretchers. A wide moon face looked down at him, grinned. "Might have known it would be you, Jim," he said. "You look like shit."

"Thanks, Clyde," he croaked. "You should see how it looks from the inside."

There came an agonized grinding from above as the gear case of the helicopter finally ran out of fluid and came apart. "Run!" cried someone as the helicopter fell out of the sky. It hit hard, the landing skids splaying out to the sides, the tail boom fracturing and falling to the ground. The main rotor, frozen in place by the seizing of the gears, snapped.

He was left on the stretcher as the others ran back to the helicopter to rescue the crew. He saw fuel spilling from the tanks, watched as it ran over the hard-packed ground toward him, tried to get up. Even the abject fear he felt could not overcome his body's refusal to act. It was as if his muscles were saying, Enough! If we die, so be it, we will go no further.

They were spraying the copter with foam from hand extinguishers, getting in so close they were standing in the fuel, while others pulled the crew out. The pilot had to be cut out of his harness, was pulled from the side, clutching his stomach. His Nomex suit was wet with blood, soaked down his legs, pooled in the crotch. He had obviously been bleeding for a long time. His face was white.

One crewman was dead, his neck at an awkward angle. The other, blood streaming down his face, insisted on helping them take the body off. So much loss. So many of the PRU dead, and now these. For what purpose? So that they could kill a couple of V.C. And some children? Don't forget that part, Jim.

"Could've been worse," Clyde said, returning to where he lay. "Could be raining."

"Fuck you, Clyde," he said weakly.

"That's the spirit. Now let's get a look at you. Where are you hit? Haven't practiced being a medic for a while, but since you cross-trained me, I shouldn't be too bad. What goes around comes around, eh, Jim?"

"My stuff is minor. See what you can do for these other guys. My captain is in pretty bad shape, I think."

"Nah. Already checked him. Knocked unconscious, but he looks okay. Don't worry, we'll take care of everybody. Hell, we're used to it. Get a recon team in here at least once a week that's been shot to shit. So lie back and enjoy."

"Where the hell are we?"

"Camp Mai Loc. Newest addition to the string of Special Forces forts which will help to monitor, interdict and harass cross-border movement of the North Vietnamese Army. According to MACV, in any case. A real shithole of a place. Better get to the bunkers now. Almost time for the daily rockets. Pick up the captain," he said to two of the Montagnards. "Treat him gently. Far as I know, he still owes me money. Can't have him dying before he pays me back."

At the underground dispensary Jim was, once again, given a shot of morphine. I could grow to like this stuff, he thought, shortly before thought went away.

CHAPTER 10

THE Medevac chopper came later that day. By the time it arrived he was able to walk around by himself, though with some difficulty. He refused further shots of morphine, thinking that he liked it entirely too much for it to be good. The pain from his wounds was intense, but bearable. Clyde True supported him as he walked to the chopper.

"What the hell happened out there, Jim?" he asked. "Tried to talk to some of your people while you were out, but they weren't saying much."

"We fucked up. Walked right into an ambush. Damnedest thing I ever saw, an ambush right out in the middle of the jungle. Wasn't a hasty either. They had plenty of time to set it up."

"You think maybe you've got a leak?"

"I think we've got a flood. I just can't figure where. Would seem damn stupid of one of the people to set up an ambush that he was going to walk into. Unless he thought he wasn't going to walk into it. Big question, of course, is whether he was one of the survivors."

"Better you than me, buddy," Clyde said. "I thought I had enough trouble keeping this camp together. NVA sure as hell don't like us. Not that we're doing that much good keeping them from crossing the border. But they know that we're a launch base for CCN. The recon boys are giving them hell over there. They've had to divert a hell of a lot of people to guard their rear areas that could be over here fighting. The recon teams avoid fighting if they can, call in some damn fine air strikes on the convoys on the trail. Used to be pretty easy to do. Not so easy anymore. We're losing a bunch of them. That's why we built the launch sites close to the border. Think you saw what could happen if you had to fly all the way to Phu Bai on a string.''

Around them the Strike Force was cleaning up the mess from the morning's rockets. There was no serious damage. Most of the camp was built underground, in reinforced concrete bunkers. The only major structure aboveground was the latrine, which got blown away regularly. The only casualty thus far suffered among the Americans had been in that latrine. One of the team members had been a bit slow in clearing the spring-loaded screen door, which had come forward and slapped him in the back. It hit the butt of his .45, which for ease of access he always carried cocked and locked. The pistol went off, cutting a groove down his leg and plowing through his foot. He was evacuated to the music of the rest of the team's jeers and catcalls.

"You take care of yourself, Clyde," Jim said as he got on the helicopter.

"Shit, that's easy," Clyde scoffed. "I've already decided I'm going to survive this war. They haven't got me by this time, they're not going to. But you keep fucking around like this and you aren't. Find out who your leak is. Get rid of him. Then seriously consider going into another line of work. Imagine you could find yourself a nice staff job somewhere if you wanted to."

"Yeah. If I really wanted to." He waved goodbye as the helicopter took off. The other wounded were in stretchers. Some of them did not look good. The medic aboard moved constantly among them, checking this one's I.V., the vital signs of another, making sure that the bandages did not come loose and let someone bleed to death.

He relaxed as well as possible, letting the vibration of the chopper lull him into a half-sleep. Soon he would have to worry about the leak. Soon he would have to confront what had gone wrong with the mission. Soon he would have to think about the children. But that could wait for just a little while.

AN ambulance was waiting for him at the landing strip of the 95th Evac Hospital in Danang. They took him to the surgery clinic where, after administering local anesthetic, they removed the claymore pellets from his legs and stomach.

He had been even luckier than he had thought. None of the fragments had penetrated the stomach wall, all being stopped in the muscle. He would be sore, but that was a lot better than the effects that could have been expected from steel balls ripping through his intestines. Some of the fragments in his legs were deeper, and he was gray with pain before they dug the last ones out.

He heard a muffled exclamation from the surgeon, who probed with the forceps, pulled something out that was white and jagged.

"Bone," the doctor said tersely. "Not yours."

"Must have come from one of the guys in front of me, Doc. They were pretty well torn up."

"You doing okay?"

"Real good, Doc," Jim lied. "You about finished? I'd like to get back to Hue tonight."

The doctor stared over his surgical mask in disbelief. Then he laughed, a short, barking sound. "You won't make it back to Hue tonight," he said. "Or anytime soon. We're going to keep you here for at least a week. Some of these wounds are pretty deep, and from the scars I see, I know that you know how easy it is to get infected over here. We'll leave them open for drainage right now, close them up later. For now lots of antibiotics, plenty of rest and a chance to get out in the sun. Looks like you could use it. You spend all your time indoors? Only man I've seen over here without a tan."

Jim started to protest. The doctor cut him off by probing more deeply in one of the wounds. "You sound just like that other asshole who came in from Hoi An. Had a hole in his leg big enough to put a fist into. Told me he couldn't stay in the hospital, he had an operation running and they couldn't do without him. They're doing without him."

"That fella wouldn't happen to look like a fireplug, would he?" Jim asked, grinning through the pain.

"You obviously know one another. Might have known. You want a bed next to him?"

"Please, if you could arrange it."

"Hell, I insist. Might keep from contaminating the rest of the ward. I'm sure you'll have plenty to talk about. Now lie still! One more piece and we're done."

• • •

"THOUGHT I told you I didn't want company," Al growled as the corpsman backed through the door pulling the gurney. "You getting that crowded here in this fucking butcher shop?"

"They thought you needed some company, Al," Jim said as he sat up on the gurney, enjoying the look of surprise on his friend's face. "Said you looked like you were getting lonely. And God knows no nurses are going to come anywhere close to you."

"That's a goddamned lie. They all love me too many. How you doing, Jimmy? You look like shit."

"That's the second time today I've been told that. Must be the truth. Even if it does come from two notorious liars. What happened to you anyway?"

Al grimaced. "Turned a jeep over," he said. "Sonofabitch rolled over my leg. Tore open the old hole from last time I was shot."

"Been telling you for years that you were a shitty driver."

"You would have been too if someone had been shooting at your sorry ass."

"Somebody trying to plug you, were they?"

"Real hard. Might've done it if I hadn't been driving so fast. One of the advantages of being such a shitty driver. Bullets tore the hell out of the backseat. I kept on going, floored the sonofabitch. Found out that an M-151 doesn't take a corner too well at about a hundred. What happened to you?"

"They 'bushed us. Tell you about it tomorrow. It's been a long couple of days, and I'm going to get some sleep. Try to keep the noise down, will you? Act like an officer and gentleman, for a change."

"Fuck you, Jimmy. Nighty-night! Want me to wake you up when Sally Suckemsilly comes by to give me my nightly blowjob?"

"Nah. I'm too tired even for that. Just don't groan too loud."

"I do believe you *are* worn out. Mr. Gonad himself turning down a woman. How the mighty have fallen!"

HE woke the next day to the sound of Al arguing with the doctor. "You don't understand," he was saying. "We've got a joint op running with the 101st, and I'm the only English speaker in the PRU. They can't do it without me."

"I know of absolutely no indispensable people, Captain. This war can go on without you for a little while. Because you're not getting out of here."

"We'll see about that shit. Did you call the Embassy House like I asked?"

"Yes, and a Mr. McMurdock will be visiting you later today. I'm sure he will tell you the same thing. He sounded like a very reasonable man over the phone."

"You've got a new experience in store for you, Doc," said Jim. "Roger McMurdock may be a lot of things, but reasonable isn't one of them."

"Captain Carmichael. Glad you're awake. I need to look at those wounds. You don't mind, do you?"

"Go ahead," Jim said, resigning himself to more pain. "Al, if he gets too eager, kill the asshole, will you?"

AL started on the ROIC before he could even say hello. "You've got to get me out of here," he insisted. "You know as well as I do how badly wrong a joint op can go when the two units can't talk to one another. Hell, they go badly enough when they can. I promise I won't go on the ground with the unit, I'll stay back with the command group. After it's over they can send me back here and be damned."

"Glad to see you too, Al, Jim," Roger said drily. "Looks to me like my tigers got into too much of a cat fight. I suppose you want to get out of here too, Jim?"

"Not particularly. Nice and restful here. With the exception of Al stirring up the staff all the time. Why don't you let him go so I can get some sleep?"

"A reasonable man! I didn't think you had it in you. Al, there will be an Air America chopper on the pad tomorrow morning at eight o'clock. It will take you to the operation. You'll coordinate from the air, you will not go on the ground at all. Is that understood? Because if that isn't good enough, I'll let you rot here in this place. Agreed?"

Al, reluctantly, agreed that it was better than nothing.

"And you'll come back here once a day to let them change bandages. You get infected and you'll be out of action for a long time. We can't afford that. Jim, how are you feeling?"

"Like shit."

"You look like it too."

"That seems to be the consensus."

"You feel up to briefing me?"

Over the next hour he did so, omitting nothing. Even the part about the district chief. They'll probably put my ass in jail for that, he thought, as he described how they had set it up. He took full responsibility for the idea, hoping in that way to avoid causing problems for Captain Vanh.

"You've been a busy young man," was Roger's only comment. "Looks like someone was letting you run out your string, get all the people you had on the list before deciding to get rid of you. Like you, I think that the ambush was just a little too coincidental. Damn shame to lose those people."

"How is Vanh?" he asked.

"Pretty sick. I had him put in the hospital. He wanted to go back to Hue, of course. Damn near had to pull a gun on him to convince him otherwise. He'll pull through, but it will be at least a month before he'll be back."

"And the other wounded? Did they put them in that shit-hole Vietnamese hospital?" All the indigenous soldiers dreaded wounds. The Vietnamese hospitals were vastly over-crowded, care was minimal and sanitary conditions were atrocious. This despite the money and medicine poured into the system by the Americans. The money was pocketed by officials all down the line, and the medicine was stolen. Often the soldiers were forced to pay if they wanted any drugs other than aspirin. Death tolls were high.

"No way!" Roger looked horrified at the thought. "I pulled a few strings and got them put aboard the German hospital ship. Vanh too. The Krauts do a good job."

"That they do," said Al. The ship was anchored just off-shore at Hoi An and he had spent quite a lot of time with the doctors and nurses when they came ashore. His ambush of the V.C. squad who had raped and killed their people had made him popular with them. "Got some good-looking nurses too. Not that you'd worry about that, Jim, what with you deciding to enter the priesthood and all. They get you in the dick again or what?"

"Just missed it this time. Couple of holes through the sac, but nothing important in the way."

"So, Jim, what next?" asked Roger. "You planning to do any more government officials? You might let me know ahead of time, next time. Lot easier to cover your ass that way."

"Sorry, sir. Didn't want to involve any more people than necessary, in case it went wrong. Isn't that what the Agency likes, deniability?"

"What the Agency likes and what I like don't necessarily coincide. Now, obviously you're in danger. If they tried to get you once, they'll do it again. Vanh is well out of it on the hospital ship, so no worry there. I think you'll be okay as long as you're here, but just in case, you'll find a pistol in the bag I brought along. Along with some medicine. Problem will be when you get out. You want to be transferred? You've set them back a hell of a long way in Thua Thien. Might be better to go somewhere else now and start over."

"I'd rather not. Like you said, they've been set back. But they'll recover. We keep pushing them and they won't. Besides, I don't know that I'm up to starting over again. All in all, I think I'd be safer if I just concentrate on getting them before they get me."

"Probably right," Roger admitted. "I'll find out all I can while you're in here so you won't be walking back into it blind. Big thing that worries me is the children. What the hell were they doing there? And who were they? Again, just a little too coincidental for my taste."

"I haven't thought of much else. The thought that somebody put those children there so they would be hit drives me crazy. Bad as we are, we're not that bad."

"Not yet," Roger said. "This war goes on much longer we may get that way. The longer you fight, and the more you see, gets easier to do things you wouldn't ever have thought about."

"Shit, boss!" Al interjected, "I hope you're wrong. I'd hate to think it would come to that."

"Me too. So let's try to win this sonofabitch before it does. Or if we don't want to win it, get the hell out of it. I'll leave you guys to the tender mercies of the medical staff now. That doctor is just going to be real pleased when he finds out that you're getting on a chopper tomorrow, Al. If he's too hard on you, I think what you'll find in the bag will help."

• • •

"I don't know how you did it," the doctor fumed. "But you're out of here tomorrow. Your boss went right over my head to the hospital commander. Guess I can't stop you if you want to do this, but I think you're making a mistake."

"I promise to take real good care of myself and come back and visit you each and every day, Doc," Al said. "Hell, I don't want to get screwed up any more than you want me to. They'd send my ass back to the States and this war might be over by the time I could get back here."

"Typical of you guys," the doctor said. "Most of the people I get in here would give their right nut to go back to the States. What did they call it in World War II, the 'Million Dollar Wound'? How long have you guys been here anyway?"

"Which trip, Doc?" Jim asked.

"How many trips have you made?"

"Three for me. I think Al got in one more TDY trip than I did, so he has four. Getting tired of all this goddamned back-and-forth, so I think I'm going to just hang around this time."

"Well, I think you guys are nuts. You can bet that once my year is up I'm getting the hell out of this wonderful country. Leave it to the maniacs like you." He swept up his instruments and stormed out of the room.

"I think he's a little pissed, Al."

"Seems like it. I probably would be too if someone went over my head like that."

"Yeah, me too. Ever occur to you that we may not be exactly the best army officers in existence? What with both of us not eager to take orders from anybody."

"That thought has run through my mind. Ever thought of what you're gonna do if, perish the thought, this war ends and you survive it?"

"Stay in the army, I guess. But we'll sure as hell have to clean up our act. Go to all the little officer parties, try to avoid pinching the colonel's wife on the ass, even when she wants it, don't get drunk, follow orders, get a nice staff job counting pencils—shit! I'm getting depressed. See if Roger brought us anything good."

Al opened the bag, looked in. A broad smile creased his

face. "Get us a couple of glasses, Jimmy," he said. "Unless you don't want any of this Chivas."

THE days after Al departed were, indeed, restful. He slept as much as he could, raided the hospital library and caught up on his reading, ate the bland hospital food with gusto and slowly died of boredom. He talked little with the hospital staff. A couple of the nurses showed interest, but when he ignored them, gave him up to work more fertile fields.

Most of the time he spent trying to figure out what to do once he got out. Who had betrayed them? How was he going to find out? The orders had to have come from someone higher. Who was that? Would it be some high-level V.C. or NVA officer, someone they didn't have information on, someone so high that even the former district chief did not know about them? Or had it been someone on the government side? Someone they had information on, who knew that they had the information and wanted them silenced. He didn't have a clue as to how to find out, and it was driving him crazy.

He kept the Browning under his pillow and carried it with him wherever he went. Even if it was to the latrine. Hospital staff learned to knock on the door before entering, after a couple of them found themselves staring over the barrel into the eyes of a sweating, very perturbed patient.

On the fourth day he was again visited by Roger McMurdock. "Brought some mail for you," he said. "And another bag of supplies. You're not taking any of the painkillers, are you? Those things don't react so good to alcohol."

Jim assured him that he was not. Only one piece of mail interested him: a letter from Lisa. "You find anything out?" he asked.

"Not yet," Roger admitted. "But we do have a problem. The province chief has reported to Saigon that your PRU unit exceeded orders, that you were going on unauthorized operations, and as a result some innocent people got killed. The kids, of course."

"How did he find out about that?"

Roger looked at him pityingly. "Someone in your unit is reporting to him, of course. Did you seriously think he wouldn't have an informant?"

"Guess not. But that makes him a pretty good candidate for the setup, doesn't it?"

"Not too bad. He certainly could have done it. And from what you tell me about the things you have on him he would have the motive. What did you do with that tape, by the way?"

Jim grinned. "It's in a safe place," he said.

"Don't trust me?"

"You're the one who told me to trust no one," he said. "I can get you a copy, but the original stays with me. Along with copies of all the arrest orders so far. Including the ones for the last operation. Which the colonel signed himself, by the way. So much for 'unauthorized operations.'"

"You're learning," Roger said, smiling. "We'll keep on trying to get some information. Should know something by the time you get out of here. Which the doctor tells me should be in about a week. You heal fast."

"All the clean living I do," Jim replied. "Share a drink?"

"Love to, but I've got to get back. Eliot Danforth is coming back into town tomorrow. With Moira, I suspect. You want me to tell her where you are?" He laughed knowingly.

Anything you don't know, you asshole? Jim thought furiously. "About as much as I want you to throw a rattlesnake in bed with me," he answered. "That woman scares me, and everybody knows I'm fearless."

"Then be a good boy, and quit scaring the staff, and maybe I won't. You're right about her. New breed there. I don't think old Eliot really knows what he has hold of. She'll have his job one of these days. Then it'll be time to really be scared. Might be okay for you, though. She seems to like you. Wouldn't want to be you when she decided she didn't anymore. She'd probably be wearing that scarred-up pecker of yours for a pendant. With that cheerful thought, I'll leave. Try to be good. I know it's hard for you."

Dear Jim,

Your letter and package took a long time in getting to me. I had almost given up hope hearing from you. I am very glad that, at least as of the writing, you were well.

Of course I will do as you ask. You didn't have to worry about that. Whatever you need, just ask.

I have missed you. More than I thought I would. Perhaps I am not quite as tough as I had thought. I welcomed your letter, and the knowledge that you think about me.

The hospital grows worse. More and more young men shipped in, bodies shattered, minds worse. It seems such a waste. I know that you are a believer in this thing, but I find myself questioning it more and more.

I try to not get emotionally involved anymore. Don't think I could take growing to care for someone again, only to see him go away. Perhaps that will change someday, I don't know. For now I live alone, with my thoughts and memories.

I hope to see you again. You will come back, I know that. I don't know what you'll be like by then, whether you'll be anything like the person I once cared for. But I will still want to see you.

Dr. Cable's son tried to kill himself. He wrote a note saying that he could not face life as a cripple. The doctor thinks the real cause was the disillusionment caused by being shot by one of his own men. He walks around like a dead man himself. But he never fails to ask about you when we talk. He liked you a lot. Perhaps a letter from you would help.

Take very good care of yourself, hero. Write me when you can. I will always answer.

She signed it, "Love." Just like I did. Did she mean anything by it? Probably not. But it makes me feel good anyway.

Will I be anything like the person she once knew? His words, his high ideals, seemed like mockery now. He had sworn he would never kill an unarmed adversary. Then he had done it, many times. No good to rationalize that there had been no other choice. Had there been no choice? Or had the killing just become easy, much easier than the alternative? Did it matter? They were the enemy, after all. There was no doubt of that. Did they deserve to die? Probably. But it did not make him feel any better.

What would he say to Colonel Cable? That his son's sacrifice was not in vain? Bullshit! That they would undoubtedly punish the soldier who shot him? That didn't bring his son's legs back. That the army was self-destructing and his son got in the way? Real good, Jim, that ought to explain things real well. There was nothing he could say that would help.

"DAMN good thing I was there," said Al, sitting on the empty bed. "What a ratfuck operation that was!"

"What happened?"

"First off, we ended up with not only the 101st involved, but also the Korean artillery unit. Nobody was speaking each other's language, nobody knew where anyone else was, nobody seemed to give a shit. I ended up acting like some sort of goddamned airborne command post, just like those assholes we used to hate so much. Got any of Roger's medicine left?" he interrupted himself, then continued as Jim poured out a half-tumbler of the amber liquid. "Anyway, first thing that went wrong was that the Koreans shot out of fan, one round landed right in the PRU C.P. area. Killed four of my people, wounded another six. I know I promised Roger not to go on the ground, but if I hadn't, the rest of the PRU was going to go over and kill some Koreans. All we need, a shooting war between the allies.

"I had to do some damn fancy talking, I can tell you that. Promised them all sorts of shit I hope we can come up with. Official apologies from the Koreans, death benefits over and above what we ordinarily pay, care for the wounded out with the Germans, big fancy funeral. Finally got them calmed down, and then the airborne called up and wondered why they weren't moving! That pissed them off again. Told the airborne commander to shove it up his ass, had to fly up there and argue it out with him. Then over to the Koreans to see what the fuck happened, and those arrogant assholes claimed that it wasn't their fault. Told those kimchi-eating motherfuckers that if I didn't get some satisfaction, I'd make sure they got some night visits.

"Pain in the ass, man. Not enough we've got to fight the Commies, we can't even get along with each other. I'm getting tired of this shit. Maybe I'll take that assignment in Germany once this is all over, see what the peacetime army is like."

"Boring as hell, I expect."

Al nodded. "I expect you're right. When are you due to get sprung anyway?"

"Another week. Doc wants to make sure all my holes are closed up. Says he suspects that sure as hell I won't stay out of the field so's I can keep the muck out of them, so he'll make sure we don't have to worry about it. I think Roger is pacifying him after going over his head about you."

"I'm hearing some bad stuff from my sources," Al said. "Something about those kids that got killed. Seems like they may have belonged to some bigwig. Don't know who, but likely someone high in the Vietnamese government. Rumors are that there is some very serious shit coming down about it. Roger say anything about it to you yet?"

The bile rose in his throat, burning like distilled pain. Everything about this screamed setup! "What else have you heard?" he asked as soon as he was able to talk.

"That's it. I've got everybody listening for more, though. Think it's time to run yet?"

Jim seriously considered it. Nothing that he did seemed to do any good. When he tried to do his job, they attempted to kill him or put him in jail. If he did nothing, the enemy would win. Did it matter? Who was the enemy? The soldiers who fought against him? Or his supposed allies, who were thieves and murderers and liars?

"Not yet," he said. "First I want to find out who's doing this shit. And take care of him. Then we'll see what happens."

"We'll keep the option open anyway. Never know what will go down next. Time for me to get back to the field. Give Sally Suckemsilly a kiss for me. Though you know what that will make you, don't you?"

"Yeah, a cocksucker by proxy. That line was old when George crossed the river."

"Hell, it was old when Christ was a corporal, and I was just a junior lieutenant. But what the hell. I like it anyway."

"Why don't you hang around for the night. I could use someone to talk to. Can't do it with anyone here."

"You know why, don't you?"

"Why?"

"Because they're scared shitless of people like me and you. I've heard them talking. Killers, they call us. Hard-eyed gunmen. Shit, almost makes me scared of myself!"

Jim was silent for a moment. "We are, you know."

"Yeah. I guess so. Helluva thing. You ever wonder why?"

"Why what?"

"Why you can do the things you do. Without a hell of a lot of remorse. Without the good old Baptist guilt. You read more than anybody I know, Jim. Have you ever read in any novel about anyone who didn't go through horrible pangs of conscience, flashbacks, bad dreams, when they had to do things like this? It always destroys them in the end, yet here we are and it doesn't seem to make a hell of a lot of difference."

"Frankly I suspect there are more of us out there than there are the other kind. People who are relatively normal, who are good citizens, whatever that means, peaceful, nice to their neighbors and all, but who have the capability of doing exactly the same thing. If they have to. They just don't get novels written about them."

"Maybe you're right. Anyway, as I was saying, we scare the hell out of people. I've got an idea. I heard there was a band at the Officers Club tonight. Want to go there?"

"Why not?"

THEY arrived at the club when it was in full swing. A Vietnamese singer was crooning. "Moon libber, wider than a mi, I clossing you in sti, sunday."

"Jesus, I love this," Al said. "Look at all the people dancing. Somehow, dancing with somebody else in fatigues never appealed to me." They took an empty table. Ordered drinks. Were amused at the furtive looks which came their way.

"Well, Captain," said the doctor who had treated them, "I see you're still alive."

Al smiled up at him. "Shit, Doc, I'm indestructible. Join us for a drink?"

"Sorry, I don't drink with patients." The doctor looked uncomfortable at the thought.

"Well then, get your raggedy ass out of the way. I think the go-go dancers have started."

"See what I mean, Jim?" Al asked after the man made his way back across the room.

"Yeah, well, fuck 'em all."

"Yeah, I know, all but nine. Six pallbearers, two road guards and one to call cadence. Let's have another drink."

• • •

ROGER didn't show up for four more days. Jim tried to call him several times, with no success. The duty officer's story was that he was out, that he couldn't be reached, that an important operation was going down, and as soon as he got back, he was sure to call. Day by day he grew more worried. If he couldn't count on Roger, he was lost. Perhaps he should have taken Al up on the offer and run. But Al hadn't shown up again either. Maybe he should just check himself out, catch a flight to Saigon, disappear. It would take them a long time to find him. Some deserters had been hiding there for years. Surely he could find a way to get out of country before they could track him down. Disappear, take a new name, go somewhere that no one cared about his background. Where would that be?

In the end he came to the realization that his original impulse had been the correct one. Stay here and fight it, find out who was behind it, do something about it. No matter what happened. Better to go down fighting than to run away only to be brought back in chains.

"I think it's time you took a little vacation," said Roger when he finally walked in the door. "You've been in country for a little over four months now, that authorizes you some R&R. So I've taken the liberty of getting you some orders cut. Where do you want to go?"

"How about Hue?"

"You make real funny jokes. Right now if you went to Hue, you'd last about fifteen seconds. Al tells me you know about the problems. I'll finish filling you in. The kids that got killed were relatives of the biggest Buddhist bonze in the country. And he thinks you did it deliberately. So every Buddhist around would like to get a piece of your hide. Now, I've got some plans on how to take care of that. But those plans include you not being around for a while. So how about it, where do you want to go? Thirty days anywhere in the world. Want to go to Hawaii?"

"You're not just getting rid of me for good? You'll let me come back?"

"If we can get this situation squared away, hell yes. You're the best PRU officer we've had."

"How about just going to another province? Somewhere down south."

"You don't seem to understand!" Roger yelled, losing his temper for the first time. His voice roared through the hallways. A nurse passing by looked startled, paused on her rounds, then hurried on upon seeing the glance he shot at her. "Every fucking Buddhist in this country is your enemy right now. You've got to leave. Trust me. We'll get it squared away. Now, for the last time, where do you want to go? Or shall it be to the States, in handcuffs?"

"Fuck it. Australia."

CHAPTER 11

HE decided he liked Sydney. The taxi taking him to his hotel passed through the Kings Cross section. Even at this early hour the sidewalks were filled with people. Beautiful women, most of them. Miniskirts so short it seemed a waste of material to wear them at all. He settled back in the seat to enjoy the view. Bursts of laughter came through the open windows. It was one big party. He suspected that he was going to enjoy the R&R in spite of himself. His attitude had changed somewhat since being told that he had to go on R&R rather than stay in Vietnam. Amazing what the sight of pretty women could do.

"Here you are, mate," the driver said, pulling up outside the big hotel. "You must be one of those bloody Green Beret types, eh?"

Jim looked at him sharply. "What do you mean by that?"

"No offense," the man said hastily. "Miller's Oceanic Hotel is a hangout for you types. Nobody else on R&R, at least nobody in their right mind, stays there. Have a good time, mate."

The extremely pretty young lady who registered him was very friendly. She explained about the hotel, about the R&R party room which was reserved for their honored guests from Vietnam, about the mixers designed to get their guests acquainted with the local citizenry, about her working hours and how she certainly hoped that she would see him again soon.

In his mind he vowed that she certainly would.

Within an hour he was in the hotel bar, drinking the first of many cold Foster's lagers. Quite a difference from the rusty cans of Hamm's which seemed to be all that was left in the PX in Vietnam after all the good stuff was skimmed off. It tasted good, ice cold, just slightly bitter. Heady stuff. He had another. Then another. Just starting to develop a pleasant buzz. Felt a hand on his shoulder. Stiffened, ready to lash out, then remembered where he was and relaxed.

"Easy mate, I'm a friendly. Name's Frank Klasic, and I run this place. You must be Jim Carmichael."

"I guess I must. Al Dougherty told me to tell you hello."

"Ah, my good friend Aloysius Dougherty. And how is the little bastard? Still as mean as ever, I expect."

"He'll be down in a couple of months. Soon as he can tear himself away. Powers-that-be decided I needed a break before he did."

Frank sat at a stool next to him and ordered two more beers. "Everyone should come to Sydney at least once," he said. "I expect you've already seen some of the things it has to offer."

"Yeah. Clean, soft beds. Beautiful women. Clean streets. Good beer. Nobody shooting at you. I'm overwhelmed."

"How long are you here for? The regular five days?"

"No. Lucky me. Thirty."

"Extension leave, then?"

"Nope." Jim shook his head. "They just decided they could do without me for a month. Al tells me that you're not exactly a stranger to the profession. Is it true that you ran guns into Palestine in the forties?"

"Some people claim that. Actually I'm just an innocent innkeeper."

I'll bet, Jim thought. The man, though he had at least twenty years on him, looked at least as fit as he was. There was a hardness about him that belied his profession.

For the next two hours they talked. Jim felt himself relaxing for the first time in a very long time. The life he had left only yesterday faded in a Foster's-induced haze. He felt at peace with the world. He thought it nice that it was unlikely that he would be called upon to kill anyone in the immediate future.

Sometime later, he couldn't have told when, they left the bar and went to the R&R room. The place was decorated with unit plaques from most of the elite outfits of the world. Jim saw the ones for all the Command and Controls, SOG, the SAS, the Royal Commandos. He felt right at home. It was full of people, some of whom he vaguely recognized from Group. Everybody was drunk, and again it seemed that everyone was happy. He switched from Foster's to screwdrivers, then to an evil concoction called Black Velvet. The young lady who fed it to him told him it was half Guinness stout and half champagne. The name was appropriate. It made his tongue feel like it was coated with velvet that someone had been wearing for a long time without bathing. The girl was taken away by someone else and another sat beside him. His vision was by this time a bit fuzzy, but not so much so that he could not recognize the receptionist. "Is it that late already?" he asked, aware that his words were slightly slurred.

"And past," she sighed. She cocked her head, sighed again. "I suppose you're too drunk to take me to dinner?

"Yes, you are," she answered her own question. "Come, give me your room key. I'll take you to bed."

He looked at her in surprise. Surely she didn't mean what he hoped she meant. She was probably just trying to keep him from making a fool of himself. Best to leave now before that happened. He handed over the key.

SHE hugged him close on the trip. Half supported him, staggering somewhat under his weight. She felt the muscles of his back rippling under her hand. Was aware that she was getting very, very wet. It seemed that they would never get there; the elevator ride was interminable, the halls longer than they had ever seemed before.

In the room he came alive. Put his arms around her and kissed her. God, he was big. His arms enveloped her, strong and yet curiously gentle. His lips were soft on hers, his tongue at first tentative, then more and more bold as she met every thrust. She felt the hardness of him insistent upon her belly.

He unbuttoned her thin dress, deftly unclipped the bra strap. With the part of her mind that still held rationality she realized that he was not quite as drunk as he had seemed. She pushed him back onto the bed.

He was in heaven. She was so soft, and smelled so good, so clean. Her lips were full and her breath sweet. She sat up, dropped the top of the dress. Her full breasts with the deliciously large nipples seemed to beg to be kissed. She arched back her head, hair tossing from side to side. Her pelvis ground into him. He thrust up at her, aching from need and from the rough friction.

"Enough," she cried. She stood up, shucked off the dress, stood before him in glorious nudity. It was the last thing he needed to convince himself that he was really here. Nobody was going to try to kill him. He didn't have to sleep with his hand on a pistol. He gave himself over to pleasure.

She blessed the American government and the Vietnam War and the R&R policy. Sex had never been this way with her countrymen. They were rough, cared only for their own pleasure. She was a sensual woman and needed more. These men, coming from a land of death and reaffirming their existence in her body, had been a revelation. She hoped it would never end.

Sometime before dawn he finally fell asleep. She looked at him, stretched out on the bed in the dim light. Such a beautiful body, marred by so many scars. Some old, some very new and angry. So young.

She got up carefully, showered and combed her hair. As she was getting into her clothes she became aware that he was looking at her. His eyes were empty. Dead. She turned away, a chill running up her spine and causing her skin to ripple in dread. Finished dressing.

"I won't see you again, will I?" he asked, his voice as dead as his eyes.

"No, love, I don't think so," she said. "You're new here. You don't realize what goes on."

"What do you mean?"

"I mean that this is a place where you do anything you want. Nothing is held back. You made it with me last night, today you'll be with someone else. And so will I. We had a wonderful time. Now let's not push it. I'll see you around, Yank." With that she left.

Outside the door she felt the tears start to her eyes. There had been so many! Too many. She could not afford to get involved again with a man who, despite promises to the contrary, promises that he may even have intended to keep, would never come back. She was too fragile to love someone who would soon be bleeding his life away on a distant battlefield. Someone she would never even know when and if he died. Her mother had done that, for a long-gone American soldier who had been killed in New Guinea. She had seen what it had done to her. It was easier to be hard. Easier than to suffer.

Inside the room he shrugged it away. Ignored the sense of loss that nagged at his brain and after some tossing and turning fell back asleep.

THE next week passed in a haze. For the first few days he scarcely made it out of the hotel except to sun himself on the beach. Each day he passed the receptionist, who was polite and proper, but nothing more. No matter. There were plenty more. All the young ladies in the area stopped in the Oceanic, hoping to meet one of the notorious free-spending Green Berets. Most of them got lucky. It was one long drunken party. After the second day he tapped into the bottle of Dexamil he had brought. The stuff was issued in Vietnam, supposedly to keep you awake on patrol. He had learned long ago that it would do that. It would also give you wonderful hallucinations after a couple of days. He had tried it once in combat, stopped after one night seeing elephants walking down the trail with Styrofoam wrapped around their feet to cut down the noise. Bright green Styrofoam, and the elephants were blue. But it was great here. No need to sleep! You could sleep when you were dead. One girl in the morning, another in the afternoon, perhaps another that night. No guilt, no shame. You were going to die anyway, might as well enjoy life while it was possible.

On the seventh day he crashed. Slept round the clock. Woke up feeling terrible. Called room service and got his usual steak, egg and fried-tomato breakfast. Took another Dexamil and waited for it to kick in. Decided to expand his horizons to somewhat past the Coogee Beach area and check out the Kings Cross.

The taxi driver was the same one who had brought him to the Oceanic, it seemed like years ago.

"Christ, mate, you must have been enjoying yourself. You look about ten years older."

"At least that," he said, his voice whiskey-rough. "Where's the best place to go in the Cross?"

"That'll be the Texas Tavern. Most of the Yanks go there. Though it really doesn't matter where you go in the Cross."

When he walked into the place, he realized what a woman must have felt when she walked into a bar in the United States. Most of the tables had two or three females; there were not a lot of men. The women looked at him appraisingly, running their eyes up and down his body, then talking in whispered asides to their friends. He stifled the urge to cover his crotch in embarrassment. Walked to the bar as quickly as he could and ordered a drink. Heard a loudly voiced comment about his ass and how nicely tight it was. Was at some loss as to what to do next.

"Saw you at the Oceanic the other night," said the girl to his left.

He turned toward her. She smiled. Her friend sitting to the other side smiled. He smiled.

"You want to get crazy, ladies?" he asked. They nodded in unison. "Then there's one for you and one for you." He handed each a Dexamil. "It's going to be a long night," he explained.

He escaped from their flat only after a very long two days. Probably would never have gotten out, he reflected, if he hadn't run out of the pills. His crotch felt raw.

Need some rest. Got to crash. It was early morning and taxis were scarce. He passed an all-night restaurant and realized that he hadn't eaten for quite some time. Went in, ordered a large breakfast.

As he ate he looked around. Most of the patrons looked as debauched as he felt. Except one. To his eye she was a princess fallen into bad circumstances. Long brown hair, petite, flashing green eyes being directed at the man sitting across from her. For his part he was clearly American, and just as clearly very drunk. Jim watched, amused, as she berated him.

The man, who may have been handsome under better circumstances, stared at her through swollen eyes. Spoke some slurred words that Jim could not hear. She spoke sharply back. The man's face reddened. He drew back his fist and lunged at her. His hand grazed her cheek.

Game time, he thought. He got up, walked over to where they were sitting, said, "Why don't you pick on someone your own size, asshole." Jesus, he thought, do I sound corny.

"Mind your own business, fuckhead," the man slurred. He made as if to get up.

With his right hand Jim pushed the man's face to the side, with his left hand reached around to the other side and inserted his middle finger in between cheek and teeth. Pulled sharply, twisting the man's neck and jerking him out of the chair. He kept the man's head twisted, kicked him behind the knees and dropped him to the floor. With a knee planted firmly in his spine, he leaned down until his mouth was very close to the man's ear.

"I want you to listen very closely, asshole. You've got about five seconds before I rip your cheek right off your fucking face. Nod if you understand me."

Slowly, painfully, the man did. The agony in his face was rapidly becoming unbearable. His mouth was stretched almost to his ear.

"Now, when I let you go, you're going to get up very slowly. You're going to walk out of here. You're not going to say anything, not turn around, and you damned well better not try to come back. Because if you do, I'm going to hurt you very badly, and very permanently. Do you understand that?"

Something in Jim's voice told the man that he should do as he said. Slowly he nodded again, felt the finger being withdrawn from his mouth and the terrible pain ease. He got up and with as much dignity as he could muster walked out.

"Who the bloody hell do you think you are?" the woman demanded. "That was none of your business."

"Sorry. Looked like you needed help."

"Typical fucking male reaction," she mocked. "Poor little girl can't take care of herself, so the big hero will do it for her. And she'll be so grateful she'll just fall right into his arms. Well, you can forget that, mate. I can handle myself perfectly well and I don't need your help or any other bloody man's." She grabbed her bag and stormed out.

He watched her go, amused. Guess I screwed that one up, he thought. He wasn't sorry for what he had done, though. The brush with violence had gotten his adrenaline flowing. He felt alive, more charged than the pills could ever make him. Returned to his seat and finished breakfast with gusto, aware of the amused looks of the other diners. He grinned. The day was beginning to look promising.

Out on the sidewalk the town was again coming alive. Time to see more of the city than just barrooms and bedrooms. It was a beautiful day, and he was alive and there was a whole world out there to enjoy. He hailed a taxi.

The next two days were spent sight-seeing. Sydney was a beautiful city. Not as crowded as major cities in the United States, cleaner, built around a gorgeous bay. Everywhere he went the people were friendly. He drank only in moderation, took no pills at all and was beginning to feel almost healthy. Time, he thought, for some more serious debauchery.

For in his semisobriety the dreams had started. He'd wake up, soaked with sweat, the dimly remembered dead faces swimming before him. Time again to wash them away, to drown them in a sea of alcohol and sex. Time to find someone who, if they could not make him forget, could at least exhaust him enough that the dreams would not come.

In the afternoons the Texas Tavern was not crowded. One could have a drink or two in relative quiet. Time enough to get a good buzz on before doing some serious hunting. He was on his third drink when he saw her in the mirror behind the bar. The not-quite damsel in distress. He wondered if she saw him. She was coming his way. What did she want? He hoped it was not to berate him again. He really was not in the mood. He tried to ignore her as she sat on the stool next to him and ordered a drink. It was hard. Her fragrance, one he could not identify, wafted over him.

God, she was beautiful! Her hair was teased up in a mane, framing an oval face. The eyes which the other day he had thought to be green looked in the dim light of the bar to be almost blue. Her features were delicate, as befitted such a small face, and yet there was a hint of strength there. She was perhaps five two, and perfectly proportioned. He sighed audibly. Too bad. He would have liked to know her better.

"I suppose you have the right to ignore me," she said without turning her head, "after the way I treated you the other night. I hoped that I would find you sooner or later so that I might apologize." Her accent, now that the hard edge of anger was gone from her voice, was enchanting.

He grinned. "You mean you've been looking for me?"

She flushed slightly. "Not the first day. I was too angry. Then I realized it wasn't you that I was angry at, but me. You were just trying to help. I was stupid for allowing myself to get in such a situation. Forgive me?" She turned to him and smiled. Her teeth, like the rest of her, were perfect.

"Hell no, I don't," he said, and watched her smile disappear. She stiffened, started to turn away. "But I will, if you'll allow me to buy dinner for you."

"You're a hard bastard, aren't you?" she said, smiling again. He loved the way she said "bastard," the "a" of the first syllable deliciously drawn out. "I suppose that in the face of such an ultimatum I can do little but give in. Though it should be I who does the buying."

"Next time, perhaps. That way I can make sure you'll go out with me twice."

"Done. At least allow me to buy you a drink. My name is Frances DeLacy, but everyone calls me Frenchy."

"I'm James NMI Carmichael, but everyone calls me asshole. Without the hyphen. But if you insist you can call me Jim."

"No, I don't think so. You look more like a James. I'd rather call you that, if I may." She took a sip of her drink. Licked her upper lip delicately. He shivered.

"What do you do for a living?" he asked.

"Work for an advertising agency. Write copy and sometimes, if I'm lucky, get a little work modeling. Though I'm far too short for that. If only I were six inches taller! Guess I have my parents to blame."

"I wouldn't blame them for a damned thing. In fact, I'd like to meet them and give thanks. You're perfect." He hoped he had not gone too far. Was that an actual blush he saw?

She smiled again. "Why, thank you, James. I've always loved a compliment. I suppose I don't need to ask what you do?"

"What gave me away? The haircut? At least I'm not wearing army shoes, so it can't be that."

"And thank God for that! They look horrible. Actually, it was your eyes. They are beautifully blue, but I see a great deal of pain there. And rage. What do you rage against, James NMI Carmichael? When you came to my rescue the other night, you frightened me. I saw you come into the restaurant, thought What a nice-looking man. Then when you grabbed Bobby, you were totally changed. As if a different person took over. A not very nice person, I think. You quite frightened Bobby out of his wits, you know. He came round the next day, very apologetic. I'm afraid I wasn't too nice either. Told him that if he didn't go away, I would call you from the bedroom. The look that passed over his face was priceless. He took to his heels, calling you and me some very nasty names as he left.''

He laughed with her at the great joke. Wished he had, in fact, been in the bedroom. Wondered if there was any chance of that happening.

By the time they went to dinner they acted like old friends. She was remarkably easy to talk to. He found himself telling her things he would never have dreamed of uttering to someone he had known for such a short time.

She was uncommonly well informed, conversed knowledgeably on a number of subjects. At times he had the slightly uncomfortable feeling that she was brighter than he. It was refreshing.

During coffee and cognac he asked her if she would care to go dancing.

"Absolutely love to. Have to do something to work off all this booze. We have sat here and got me more than slightly tipsy."

"Good. My hotel has a live band almost every evening. It's a bit far from here, the Oceanic.''

"Ah, Coogee Beach. I love the place. Shall we go?''

During the long taxi ride she sat rather closer to him than he could have hoped. Placed a hand on his knee. It seemed so much an innocent gesture that he thought little about it. Until they went around a curve and she leaned into him, turning her face up to his.

Her lips, which had looked so small, were full and warm against his. He kissed her softly, marveling at how good it felt. Her lips parted slightly and the tiny tongue came out to meet his, touching slightly, teasing his lips, then withdrawing.

She pulled away. "I've wanted to do that all evening,'' she said. "You kiss as well as I'd expected. Look, here we are.''

Frank Klasic met them in the lobby. Looked approvingly

at Frenchy. "Good to see you, Jimmy," he said. "Haven't had much chance to talk lately. Going to the dance tonight? Good. I'll get you a good table."

The place was crowded, but Frank found them a table that had for some reason been reserved. Winked at them as he took away the sign. "Knew I'd reserved this for something," he said. He whispered something to the waiter. "Enjoy yourselves, now. Jimmy, give me a call when you get time. Perhaps we can go down to my club and play some squash." Then he was away.

Frenchy eased her hand across the table, clasped his. "God, your hands are warm," she said. "I like that. I'm often so cold. I think Mr. Klasic likes you. I can understand that. You're a likable person."

"Not to some people," he replied.

"You just think that. I think that if you would just allow it, you'd be surprised."

A bottle of good Hunter Valley wine appeared on the table. "Compliments of management," said the waiter.

"Nice man, your Frank."

"He is that. And you are beautiful. And would you like to dance?"

On the floor she molded against him. Her head was tucked just under his chin, her breath soft against the opened collar of his shirt, stirring the hair on his chest. Her hair smelled of cleanliness and that strange perfume. They moved hardly at all, swaying slightly to the beat of the music.

The song ended and they stood there for a moment, she looking up into his face and smiling.

"You know," she said, "I'll just bet that Frank wouldn't mind terribly if we take his lovely bottle of wine up to your room and share it there."

His mouth felt suddenly dry. "I'm sure he won't," he managed to croak.

In the room she matter-of-factly stripped off her clothes and lay on the bed. He stared at her, not knowing what to say. The clothes had hidden no faults. Her breasts were small but nicely rounded, the nipples childlike. But that was the only thing childlike about her. He hurriedly stripped out of his clothes.

She pulled him down onto the bed and wrapped herself

around him, surprising strength for so small a person. "Ah, God, I've wanted you so badly ever since you stood there with such a hurt look on your face because I was so nasty. And if you don't make love to me *now*, I'm going to explode."

Afterward she propped herself on an elbow, face hanging over his, mane of hair a tent protecting them from the world. "Do you think I'm terrible?" she asked.

He kissed her, then shook his head. "I'm only amazed. And feeling very lucky. I haven't figured out yet why you wanted me. Won't try to. I'm just glad you do."

"How could I not? You're very sexy."

He laughed in delight. "I'll bet you say that to all the guys," he joked.

Her face clouded quickly. She drew back. "What do you mean by that?" she demanded.

"Sorry, I was just making a joke," he said hastily. "You know, the one about every man in the world thinking himself well hung and loving to hear it confirmed. Even if he's built like a stud field mouse."

"A stud field mouse!" Her laughter filled the room. He was glad that the moment was defused. Wondered why she had reacted so strongly to what he had thought was a harmless joke.

She quieted, seized him by the face, looked him in the eyes. Her eyes, he noticed, looked green again, but with a fringe of gold around the pupils. "I will never," she said quite seriously, "tell you something I don't mean. You are a wonderful lover, and very gentle, and very considerate."

Some time later she was tracing lazy patterns over his body with a feather-light touch. She encountered a ridge of scar tissue high on his shoulder. "What was this from?" she asked.

"Carbine bullet," he answered. "First trip over."

"And this one?" touching the sunken place on his thigh.

"Second trip. AK-47. The small ones are from shrapnel. The new-looking ones are from this trip, claymore mine." He turned over. "Back side still looks pretty good, though. I've got lots more room."

"My God, you've been in that place three times? Why?"

He was getting tired of the question, and disgusted with

his inability to answer it. "Only war we've got? No, I'm sorry, that's a flip answer. I don't really know. All I know is that I don't fit in anyplace else. At least in combat I know who my friends and enemies are. Usually," he amended.

"I hope you'll let me be your friend."

"You have to ask?"

They talked into the early hours of the morning, slept, woke up and made love again, slept more.

He woke before she did. Spent some time looking at her. She was curled up like a cat, hair partially obscuring her face. He gently brushed it back, saw her lips curl in a small smile, as if she were having a particularly pleasant dream. Funny, he thought, he didn't feel the need to get away from her as he so often did with the others.

After a while she woke. Smiled up at him. Pulled him down for a kiss. "I was dreaming that we were making love," she said. "It was almost as good as the reality. You look happy this morning. Are you?"

"Immensely. Now get your little butt up out of bed and let's eat some breakfast. I'm so hungry I could eat the south end of a skunk headed north."

"You have such a way with words, darling." She made a little face at him, then flounced off to the bathroom.

The next few days were wonderful. Frenchy knew the city from top to bottom, took him places he would never have been able to find on his own.

After the first week he asked about the job. They spent every moment together. Didn't she have to work? She told him that she had called her boss and was taking a long-overdue vacation. Why did he ask, was he tired of her already?

During their second week together she told him that she would not be able to see him a couple of nights hence. That there was an out-of-town meeting that she would have to attend. It had been scheduled since before she met him and she couldn't possibly get out of it. She hoped he would understand.

When the night came, he was at a loss. Didn't feel like drinking, certainly had no desire to carouse with anyone else. Funny, he thought, in the old days I would have welcomed such a break. I would have been out meeting someone else, out burying myself in yet another body. Using sex as a bludgeon to drive away the loneliness. Tonight I have absolutely no desire for it. He was glad, and yet a little frightened. It served to reinforce what he had gradually come to admit to himself. That he was feeling far more than infatuation or even great lust. He hesitated to call it love. He did not know what love was, or if he would or could recognize it when and if it hit him. But he knew that he cared for this woman more than he thought he could care for anyone. For some time he had thought his emotions were gone, that he was dead inside. The dispassionate killer, the dead-eyed one, the stalker of the night. Now he was feeling the stirring of long-buried enthusiasms. He was afraid. Too soon he would have to leave this. And there was no room for emotion back in country, no use in trying to cling to a life that suddenly seemed much more worthwhile. Such an attitude could get you killed much quicker.

He had a quiet dinner and a couple of drinks and went to bed early. And tried not to feel empty when he woke during the night reaching for her, only to find that she wasn't there.

She returned at noon the next day, seeming a little distant, more reserved. He attributed it to other concerns, perhaps trouble at the meeting. She was not disposed to talk about it, and he did not press. By midafternoon that attitude had dissipated and they were once again enjoying one another's company without reserve.

That night she insisted on taking him to dinner, claiming that after all he had done she owed it to him. They went to a rather more fancy place than usual, had a bottle of champagne, then another.

During the second bottle she suddenly grew serious. She looked directly into his eyes for a moment. He felt pinned by her stare.

"James," she began, "what do you really feel for me? I want the truth. I'm a big girl and I can handle it. If this is just an R&R romance, I want to know. I can live with that. But if there is something else, if you feel more, I need to know that too. Because I'm feeling far too much for you. More than I should, I know. For such an impossible situation."

"Impossible?"

"Yes, impossible. Soon you'll be returning to Vietnam. I'll be returning to my life. I don't know if I'll ever see you again. Won't know if anything has happened to you, won't know if you're alive or dead. I don't know if I can stand that."

The candlelight illuminated the tears standing in her eyes. She was clasping his hand so hard it hurt.

"Why did you bring me here to ask me that?"

"Because I was afraid I'd bloody well dissolve into a mess of tears if we were alone. And I didn't want that. I wanted to discuss this rationally, as two adults. And I'm less likely to cause a scene here."

He smiled at her, took her chin gently in his hand. She clasped him, kissed his palm. Her cheeks were wet.

"No, this isn't just an R&R romance. In fact, I'm going to tell you something I've never said before. I think I'm falling in love with you. And I don't know what the hell to do about it."

"Aren't we a pair?" She laughed. "So afraid to feel anything that we've let a lot of life pass us by. I was almost hoping that you would say that this meant nothing, that it was pleasant and a lot of fun, but don't expect too much of it. Because I know now that I love you too. And I thought that if that feeling wasn't returned, perhaps I could get over it. Now what do we do?"

"Get out of here, for one thing. For some reason I don't have much of an appetite. And I think we need to talk. There are a lot of things you should know about me."

THAT night he told her of the things he had been doing. He left nothing out. He wanted to shock her, wanted her to know the kind of man she thought she loved. He felt that once she heard it all she would no longer care for him. Nobody could love such a monster. And the problem would be solved.

Finally he finished. He had not looked at her the entire time. She had made no comment, no move. He dared to look over at her. She was lying there, silent, staring at the ceiling.

"So you see the man you thought you knew doesn't exist. Never has. What you have instead is a not very highly paid professional killer."

She came up off the bed in a fury, pushed him back and held him down by the shoulders. "Don't ever say that," she hissed. "The man I know is the one who is really there. Don't you think I can see that? What you have done, what you have been forced to do, is not you. That person is not in your eyes. That person could not look at me with the love I see there. He couldn't be gentle, couldn't be warm. And he wouldn't have that look of ineffable sadness that I see so often. I love you. I don't care what you've done. It means nothing. The only thing that matters is that you love me too."

"I wish it were all that mattered. But it's not. I've got to go back to the war. I have no choice. They own me. I'm bought and paid for."

She winced. "You do have a choice. I haven't told you before, but I'm not poor. I have enough money for the both of us. You can stay here, not go back. There are at least a couple of hundred G.I.s in Australia who haven't. It's a big country, easy to get lost. The government doesn't look for them too hard. You've served your time. My God, three tours and more scars than I care to count. Let someone else do it for a while. Let them find another tool. They will, you know. They always do."

"I can't do that. I don't like what I'm doing very much, but I can't quit."

"Why not?"

"Because it's what I do! What the hell would I do down here? Lie on the beach? Let you support me? I couldn't live that way. I have no other skills. Christ, I've been in the army since I was seventeen. It's the only life I know, bad as it is."

"Is that what's really bothering you, that you'd be living off me?"

"Not entirely, no. I wouldn't feel right, but I just might be able to get used to it. I'm not one of those old-fashioned types who think that they always have to be the provider. No, it's more than that. It's more that I started this damned thing and I will, by God, finish it. I have no choice."

"Then you're telling me that we have no future."

"Don't say that," he begged. The look of sadness in her eyes was more than he could take. "I've got the rest of this tour to get through. After that I owe them nothing. I can resign my commission, or try to. They may even let me go.

Then we can be together. I could come back here, or you could come to the States. Even if they won't let me out of the army, you could still come to the States and we could be together.''

''That presupposes that you'll survive. James, you must realize that everything you've told me so far indicates that you don't expect to. It's almost as if you want to die.''

''That may have been true at one time. It's not anymore.''

''Do you really mean that?''

''More than anything I've ever said before.''

''Ah, God, this is impossible. But I have no choice but to love you. I can't help that. May we make love now?''

Afterward she snuggled close to him and fell asleep. He lay there watching her soft breathing, unable to sleep himself. His mind was far too busy.

Why was he going back? She was right, he had done far more than his share. There were but a handful of people who had pulled more than one tour, far less three.

Because, he told himself, what he was doing was important. It might be unpleasant, though he had long ago stopped being bothered by the unpleasantness, but it was getting the job done. Because of him there were a lot of murdering bastards who would kill no more. He held no illusions that it would affect the outcome of the war one way or the other. The outcome would depend on the politicians, and it looked like they were already preparing to give it up.

On the other hand, the people he opposed probably considered him to be a murdering bastard also. Was he any better than they? True, he had never, on purpose, killed innocent people. Of course the other side could say, and did say, that there were no innocents. That if you did not support them, you were not a revolutionary, and were therefore as much an enemy as the soldier in the field.

That way lies madness, he told himself. When you lose all sense of right and wrong, you are no better than those whom you fight. Are you any better? Maybe not. Shouldn't we stop this shit? Yes, we should. He closed his eyes and tried to sleep.

Sometime before morning his nemesis came for him again. Teeth shining, pistol gleaming softly in the half-light, eyes glittering and cold and black. The pistol was pointed at him.

He was on hands and knees trying to get away. Tried to get up, but did not have the strength. Pushed himself forward, but the air itself resisted him, seeming to become a viscous substance. He struggled, aware that the man's finger was tightening on the trigger, felt the hair on his neck standing on end at just about the point the bullet would go in. Heard the explosion of the gun—only a fraction of a second to live . . .

Opened his eyes to see beautiful hazel ones looking into his. "You were dreaming. I couldn't wake you. You were struggling so hard. Look, you're covered in sweat. I was frightened."

"I'm okay now. Just an old familiar dream. I'm almost used to it."

"You want to talk about it?"

He shook his head. "Not now. Maybe someday." The memory of it was already fading, as it always did. His mind protected itself, perhaps knowing at some subconscious level that to dwell on the dream would destroy him. "I'm going to take a shower. Want to join me?"

PERHAPS, he thought later, it was the dream that caused him to more seriously consider what she had proposed. Would it be so bad? True, he would be a deserter, but there were any number of those. Sweden and Canada were full of them. He doubted they would look for him for long. If he played it cool, didn't draw attention to himself, he could last for a long time. Perhaps forever. Certainly until the war ended. He had no real desire to go back to the States and be spat upon again. Australia wouldn't be so bad. People here still seemed to like Americans. Frenchy had said she had enough money to support them. He would consider it to be a loan, and when he got a job he could pay her back. He wondered where the money came from. Her job at the ad agency, from what she had told him of it, didn't pay all that well. Perhaps there was some family money. He would ask about it. For a time he sat and fantasized about life without war. It was hard to imagine.

They had another wonderful week. Went to the zoo, where he had a koala try to climb up his leg. They had sharp claws. Met a fading English movie star at one of the bars. Sat entranced as he told them all the Hollywood gossip. Went to Bondi Beach, where he became the center of attraction because of his scars. At least until Frenchy tried body surfing and came up from a big wave with her bathing suit down around her ankles.

Then she told him she had another business meeting that she absolutely could not get out of.

"When?"

"Tonight."

He was irritated but tried not to show it. After all, she'd had a life before he had come along. He couldn't really ask her to abandon it. Especially now, when he was considering becoming a full part of that life.

"I'm very sorry," she said. "I know it's our last week together, and I want to spend as much time with you as possible, but I'll make it up to you, I promise."

"I wanted to talk to you about that. I've been giving a lot of thought to what you said. We'll talk about it when you get back. Now, get out of here before I don't let you go, and you get fired."

That night he was again assailed by doubts. He was ready to change his entire life for her, give up all that defined him. Yet he knew so little about her. He had told her so much about himself, and she had told him so little of substance. He knew that she'd had an active life before him, that much was obvious. Early on in the month, in a fit of false nobility, he had told her that he would understand if there were other men. He told himself that he was being quite worldly, that he was showing a remarkable degree of maturity. That she was a passionate woman with needs that he would not be able to satisfy when he was away, and that he did not want her to feel guilty.

Now he cursed himself for that little speech. Had she taken it to mean that she was free to go out and sleep with someone at whim? He had not meant that, not meant it at all. And if he admitted the truth, as he was now belatedly doing, he did not want her to do it while he was gone either. Call it selfish, he told himself, call it unreasonable, so be it. It tore at his stomach to think of her with someone else. He was cursed with a vivid imagination. Now it took hold. Was she with someone else right now? Perhaps keeping up an old relationship, one that she could return to while he was gone? The excuse of the business meeting was pretty flimsy, if you just thought about it.

He did not have to worry about the dream that night. He slept not at all.

He resolved to confront her when she came back the next day. But when she came in the door she was already stripping her clothes off, telling him how much she had missed him, pushing him down on the bed and loving him with a frenzy that washed his doubts away.

For a while.

They slept, woke, made love again. Finally she said, "Enough! You're insatiable. I need a break. Let's go out to dinner, perhaps a little dancing, then we can come back here. How about it, you horny bastard? Bring that lovely tool of yours to the shower, and we'll get it all clean. And perhaps, if you're a very good boy, I'll give you something special."

The meal was superb, the wine better than it should have been. One bottle didn't seem enough, so there was another. The band seemed to play only the right songs. They held each other close, swaying to the music. "I missed you last night," he said.

"Mmmm, and I you. I hate to be away from you."

"Where did you go?"

"Oh, you know, to a hotel. Had meetings, then dinner, then more meetings. Then to bed."

"Alone?"

She stiffened in his arms. "What do you mean?"

"I mean, is there someone else?"

She pulled away, a shocked look on her face.

"Look," he said, "I can handle it, okay? I know you've had a pretty active life before I came along. I've suspected that I wasn't the only one in your life. I mean, come on! All-night business meetings? I can't lie to you and say I don't care; I do. Very much, and I'm jealous. But what's really important is, how much does he mean to you? Do you love him? Because if you do, I'll step away and quit bothering you. I just need to know." She had not yet said anything, a look of anger melting away into sadness. He took this to mean that his conjecture had been right. His heart was being ripped out.

She refused to look him in the eyes. "No," she finally whispered. "He means nothing to me at all."

He wondered if his meal was going to stay down. "Then why?" he demanded. "Why would you see someone who means nothing to you? Why take part of the little time we have left together to see him? You tell me you love me, and then this. Why?" His throat was constricted, he couldn't trust himself to say more, aware that he was dangerously close to tears.

"Oh, James, you really don't realize what's going on, do you? For someone who has gone through so much you are incredibly naive. I thought you knew. The night you told me it would be all right if I saw other men, I thought you knew."

"Knew what?" he asked. "I've wished a thousand times that I could take those words back. What I thought I was saying was that I realized you would be seeing someone else when we weren't together, though I was hoping you wouldn't. I sure as hell was not saying that it would be okay while we were together."

"You still don't see it, do you?" Her voice was hard and pitiless. "I thought you had to know. James, don't you realize I'm a pro?"

His mind skittered away from what he was hearing, refusing to acknowledge the words. Finally, stupidly, he asked, "A pro? What do you mean, a pro?"

She shook her head in exasperation. "God, how can I be more clear? I mean that occasionally, not very often, I have dates with very nice, older, very wealthy gentlemen. And they give me lots of money for making them feel good. I'm very good at making them feel good. How did you think I was going to get the money to support us? As an advertising copywriter? Shit, I barely make enough money there to pay for my clothes. Didn't you know? How could you not have known?"

He felt empty, drained of emotion. He thought he should feel angry, or hurt, or embarrassed, but felt nothing at all.

"Say something," she pleaded. "Don't just look at me with that horrible dead stare. Call me a whore, hit me, but say something. I can't stand this."

With a visible effort he pulled himself together. "I guess

I've been pretty stupid," he said. "We need to talk. And I don't think this is the place to do it. Shall we go?"

They made it to the parking lot before it hit him. The embarrassment of being so well and truly fooled. And the rage; ah, yes, the rage. Choking him, suffusing every tissue with uncontrollable energy. Energy that had to be released somehow. Else someone would die. His arm whipped around almost of its own volition, smashing forward, obliterating her reflection in the side window of an automobile in a million shards of glass. As soon as it had come, the rage vanished, leaving him staring at his rapidly swelling knuckles.

She was looking at him with such a look of sorrow and hurt that he wanted to take her into his arms, comfort her, pretend that this had all been a nasty dream. Instead he sat down heavily on the curb, cradled his shattered hand, asked, "You want to tell me about this?"

She sat beside him. "You don't know what it's like being a woman," she said. "Especially an attractive one who wants, or wanted, to work in a man's world. Oh, I could have been a secretary, or nurse, or any of the other 'traditional' female roles. But I have a brain. I was foolish enough to think that was enough. So I went to college, and my professors let it be known in no uncertain terms that if I really wanted to do well, all I would have to do was 'be nice' to them. Oh, they weren't so crude as to say that I'd have to fuck them for a grade, but that's what they meant. But I said no, I have a brain, I'll do this on my own. And I studied, and I worked, and I was better than any man there. And I got my good grades. But not as good as the men. I got no awards, no recognition. When I asked about it, I was told that the men would need it, I wouldn't. They'd have to compete in the workplace, I'd soon have someone to support me.

"But, I told myself, that's just academia. Old fossils, out of touch with reality and a changing world. Business would be different. If I was good enough to contribute to the success of the firm, they'd recognize my worth.

"My first boss waited for almost a month before he cornered me in the office one night while we were working late. He tried to rape me. This very intelligent man, this man I admired so much because of what I had seen of his business sense, this man with whom I might have slept if we had not been working together! I finally beat him off with a stapler.

"And went looking for a new job the next day. It didn't take me long to find one.

"The next boss wasn't as crude as the first. He never came right out and said it, but it was made clear that if I wanted to go very far, I'd have to sleep with him. I lasted two years there, and when I left I had the same position in which I'd started.

"My next job was with a very successful older gentleman. He owned his own agency and was always picking off clients from the larger agencies. Nobody could understand it.

"And he was very nice to me. Never pushed, never suggested. Gave me interesting projects, the occasional raise. I thought, my God, I've finally made it. I won't have to sleep my way to the top. And realizing that, I decided I did want to sleep with him. He was nice, and polite, and attractive, and I wanted to thank him. I maneuvered him into inviting me to dinner.

"We dined in the finest restaurant in the city. Then when he invited me to his apartment, I said, why not?

"We spent the night. I enjoyed it. He was very attentive, and I wanted to make him feel good. He told me that he had wanted me from the moment I walked in for the interview. Told me that I had a very special talent. That I shouldn't waste that talent.

"He took me home the next morning. As he was letting me off, he kissed me and handed me an envelope. I went up to my flat and put it on the table and looked at it for a long time. Finally, later that afternoon, I opened it. It contained five hundred dollars in cash and a thank-you note. To the effect that it was simply a gift, and that I should think of it as nothing else.

"At first I was insulted. I wanted to take the money and throw it in his face. Tell him to take the job and stick it up his hairy arse.

"Then I felt hurt. I had gone to bed with him because I wanted to, not because I wanted anything from him. What must he think of me? Had I acted like a whore?

"In the end, I think it was the exhaustion that got to me. I was tired, tired to the bone of trying to make it in a man's world. What had it gotten me? A low-paying job with little chance of advancement. A bunch of horny men who, if I wouldn't fuck them, would make sure that I didn't get very far. Oh, I had heard the stories they told. That I was a troublemaker. Couldn't accept authority. My name was becoming poison in the industry. If I quit this job, I could forget about ever working in the field again. Four years of college, four more years of work experience, all down the drain. And for what?

"So I thought, why not? It was what they wanted of me. Wouldn't rest until they got it. So I would give it to them, but by God I would make them pay for it. I'd use what had been given to me, what had turned out to be a curse, and I'd use it well.

"Nigel, my boss, was very glad to see that I'd finally come to my senses, as he put it. Once a week we'd go to his flat and there would be the envelope in the morning. It was easy, and became easier with each time. I wondered why I'd resisted so long. Surely this was easier than beating my head against the wall of the bloody male establishment day after day.

"So when Nigel told me he had an extremely important client coming in from the States, and that he'd like me to escort this man around town, I didn't think it was so bad. He said there was no one else he could trust, and that this account would put him into the big time, and that if I helped I'd share in the good fortune. He needn't have given me such a hard sell.

"I met the gentleman in his suite in the best hotel in Sydney. He was very nice, and I liked him. He was very considerate. Bought me jewelry, a new watch. He was very rich; spending a thousand dollars was to him as spending ten is to me.

"Since then I've managed to build up quite a decent bank account. I haven't progressed very far in my other career, true, but I really don't care anymore. It's a very easy life, I don't go with many men, one per week at the most. And I make more money than any woman, and most men, that I know."

She was silent for a few moments. Finally she said, "And now I suppose you hate me?"

He shook his head. "No, I don't hate you. I don't suppose I can hate you, else I might. What I am is very, very sorry."

"Don't feel sorry for me," she shouted, suddenly very angry. "Can't you see, I've won. I'm using them, using them quite thoroughly and getting paid for it."

"You haven't won anything at all. Money means nothing to them. They find it easy to give away. Especially when it gives them power. And power is what they have over you. Power to command your body, to make you do the things they want. How could I hate you when you and I are very much the same? They own me just as surely as they do you. We're possessions, to be used as they see fit. Aren't we a pair! The assassin and the whore. In a way, I guess we're both whores. Only difference being that when I fuck someone, they stay fucked. No, I don't hate you. Strange as it may sound, I still love you. I was ready tonight to tell you that I'd changed my mind. That I'd stay here with you. Amazing how things can change in just a couple of hours."

She looked stricken. "Why does that have to change? Is what I've done so awful? Any more awful than what you've done?"

"Are you prepared to give it up?"

She lowered her head, was silent.

"I didn't think so. Let me see if I've got this right. The money you said you had to support us came from this. Without that, there wouldn't be enough. Is that right?"

"Is that so terrible? I've told you that it doesn't bother me. Why should it bother you? It means nothing. It's just my body, not me. It's not that often anyway."

"Now it's your turn to not understand. Can't you see what that would do to me, to us? I'd hate it, couldn't stand it, knowing you were out there with someone else just so I could go on being with you. And I'd take it out on you. And soon we'd hate each other. I can't live like that, and I think you know it."

"So you'll go back to not living at all. To surviving from moment to moment, doing something you hate. Until you meet someone who is as good or better than you. Or just more lucky. Is that any better?"

"Perhaps not better. But inevitable. It's all I can do. I can't do what you want."

"Then there's no chance for us?"

"Afraid not."

"Then we'd best enjoy what little time we have left."

The last precious days they spoke no more of things serious. They shut out the world and its ugliness, glorying in one another, in pleasure taken from a love that had no chance. It was as if they were newborn, with no past to cast its shadow upon them. There was no future, so there could be no past. There was only the now. On the last day, when she saw him board the plane, she cried not at all.

CHAPTER 12

"I think we're in pretty good shape," were Roger's first words to him. "We spread some money around, paid off several high-ranking bonzes, put out the story that the kids had been kidnapped by the V.C. and that it was just an unfortunate occurrence that they were in the kill zone just when you attacked. My sources tell me most people are buying the story."

"And did we find out what really happened?"

"Probably pretty much like the story, except we doubt that the V.C. kidnapped the kids. More likely it was someone on our side. If I've guessed right, the kids were supposed to be the only ones in those huts when you attacked, but you got there a little sooner than they expected. I figure they probably planned two ambushes. First one would have been right after you shot up the huts. Then if something went wrong, as it did, they'd ambush you on the way back, somewhere close to the pickup zone, so they'd know where to hit you."

"And do we know who on our side did it?"

"No. Whoever it was covered his tracks pretty well. But we'll find out, sooner or later. Of course you realize that means you're going to have to watch yourself. If he tried once, the likelihood is that he'll try again."

"What a cheerful thought! You guys don't expect much, do you?"

"Nothing more than we figure you can do. You were the one who wanted to go back to Hue. Changed your mind?"

"Fuck you. I can't wait. Go back out and get my ass shot at in the field, and come back in and wait to get it shot by our own side. Sounds like a hell of a lot of fun. Wouldn't miss it for the world. How is Al, by the way? He healed up yet?"

"Pretty well. I guess his leg still bothers him a little. Keeps opening up at the scar. But you can't keep him out of the field. He's out on operation now. Another joint op. Had a hell of a time talking him into it."

"I can imagine, after the last episode. Glad there aren't any Koreans in Thua Thien. The American troops are bad enough."

"Speaking of which, the 1st Brigade commander of the 101st sends his compliments. Seems that a battalion of North Vietnamese troops just got their clocks cleaned. They'd just come down the trail, crossed over into the province. Couldn't find any trail watchers, no guides, nobody. They were lost for three days, wandered around until they ran into the 1st Brigade. Survivors say they just couldn't understand why there was nobody to meet them. They'd been promised before they left that all the people down here would welcome them with open arms."

"You figure that's because of what we did?"

"I know it is. People are giving themselves up right and left. When you ask them why, they say they don't want to die in their sleep like so many of their comrades did. Lots of low-level people weren't that motivated anyway, just stayed in the movement because they were afraid not to. Now we're hitting them double; they're more scared to stay in, and the people who threatened them if they fell out aren't around anymore."

"Nice to know we're appreciated."

"More than you know. Now for the bad news. We've been getting rumors that the NVA know and appreciate what you're doing too. And they want to do something about it. So they've sent for a special team to come up here. One that's had a lot of success in the past, especially down in III Corps. Guess who they're going to be looking for? Rumor also has it that there's a price on yours and Al's heads."

"How much?"

"Ten thousand dollars on you, eight on Al."

"That probably pisses him off."

Roger smiled. "Very much so. He wanted to know what he was doing wrong." He grew serious again. "So you're really going to have to watch your ass now. Whoever set you up for the last one is still out there, and it looks like you'll have not only a professional hit team but everybody else who wants to make a little money, gunning for you."

"We have any more information on this team?"

"Only that they've been very successful. Started out in '63, killed a couple of S.F. captains and a sergeant in an ambush." He started to go on, then saw that his words had made a visible effect on Jim. The young man's face looked haunted, drained of blood. "What's wrong?"

Jim found himself shaking, his insides so tightly clamped it felt like his heart was being squeezed. He said nothing for a couple of moments, not trusting his voice. Finally he said, "I think I've met these guys before." He told Roger of the day long ago. He did not tell him of the dreams.

"Shit," Roger swore. "Glad I don't particularly believe in fate. Because if I did, I'd be even more worried."

Jim assayed a smile. He wondered if it looked as weak as it felt. "In a way there's a little advantage in it," he said. "Because if they are the same people, I'll sure as hell recognize them. And they can't know that. So if you hear of me gunning someone down in the street, you'll know why."

"Just make sure you get the right ones. Which is the other bad news. There are some rumblings from Saigon about you. That you may be just a little too aggressive. I've had to field a couple of inquiries from Moira Culpepper already. On behalf of her boss, she says. I wonder about that."

"Now, that really pisses me off! Everything else you've told me I can deal with. What the fuck do they expect anyway? Some clean little war, where nobody gets hurt, and everybody goes home with a bunch of medals and some wonderful stories? God save me from my friends! The enemies I can deal with myself."

"Well, now that I've given you a proper welcome back, how was Australia? Come on, let's have a beer."

THE woman in question was at that moment briefing her boss. He'd looked even worse than usual when he came in that morning. Too many Scotches with his French friends, she suspected. The greenish alcoholic pallor was beginning to show through his tennis tan. But at least he wasn't bothering her too much now. The last time he was in her room he had failed miserably to function, and it had affected his attitude toward her. Perhaps because for the first time she had not bothered to hide her contempt for him.

"Captain Carmichael returns to duty today," she said. "Apparently fully healed and ready to go. McMurdock, despite your wishes, intends to send him back to Hue. He should be back there by tomorrow."

Eliot Danforth swore horribly. "One of these days," he vowed, "Roger is going to fail, and I'm going to make sure when he does the right people know about it. I've had it with his operating as if he's a law unto himself. He wouldn't have gotten away with it the way he has so far if he didn't have friends from the old days sitting at the top."

And if he wasn't so good at what he does, Moira thought, but did not say. McMurdock had shown no inclination to help her career, so she had no intention of standing up for him.

"Carmichael is a loose cannon," Danforth continued. "He stands a good chance of blowing some very sensitive operations in that area. We can't let that happen. Do we have any more word about the team that's supposed to be going up that way?"

Moira frowned, consulted her notes, though she knew them by heart. She had learned not to have all the answers at her fingertips. It scared people, made them worry for their jobs. Best that they didn't worry, until it was too late. "Yes, here it is," she said. "We're getting some very good information from III Corps these days, far better than from anywhere else in the country. The new man there is doing a very good job."

Danforth sniffed disdainfully. "Yes, I've heard. Former Army CID, isn't he?" By his manner of speaking he fully conveyed the contempt the career CIA men had for anyone who did not share their Ivy League upbringing. Moira had no doubt that the new man in III Corps would not have a long and profitable career in the Agency, no matter how good he did and how much intelligence he produced.

"The team appears to have departed their base in the Ho Bo Woods, crossed back into Cambodia and are headed up the trail toward the north. The agent who reported this indicated that they said they had an important mission, and had been told by COSVN, the Central Office of South Vietnam, that they had to accomplish it at all costs. The commander didn't seem to think that it would be much of a problem, and told the agent he'd be back within three months. So that should give our people at least an approximate time frame as to when to expect them. Would you like me to send the wire?''

''No,'' he said without hesitation. ''Not just yet. Plenty of time, isn't there? After all, it's a long walk to Thua Thien. If we send it now, there's too much chance the information will leak, thus jeopardizing our information sources.''

Moira was speechless. The audacity of the man! His reasoning was, of course, ridiculous. There were ways of passing the information which would ensure that it could never fall into the wrong hands. He was allowing the V.C. assassination team a clear shot at Jim Carmichael. She had no doubt that, if she were to ask again in a month if it was time to let him know of the danger, she would be put off with an equally specious reason. It was breathtaking in its callousness. By refusing to pass on information, with a reason he could later justify, he was very possibly condemning one of his own men to death. It would get rid of an irritant, protect an ongoing operation and serve as a warning to Roger McMurdock. She hadn't thought he still had it in him. She felt a sudden surge of desire. Perhaps she had been wrong to dismiss him so quickly. There were so many things he could still teach her. She moved around the table and stood behind him, softly massaging his neck.

''I'M putting two people with you,'' said Vanh. ''They are to be trusted. Not like that dog Quanh, who if he hadn't died in the ambush I would have killed.''

''You figure he's the one who set us up?''

''No doubt of it. We went through his things. He had money, much money. And documents. Methods of contacting his handler. We tried to establish contact, but they obviously already knew he was dead.''

''And you think he was the only one?''

Vanh smiled. In his face Jim read the bitterness of one who knew all too well that no one could really be trusted, that anyone could be your enemy in a war that had gone on far too long and made people change sides with the wind. ''I trust only myself. And you. And the people I will put with you. One is my brother. The other is my uncle. You are in much danger, Jim.''

"And you?"

"I, too, I suppose. But I am always surrounded by my PRU. I go nowhere alone. But many times I have seen you go out by yourself. You cannot do that anymore."

"There will be times when I must," Jim said. "But I will keep them to a minimum. I accept your offer. How did you like the hospital, by the way?"

Vanh smiled again, and this time the smile was genuine. "The Germans were very kind," he said. "I am grateful that Roger made it possible for me to be there. I have had the malaria for a long time, but I was afraid to go to one of our hospitals. One goes in there and all too often does not come out."

"Good. Now, what do we have going?"

For the next few minutes they went over the current intelligence, which was, as usual, sparse.

"Christ!" Jim exploded, exasperated by the prospect of once again having to operate blind. "What the hell do the people at the PIOCC do? We haven't gotten anything we could use out of them since I've been in country."

"Since long before that, I'm afraid. There is no organization there, no one who knows how to set up an intelligence net, no sources, no agents. I am a simple soldier, yet I know what they do not. That if you wish to know about the enemy, you must have someone within the enemy ranks. And they have none. But the enemy seems to have no problem. They always know what we are doing."

"Well, shit. Looks like we'll have to do it ourselves again. Any ideas?"

"We hear that the enemy is replacing the ones we took away. But they are not Viet Cong, they are North Vietnamese. The Northerners say that there are not enough experienced ones in the ranks of the V.C., that too many of the cadre have been killed. The ones they send are inexperienced with the ways of the South. It is creating problems. The people of the South do not like the newcomers. They are afraid, they say that the Northerners do not care about the needs of the people, that they are only interested in the victory of the NVA and that they will sacrifice anyone to make sure that happens. And the Northerners say that the V.C. are lazy, that they are not sufficiently motivated. And that they are not grateful enough for the sacrifices the North has made. The Chieu Hoi center is full of former V.C. who have grown tired of it. But the people of the PIOCC only interrogate them for information of immediate military value.''

"And you think they could be made use of?''

"Yes. I think that they can be turned.''

Jim looked doubtful. "I don't know," he said. "Just because they're tired of war, and pissed off at the NVA, doesn't mean that they'd betray their friends.''

"If they were Westerners, no. But that is one thing that you do not understand about us. You have individual loyalties. Even if you stop believing in a cause, you still believe in the friends you left behind. For us it is different. When a Vietnamese stops believing in a cause, he stops believing in anything that goes with it. Yes, they will cooperate. They have already made the first step, by turning themselves in. Now they must support us, because if the other side wins, they will be the first ones to be executed as traitors. So they must make sure the other side does not win. We can use them.''

"So let's do it. Why haven't you started already?''

"Not that easy. The officials at the Chieu Hoi center do not wish to let us have access. They say that they are afraid of what we will do. That many of these people have been responsible for many crimes, and that we will kill them. But the real reason is that they are, as you say in English, shaking them down. The longer they hold them, the more they can charge their families to get them out. Many people are making much money this way.''

"Time for some more pressure on the province chief?''

"I think it will be the only way. But it is dangerous. He also is one of those who profit. And I think that he will be very angry to be challenged again.''

"One more to add to the list," Jim said. "We're going to be real popular guys. I hope the people you're putting with me are good. They may have to earn their money.''

THE province chief, after Jim's departure from his office the next day, let rage suffuse him, dangerously raising his blood pressure, reddening his face, bulging his eyes. He stormed through the office, kicking over his trash can, screaming, swearing terrible oaths. When his secretary rushed in to see what was the matter, he was met with a stream of abuse and rushed out again. The colonel had an overwhelming urge to hit something, anything, preferably something that could feel it. Nothing was immediately at hand. He stared wildly about, eyes finally alighting on a framed picture of himself and the former Vice President of the United States, taken during that personage's visit to the country. The bland Minnesota politician's face particularly infuriated him this day: so self-righteous, so sure that the "American Way" was best. He snatched the picture from the wall and smashed it to the floor, taking great pleasure in grinding his heel into the face, obliterating it as he would have liked to do to Captain Carmichael. He felt much better afterward.

He sat back down, fury expended, and attempted to achieve the equanimity his religion held in so much esteem. It would not come. Something would have to be done about the PRU. He did not know what. Captain Carmichael had left no doubt that if something happened to him, the information he had on the colonel's illegal dealing would go to those who could do the most damage. Was the young American foolish enough to keep the information near him, perhaps in his quarters? Sadly, he realized it was unlikely. He felt helpless. And that angered him again. He was worried about what the American, and by extension, the PRU, would find out from the Chieu Hois. Frantically he racked his mind. Who was in the center now? He couldn't think of anyone important. Lots of small fry, but it would take more of an effort and more knowledge than the American had to piece together the whole thing from them. If anyone important came in, they would be taken care of. There were secrets which must be guarded at all costs.

He finally came to the conclusion that there was nothing he could do. Now. But sooner or later the American would make a mistake. The colonel took the long view, something that he knew was foreign to the Westerners. If you waited long enough, opportunity would arise. You just had to be smart enough to recognize that opportunity and take advantage of it. And he was very smart.

THE first "recruits" from the Chieu Hoi center were understandably nervous. They knew the PRU; for many of them it was the primary reason they had regrouped to the government. The death that came in the middle of the night had visited a little too often those whom they knew and worked with, and they had known that sooner or later it would visit them too. So to be taken out of the center, which, despite the bad food and lack of amenities, was better than what they had experienced in the jungle, and by the American they knew to be the driving force behind the killers, was a terrifying experience. They fully expected to be driven away to an isolated place, probably tortured, almost certainly killed. Thus it was an even greater shock to be put into a nice villa, fed well, given conjugal visit privileges and treated better than they had ever been in their lives. It softened them for the approach.

The questions came, but they were offhand, almost casual. They came in conversations in which the interrogators compared their experiences in the war with those of their V.C. counterparts. How did you survive, during those times when we were so close that you could not have had time to rest, eat or sleep? Where did you go during the bombings? You must have been very strong to stay dedicated so long. Who were your inspirations? The political officers, you say? What were their names? Do you know where they are now? Slowly, almost imperceptibly, they found themselves talking more and more with the men they had so feared, but now found were so much like themselves.

And slowly the intelligence grew. Items gathered from one person were cross-checked with others. Bits gathered from various sources allowed the PRU to piece together a picture of operations and personalities that, while it would never be whole, was much more clear than anything theretofore available. The more they knew, the easier it was to find out more. Now they knew what questions to ask, could confront a liar with the truth, could show the one being questioned that they already knew what he knew, so why should he hide anything?

Vanh and Carmichael had agreed that they would take a break from operations until the intelligence operation was fully under way. Neither wished to work blind again, and both wanted to make sure that no disasters such as the one which had come so close to claiming their lives happened again.

Besides, it was a full-time job just staying alive.

• • •

THE first attempt at Jim came when he had been back in Hue for less than a week.

He'd intended to go and visit the Indian, had dismissed his bodyguards, much to their displeasure. He figured that it was safe enough; the assassination team from III Corps could not have had time enough to get there.

Still, he remained alert. There were few danger zones between the Embassy House and downtown where the Indian kept his shop, but who could tell what was really a danger zone anymore? He pulled out of the gate, satisfied to see that the guards were still doing the procedures he had taught them. One man opened the gate, the other took up position in the road to stop traffic. He pulled out, carefully looking both ways, trying to sense anything out of place. Nothing. Satisfied, he accelerated, moved in and out of the sparse traffic, turned left on the main road leading into the city. On both sides were friendly installations. He waved to the Special Branch advisor, who was in the courtyard supervising training. An over-the-hill former L.A. cop who loved his booze, he still brought street smarts and hard-nosed realism to his job. Jim had spent a couple of nights talking to him in the MACV bar, and had liked the cynical attitude and profane manner of expressing himself. And his cop stories were great, funny and sad all at the same time.

Just beyond the compound was the double-span suspension bridge across the Perfume River. It was jammed, as usual; military vehicles of all sizes from giant gasoline tankers to jeeps jammed cheek by jowl with bullock carts, three-wheel cyclos, motorcycles of all types, pedestrians. Beneath the bridge, which always seemed to be groaning with the weight, the broad brown river flowed, carrying its own cargo of sampans, fishing boats, trash, logs, dead fish and the occasional body.

To Jim this was the only real danger area, and he didn't feel good about joining the crush. But unless you intended to swim, this was the way you went downtown.

He heard the popping of the 50cc Honda coming up on his left. Nothing strange about that: the small motorcycles threaded their way in and out of the traffic all the time. It was the fastest way to travel. Except perhaps walking. Still, caution made him reach over and adjust the rearview. Two young men on it, approaching from his left rear. Nothing strange there either: few motorcycles carried only the driver. He had seen them loaded down with entire families and a pig.

He saw the one on the rear reach into his jacket just as the cycle approached the rear bumper. Shit! No way to escape by vehicle, he was thoroughly jammed in. Danger! his nerves screamed, even as he threw himself to the side across the other seat, scrabbling for his gun. It was under him, squeezed between his waist and the seat. His legs were kicking, vainly trying to push him out of the way of danger.

The first round shattered the windshield, in front of where his head had just been. The second went into the seat, hitting the top brace and whining away crazily. The third was slightly lower, punching out cushion material, the heat from the round causing it to smolder. He twisted, finally got the gun free, sent the first round over the head of the driver just as they came even with the front of the seat.

The driver jerked away, spoiling the aim of the shooter. The fourth round hit in the dashboard, shattering gauges and showering glass and metal all over Jim. He fired back, totally missing. The man's face was clear over the sights of the gun, nervous, scared, concentrating and trying to hit him, registering surprise when none of the bullets scored.

Then they were by, and he was trying to get up, his body refusing to act properly. He was trembling, unable to reload the pistol, thinking in some recess of his mind that he could not believe that he had fired fourteen rounds of 9mm and had done nothing but punch holes in the air. Finally he got reflexes and muscles able to react in some sort of coordinated way, braced himself across the hood of the jeep, and shot again and again at their receding backs. The bullets were whanging off vehicles, ricocheting crazily, striking great showers of sparks off the bridge members. People were screaming, crawling, trying to get themselves under anything available. His hands were shaking uncontrollably, the barrel wavered, but still he fired on the off chance one of the rounds would connect. The heavier crack of a rifle sounded over his head, scaring the driver, who veered to the side. And hit the rear bumper of a truck, shooting the cycle and both riders off the side of the bridge like a rock from a slingshot. Out in a graceful arc, the driver staying with the bike as if he expected to land on the surface of the river and drive away. The rider kicked away, tucked, hit the river with somewhat less of a splash.

The police advisor ran by Jim, stationed himself at a bridge stanchion, aimed his M-16 down at the splashes, fired off a magazine. The bullets pocked the water. He reloaded, waited. By this time Jim had gotten enough control of himself to run to his side. Just in time to see him grunt in satisfaction, aim carefully and fire again. Jim looked down to see a body disappearing, blood mixing with the brown water. They waited for the other one, but he never came up. "Didn't think he would," said the advisor. "He rode that cycle right to the bottom."

"Thanks, man," Jim said. He was trying to get his pistol back into the holster, missed it twice. The advisor gently took it from him, engaged the safety and tucked it in place.

"Don't mention it," he said. "Looked like you could use some help. Shit, don't think I've run that fast since I was a rookie chasing purse snatchers. You got any idea who they were?"

Jim shook his head. He was still trembling. "No idea. Somebody who wanted to collect a pile of money, I guess."

"Yeah. Heard you had a price on your head."

"Let's get the fuck out of here before somebody else gets another bright idea." They could hear the sirens of the Quanh Canh approaching. "I'm not in the mood to answer a lot of questions right now. Think we can get the jeep out of here?"

"Jim, I don't know much, but I do know that jeep is broke." The bullets had shattered much of the instrument panel, punched through the transmission, hit the engine at least twice. They had hit, it seemed, everywhere except where he had been. Grease dripped on the bridge and flowed out around their boots.

"You may be right, Billy. I'll send somebody back for it. Let's go to your place. I feel a need for something very strong and very wet."

"Good idea. You get the shit shot out of your jeep, you expend over twenty rounds without hitting a fucking thing, you scare the hell out of about a thousand people on the bridge. Not a bad morning. I'd better get you drunk and put you to bed. I don't think this town can take an afternoon of you. What'll you do for an encore? Blow down a building or two?"

"Fuck you, Billy. Fuck you very much."

CHAPTER 13

"You find out who they were yet?" he asked Vanh later.

"No one special," Vanh answered. "No known V.C. connections. One was a deserter from the army. The other was sixteen years old. Both had criminal records—petty thievery, shakedowns. Looks like they were just two cowboys who wanted to cash in on the reward."

"Wonderful. Damned near did too."

"If you'd had the bodyguards . . ."

"Please don't say it. I know I screwed up. You haven't seen me go anywhere without them lately, have you?"

Vanh smiled. "It seems that even you can learn."

He finally got to the Indian's place two days later. This time he let the bodyguards accompany him, telling them to stay outside while he conducted his business. They smiled at one another when he went in. The American was not so incorruptible after all. He manipulated currency just like all the rest. It made him seem more human.

Chandragar looked pained to see him. "Please," he said, "it is not safe for you to be here. You must leave."

"You worried about my health or yours?"

"Both," the Indian admitted. "Many people want you dead. On both sides."

"Tell me all about it. And quickly! That way it'll be safer for the both of us." Jim laughed. "I'd hate to have someone throwing a grenade in here, wouldn't you?"

"You know, I'm sure, about the Communists. They are very angry and frightened. You have been far too successful, more successful than your predecessor, and you know what happened to him. They know what you are doing with the

Chieu Hois and see it as a threat. Some of those people know everything about the structure in this province. They even know some of the deep-cover people, their real names. And the Communists want to keep you from finding it out. I am told that you are one of the highest priorities for assassination, with orders being sent down directly from the North."

"No surprises there. I've heard about the hit team on its way here. Makes me feel almost famous."

"That's only part of the problem. The Buddhists are also angry. They have told your Roger McMurdock only a part of the story. It's not about the children. They seem to think that you know something else about them, something that would make the Saigon government come down even harder on them. They are very afraid, and have made contact with someone within your government asking them to remove you, or if they cannot, get rid of you. I do not know what it is that you are supposed to know, or with whom they are dealing on your side. But he is very powerful."

"Neither do I. Shit, I don't have anything on the Buddhists!"

Chandragar looked at him in such a way to clearly indicate that he did not believe him, but did not press the subject. "And," he continued, "there are people inside the Vietnamese government who would like to see you out of the way. I'm sure that comes as no surprise to you either. The things you found out from the late and unlamented major make them very nervous. They have not moved yet because it is rumored that you have insurance in the form of documents, which they cannot find, though they have searched many times. They are perhaps the most dangerous of all. I recommend to you, young Captain, that you take care to stop angering them. Sooner or later, insurance or not, they are going to come to the conclusion that you are just too troublesome to allow to live."

"Anybody in this province who isn't my enemy?"

"Only your PRUs, I think. The one who betrayed you is dead. He was killed by his own people, as an example of what happens to those who fail. And of course," he said with a smile that was a model of insincerity, "you can trust me."

"Only because you know that if I go, you go," replied Jim. "And that's the best possible kind of trust. But I think that it would be best if we did not see each other again. We'll go back to clandestine communications. I'm sure you won't mind that. Only one thing, I'm going to leave you this radio." He handed the Indian a small Motorola. "I need to know, just as soon as you know, even if it blows things, when you get word about the team from the South. Put all your people on it; drop everything else. You may think the province people are my greatest danger; I don't. I want to know about that team, do you understand!" His face was very close to Chandragar's. His eyes held a haunted look. He did not bother to explain why it was so important. His look convinced the man that it was.

So you are finally afraid, Chandragar mused after he left. Good! Now you can begin to understand what we have lived with for so many years. Every man's hand turned against you, living only because you were useful and because you became adept at deflecting the threat to someone else. Now you will know what it is like to wake in the night to the slightest noise, knowing that it could be the last sound you ever hear. Know the agonies of the imagination, neck tingling, feeling the garotte. It was in many ways worse than dying. If you were dead, these things could not bother you, you would at last find peace. Perhaps that was why so many did not survive; they found it easier to perish than to live with the fear.

Do I feel sympathy with him? Yes. The arrogance of the Westerner was gone. He was a man. A young and frightened man. I will do as he says. It would be easier to let him perish, and yet I will not. Would he be grateful if he knew? Probably not. He would just say it was being done to save my own hide. No matter. He chuckled softly. I must be getting old— and soft.

HE wasn't satisfied with the new jeep. It hadn't been modified to his specifications. His old one had a locking gas cap so no one could plant incendiary devices in it. Or hand grenades with the pins removed and a rubber band holding down the spoon. The gas ate away the rubber band and *boom*! The tank was directly under the seat, a detail he'd always felt must have been designed by saboteurs. He'd also had bolts inserted through the muffler so no one could put a device up his tailpipe. The hood had been fitted with a hasp and a Yale lock. Copely had assigned his own jeep to him until the old one was repaired, and it had none of these precautions. Which was perhaps why he took more care to inspect it before he got into it and started it up. Which was also undoubtedly why he spotted the small piece of colored insulation from 24-gauge wire lying on the ground beneath the engine.

"Sonofabitch!" he cursed, scrambling to his feet and backing away from the vehicle. He looked vainly around, hoping that someone was not sitting within range with a radio transmitter on the correct frequency. He was shaking again.

"Trung Si," he yelled to the nearest guard, "keep everyone away from this jeep. You stay away too. There's a bomb in it."

The Vietnamese immediately retreated behind the nearest sandbagged bunker, peering out from around it. Not a bad idea, thought Jim. I think I'd better get the hell away from it too. He went back into the Embassy House, where his old friend Alfred Fitzwilliam was again on duty officer.

"How about calling up an EOD team," Jim requested, marveling that he could keep the quaver out of his voice. "There's a bomb in my jeep."

The young agency man looked at him in surprise and disbelief, then saw Jim was not joking. He thought the PRU advisor remarkably cool, finding a bomb in his jeep and standing there as if he didn't have a care in the world. I'd be shitting my pants, he thought.

Jim's guts were churning. What the hell is wrong with me? Shit, I've been through worse than this and it never affected me this badly before. First the attempt with the cowboys, and I was shaking so bad I couldn't shoot, and now it's all I can do to keep from throwing up. Am I losing my nerve? Is it like the guys from World War II used to say, that you can only go to the well so many times? Am I going to crap out?

"They'll be here in fifteen minutes," Fitzwilliam said, hanging up the phone. "I told them to put a rush on."

"Good. I've got a guard on it in the meantime. No use in hanging around. I'll go get some paperwork done in my room. How about letting me know when they've finished?"

He left without another word, leaving the CIA man to wonder again about his lack of emotion. He no sooner got through the door to his room than he was frantically unbuttoning his pants, making it to the stool just in time. His bowels evacuated in a flood, fouling the air with a stench that was as fetid as the fear washing through his mind. He cleaned himself, pulled up his trousers and staggered to the bed. In his mind he saw himself getting into the jeep, inserting the key, turning it. Then the split-second realization that something was very, very wrong, as the electricity rushed down the thin wires, sending a spark across a gap in the blasting cap, detonating the cap and sending the shock wave into the explosive charge, causing it to deflagrate at blinding speed, quicker than the mind could imagine. But it would go on obstinately imagining, seeing the fireball expand, forcing pieces of metal in all directions at speed exceeding that of a bullet. Pieces that would rip through him, stomach and pelvis first, cutting and slashing like tiny jagged saws. The shock wave would tear parts from his body. The flames would reduce what was left to a vaguely human-shaped cinder, hands curled up, body trying to assume the fetal position as heat-shortened tendons pulled it together. As we begin, so shall we end.

The knock at his door startled him, mercifully chased the images of his own death to the back of his brain where they would patiently wait in ambush. He tried to compose himself, ran a hand over his hair, looked to see if the hand was shaking.

"You had a real good one there," said the short, squat man who had knocked. "Sergeant Snyder, EOD. You wanna see it? Damn lucky you spotted it. How'd you do it anyway?"

Jim explained about the insulation, the sergeant shaking his head in wonder at his good fortune and acumen.

"Most people would'na known that," he said. "Lookie here. They had dual firing circuits on this baby." He hefted the tape-wrapped packet. "We took it out from in front of the fire wall. They wanted to get you, all right. Two pounds of C-4, shaped like a platter charge. Would've sent a fireball right into your gut. Had one circuit hooked into the ignition system, and another to a trembler switch. Looks like they made it from the spring from a ballpoint pen and a piece of copper wire. Had enough of a gap that it probably wouldn't have gone off when you got in the jeep. That way if something had gone wrong with the ignition circuit, the first time you hit a pothole the two wires in the trembler would have made contact, and you'd be a memory.''

"Not too much chance of this one being made by some amateur, was there?'' Jim asked. He wondered at his ability to hold it together. When all he wanted to do was scream and cry.

"Amateur? Fuck no! Whoever made this one knew what he was doing. Or she was doing. Some a these cunts are gettin' as good at making bombs as the dicks are. Nah, you got a pro here. And you're one lucky sonofabitch. Ain't you the one who got shot up in the jeep the other day? You got more lives than a fuckin' cat. Wouldn't want to be in your shoes.''

Jim thought this an amusing statement from a man who disarmed bombs for a living. The humor of it brought him back to himself. He laughed aloud.

The EOD sergeant took it as bravery, someone who didn't care what happened, a man who could defy the odds and win. He wondered what made up such a person. His own job he took as a matter of course. "You want to keep this?'' he asked, offering the device. "I've disarmed it,'' he added needlessly.

"Sure. Why not?'' He had noticed that the sergeant was wearing gloves. "Might even be able to get some prints off it. Though I can't for the life of me think of what good they'd do us. But we might get lucky. And if not, think of what a great souvenir it will be. It and fifty cents of scrip might get me a beer at the club.''

"You come around the club anytime I'm there, sir, and I'll buy you that beer. Hope you last that long.''

I hope I do too, thought Jim. I sure as hell hope I do.

"THIS is getting ridiculous!'' said Copely. Jim had been called to his office as soon as he had heard about the bomb. "I'm going to call up the ROIC and ask that you be recalled. You're becoming a danger to the entire compound.''

Why, you beer-bellied asshole, Jim thought. You could give a shit less about what happens to me, you're just afraid that one of the other people around here could get hurt in the fallout. Like yourself.

"Don't worry about it,'' he said. "I'm going to move in

with the PRU. I trust them.'' More than I do you, he thought, but did not say. Then, unable to resist the cruel twist, he added, ''Whoever did this came from the inside. One of the guards, probably, or maybe the cook, or a houseboy, or one of the girls some of your people keep bringing back here. And I don't want to be around for them to try again. Hell, they may not have been trying to get me anyway. It *was* your jeep.'' Leaving the POIC to wrestle with that thought, he walked out. In an hour he was packed and moved. Vanh gave him a cot next to his own.

FOR the next week he bunkered up, ventured outside the compound not at all, and within it very little. His requirements he communicated to Vanh or to the intelligence sergeant. At times the reasons for the requests were obvious, at others they made no sense at all. But by now Vanh knew to trust in his friend's instincts, and asked no questions. Jim worked late every night, took all his meals with the PRU, ate quickly and went right back to work.

When, during the second week, Jim continued to do the same, Vanh began to worry about him. He looked haunted, blue bags under his eyes, weight falling away from him. Vanh had grown to like and admire the American, a feeling he had never thought he would have. He did not want to see anything happen to him. And it looked as if he was going to pieces.

''My friend,'' he finally said, ''come. The PRU wish to have a celebration. It is a Vietnamese holiday, and they would be honored if you would share it with them.''

Jim frowned down at the mass of scribbling on the papers in front of him, unwilling to break concentration for even a moment. ''Tell them I appreciate it,'' he said brusquely, ''but I'm way too busy. Maybe next time, after I finish here.''

Vanh shook his head. ''No, not next time. I wish you to come now. It is important. Important for them, important for me, but most important for you. In this I must insist.''

Jim looked up in surprise, saw the look of concern in Vanh's eyes. Felt gratitude, affection for the little captain. Realized that he did want to give up, just for a little while, the project. Strange that the only person who cared whether he lived or died was this Vietnamese. And Al. Perhaps Roger, though he could not be sure. No one else.

"You win," he said, grinning, a flash of the old spirit showing on his face, heartening Vanh. "Let's go to this celebration. But if you try to get me to eat hundred-year eggs again, I'm gonna break both your legs."

"WHAT are we celebrating?" he asked, noticing that his tongue was not working well. Must have been the half bottle of Johnnie Walker, he thought.

"The liberation of our country," Vanh replied. He was smiling happily, well lubricated by the Scotch himself. "One of the many liberations. We have been fighting the outsiders for so long. The Khmer, the Chams, the Chinese many times, and the French. And we have always won. Sometimes it took hundreds of years, but we won in the end, because we knew that as long as we fought, the outsiders would inevitably grow tired, and decide that we were not worth the trouble, and would go away.

"But now," he said, and the happiness left his face, "I think we lose. Because we are not fighting against someone from the outside, but against our own brothers. Our brothers who are infected with ideas from the outside, alien ideas, ideas as foreign to our culture as the French were to our country.

"And how do you fight against ideas? How do you combat madness, for madness it is? Especially when it is an idea that, on the surface, seems to make such good sense. I too at one time was a Marxist. When I was young, at university. That is the best time to be, when one has unbounded faith in the inherent goodness of man; when one believes that people should and will work together for the betterment of mankind. 'From each according to his ability, to each according to his needs.' It's a very seductive idea, especially when all that you have seen is the gap between the rich and the poor, and how the poor seem never to be able to shake that condition.

"Then you see the reality. You see that Marxism does not change things, that there are still two classes. You have merely changed one set of oppressors for another. An ideological elite for a hereditary. And have got in the bargain an economic system which simply does not work. One in which you must suppress the natural instincts of man, usually by violence. As happened to the farmers in the North shortly after the Communists took over. As happened in Stalin's Russia, when all the kulaks were killed. You look at me in surprise that I should know such things? Like you, I am not just a simple soldier. I am a soldier because that is the only way I can attempt to keep away the horror I know is to come. But it will come, no matter what we do. You too will sooner or later grow tired of us, and will think that it is better that we be left to ourselves. A pox on both your houses, is that what one of your writers said? You will go away, and we will fall, and I will die."

"Bullshit!" Jim said. "We sure as hell aren't going to abandon you. Not now, not when we've got this much invested in you. No way the American people are going to let us lose a war. That has never, never happened, and it isn't going to happen now. Shit, you got me here to cheer me up, and now you're bringing me down. Got any more Scotch?"

Sometime later Van got up, silenced the soldiers with a shout. Speaking slowly in Vietnamese so that Jim could understand, he said, "Men of the PRU! Tonight I wish to honor those who have shown bravery in the face of the enemy, both living and dead. For the dead, who are with us in spirit, we offer prayers. And recognition. The government of South Vietnam has authorized the Cross of Gallantry with Silver Star for the following men." He read off the names and presented the medals of the operations sergeant, who would make sure they got to the families. "And for those who live, please come forward."

What we will do for a little piece of ribbon! Jim mused. Who was it—Napoleon?—who said give him enough colored ribbon and he would conquer the world? We fight for it, we die for it. Not for the ribbon itself, but for what it says about us, for the recognition we see in other men's eyes.

He was startled by the sound of his name. "For Captain James Carmichael, I am authorized by my government to give the highest award, the Cross of Gallantry with Gold Palm Leaf. Captain Carmichael has shown bravery far above what we have seen in other advisors. He has been there with us, has fought at our sides, has suffered and bled for a cause that is not his own. He is our brother and our friend. What we give him is a small thing. But soldiers know what it means. And that is enough."

It is enough indeed, Jim thought as Vanh pinned the medal to his chest. It meant more to him than the Silver Star he had been awarded by his own government. This was given by soldiers he liked and admired, not by some faceless bureaucrat. He felt tears start to his eyes. Abandon them? Never.

"I need to talk to you," he said to Vanh two days later. Vanh followed him into the small office where he had been closeted for so long. Taped to the walls were sheets of butcher paper, their surface covered with blocks connected by lines, names in most of the blocks. Other pieces of paper covered the small desk, some stacked so high they were in danger of spilling on the floor. Vanh recognized his writing on much of the material, that of his intelligence sergeant on more. The rest he could not identify. The staleness of too-often-breathed air hung about the room. It smelled of frustration.

"Help me, Dai Uy," Jim said. "I think I've put part of the puzzle together, but there's some things I don't know."

Vanh walked closer to the wall charts, read some of the names. Some he did not recognize. Others made him blanch.

"Yeh," said the American. "Pretty nasty shit here. Connections all over the place. Right here we've got the right-hand man of the chief Buddhist monk, his private secretary, cooperating with the military proselyting chief of the V.C. Meets him regularly when the man comes to the temple disguised as a monk. Over here we've got the province chief, who also talks to the secretary on a regular basis. Even got the Catholics in this. Some of them on the neutralist side don't appear to be so neutral."

"You got all this from the Chieu Hois?"

"Not all of it," Jim admitted. "I have a few other sources of my own. And I'd appreciate it if you didn't ask about them. What I don't understand is, if I could take a few days and figure all this shit out, how come nobody did before?"

Vanh did not answer, instead focusing his attention on the charts. The connections were, indeed, everywhere. Some of them confirmed long-held suspicions. Others were completely unexpected. One name stopped him short. He hoped that the surprise he felt was not reflected on his face. Why was this man here! Vanh vowed to find out.

"Perhaps they have figured it out before," he said. "And for some reason of their own have left it alone. Until they decided to use it for their own purposes. It would not be the first time, Jim, that your CIA has done things that no one else knows of. In fact, I would be surprised if someone does not already know. Someone high. Perhaps Roger McMurdock?"

That brought Jim up short. For the last few days, as the information kept pouring in from the Chieu Hoi interrogations and the reports from Chandragar, as the connections kept forming, he had been haunted by the feeling that forces were at work here that he did not and could not understand. Forces that were far above him, and more powerful than he could imagine. Roger a part of it? Couldn't be! He trusted Roger, trusted him instinctively and with perhaps unreasonable force. Still, he had to admit that it was possible. Roger was a pro. If there was a good purpose behind what he was doing, it could be that he did know, and did not trust the information to anyone else. Even someone for whom the information was vital. Whose life depended upon it.

"I don't know," he admitted. "But I intend to find out. Question is, what do we do with it? Sure as hell can't trust anyone else with it. And I don't think we can get away with pulling in most of these people for interrogation."

"How about the proselyting chief? He's V.C., been on the blacklist for a long time. A big target. And one that shouldn't be too hard to hit. We wait until he comes back in for a meeting, pull him in, talk to him, find out what's going on."

"Good idea," Jim said. "We're going to have to keep it damn quiet, though. Don't think we should bring him here. If this is what it appears to be, we don't stand a snowball's chance in hell of keeping him for more than a couple of hours."

"I'll set it up. I have a house outside the city no one knows about. We'll use only a few of the most trusted PRUs. We'll keep him until we get what we want, then decide what to do from there. You know that we may have to kill him afterward?"

Jim shrugged. Such deaths bothered him far less than they formerly did. He hardly wondered at his callousness. "If that's the way it is, then that's the way it is. Let's worry about getting him first.''

        ''DAI UY,'' said the PRU soldier, ''you have visitor.''

Jim shook the sleep from his eyes. After leaving Vanh to study the materials in the room, cautioning him to make sure to lock it up after he left, he had come to his cot and flopped down for a much-needed sleep. It seemed that he had just closed his eyes, though looking out the window at the setting sun, he realized several hours had passed.

''May I come in?'' asked Alfred Fitzwilliam. He was at the door, the PRU soldier standing suspicious guard.

''It's okay, Tu,'' he said. ''Come on in, Fitz. What can I do for you?''

''I brought over your mail,'' the young CIA man said. ''Thought you might like to have it. Didn't figure you'd come back to the compound to get it.''

''Thanks. I appreciate it. How are things going?''

''Much more quietly. No more bombs, no shootings. Boring, in fact.'' Fitzwilliam smiled. ''Copely is much more happy. Some of the rest of us aren't.''

Jim looked at him in surprise. He had been going through the envelopes, seeing one from Lisa, and another from a name he did not recognize in Australia.

''I just wanted to tell you,'' Fitzwilliam continued, ''that some of us think it's pretty shitty, Copely being so fucking scared that you have to live over here. Not much we can do about it, but we did want you to know. And that if there's anything we can do for you, please let me know.''

''Thanks.'' He was genuinely touched. There was little they could do, but the offer was appreciated. In fact, since he'd had time to think about it, he was just as happy he'd moved out. He was a danger to the other Americans, and they were very little help to him. He didn't want to die, but he wanted even less to die and have innocent bystanders killed because of someone's determination to get to him.

''Just wanted you to know,'' said the CIA man, ''we appreciated the training you gave us. We're still the amateurs you called us, but maybe a little bit less so now. Anyway, I'll keep up with your mail for you.'' He turned to leave.

"You guys take care of yourselves. Maybe you aren't the shitheads I thought you were."

Fitzwilliam turned at the door, smiled. "Nobody is the shithead you thought we were," he said. "Except maybe Copely. We're just a bunch of people with very little useful training, no experience in this sort of thing, no guidance as to what to do, trying to muddle our way through and even do some good, if we can. Not that we get much of a chance for that." He left.

He turned the letter from Australia over in his hands several times, a sense of foreboding making him reluctant to open it. Wondered if he should take a drink first to fortify himself. Cursed himself for being so weak as to seriously consider it. Thought that he would first read the letter from Lisa.

I know I said that I would wait for you. But something has happened. I have met a man, another who was shattered like you, but unlike you, will bear the burdens of his wounds forever. You know of him, though you never met. His name is Neil Cable. Colonel Cable introduced us, thought that it might help him to talk to someone. It did. We have grown very close in the short time we have had together. Not as close as you and I, but I don't think anyone will ever be like you.

Unlike you, he needs me. As I told you once, you need no one. I doubt that has changed. You are a very self-sufficient man, and as I also said before, a survivor.

I cannot turn my back on Neil. He is very fragile. Since we have been together he has started to think once again about life. I cannot take that away from him.

I hope you will understand. I think you will. We had wonderful times together, and I will always think of you and wish that it might have been different.

Take very good care of yourself. Come back home from that war. Build a life for yourself that does not include hate and killing. You deserve it.

Know that I have loved you as I never loved anyone before, or ever will again.

P.S. I will continue to keep your secrets until you need them.

Didn't need anyone? He had never felt so alone in his life.

He opened the other letter. A clipping fell out. He ignored it at first, concentrating on the letter, which was brutally simple.

Dear Captain Carmichael,

Frances asked me, days before the accident, that if anything should ever happen to her, I should inform you. Perhaps she had a premonition. Our family seems sometimes to have that power.

In any case, the clipping should explain all the details. They are too painful for me to cite again.

I sensed something was wrong when I last spoke with her. She said at that time that she felt very bad and that she wanted to change her life. That she had lost something very important when you went away, but that perhaps it was not too late to fix it. She said she was going to change her life, quit what she was doing, that some people wouldn't be too happy about it, but that was their problem. When I asked her what she meant, she said that she would explain later, after it was all over. She never got the chance.

In any case, I have discharged my duty to her. You will understand, I am sure, that we do not wish to have further contact with you. I think that you hurt her very badly. I may be doing you a disservice, but this is the way I feel.

It was signed by Frenchy's mother.

DEATH AT HOTEL

A young woman was found this morning by hotel staff. She had been the victim of foul play. Police, summoned to the location, stated that she had been beaten and strangled.

Upon questioning of the staff, information was gathered that suggested that the victim, Miss Frances DeLacy, had checked in the night before with Mr. Nigel Archimedes, owner of the Acropolis Advertising Agency. Mr. Archimedes was later seen leaving the room, according to witnesses, in a state of agitation. Mr. Archimedes is being sought for questioning.

Police request that anyone else who may have information pertaining to this matter come forward.

Why was he crying? Friends had died, sometimes in his arms, and he had not cried. Why was his chest hurting so? Why this terrible bleak feeling that he had lost something that would forever leave a hole in his soul? Why did he have this overwhelming urge to kill someone, anyone, but particularly the exploiters who took advantage of your weakness, seduced you with pretty words and seemingly generous deeds, made you do things, and when you were of no more use, discarded you like a piece of trash? Someone had to pay.

CHAPTER 14

VANH left the compound the next day. He'd sent a message notifying them that he was coming; a risk, he knew, but one he felt forced to take. He took pains not to be followed and was sure that he had not been. His destination was just outside Hue, in one of the few outlying villages that had not been totally destroyed during Tet. It looked, in fact, hardly scarred by the war. Water buffalo slept in the shade of the banyan trees, occasionally flicking away the flies with their tails. Elders squatted in the town square, slowly chewing their betel nut and spitting the bloodred juice at their feet. The heat beat down, shimmering. Dust devils sprung up here and there, carrying the dirt and omnipresent trash high into the air. He was being watched, he knew, from the shadows behind many windows. He felt safe. His cousin was, after all, the village chief.

He was received with honor, as befitted his position. Tea was brought, ceremonially drunk. He politely refused the offered food, knowing that to eat would delay serious conversation for hours. He did not have hours to spare. The tea bowls were cleared away. His cousin's wife left the room. It was time to talk.

"My cousin," he began, "I have seen something that disturbs me greatly. I am sure that there is an explanation for it. But you must answer me truthfully. There is great danger for you."

"Danger, honored kin?" The village chief tried to give nothing away, but the tiny twitching of his cheek indicated his agitation. Vanh had the fleeting thought that it was strange the Westerners thought his people to be, as they called it, inscrutable. This one's face was easy to read. Of course, he knew him well. In the typical Vietnamese extended family they had been raised almost as brothers.

"Danger, yes. Your name has been linked with some very strange ones. Buddhist militants, neutralist politicians; even, I am told, with high-ranking V.C."

"And you believe this?"

Vanh considered a moment before answering. He was on dangerous ground here. Finally he nodded.

"And what do you intend to do about it?"

"Nothing, at the moment. But I wish to understand. Why would you consort with the enemy? It was your mother and father too that we dug from the sand dunes. And your brother and two of your sisters. And their children. Why?"

His cousin sighed. "You were always one," he said, "for absolutes. You should know by now that there are none. Perhaps it is because I stood there that day gazing down upon my family's faces, sand in their eyes, the ants crawling all over them, knowing that there would be many more like them, that I do the things I do."

"I do not understand."

"For an educated man, you can be remarkably stupid! Perhaps it is because you have been around the Americans for too long. I belong to a group who think that this war must end. Soon. Far too many of our people have died fighting against one another. More will die, unless we stop it. We belong to no side. The ones you call V.C. know that if it goes on much longer, they will no longer exist, and the ones from the North, who do not know our ways and would wish to impose themselves upon us, will be the only ones left. The Buddhists wish autonomy, to stop being persecuted by the Saigon government. And the ones you call, with such contempt, neutralists know that compromise is the only way out. The Americans must and will go. It might surprise you to know that there are some of the Americans who know this, and who help us. All they wish is for the Northerners to not be able to take over, so that they can go home and say they won. Our movement is not large yet, but it is growing. And if you know what is good for you, you will join us."

"Now it is you who are the fool." Vanh was furious. "Do you think the Northerners will allow this? Do you think that, even if you can come to some sort of accommodation with the V.C., they will just give up and go back North? You have been listening to far too much of their propaganda. They only came South to help their fraternal socialist comrades? Nonsense! They are fighting a war of aggression, and they will not be satisfied until there is no more South Vietnam. That has not changed from the earliest days, when Ho was just another guerrilla in the Cordillera. They will allow you to do their work for them. They will it to dishearten those who oppose them, spread defeatism among our ranks. And when you have served your purpose, they will sweep you away like the chaff after the rice has been sifted. Your V.C. friends take their orders directly from Hanoi. I do not doubt that they are very tired of their overseers, but if you think they will disobey them, you are not only stupid but crazy.''

The two men were still kneeling, facing one another. Both internalized the rage they felt. The only sign of emotion was the slight trembling of their bodies.

After a moment his cousin shrugged, ever so slightly. ''I should have known that you would not understand. It is unfortunate that you have found out. We had planned to be much further along before that happened.''

''Perhaps I should now ask you the same question you asked me. What do you intend to do about it?''

''That would depend, I suspect, on what you do. You have seen the size of our organization, who it contains. It would be very dangerous for you to oppose us. I will not have the blood of a kinsman on my hands. But there are others who would not be so fastidious.''

''And what of the American?''

''Ah, that one. What do you care of him?''

''He is a friend and a brave soldier.''

''And very dangerous. You have not said so, but I know it must be that he is the one who discovered us. I respect your feeling for him. So it must be you who keeps him from doing harm. Otherwise, I fear, his fate is sealed. He has made many powerful enemies. Now you must go. I cannot guarantee your safety if you stay in this village much longer. Already the word has gone out that you are here, with no bodyguards. And you have made many enemies also.''

• • •

THE man who had been waiting there came from the next room after Vanh left. He waited for the village chief to speak, knowing that if this man said the wrong thing, he would have to go. The revolution had no place in it for these outmoded family connections.

"I fear that he will not listen," said the chief. "He must be taken care of."

The man nodded, satisfied. This one would do well. He departed as he had come, silently.

VANH reached his jeep where he had hidden it behind a clump of bamboo outside the village. The light had started to go, but the heat had not yet lessened. It would not, he knew, until early in the morning hours. There would be much time to sit in his room and sweat, and think, and fear. Perhaps he should talk to Jim? He, and only he, might understand. It was a strange thing, that he should come to trust this foreigner more than his own people. No, it would keep until the morning. Then they would make plans. This plot could not be allowed to go on. Between them, and with the PRU, they could stop it.

He was in a hurry to get back. It would not do to stay in this area past dark. Even this close to Hue ambushes could happen. He knew that he was taking a chance, starting the vehicle without checking under the hood, but had long ago consigned his life to fate. If it happened, it happened. Still, he felt a wash of relief as the engine caught. He put the vehicle in gear, started to pull away.

The watcher from the clump of bamboo gently squeezed the device, sending a burst of electricity down the wire which had been buried beneath the sand, to the claymore mine placed, faceup, under the seat. The two pounds of C-4 alone would have been enough to ensure death in the target; the hundreds of steel bearings they propelled upward just added to the effect. The explosion moved faster than nerve impulses. There was no pain.

IT was not real. The bits of stray flesh, the charred legs still in the blackened jeep, these were not his friend. They had nothing to do with Vanh. They had contained him, but now he was gone. Why were the PRU soldiers crying?

Didn't they see that it did no good, that you could cry until your tears filled the Perfume River and it would not bring him back? It was no time for tears. It was time for revenge, to wash this place in a river of blood. Snatches of the hard-shell Baptist sermons he had heard as a child came back to him. "As ye live by the sword, so shall ye die by it." There will be weeping and wailing in your tents, and your huts, and your fancy villas. I will root you out, stem and branch, and I will not rest until you all perish, or I do.

SLOWLY now. Make no noise at all. Move by inches and fractions of an inch. Soft black pajamas blending with the night. Face blackened so that the soft moonlight coming through the window does not reflect. Eyes slitted so the mad glitter does not shine through the room. If the intensity of the hate they held were light, they would illuminate the room like spotlights. Vanh's T-shaped tool is clutched in the hand, the point honed needle-sharp. The body on the bed, strangely, does not sense the black menace. Surely he should feel it! Death is near, and he lies beside his wife, softly snoring. You were the last man to see Vanh alive, his brain is shouting, with such force that he thinks that the whole village must hear. You were his kinsman. You were on the list. You are dead, only still breathing at this moment because I have not yet reached you.

Hand over the mouth, press his head down, hold it solid. The black eyes snap suddenly open, full of terror. Only for an instant, because the sharp probe is already crunching through the soft bones behind the ear, driving deep into the brain, twisting around, scrambling the centers which control breathing and heartbeat. Safe to pull the hand away now, nothing escapes the mouth except a soft sigh.

The woman is awake, looking up at him with resignation written upon her features. She closes her eyes, waits. Hears the tiny sound as the probe is withdrawn, hardly more than a soft scraping. Was that what had woken her in the first place? She wished that she had continued to sleep, that the act would have been performed without her knowledge. Now she had to wait for it to happen. She prayed, consigning her soul to the gods. Perhaps in her next incarnation she would not be so unlucky.

But death passed her over on this night, gone as silently as it had come.

ROGER came to attend the funeral of Captain Vanh. It was an astute gesture, and important to the men of the PRU. That such an important man would come to do honors to their captain showed them that they too were important.

"You okay, Jim?" he asked afterward.

"Okay? Sure, I'm okay. Just someone else dying, isn't it? Don't you think I've gotten used to that by now?"

Roger looked doubtful but did not press it. He had seen the reaction before. It had not become real to him yet. It would. Some dime-store shrink would call it repression. Roger thought of it as the shock necessary to shut down the systems long enough for you to function. For a little while. Then it would hit with more force. It always did.

"Listen, I think you should move back to the Embassy House. I heard what Copely did. Told that stupid mother-fucker that if I heard even a hint of any of that kind of shit again, I'd fire his ass. You need to be back among your own kind."

"My own kind? Can you tell me what that kind is? Because I've sort of lost sight of that. Is my kind Copely? I don't think he was really afraid of the actual danger, you know. It was more that it was a messy situation, and he didn't want to have to explain it when something went wrong. Or is my kind those kids who are working for him; who aren't bad people in themselves, but just don't have a fucking clue as to what's going on? No, it seems to me that my kind is in that urn they're carrying away. Vanh fought as well as he knew how. He was a good soldier. And a good man. I'll stay where I am. I feel safer there anyway." He did not add, "And because none of the Americans will know when I leave the compound at night and do the work I must do."

"Okay, I understand," said Roger. Privately he was wondering if it was time to withdraw the captain. He was showing signs of incipient burnout. His hands held a slight tremble, which he tried to suppress. He had lost weight, his eyes sunk back into his head so far that it was like looking into a burrow. A burrow with something glittering and very, very deadly inside. "What have you found out with your Chieu Hoi program?"

"Not much," Jim lied, not knowing why he did it. He had before trusted Roger, still did, he supposed. But something held him back. Roger was, after all, a part of the structure. Perhaps as much a manipulator as any of the others. "I don't know if it was such a good idea," he continued. "But we've come too far to stop now, so I guess we'll keep it up for a while. Hate to pull the plug on something too early. Might come up with something yet." He was chattering, filling the air with words to hide the lies he was telling. He wondered if Roger could tell.

Apparently not. "Right," he was saying. "Don't give up too early. It's been my experience in work like this that nothing comes too quickly. Not like in the movies. Mostly it's just a shitload of work, one detail piling up atop another, until finally, and you hope it's not too late to do any good, you start to be able to see a pattern."

"How's Al doing?" Jim asked to change the subject.

"Slow going for him too, right now. You guys were just too efficient when you got here. Most of the hard-core V.C. in his area have pulled back, are living with Main Force NVA units. Shows how scared they are. But up there they can't do as much damage either. Can't get out and visit the villages, having a hell of a time recruiting, having peasants actually refuse to turn over a part of their rice harvest. So either way, whether we capture or kill them, or make them so scared they stay away, we're neutralizing them. And that's the name of the game."

Not quite, thought Jim. There are things going on right under your nose that you know nothing about. Or do you? If we have this kind of secret structure in Thua Thien, it must exist in other places as well. He wondered if he should tell Al; could think of no good way of doing it without giving the whole game away. Time enough for that, after he did his work.

"Any more word on the people from the South?" he asked.

"Dead quiet. Sorry, bad choice of words. Haven't heard anything from Saigon. I'll get off a query when I get back. Maybe they've decided that you weren't that important."

"Maybe." Jim was doubtful. "Or maybe everyone has just

lost track of them. And they'll show up at my back door in a few days. Doesn't matter anyway. I'm taking all the precautions I can. If they get me, they get me. Nobody lives forever.''

HE waited until McMurdock went back to Danang before putting the next part of the plan into operation.

He knew that they would soon replace Vanh. And his replacement would be an unknown quantity, though he would have placed bets that the man would be a creature of the opposition. After all, he would be appointed by the province chief. Best, then, to do what was necessary before that happened. Then it wouldn't matter who the new man was. He called in the intelligence sergeant, Tu Van Tuyet.

"Trung Si," he said, "I know that you loved Vanh. I think that you are a man who can be trusted. Are you?''

Tu's answer was simple. He pulled the knife from its sheath on his web gear, pulled the razor-sharp blade across his hand. A thin line of blood sprang from the cut. He offered the hand.

Jim took the knife, did the same. Clasped bloody hands with the sergeant. The cynic's part of his brain said that anyone who saw them doing this would think it insufferably melodramatic. But he knew what the gesture meant. Any doubts he may have had about the sergeant's trustworthiness went away. And he'd had few in the first place. They had already been through too much together.

"I have a plan to avenge the captain," he said. "Although the man who probably ordered his death has since suffered the same fate, there are others in on the conspiracy. To fully avenge him, they too must be stopped. Do you agree?''

Tu nodded. He had already suspected that the sudden death of the village chief had been the work of the American. The method, using the same tool that Vanh had so often employed, had been a stroke of genius. It was fitting.

"Then we have an appointment at the temple. Get the men ready. I'll brief them just before the operation. After that, we isolate everyone. No one leaves, no one gets close to a radio. Do you understand the need for that?''

"D'accord, mon capitaine," said Tu, who had received his original training with the French Groupement de Commando Mobile years before Dien Bien Phu. In English that was equally accented by Vietnamese and French, he asked, "And will we be bringing a prisoner back?"

"This time, I think so. So it will also be necessary to keep only a few people privy to the plan. I think that six will be enough. I don't have to tell you to pick only the best men."

"It will be done."

"I'll also tell you that you will soon be in as much danger as was Vanh. I wish you to understand that."

"*Mon capitaine,* I gave up my life many years ago. I have lived much longer than I had ever planned. So it does not matter if it ends now, or next week. I will go for now to pick the men. At what time would you like to brief us?"

"Six o'clock. That gives us enough time to get into place before evening prayers."

THE operation itself went so smoothly it frightened him. The monks were converging on the temple in ones and twos. He'd taken position at a point where he could observe all who came and went. The Chieu Hoi who had given him the information in the first place was by his side. Suddenly he stiffened, pointed out one of the saffron-clad monks. Jim whispered into the radio, and two other monks converged on the man. One pulled from his robes a silencer-equipped .22, poked it into the man's ribs. The other took position in front of him, spoke to him briefly. There was a flash of movement as the target decided he would try to run. The .22 was inclined downward slightly, trigger jerked once. The bullet smashed through his pelvis, the noise it made inaudible over his scream. "Brothers!" the one monk called. "Please help us." He stooped over the fallen man, his robes covering the chloroformed rag placed over the mouth. Two other monks hurried to the spot, helped pick up the fallen man and carry him to a waiting vehicle. They were away before anyone from the temple knew that there had been a problem.

THE man stared at him in undisguised hatred. "Colonel," he said, "you must know by now that you are in the hands of the PRU. You don't have much of a chance. If I were to tell them who you actually were, they'd kill me to get to you. So let's talk."

He'd already given the man a shot of morphine to dull the

pain of his shattered pelvis. They'd brought him in still unconscious, and Jim had carefully monitored his blood pressure and pulse, hoping that the round had not hit a blood vessel. That was the chance you took, but the slowness of the silenced round at least kept it from ricocheting around a lot. So far there had been no sign of major vessel involvement, but you couldn't tell very much without exploratory surgery. So he had to get as much as he could as quickly as possible.

The colonel held his silence. "We don't have much time," Jim said. "If you're holding out until we turn you in to the province officials, you can forget about that." Jim was using an old interrogation trick: show them that you already know most of the details, so that it becomes pointless to hold out. "We already know about them. You won't be turned in, not at all. At this point, all you can hope for is that I can somehow get you to Saigon. I'll put you in the hands of people there who I can trust. But you have to give me something."

The collapse was obvious. The colonel's shoulders drooped, he looked exhausted. Jim pressed the point.

"You must tell me the purpose of this whole thing," he said. "We have brought in most of the other people," he lied. "They are telling us everything they know. How do you think I found out about you? You will do yourself no good by telling me lies. We are not unreasonable men, Colonel. You are a soldier, as am I. As soldiers, we know when the battle is lost."

The proselyting chief of the northern provinces started speaking in a dull, morphine-induced monotone. Jim checked to see that the tape recorder was working. He did not want to miss an instant of this.

It took hours. At the end he had to prod the colonel awake, to get the final, almost unbelievable details. When it was over, he let him rest, telling the guard to keep good watch on the hut. Not that he thought the man would or could escape. The broken pelvis would make sure of that. He needed his own sleep. There was much to do in the morning.

THE man was dead when he looked in on him the next morning. There were no obvious marks. He checked quite thoroughly, questioned the guard at length, assured himself that no one had been in there. Must have been more internal bleeding than I thought, he told himself. Not that it mattered. He had not yet figured out what he would do with the man. The problem did not exist anymore. Just another corpse to dispose of. There had been many of them. There would be many more.

"I have to go somewhere," he told Tu. "I need a couple of people. P.X. shopping at Camp Evans," he lied. "You need anything?"

"Non, capitaine," replied Tu. "We will rid ourselves of the offal while you are gone. You will give us orders when you return?"

"Lots of orders, my good friend. Lots and lots of orders. Get the PRU ready. We have much work to do."

HE put a copy of the tape into a mailing packet, addressed it to Lisa and deposited it in the Army Post Office at Camp Evans. All around him was the bustle of a major U.S. Army base. The 101st Airborne was in residence, a good unit and one which had been blooded in hundreds of useless battles for insignificant pieces of terrain which were immediately abandoned. Thousands of young men, strong, healthy, whole. The rot that had begun to affect the rear-area troops had not shown itself to any great extent here. These troops were confident, hardy, brave fighters. Most of them, he figured, still believed in what they were doing. Wonder what you'd do, he thought, if you knew that your own leadership was getting ready to give it all away. That all the sacrifices you made, all the buddies you watched being shipped out in body bags, were all for nothing. Would you stand up, demand of your leaders the commitment and bravery that you have shown? Or would you just go on believing that the people in power probably knew best? That if they were doing something, they must have a good reason for it, perhaps one that you did not understand, but after all, you were a simple soldier and were not supposed to be able to understand. What would it take to rip that veil from your eyes? To see that the leaders were just men, all too fallible men, who for a host of reasons made mistakes too? Disastrous mistakes, which made a mockery of what you were doing. More evidence than I possess, certainly, though the tape which just went out of here might someday help.

He kept to his cover story by going to the P.X. and purchasing a few supplies: shaving gear, writing paper, a couple of cases of beer. The P.X. was as well stocked as any in the United States. Clothes, expensive jewelry, concessionaires who sold cars for delivery when you got home, tailor shops where one could get the latest fashions made to measure, mountains of beer, liquor stores selling booze at a fraction of the cost of what it would have been in the States. No wonder the Vietnamese think we're so rich, he thought. And no wonder one of the biggest businesses in the country was dealing in black-market P.X. goods.

Time to go. He had his mission, and he knew how to carry it out. He needed no logistics for it, no helicopters, no air strikes, no artillery. Just a few trusted PRU. And while he did not know if it would do any good, at least he had to try.

MOIRA Culpepper dropped the sheaf of flimsies on Eliot Danforth's desk, announcing that they were the latest reports from I Corps. Waited for him to read them, and the explosion she knew was to come. She was not disappointed. His nose grew even more red than usual, the flush climbing into his receding hairline. He was breathing harder and harder, almost as hard as he did when he was atop her. I wonder when he's going to have a heart attack, she idly thought. The prospect did not dismay her. Though she hoped it would not be in her room. That would be messy and hard to explain.

"If I had any hard evidence at all that he was the one who killed our man," he hissed, "I'd have him shot."

"What more evidence do you need?" she asked. "The man was killed in his bed, the night after Vanh was blown up. With a tool of the type known to have been used by Vanh in any number of assassinations. The wife says that it was a large figure; never mind the mumbo jumbo about it being the black form of death itself. Who else could it have been?"

"That, my dear, is not evidence. Not evidence I can carry to a court of law and justify the act. And justify we would have to do. We can't get away with just everything. Surely even you can understand that." He ignored the stiffening of her lips caused by the insult. "He's going to ruin everything! All that I've worked for during the last year."

''There's more,'' she said. ''Colonel Binh didn't return to his headquarters last night. He's done that before, so no one is getting too upset just yet. But I thought you ought to know.'' She enjoyed the discomfiture this news caused.

''We cannot allow this to happen,'' he said. ''The plan must go forward, and it cannot without the key people in Hue.''

''Why don't you go to Roger again and demand that he be removed?'' She had been thoroughly briefed on ''the plan'' after she'd asked why it was so important to keep a close eye on Captain Carmichael. After some initial misgivings, she had seen how career-enhancing it would be for Eliot, and by extension for her, if it succeeded. It was, therefore, a brilliant plan. And if it did not work, there would still be time to distance herself from it. She kept two journals, one in which she recorded her work in support of the plan, the second in which she recorded nonexistent misgivings about it, and complaints that she was being forced to go along with it by a supervisor who was showing increasing signs of megalomania.

''No possibility of that, without telling him what's going on. And we can't do that. First, I doubt that he would go along with it. He's still of the opinion that we can win this war. Second, even if by some chance he did go along with it, he'd at some point want to claim some of the credit. And I'll share credit with no one. This is all mine. No one else in this country, on our side, knows about it. Except you. And I know that I can trust you. Because I'll bring you down with me if it goes wrong.''

You just think you will, you old fool! she thought. Aloud she asked, ''So what's the answer?''

''Do we have any further word on the V.C. team?''

''No,'' she admitted. ''They dropped from sight once they entered Cambodia. We can only surmise that they are on their way north. They could even be there by now.''

''Or they could have been killed in a B-52 strike, or by one of the Special Forces recon teams, or could have just died of malaria,'' he said. ''Not good enough. The young bastard is very lucky. Two attempts on him so far, and neither worked. His luck may run out, but it could be too late by then. No, we're going to have to do something more positive." He looked at her speculatively, eyes hooded and glittering. "I think we're going to have to put you into play."

"Me?" She felt foreboding. She hadn't signed on for this part.

"It shouldn't be too difficult. You're the only one who stands a chance of getting close to him. Certainly he's not going to trust me."

"And what makes you think he'll trust me?"

"Don't act naive!" he snapped. "It shouldn't be too difficult for you. You're used to using your body to get what you want. The young captain may be suspicious, but he's still a man. Pack your bags for a long stay. You're going to Hue on an inspection trip, and it may take you a week or two. I'll cable Copely."

"And what am I supposed to do, once I get 'close to him'?" she asked, wanting to hear him say it.

"Stop him, by whatever means you have to use. Do I have to be more specific than that?"

It was enough. A full-blown sanction. She felt an almost sexual shiver of excitement.

CHAPTER 15

HE still needed more evidence. He did not know who the conspirator or conspirators were on the American side. He could not let himself believe that they were numerous, that this was the hidden agenda of the U.S. policymakers. If that was so, the game was up. He might or might not be able to prevail if this was a plot of one or two rogue officials. If it was more, he was doomed. Not that it frightened him. He'd already decided that he did not much care if he survived or not.

In the dark watches of the night, coming awake fighting from a dream that was all too real, sleeping not again until dawn lightened the sky outside his window, he would lie rigid and think. Mostly he thought about what a piece of bad luck he was. Not for himself, necessarily. He seemed to be very much the survivor Lisa had called him. But he was a disaster for others.

People perished around him, while he walked through it with little or no harm. It seemed to be a certain death warrant, for him to care about someone. The list seemed endless: Captain Buon, Vanh, Frances, literally hundreds of soldiers whom he had led, old friends and compatriots. Everyone was dead. They called to him at night, demanded to know why. And he could not answer them. Nor, it seemed, could he join them.

Mostly he blamed himself for the deaths. His rational mind would argue, telling him that these things happened, that most would have occurred with or without him. These arguments were always lost. He *knew* they would not have happened if it had not been for him. If he had only shown more compassion for Frenchy, if he had asked Vanh where he was going and insisted that he take a bodyguard, if he had not decided to assault a hill against insurmountable odds, if, if, if . . .

At times he would get up, unable to stand the silence magnifying the voices in his brain. Play a tape on the P.X.-purchased Teac tape deck. The Doors often suited his mood. "Summer's Almost Gone" and especially "The Unknown Soldier." Other times it would be Edith Piaf, though the sentiments expressed in "Je Ne Regrette Rien" were exactly the opposite of his. Better was "En Avant la Légion." Because in the final analysis, what choice did you have but to go on?

Sometimes he contemplated placing the pistol behind his ear and ending the whole sorry mess. Would take it from beneath his pillow and stare at it until the cold metal grew warm from his hand, as warm as the touch of a seductress. Then he would sigh, regretfully, and put it away. What held him back he did not know; cowardice, perhaps. Or the realization that his work was not yet done. Or perhaps it was the desire for revenge which glowed within him like a furnace. Or perhaps it was sheer obstinacy, unwillingness to further the opposition's cause. Why should he make it easier for them?

He would doze again then, fitfully, rising a couple of hours later when one of the soldiers knocked on his door, bringing him a steaming cup of strong French coffee. Get into his clothes, which were starting to hang on him like rags. Look at himself in the mirror while he shaved, seeing how much further his eyes were sunk into his head today. Occasionally a flash of the old humor. God damn, he told himself, a little more of this and you're going to look like Twiggy. He smiled a little bit. It felt strange.

A knock on the door. The guard again, telling him he had a visitor. Must be Fitzwilliam bringing me mail, he thought. Don't think I can stand any more good news. Maybe I'll just tell him to burn the shit when he gets it.

He was surprised, and immediately suspicious, to see Moira Culpepper standing there. I was expecting bad news, he thought, and here it is in the flesh.

SHE was nervous. Not at all the self-assured, poised woman he had known. She had not stopped chattering since she perched herself precariously on Vanh's old cot. Bullshit about an inspection visit, and how she had seized the chance for it because—and at this she looked at him from under seductively lowered eyelids—it would give her a chance to spend some time with him, to get to know him better. She looked very good, sitting there in a vaguely military pants suit. But the military never issued material that clung so lovingly to upthrust breasts and artfully stretched itself along crossed legs. She talked about Saigon gossip, dropping names that meant little or nothing to him. What difference did it make that this general was banging that secretary? That so-and-so was a closet homosexual and couldn't keep himself away from young Vietnamese houseboys? Frenchy thought of herself as a whore, he found himself thinking. And I couldn't understand it and left her because of it. But she was nothing compared to you. She, at least, knew what she was. You, on the other hand, feel no remorse, no shame. Your morals are not underdeveloped, they don't exist at all. I feel nothing at all for you, no desire, no lust, nothing. And realizing that, he felt liberated.

It's not working, she thought frantically. He sits there and looks at me with no emotion at all. His eyes are empty, dead. Looking at me as if I'm some sort of foreign creature. It angered and frightened her. The one constant in her life had been her ability to control men through her body. Now she was beginning to realize that it was she who was being controlled. First Eliot had sent her here with the unspoken order to use her sex to get close to this man. Not caring that she would have to sleep with him, treating her like little more than a common whore, when she would have thought it would make him wildly jealous to think of her in another man's arms. The control she'd thought she had over him obviously did not exist.

Now this dead-eyed one, whom before she had found so easy to manipulate, responded to her not at all. She uncrossed her legs, let him see where the tight material cleaved into her sex. There was no flicker in the eyes.

"Eliot wanted me to ask you," she said, changing tack, "about the PRU operations. There haven't been many reports coming from Thua Thien."

"That's because there hasn't been much to report," he lied. "By the way, does Roger know you're here?"

"Certainly," she replied. He hadn't been told, of course. He'd have been suspicious of such a visit. One did not just come down and inspect province operations without the knowledge and permission of the regional office. She hoped to have her business done and be out before he found out. After that, he wouldn't be able to do anything about it, except complain to the deaf ears of Eliot Danforth.

In reality, she wasn't sure exactly what she was supposed to do. Eliot had been purposefully vague on that point. He'd told her to get close. Then what? Stop him, he had said. Surely he hadn't intended that she be the one to kill him! She was not sure she could do that. She'd been to the training at the Farm, of course, and was thus technically qualified. But technical qualification, shooting at paper targets, and stabbing a dummy were not like the real thing. She had never had to do that and was not sure she could. Still, if it came to a choice between him and her . . .

But right now she'd continue to try to gather information. "You stated in a report a few weeks ago that you felt you'd be able to build up a comprehensive information base from the Chieu Hoi program. How's that coming?"

He smiled for the first time then, a painful rictus which bore no resemblance to the open grin which had attracted her so much the first time they met. "Not too well. I'm afraid I may have made a miscalculation. Appears that they know less than I'd expected, or they're a hell of a lot better at concealing it. I'm not ready to give it up yet, but I think it's going to take a lot longer than we'd hoped."

He's lying! she thought. Captain James NMI Carmichael, you've learned a lot, but not enough. Not enough to fool someone who lies as a profession. In this, at least, she still felt confident. "I know how the loss of Captain Vanh must have affected you, Jim," she said, putting all the sincerity of which she was capable into her manner. "I just wanted to tell you how sorry all the people in Saigon, and especially myself, are. Your early reports made it evident how much you thought of him."

You lying bitch! he raged inside. You and all your ilk could give a fuck less about Vanh. Just another slope, you'd say, if you said anything at all. More likely you wouldn't even have taken notice if it didn't suit your purposes to use it to try and fool me. "Yes," he said, his face smooth and noncommittal. "He was a good man. This sets the program back even worse. He was essential. He'll be hard to replace."

"Yes, well, I guess I'd better get back to the compound now." She was seething. Nothing seemed to work on him, not sex, not sympathy, not official queries. Eliot would be very angry, and that would not be good for her career. And anyone who stood in the way of her career was in a great deal of danger. She made one last halfhearted attempt. "I'll be at the compound every night," she said. "They gave me your old room to sleep in. Will you come by and see me?"

If you don't get out of here very quickly, he was thinking, I'm going to cross the few feet that separate us and take you in my arms and turn your head around until I hear the bones snap and feel you quiver as the life drains out of you. "Maybe," he said. "But I haven't been feeling too good lately. Maybe it's the malaria making another visit. I can't guarantee anything."

You've made your choice, Captain, she thought as she made her way back to the Embassy House. Eliot was right. You're a rogue player. And we can't have that.

She swept into Copely's office. "Please make me an appointment with the province chief," she said. "This afternoon."

SHE'D said Roger knew she was in town. Was that true? If so, he was in on it. He still hadn't made up his mind as to that point. He hoped not. Roger might be his only chance for survival. And while he wasn't sure he would survive or even wanted to, he did not yet want to close off that option. Perhaps he would know tonight. "Sergeant Tu," he called, "come on in here. We need to plan an operation."

ROGER was, at that moment, finding out about the visit. A friend of his from Air America with whom he had served in Bolivia gave him, as a matter of course, all Air America manifests. He liked to know who was traveling in and out of his region. Usually the names meant nothing: AID, Embassy, CIA and other personnel going about legitimate business; Vietnamese of enough rank to be able to qualify for the flights going to or coming from Saigon, usually so heavily laden with black-market goods the C-47s had to strain to get off the runways. But this day it paid off. Why would Moira Culpepper go to Hue without notifying him? True, Eliot had the authority to send anyone anywhere he wanted, but in practice it was simply never done. Turf was zealously guarded in the Agency, and for very good reason. There was not enough time to brief everyone on every operation, every agent. So you could be sending someone in on an ongoing op, where anything could happen. Simply not good tactics.

He knew that it would do no good to question Danforth. He would get the usual smooth explanations, be reminded of Danforth's authority and learn nothing.

He unlocked the small room off his office, went inside, turned on the radio. While he waited for it to warm up he reflected that Danforth must be running something very funny indeed. He wondered who else was in on it. He needed to know.

He spoke into the handset, the electronic device inside the radio garbling his speech into unrecognizable electronic signals. Unrecognizable to anyone who did not have a similar device at the other end. When he finished, he went to his desk. Paperwork to get through while he waited for the red light that would indicate he had return traffic. It might come today, it might not be for several days. But he would have an answer.

He thought for a moment, something that he must have missed nagging at his brain. Called himself stupid when it finally occurred to him. Went to the other radio, called Al Dougherty in Quang Nam and told him to get on the next thing flying to Danang.

HE thought it would have to be the hardest thing he had ever done. Invading a Buddhist temple in the middle of the night, securing one individual and bringing him out alive. All without drawing any attention, without alerting any one of the hundreds of monks resident in the temple. Some of them, he knew, did not fully subscribe to the nonviolent tenets of their religion, and could be expected to react with force if his group was discovered.

Tu had an idea. "*Capitaine*, can you provide me with something which will make the man sleep?"

"Sure," he said. "I've got some chloral hydrate, what we used to call mickeys. They'd put a bull elephant to sleep."

"One of the acolytes is a kinsman of mine. He often serves the ranking priests. Perhaps he can get it into the drink. And if he can't, we're no worse off than we are now."

They had been laboring at the plan for hours. It had seemed impossible on the face of it, but after many false starts and discards it seemed they were on the verge. Give me a nice easy smash-and-grab anytime, Jim thought. Still, this might work. The hardest part had been how to secure the man quickly so that he did not make any noise to alert the others.

"Let's go for it," he said. "I'll get the drops. They'll take just a few minutes after he drinks them. Then he'll be out for at least four hours. Make sure your man doesn't give them to him before last prayers. Tell him to be careful. This guy is bound to be jumpy now that the colonel hasn't shown up for the last few days. He has to suspect something's wrong."

"It will be done. I shall depart now and will meet you at the rally point tonight."

He was about to stir up a hornet's nest, he knew. The Buddhists would not take lightly the disappearance of the secretary of the chief bonze. This time payoffs to the hierarchy would not work. They'd be after him all over the country. He planned to drop from sight until he had all the information he needed. Then he'd surround himself with the PRU, get to the airport and commandeer a plane to Saigon. There he could lay it all out to COMUSMACV. He did not trust anyone on the civilian side. He did not know who might be in on it, but doubted the military was. The brass might not know how to fight this war, and didn't, in his opinion, but he doubted that they would be party to just giving up. After that, he didn't know what would happen. And didn't much care.

He busied himself by gathering a few things together, placing them in a small pack. He doubted that he'd be seeing this place again, no matter what happened. There was surprisingly little. The letter from Australia, Lisa's address. A small framed picture of his mother, taken in the thirties. All he needed. The tape recorder, tapes, other detritus he would leave for the PRU. It was time. He went to the bathroom, stuck a finger down his throat, caught the watery results in a plastic bag. Tied it off and stuck it in the pack too.

• • •

"COLONEL," she said, "we have a problem."

She was, he thought, quite beautiful. For an American. Ordinarily Westerners did not attract him; he thought them too big, and unfeminine, and gross. But something about this one made him put her in the excepted category.

"*We* have a problem, Miss Culpepper?" he said, acting as if he did not know what she was talking about.

"Cut the bullshit, Colonel. I'm speaking of Captain Carmichael. And I speak with the full authority of Eliot Danforth. Now, do you wish to speak frankly, or shall I go back to my superior and tell him that you refuse to cooperate?"

Desirable or not, she was still a Westerner, with their insufferable ways, he thought. Still, it would not pay to anger her. "Yes," he said. "The captain has become a thorn in our sides. Already he has done much damage."

"He cannot be allowed to do more. Do you understand me?"

"And in this you speak also with the voice of Mr. Danforth?" he asked, hoping that the tape recorder he had concealed in the desk was picking up the entire conversation.

"I do," she replied.

"And do you have any suggestions?"

"That, Colonel, is your department. I have every faith that you can manage."

If only it were so easy, he thought. Already the two attempts I made did not succeed. Still, I only need to be successful once, and he must be successful all the time. It will be done. Better this way anyway, with the Americans telling me to do so. If anything goes wrong, I can always blame them. It would be very embarrassing for them, having it known that they authorized the assassination of one of their own.

"Would you like a drink, Miss Culpepper?" he asked. Perhaps she would be more friendly, now that they were co-conspirators. He was aware that he had grown an erection from watching her breasts poke against the thin green fabric of her suit. So much larger than the Vietnamese women he was used to. Even those who were half French.

"No," she said disdainfully. "My work is done here. I'm going back to the Embassy House. You can reach me there, if you need anything." She knew the effect she was having on him, and was glad of it. Her self-confidence had taken a severe blow when she was unable to arouse Jim Carmichael. Still, a Vietnamese? The thought repulsed her.

He did not let her see his anger as he showed her out. Someday, he vowed to himself, someday I will repay these Americans for their arrogance.

"WELL?" he demanded of Tu when they met at the rally point in a small hut just outside the temple compound.

"It is done. The man likes to have a cup of tea just before going to bed. My nephew says that he sleeps like the dead."

"Then let's go." They were again dressed in saffron robes. The robes were convenient for hiding much: Uzis strapped to their sides, pistols, ropes for binding and tape for muzzling mouths. He hoped they would have to use none of it. If they did, the game was as good as up before it started. He was not too worried about his height. Some of the Buddhists of Chinese extraction were almost as tall as he, and he was wearing a hood to disguise his hair and features. That, and the dark, should be enough.

They slipped into the temple by ones and twos. The mental map he had constructed from the sketches of one of the PRU soldiers who had spent much time there served him well. Not that it was a terribly complicated building anyway. Tu was by his side. They occasionally passed others: monks who could not sleep and wandered the halls, or those on business of one type or another. No one challenged them. The Buddhists regarded this place as sacrosanct, invulnerable to threat from either side. Jim had counted on that attitude. It seemed to be working.

Their group took up positions: two by the front door, ready to cover the escape; two more on each floor to cover the rear; Tu, himself and two others at the room of the target. The door was unlocked. He was relieved. He'd brought along a pick kit but had never been particularly good at surreptitious entry. His instructor at Fort Holabird had despaired of him, told him that his best bet if he had to open a door would be explosives, and a hope that everyone was deaf.

The man on the bed was snoring loudly. The two men with them took position on either side of the door, and he and Tu went in. Christ, he thought, helping Tu to pick him up, this guy must weigh two hundred pounds. They roughly stood him up between them, supporting his weight with his arms over their shoulders. He did not stir, though the snoring stopped. "Wait a minute," he whispered to Tu. He took the plastic bag from a pouch inside his robe, ripped it open, and poured it down the front of the sleeping man. The sour smell of vomit immediately flooded the room. Tu wrinkled his nose in disgust.

They walked, half carrying and half dragging the man between them. The two men at the door fell in behind them, close enough to assist and far enough away not to attract attention. Jim was sweating. He was beginning to wish he had kept himself in better shape over the last few weeks. The man was totally dead weight, his head lolling on his chest, flecks of vomit attaching to his chin. Down one flight of stairs, another long hallway. They hadn't seemed so long when he was coming up. They were becoming a spread-out column now, with the hallway guards from the last floor taking position still farther to the rear.

Someone approaching, not one of ours. "My brothers," the man said, "is there a problem?"

"Our brother is sick," said Tu, moving closer to the other monk so he would be assured of smelling the vomit. He did, backing up quickly.

"Can I be of assistance?" he asked, hoping they would say no. He knew that he should be of service to his fellow-man, but this one smelled so bad!

"You are kind," Tu replied, "but no. Our friend had too much to drink after evening prayers, and you know how that is regarded here. We would ask you to tell no one of this. He is a good man, but sometimes he is weak. We wish to get him into the fresh air and clean him up. He will be well in the morning."

"I understand," the monk said, who had weaknesses of his own, the most prominent of which was that he loved the form of little boys. He hurried away.

Down another staircase, the front door in sight. He had to keep himself from hurrying. All had gone well so far, no need to attract attention now. Not, he thought, that he could have hurried very much anyway. The man seemed to be getting heavier.

Then they were outside, and the cool night air washed over them, diluting the sour smell of the victim. Two of the PRU relieved him and Tu of the weight. He was panting, was glad to see that Tu was also. "Next time," he whispered between breaths, "let's get somebody who doesn't like to eat quite so much, okay?" Tu's flashing grin in the moonlight rewarded him.

They could not take the man back to the PRU compound. That would be the first place the searchers would look. That had been one of the sticky parts of the plan: where to go. Finally Tu had volunteered the fact that yet another member of his family, one who could be trusted as much as his nephew, since it was that nephew's father, had a large sampan. They headed for the Perfume River, only a couple of hundred yards from the temple, where they took up position on the bank. Tu produced a flashlight with the lens taped so that only a slit of light escaped, flashed it twice. Received an answering flash immediately, followed in a few minutes by the soft plash of oars. They loaded the unconscious man aboard the little boat, along with Jim, Tu and one other PRU man. Smoothly the boatman pushed them away from the bank and steered them out into the river. Within moments they were bumping against the side of the sampan.

The transfer was made, the small boat tied to the rear of the sampan, and they cast off downriver. It would be a few hours before they could reach the sea, there to become just one more boat among thousands. Jim was exhausted. Sleep came quickly.

THE chop as the sampan exited the mouth of the Perfume River into the South China Sea woke him. He'd slept only a few hours, yet felt curiously refreshed. His demons had not visited him at all. Perhaps because now he was committed upon a course of action from which there could be no turning back. No matter what happened, nothing would ever again be the same.

There was an R&R beach off to the right, barbed-wire-encircled and reserved for the relaxation of the American troops. No Vietnamese were allowed, except for the drink sellers, massage girls and whores lucky enough to get an invitation to accompany some G.I. Few combat troops ever came here; when they got out of the field, they had no desire to go to a beach somewhere in Vietnam, opting instead for Bangkok or another of the out-of-country locations. Mostly rear-echelon types came, people who had plenty of time off and took not only the out-of-country R&Rs but any other little benefits they could lay their hands on. This early in the morning there were yet no sunbathers. At one end a group of soldiers with mine detectors slowly advanced, sweeping from side to side in case the V.C. had come in during the night and left unpleasant reminders of their visit. The sun was coming up over the water, its glare an unpleasant reminder of how hot the day was going to be. Time to get to work.

He went below, where Tu was presiding over a very groggy prisoner. Chloral hydrate was effective, but it gave one the grandaddy of all hangovers. This guy was not going to feel very good. At least someone had cleaned the puke off him.

"We need him to be out from under it a little bit better," he told Tu. "Maybe another couple of hours. You want to get something to eat?"

Tu nodded, making one last check of the prisoner. Not that there was much chance of his getting away. He was handcuffed to eye bolts in the hull. His feet were tied together, and there was a strip of duct tape across his mouth. "Take the tape off," instructed Jim. "There's no one to hear him now."

Up on the deck Tu's brother's wife had cooked up a pot of *pho*, the Vietnamese soup that was a full meal in itself. As befitted a maritime family it was thick with chunks of crab, shrimp and fish. Jim took a bowl, doctored it with a hefty shot of *nuoc mam* and squatted next to the rail. He enjoyed the motion of the sea. Perhaps, after this was over, if he survived, he would become a fisherman. It seemed a good, honest life. But that "if" was a very big one. Tu squatted next to him.

"A very smooth operation, *mon capitaine*," he said between slurps of the tasty soup.

"So far, my friend, so far. I just worry that this was the easy part."

Tu's silence was in itself an eloquent comment. They did not speak again until both finished their meal. They politely refused another helping, disappointing the woman. Both had noticed that there was very little food left after their bowls had been filled. The woman would have given them all of it had they allowed it, and the family would have gone hungry.

They continued out to sea, and even as slow as the sampan cruised it was not long before they were out of sight of land. The engines were cut, and the boat allowed to drift. The family dropped lines into the water. To anyone who looked, it was just another fisherman at work.

The man was fully awake when they went back below. It was obvious that he recognized Jim, because upon seeing him he shut up the complaints he had been voicing to the guard. Perhaps he felt it would be no good. Instead he started praying.

"We wish you no harm, esteemed one," started Tu. "You know who we are. We do not regard you as an enemy. We may even be on the same side. But we must ask you some questions. There is much we know. We only need you to fill in the details. Then you will be released, unharmed."

Couldn't have said it better myself, thought Jim. He had already decided to let Tu handle the interrogation, remaining in the background as a distant, unspoken threat. They already thought he was crazy, and capable of anything. Let them go on thinking that.

"Tell us," said Tu, following the line given him earlier by Jim, "what is the purpose of this effort? We already know of the people involved. Some of them we have already picked up. The others we soon will. We have the backing from Saigon," he lied. "So you must know that your plot has failed. This is your chance to prove to us that you were involved only because the enemy promised you, false promises, that your order would be spared if you cooperated. They threatened you or your leaders?" Tu was by this allowing him a way out.

It was effective.

"We are a group of people," the monk began, "from both sides, who are tired of the war. We know that it cannot be won, not by either side. So it will go on, and many more people will die, and to what purpose? We wish a country which will be aligned to neither side, which would be neutral."

"And what do the Northerners say about this?"

"As soon as we take over, we will ask the Northerners to leave. We will no longer be a threat to them, so they will do so. We will then set about establishing economic and commercial ties, so that both countries may prosper."

"And how did you plan to go about this?"

"There are high-ranking officers in the South Vietnamese forces who think as we do. Some of them in critical positions. When the time is right, we intend to capture the warmongers in Saigon and establish a new government."

"Yes, yes, we know all about those officers. Most of them have already been picked up. They will be court-martialed. We will wish to check our list, to make sure we have them all. You are to write down all who you know. We will know if you leave someone out! So do not play us for fools. The American, there, who luckily does not speak our language, already wishes to kill you. I do not know if I can stop him if he finds out you have been lying to us."

AN hour later Tu handed Jim the completed list. He eyed it briefly, then smiled. So that was why Moira had visited! A lot of people had a lot more explaining to do. Perhaps it wouldn't be necessary to flee to Saigon, after all. Danang would do. But first there was just a little bit more work to do in Hue.

"Come, my friend, up on the deck," he said. "We will talk of things important."

CHAPTER 16

SHE hadn't slept well. Several times she had wondered if she should give Jim Carmichael just one more chance. She had never before consigned a man to death, as she had effectively done that afternoon. She'd thought she was hard enough. Now she didn't know.

She'd had several more Scotches than she should after dinner at the Embassy House, played at charming the young officers, had been satisfied with the attention they showed her. Had in the end gone to bed alone, though she could have had her pick. It took forever to drop off, and when she did, the dreams came, tormenting her with visions of broken bodies and blood spraying from bullet wounds. And all the bodies looked like Jim, until at the last one of them was her. She woke up screaming, her throat sore. Turned the light on and tried to read. But she could not concentrate, found herself reading a paragraph over and over again, and then could not tell what it was about. Early the next morning she started dozing again, stayed awake long enough to turn off the alarm clock. No reason not to sleep in. *Things are in motion now, and I can't stop them.*

Shortly before noon she was woken by someone banging on the door. *Who the hell!* The sense of foreboding that came over her was as strong as the taste of stale Scotch in her mouth.

It was one of the young CIA officers, Fitz something or other. She remembered thinking that he was the most attractive of the lot, in an immature sort of way. What was he saying?

"I said," he repeated, "we just got a message from the province chief. He wants to see you right now. He sounded pretty agitated. Is there something we can help you with?"

"Yeah," she said. "Get out of here while I get dressed, and get me a car and driver. Think you can handle that?"

Had it happened that quickly? she wondered as hurriedly she got dressed and ran a brush through her hair. Were my dreams for real? She felt a sudden, unexplainable sense of loss. Interesting, she thought, storing it away for later analysis. I'll use it in the novel I'll write about this place someday.

"He's gone," said the colonel.

"My God, that was fast," she said, hoping her face did not give away the shock.

"No, you fool! He's gone. Disappeared. Along with some members of the PRU."

Was it relief she felt? "I'm sure he'll show up again. And you can do what is necessary. Don't be so eager." And who was this fucking slope, to be calling her a fool!

"If only it was so easy," he said, settling back behind the desk and making sure the reels of the tape recorder were slowly spooling. "We hadn't intended to go after him last night. It takes more planning to catch a tiger than a dog."

"Then what's the worry?" And why did he get me over here in such a hurry? No wonder these fools were losing the war, if they got so excited over every little thing.

"The worry, my lovely colleague, is that Nguyen Dinh Minh has also disappeared. He did not report for morning prayers, and when they went to find him, there was no sign. One monk gives a confused story about three people walking the halls last night, one supposedly very drunk. He thinks the drunk could have been Minh, though he cannot be sure."

"Oh, my God," she whispered, the color leaving her face. "And you think it was Captain Carmichael?"

"I see no other explanation. The question is, what are we to do about it? Minh was privy to all the secrets. He knows the identity of everyone. By now, we must expect that the captain does also. He has so far been very skillful at extracting information from even the most hardened."

"Kill him," she said without hesitation.

"And if we cannot do it without also harming Minh?"

"Then kill him too. We can always blame it on Carmichael. He's now a rogue, beyond all help. Minh can be replaced. We cannot afford for any of this to be made public. It's too early. And make sure you take care of any of the PRU who were with him.''

"And in this you also speak with the voice of Mr. Danforth?''

"Yes,'' she said simply. "Would you like to speak with him to confirm that? We can get him on the single sideband.''

"That will not be necessary. It will be done. Already my men are searching. I will also notify our friends in the Viet Cong. He will be shot on sight. It will be easier to explain that way. We would not want him brought in, where he might talk.''

"Indeed we do not,'' she replied. Gone was any residual feeling for her former lover. Now he was in the way, and dangerous for her plans. He could not be allowed to spoil her career, not after she had worked so hard and come so far.

"THERE'S a couple more questions I'd like you to ask him before we drop him off,'' said Jim, handing Tu a sheet of paper. There was much more he would like to know, but there wasn't time for a leisurely interrogation. These few questions, distilled from the many which ran through his mind, would have to do.

Tu read quickly, looked up at Jim and smiled. "Revenge?''

"Only honest emotion I have left,'' he replied. "Plus it's probably the only way the PRU will be able to survive. One thing the Communists have right, get rid of all your enemies, stem and branch. Can you think of any other way?''

"No,'' Tu admitted. "And even if I could, I'm not sure I would want to take it. Someone must pay for the captain's death.'' He went below.

Jim continued to enjoy the sunshine. It seemed like forever since he had been able to sit back and relax like this, though it was only a little over a month ago that he had been in Australia. He watched as Tu's brother pulled in yet another fish. They'd been very lucky today, catching more in a long morning than they usually did in a week. They'd told him that he brought good fortune. He'd smiled at that. But he hoped that his own luck would also continue to hold.

He was almost asleep when Tu returned, lulled by the gentle rocking of the boat. "It was as you suspected, *mon capi-*

taine. Our friend below was very happy to be of service. He thinks that he has been badly served by his fellow plotters.''

"It had to be. Time to get under way.''

They dropped the prisoner off on a tiny uninhabited spit of land two miles from the coast. They provided him with enough drinking water for two days, some of the fish the family had caught and a hook and line. "Heavy as this sonofabitch is,'' Jim had said, "I don't think it'll hurt him too much to go without a meal or two.'' The plan was to notify the temple in a couple of days where to find him. After it was all over.

The monk went over the side happily, glad to be out of the reach of the crazy American. He had not expected to survive. He thought he would stick to religious matters from now on.

A couple of hours later they were again chugging up the Perfume River. "May I accompany you?'' asked Tu.

"No, my friend, this is one I must do alone. No matter what happens, I will be leaving you after it is finished. You must stay here and live with the consequences. It will be easier if it is regarded as the work of a lone man. Besides, you have your own mission to take care of.''

"I think,'' said Tu, "that after I perform that, it will be time to take my cousin up on his offer, and go to France to help him with his restaurant. I need a rest. I have been fighting for over twenty years.''

"Good idea. We make it through this, anything I can do to help you, let me know.''

"We will make it through, *mon capitaine*. Luck rides with you. You will always survive.''

Jim shivered. "Yeah. I've been told that. Like the fucking Ancient Mariner. Not sure the world wouldn't be better off without me, but too late to worry about that.''

ONCE again creeping through darkened rooms. Slowly and softly moving, no maps or sketches to help this time. Not as much to worry about here, the target and his guards aren't here yet. Just an old houseboy who was easy enough to subdue and leave, taped up, inside a wardrobe. He'd gone to the office first to make sure everyone was still there. The place was a hive of activity. Still running the search for me, I suppose. But the target would not be up all night.

It was not his style. Into the bedroom, take a seat beside the bed. The colonel lived well. The furniture was old, obviously expensive. Some of it, he felt certain, had come out of the old Imperial Palace. He was sure the colonel, if asked, would make the excuse that he was saving it from further damage. There was a bottle of Scotch on a silver tray beside the bed, Chivas Regal. Not my favorite, but what the hell? A little shot won't hurt. Been a long time since I've had a drink. Know what? Hasn't been all that bad. Wonder how much of my life I've fucked up because I was too drunk to know better. How many decisions I thought I made, but were actually being made by the other person who resides inside me. He put the bottle back, unopened.

He heard the jeep pull up outside. Footsteps on the marble floors, two sets. One bodyguard, a better situation than expected. He cocked the pistol, a Ruger .22 with silenced barrel, got down behind the bed and laid it across the mattress. The door opened, flooding the room with light. The guard had only a fraction of a second to see him, start to reach for a holstered gun. Bad move, asshole, he thought, squeezing the trigger. A tiny red hole appeared between the man's eyes.

"Don't even think about running, Colonel," he hissed. "I'll drop you before you get an inch. Come on in here and close the door. Then drop that little gun you carry on the table."

"You are an idiot," the province chief said as Jim taped his arms to the chair. "Everyone in the province is looking for you. You will be dead within hours."

"Which means that I'll probably survive you by at least half that time," replied Jim.

"What do you hope to accomplish by this?"

"Not much," he admitted. "Maybe find out a few things. Maybe not. I know most of it already. Maybe I'll just shoot you now and get it over with."

"Wait! There are things you don't know. You cannot know them. Let me live. I will tell you."

"Things like Eliot Danforth being in on this? Is that what you want to tell me? Not good enough." Jim ostentatiously checked the chamber of the Ruger, though he knew a fresh round was already seated there.

"You know it, but do you have proof?" the colonel protested. "Only the word of unreliable witnesses. I have better." He was beginning to sweat profusely. He had no doubt the young madman intended to kill him. His only hope lay in delaying it long enough. Perhaps someone would notice that he had not called in to inquire as to progress in the search for the American.

"Oh? Tell me more."

"I have tapes," he said. "In my office. I taped every conversation I had with the Americans. From the earliest days, when Danforth first came to me with the plan. To the last, today, when the woman directed that you be killed."

Jim did not allow the surprise to appear on his face. "Still not good enough," he said. He pointed the gun at the colonel's left eye.

"Wait! There is money, much money. You can have it, all of it. We can leave here, go to Hong Kong. The bank will release it to you if I say so."

"That's what it was all about for you, wasn't it? The money. You ordered Vanh's death, didn't you?"

"You already know that."

"Yeah, but I want to hear it from your lips."

"Yes! Of course I did. He knew too much, and I knew that he would not go along with it. He thought of himself as a patriot!" The word, from his lips, dripped with contempt.

"Is that so wrong?"

"It is foolish. It is not enough to die for."

"So it is better to die for what you did?" Jim took the T-bar from his pocket, drove it forward in an uppercut, jamming it underneath the colonel's nose, up into the brain. The cross-eyed look frozen on his face was almost comical. Jim didn't feel like laughing. He left the instrument where it was and departed as quietly as he had come.

Early in the morning, after the staff departed the Province Headquarters, he broke in. After only a little searching he found the tapes.

COPELY was roughly shaken awake. "Captain Carmichael!" he said. "What . . . Where . . . We've been hearing all sorts of strange stories. What the hell is going on?"

"I've got something I think you ought to listen to," the

shadowy figure said. "I think you'll find it interesting. If you want to talk to me later, I'll be at the PRU compound."

"GOD damn, Jimmy," said Al. "You be in a heap of shit, boy."

"Guess I shouldn't be surprised to find you here. Roger send you?"

"Uh-huh. He thought you might be needing some help about now. Looks like to me a whole bunch of other people might be the ones needing the help. Though I guess there's no helping them now. You've been very thorough, my man."

"You talk to Copely?"

"Yeah. He's about to shit himself. Put Moira Culpepper under arrest. They're shipping her out this afternoon."

"What about Danforth?"

"Took the 'gentleman's way out.' I can just see some of these Agency types, seen too many movies, I think. Probably talked to him, left him a gun, told him they'd come back later."

"You think it was just him?"

"Shit, I don't know. I'm just a simple soldier, remember? I'll leave the big picture to people like you, want to save the world. Roger tells me he thinks that was the case, though. Danforth found out about the movement, figured if he could use it to end the war, it would do a hell of a lot of good for his career. He'd be a real hero, become DCI, go into politics. Roger says he always was too ambitious for his own good."

"What are they going to do about Culpepper?"

"They've been trying to figure that one out for the last couple of days. They're trying to keep a lid on this thing. Wouldn't do for the government in Saigon to find out that one of their American allies was ready to sell them down the river. She keeps her mouth shut, she may be allowed to resign. She doesn't, I imagine she may be seeing the inside of a jail cell. If she doesn't have an accident before that."

"And what about me?"

"You, my good friend, are going to have a short tour. Orders already been cut. You're going back to the States for early attendance at the Infantry Officers Advanced Course at Fort Benning. Needs of the army, and all that shit, you know. Then you're going to get a nice tour in Germany."

"And suppose I don't want to go back?"

"You don't seem to understand, *mon frère*. That's not your call to make. You got more enemies than Dick Nixon. All the Buddhists are still pissed at you. We got the P.C.'s people calmed down, mainly because your man Tu went to the second-in-command and told him the story. He realized the colonel had put a bum rap on you. But there's still the little matter of the price on your head, which, in case you hadn't heard, has been doubled. And finally, the boys in Saigon would feel a lot better if you weren't around to talk too much about this either. I'm here to escort you to Danang, where you'll get on the next thing smoking back to the land of the round-eyes, and I'm not to let you out of my sight. Else Roger has threatened to cut my balls off. And I think he would too. So you can go easy, or you can go hard."

"Al, on your best day you couldn't make me do anything."

"Want to bet, you big skinny motherfucker?"

Jim looked at his friend, speculatively. Jesus, why have I never noticed his arms are as big around as my thighs? "Ah, fuck it," he said. "I was getting tired of this place anyway. Goddamn war isn't fun anymore. What are you going to do?"

"Serve out my tour. Get drunk occasionally. Go on as many R&Rs as I can get away with. Try to stay alive. The usual shit. Way I hear it, my tour may not be too long either. Roger tells me that Senator J. William Halfbright is making a lot of noise about us conducting an assassination program. Word is, we all may be thrown out of country. Then the Viets will kill every-fucking-body they catch, instead of just most of them."

"And then?"

"Then I'll probably see you at Benning. Got to get my ticket punched too. This thing isn't going to last forever. God, I'm not looking forward to the peacetime army. I think I've probably forgotten how to shine boots."

"You ever thought of just giving it up?"

"Yeah. Thought about it. For about ten seconds. What the hell would I do? Other than maybe in the Mafia, there isn't too much call for my peculiar skills in the civilian world."

"You could go to school. G.I. Bill."

"Can you see me as a college student? Among all those

little draft-dodging cocksuckers? I'd be in jail for wringing a couple of necks before the first semester was out.''

''You paint a pretty bleak picture. Shit, I never expected to survive this thing. Now I'm gonna have to figure out what to do with the rest of my life.''

''One thing you can do, Roger asked me to tell you, was keep an open mind about doing a little work for the Agency, off and on. As he puts it, 'You have developed some unique skills which may very well be of use to us now and again.' ''

''Christ, isn't that something to look forward to? Like a dose of clap.''

''Yeah, well, you'd have to be the one to be the judge of that. I got no experience in that area, bein' the foine Irish Catholic lad I am. Faith and begorra. And all that shit.''

''You are such a lying asshole. Okay. When do we leave?''

''Couple a hours. We got a special flight for you. Unless you want to leave on the same plane as your girlfriend.''

''You are a slime-sucking pig. And if I didn't love you, I'd shoot your ass.''

''God, I love it when you talk dirty. Want a drink?''

AL was very surprised when, at the bar of the nearby MACV compound, Jim ordered a Coke. ''Damn, boy,'' he said after taking a long pull of his beer, ''you have been through a hard time. You're not going to get holy on me, are you?''

Jim shook his head. ''Just don't feel like drinking right now. I get drunk, I'd probably be maudlin. Cry on your shoulder. Start talking about what a worthless asshole I was.''

''And I'd probably agree with you. I'm very qualified to talk about worthless assholes, you know. Enough people have called me that.''

''At least you're not jinxed.''

''Oh, come off it,'' Al said. ''I know what you think. And you're full of shit. People die. All the time. You've had the bad luck to be around a lot of them. Most people go through their entire life without having to see anybody die, except from old age. Not that way for you and me. You watch people get hit, you start to think too much about it. You start to think, Why not me? Is it my fault? Am I doing something wrong? Or am I just bad luck? You think I haven't had thoughts like that? They're bullshit! And I don't want to hear any more about it. Or I might just beat the shit out of you yet.''

''Well, tell me something else, Mr. Deep Thinker. What about what these guys were trying to do. Would it have worked? Would it have ended the war? Maybe I fucked up.''

''I was wondering when you'd get around to that one. Barkeep! Another beer for me and a soft drink for my fairy friend. Roger says no. Says there's been talk in the High Command in Hanoi for some time about a new tactic to shorten the war. But their man up there couldn't find out what it was. They kept that tighter'n a nun's box. All he did know was it was supposed to get the Americans out. Then the NVA was going to mass troops, tanks, artillery, a regular fucking invasion, at the border. They'da gone through the South like a dose of salts. So looks like you set that one back a little bit. You're a regular fucking hero! Not that anybody will ever know about it. Roger told me to tell you that you'll have to sign a nondisclosure statement before you leave. Something like if you ever breathe a word of this, they'll find a real good assignment for you in Leavenworth.''

''That's a relief. I guess. Who says you can't change things?''

''Yeah, you've changed a lot. Which, we suspect, has made you a very unpopular boy in Hanoi. Best thing for you is get on the other side of the world, real quick. Oh, and by the way. Roger also told me to tell you that you're going to get another Silver Star. My, my, won't you look pretty!''

Billy Martinez, the Special Police advisor, saw them sitting at the bar, came over. ''I hear you're leaving, Jim,'' he said. ''Real sorry to hear that. You sure made life interesting around here. Couple days ago my troops got the word to shoot you on sight. Then it was rescinded a few hours later. You want to tell me what the fuck was going on?''

'' 'Fraid not. You wouldn't believe it anyway.''

''Well, shit. Ain't that the way everything goes on around here? So many secrets sometimes I don't know if I'm tellin' the truth to myself. The mushroom theory. Keep 'em in the dark and feed 'em horseshit. When you leaving?''

'' 'Bout thirty minutes,'' interjected Al. ''You drink beer?

Siddown, I'll buy you one. I hear you're a pretty good shot with an M-16.''

THE bar boy doubled over in pain. Told the bartender he had diarrhea, had to go. When he cleared the place, his pain magically went away. He started to run.

CHAPTER 17

"HEY, Billy," Al said to his newfound friend, "you could do us a real big favor."

"Why does my asshole pucker when I hear you say that?" replied the police advisor. "Last favor I did was back on the force in L.A., took a guy's shift for him. Later that night we had to respond to a small civil disturbance. Watts."

"This one's easy. We got to go to the airfield, and I've got the POIC's jeep. I could just leave it out there, let them pick it up later, but what the hell, you could ride out with us and bring it back. I'll get us a couple a beers to go."

Billy considered it for a moment, didn't see anything wrong with the idea. He was enjoying the company, especially Al. Jim seemed a little taciturn, but he ascribed that to the fact that he wasn't drinking. In his opinion, there wasn't anything so bad that a drink or two wouldn't make better. "Sure," he said. "Why not?"

"Attaboy," Al said in his best W. C. Fields imitation. "Stick with me, son, you'll have diamonds on your cuffs big as golf balls. So many medals they won't be able to close your casket."

"I'll leave the medals to you heroes," he said as they walked, six-pack in hand, to the jeep. "Me, all I want to do is finish this contract and get back to good old LAPD. Where I'll never complain about anything again. Christ, I didn't realize what a good life I had! Gettin' shot at maybe once a month instead of once a day. Goin' out with rookies who, though they may not have been too smart, you could be pretty sure they were on the same side you were."

They got in the jeep, Billy refusing the front seat. "You get the place of honor," he told Jim. "Us beaners don't mind riding in the back. Hell, we're used to it."

"I thought the POIC's jeep had a top on it," Jim said to Al.

"It did. I got rid of it. Anybody stupid enough to be riding around this country with a top on the jeep is just too stupid to live. So, Billy," he said as he started the vehicle, "what chance do you think I'd have if I was to apply for a job with the force?"

"Don't know," Billy admitted. He opened one of the beers, gave it to Al, offered another to Jim, who refused. "The department has all kinds of stupid rules. Education requirements, age limitations, height and weight restrictions, that kind of shit. Don't matter what you might know, how much experience you could bring to the job. I've heard a lot of cops say they'd rather have someone completely green. That way they don't have to unlearn a lot of bad habits."

"See what I'm saying, Jimmy," Al said. "We don't have a hell of a lot of career choices. Peacetime army, here we come. Ready or not. Somehow I think they're not going to be."

"Hey," he said moments later, after they pulled out onto the road. "Looks like we've got company. Some of your PRU want to say goodbye."

Jim looked around, saw that a jeepload of PRU, including Tu, had pulled in behind them. He was glad. It had seemed so anticlimactic, leaving without saying anything to anyone. He reminded himself to try to get the address of Tu's cousin. If he was going to have to go to Germany, perhaps he would be able to get over to Paris for a visit.

On the way to the airfield he soaked up last impressions, letting the activity of the city imprint itself upon his brain. They went over the bridge, Billy pointing out the fresh bullet scars from his M-16. Soon they would blend with all the others. Past Chandragar's shop. Wonder how he'll get along with the new advisor? One thing I know for sure is that he'll survive. The old imperial city came up on the right, scarred and torn from the battle. As nearly destroyed as it was, it still held a certain sense of majesty. On through the shanty village which had sprung up on the other side, hundreds of refugees living in conditions little better than that of animals. But it was preferable to the slaughter that went on in the countryside.

They seemed happy enough. The old men squatted beside the huts, talking about God knows what. The children, in the way of children all over the world, played in the dusty street, inventing games in which the rules changed by the moment.

Usually, that is. Today the street was deserted. No sign of anyone. "Al!" he yelled, flipping the safety off on his M-16. "Ambush!"

THE V.C. commander had been cursing his luck. He'd been far too rushed, after he got the word that his target was coming, to set up a proper ambush. Time only to set up a rough L-shape, with the RPD machine gun on the short leg, where the road made a sharp curve. The other members of his squad were deployed on the long leg, taking as much cover as possible in the flimsy huts. No time to place any mines, emplant claymores. He was not satisfied at all; still, he had set up many ambushes in even worse conditions and they had been successful. No choice anyway. It was this shot or none.

He had been shocked to hear, after the long trip north specifically to hit this one target, that the target would soon be irrevocably out of reach. It had been a long, hard trip. He hoped it was worth it, though he did not see how it could be. Out of the eighteen men he had started with, only twelve remained. Of his losses, one had succumbed to malaria, two had been killed by the random bombing that went on incessantly up and down the trail and another three had been lost when they themselves were ambushed by one of the accursed teams the Americans were using in the rear areas. When this was over, he intended to write a scathing report to COSVN, to the effect that if they could not protect their own rear areas, what use was it to have all those North Vietnamese security troops? Better to send them into the South to fight against the Main Force American and South Vietnamese units, and give the mission of protecting the rear area to units such as his. Who would stalk and be stalked, man against man, team against team, in a very close and personal war.

The target came in sight. Three Americans in the jeep. Good. Another jeep following a hundred yards behind. His agent had not warned him about that! Still, it should provide no real problem. Plenty of room to get them both in the kill zone. A few more seconds, when the first jeep was within twenty-five yards of the machine gun. He placed his hand on the gunner's shoulder, ready to give the signal.

Then watched, frustrated, as the first jeep slewed broadside, tires skidding in the soft dirt, sending up rooster tails as they spun. "Fire!" he screamed. "Fire!"

"Noooo," he was moaning as the first rounds smacked into the jeep. It was all a bad dream, one he'd had so many times. The deserted street, the sense of foreboding, the threat weighing so heavily it was palpable, the feeling that he had come here, finally, to die. The muzzle flashes were everywhere, rounds snapping around him in a continuous song. He was returning fire, pouring magazine after magazine at the unseen enemy, but it was as if the bullets were disappearing.

Al wrenched the wheel back and forth, zagging the jeep all over the road. A burst came through the windshield, showering them both with glass. He heard a cry from the backseat, risked looking back, saw Billy looking in horror at a shattered arm from which the blood pumped in heavy dark jets.

It's happening again, it's happening again. My God, it's happening again.

Al let out a great whoosh of air as a bullet slammed into his stomach, causing him to slump over the steering wheel. The jeep slowed momentarily as his foot came off the accelerator, then jumped forward again as, ignoring the pain, he pressed it to the floor.

"Gonna . . . hit 'em . . . Jimmy," he grunted, steering the vehicle toward the nearest hut. "Get . . . down."

The jeep smashed through the bamboo hut like it was made of paper, shattering the cheap furniture and two men who had been sheltering behind it. Another got up to run and Jim zippered him from pelvis to head.

Al slumped over the wheel. Bullets were starting to come through the sides of the shattered hut. Jim took only enough time to reload, then pulled his heavy friend from the vehicle and dragged him forward where the tire and wheel gave cover from at least one direction. Scurried back and pulled an unconscious Martinez from the rear. The blood was still pumping, though not as strongly as before. He pulled a cravat bandage from a pouch on his belt, wrapped it quickly above the wound, inserted a small piece of wood and twisted the fabric tight. The bleeding slowed to a soft ooze. It was obvious the man was in shock; not too much he could do about that now.

"Jimmy," whispered Al, "get the fuck out of here. Save yourself."

Tears were streaming down Jim's face. "I thought you were dead, you sonofabitch, I thought you were dead. Don't you die on me, you bastard."

Al managed a smile. "Don't make me start laughing, you asshole," he said. "My belly hurts too much."

"Boy, do you look like shit." Al's face was cut in several places from the glass. A large gash had been opened in his forehead when he impacted against the steering wheel, blood flowing freely from it. He took a pressure bandage and covered the wound, tying the tails around his friend's head, cradling it in his lap.

"Don't put the motherfucker around my eyes! And get my gun. They're gonna be in here in a minute or two. I'll cover for you, try to hold 'em off. You get out of here and get some help."

"Not this time, my friend. Not this time." Jim felt as if a great weight had been lifted from him. "This time, I don't leave anyone behind."

IT was going very badly wrong. He was almost sure the Americans had been wounded before they hit the hut, but that wasn't good enough. His superiors had been very insistent that he had to make sure this particular one was dead. He took stock of the situation. His troops were now separated: himself, the machine gunner and four others on one side of the shattered hut, three more to the other side. He had to assume that the men inside the hut were out of action.

The three on the other end were at least pinning down the PRU men from the other jeep. He made a quick tactical decision. "Stay here and give us covering fire," he told the machine gunner. "I'm going to take the others and assault. We'll finish them off, then get out. Cover our retreat."

The gunner signaled his understanding, sighted down the gun and sent another burst into the hut. Good man, the com-

mander thought. They had been together almost from the beginning. Owed one another their lives on too many occasions
to count. He would remain here and cover them, even if it
cost him his own life. With enough men like this, the V.C.
thought, I could rule the world. There had been many like
him, once. But they had all died.

Out of the hut, using all available cover and concealment.
A few scattered bullets came his way, but for the most part
the PRU soldiers were more concerned with the men pinning
them down. Into the next hut, where his four men lay.
"Come," he said. "Let us finish this."

"THEY'RE gonna come from this side," Jim said.
"I think the ones on the other side are too busy to bother
us." He had cleared just enough of the debris away to give
them reasonable fields of fire, had pulled what remained of a
teak table to their front to give a little bit of cover. It wasn't
much, but it would have to do.

Billy, who was intermittently conscious, moaned in pain.
Wish I had some morphine, Jim thought. Though I don't
think any of us are going to feel much pain pretty soon.

It comes to this, he thought. He felt curiously happy. No
more dreams, no more running away, no more worries. This
is where I was meant to be. This is the way it started, this is
the way it will end. Once again he checked magazines. Plenty
of ammunition. The pistol was close at hand, its checkered
grip gleaming beautiful and smooth in the dim light.

"Jimmy," croaked Al, "I don't suppose you've got any
water in your little bag of tricks, do you?"

"You know better than that. Gut-shot people can't have
water. Washes all the nasties into the belly cavity, sets up a
hell of a case of peritonitis."

Al grinned. "Medic until the last, ain't you? It ever occur
to you that I'm not going to have to worry about peritonitis?"

"We ain't dead yet, buddy. Don't you believe in mira-
cles?"

"Not since I quit being an altar boy. Do you?"

"No," he admitted. "But I could be wrong too. Shit, here
they come!"

They were good. They used every bit of cover and concealment, moving forward in short rushes, the others cover-

ing with well-aimed semiautomatic fire that came uncomfortably close. It would have come a lot closer, he knew, had they known exactly where to shoot. He and Al held their fire; the targets disappeared too quickly for it to have done any good, and the muzzle flashes would have given their position away. He counted five of them. Plus another one or two with the machine gun giving covering fire. Not good odds. But the feeling of peace would not go away. He turned to Al, smiled. "How you doin', buddy?" he asked.

"Other than being gut-shot, not too bad." Al returned the smile. "We be in deep shit, you know."

"I figure if we can hold them off for just a little while, maybe it'll give the PRU enough time to get to us. Sounds like they're doin' okay." The firefight to their other side had tapered off somewhat, with the heavy thud of AK-47s sounding less and less often against the higher-pitched crack of the M-16s.

"Yeah, and maybe God'll strike these guys by lightning. Watch it!" A stick grenade landed several feet in front of them, the crude fuse smoking. They had just enough time to take shelter behind the table before it exploded, sending heavy pieces of shrapnel thudding into the wood.

Jim peeked back around. Dust and smoke obscured his view, but not so badly that he could not see the man rushing the last few feet toward them. Before he could fire, Al's M-16 spoke, sending the man backward in a flurry of blood and shattered flesh.

That was the sacrifice, he thought. Now they know exactly where we are. As if in answer, the firing grew much more heavy and exact. The rounds thunked into the table, exited whining in a burst of wood from the other side. For some reason they were still firing a little high. They'd correct that in a moment, he knew. The machine gun was getting the range, the gunner walking the rounds ever more close.

IN the other hut Tu belatedly remembered that there was an M-66 light antitank weapon in the jeep. "Cover me!" he yelled to the others as he scurried to get it. The V.C. fired a few rounds at him, but they went wild. Tu did not even bother to duck. He grabbed the fat tube, trying to remember the exact firing sequence. Press the indents, pull both ends, the launcher extending to almost twice its original length. The sights popped up, cheap clear plastic with stadia lines meant for estimating distances. Pull out the safety, ready to fire. Automatically he looked behind him to see that the back-blast area was clear. Sighted directly at the hut from which the machine-gun fire was coming, gently squeezed the rubber pad with the trigger underneath. The rocket was away with a great *whoosh*, coughing up a great dust cloud around him. Straight and true it flew, exploding just as it hit the barrel of the gun. The resulting shaped charge, thin as a pencil, thousands of degrees hot, needled straight through the gun, carrying the molten metal with it as it struck the man behind. Intended for use against tanks, though as the Special Forces soldiers at Lang Vei were to find out months later it wasn't particularly good against them, it was extremely effective against unprotected targets such as this. The man became fused to his gun, pieces of it sticking out of him at odd angles, so that you could not tell where man stopped and gun began. Tu wished he had another to fire at the man who was keeping them from going and helping the Americans. If they did not get there soon, he was afraid it would do no good to get there at all. He used the jeep to shield himself as he crawled around to the side. Perhaps he could get a better angle of fire from there.

As the hut with the machine gunner blew up, Jim saw his chance. Hoping that it had distracted his opponents for just a couple of seconds, he rolled away from the table, scurrying to the back side of the hut. Al gave him an ironic little salute, then started firing burst after burst into the spot where he had last seen a man disappear. Come on, mother-fuckers, he was yelling, show yourselves!

Jim looked back one last time at his friend, the bullets striking all around him, said goodbye in his mind. He burst from the hut, sprinted to the next one, smashing through the flimsy door and rolling. No firing had followed him. For the first time he allowed himself a little hope. Took the chance and peered up over the windowsill. They were still pouring the bullets into the hut he had left. As he watched, another grenade arched over a mound of dirt and exploded in almost the same place as the last. He ran out of the hut, into another, finger tightening on the trigger as he saw life. No, not enemy, don't shoot. The family cowered together in a corner, looking at him in terror, seeing death only a couple of pounds of trigger pressure away. "Stay!" he commanded in Vietnamese, again looking out the window. There the sonofabitch was, the one who was throwing the grenades. He was just now pulling the fuse on another. Snap shot, just like they taught in the Quick Kill course, stock of the M-16 just kissing his cheek, both eyes open, no time to take a sight picture, pull the trigger. Watch the man's head dissolve in a spray of blood, the grenade falling at his feet. Away again, in another hut before he heard it go off. Where were the rest of them? They had to be within a few meters of Al, but he couldn't even see the muzzle flashes from here. Wait a minute! Was that a foot? He sighted very carefully, aligning the front post directly in the center of the rear peep sight. Take a deep breath, let it halfway out, squeeeeeze the trigger. The weapon bucked in his hand, and he was rewarded with a howl of anguish clear even over the gunfire. There was a bloody spot where the foot had been. He moved again, trying to get another clear shot.

THE V.C. commander was having serious second thoughts as to the wisdom of his action. The target was almost within grasp, but he was losing too many people. His practiced ear told him that the men on the other side of the hut were fighting a losing battle. The machine gunner was gone, the hut he had been in blazing fiercely. And now his right-flank man had apparently blown himself up. Why couldn't their socialist brethren in China make decent grenades? All too many of them went off in the hands of the people trying to use them. All or nothing now. He signaled the two remaining men to get ready to rush. Heard the cry of anguish from one, saw him cradling a shattered foot. Enough! He knew when it was time to break off. The mission was a failure, but it would be a worse failure if he were killed. It was a strange feeling, defeat. But there would be other chances. Other hunts, other ambushes. He leaned over the wounded man. "Comrade," he whispered, "we must go. Can you hold them?"

"*Ya phai*, Dai Uy," he said. Yes. A look of resolution was

set on his face. The commander gave him two of his own magazines, and one of the two pistols he carried. They would not take this one alive.

He signaled the direction he wished the other man to go, gave him a nudge. The man took off, staying low and zig-zagging. The captain waited until he had drawn the fire of the man still in the hut and took off in the other direction. They would meet later at the rally point, if both were still alive.

JESUS! was all he had time to think as the man burst from cover and ran almost directly past him. He fired a short burst, cursed as he saw the bullets strike behind the running figure. Lead him, you asshole! he thought furiously. He aimed again, this time a foot in front of where he judged the man's belt buckle to be, fired a longer burst. The man ran into them, the little lead pellets cutting him almost in two. He flopped down, then started trying to crawl, his lower body dragging uselessly behind him. Jim took very careful aim and shot the man through the head. *No more suffering, not even for you.*

He saw the other one running away in the opposite direction. *No, you sonofabitch, it's not going to be that easy, not now, not ever. You'll never stand over me again in my dreams, you'll never look at me with those dead eyes as you pull the trigger, no way.*

He was out of the house and running, paying no attention to the bullets which followed him, striking all around his feet, snapping through the air, hitting the ground and whining off with angry moans. *Nothing could hit him, not now. He was invincible! The bullets would not kill him, he could not be killed,* not by anyone except the man he was chasing into the faraway tree line.

THE motherfucker's gone crazy, Al thought as he saw Jim running. He concentrated his fire at the man who was shooting at his friend, ignoring the pain eating its way through his bowels, was rewarded when the firing again came at him. *You and me, motherfucker,* he told his unseen antagonist, *just you and me. Leave those other two alone, this is just between us.*

• • •

RUNNING on, neither gaining nor losing. He thought about stopping for a few seconds, trying to get a clear shot. No. It needed to be closer. I need to see his face. Each step was agony. Can't stop, he must be as tired as I am, staggering now, but still running. The tree line, a thin stand of coconut palms, not so far away now. That's where it will be. Ignore the pain in your chest, the great heaving breaths, the legs that feel like pig iron. Keep running, not too far now.

He saw the man reach the poor cover of the trees, flop down, jam a fresh magazine into the AK. He became aware that he was laughing. The bullets whined around him once again, missing him by fractions, but missing. They could not hit him, not yet. He fired a burst at the muzzle flashes, saw the bullets stir up dust all around, knew that just as the man could not hit him, neither would his bullets find their mark. But the gun felt good, bucking in his hands; no need to run now, load another magazine and fire again, keep walking forward, I want to see his face.

The man threw down his obviously empty rifle, stood up. He pulled a shiny pistol from his belt. ''Yes!'' Jim yelled, dropping the empty M-16. He pulled out the Browning.

They faced one another from little more than twenty paces. A duel, he thought. It had to come to this. They looked each other in the eyes, the big Vietnamese's mouth finally curling into a smile, his gold tooth shining in the sunlight. Jim's smile disappeared, he felt his arm jerk as of its own volition the pistol spoke. Saw the smoke coming from the muzzle of the other gun, heard its heavy bark, wondered why the round had not hit him, it was so close, how could he miss? Again and again they fired, the rounds passing in the air, some plucking at clothing, others missing cleanly. A hail of death all around on this bright summer day, and it was passing them by.

WHO was this maniac? He felt fear like tiny rats eating at his guts. The last rounds rattled out of his rifle. Too late he wished he had kept the two magazines he had given to the man who stayed behind. He pulled the pistol from his belt, his favorite one, the one which had served him so well, had killed so many vanquished enemy. The heavy weight of it was a comfort in his hand. He stood up, facing his tormentor. He sighted carefully, the shiny pistol glinting in the sun. Saw the smoke coming from the barrel, obscuring the paddies, the peasants watching from a distance, the beautiful green of his homeland, the weapon bucking again and again. He heard the hammer click on an empty chamber, found himself still pulling the trigger uselessly. Relentlessly the American came on. He dropped the revolver, pulled the knife from its sheath, stood there waiting, his opponent only feet away. Gave himself over to death.

SIX rounds to fourteen, he thought inanely. Automatic against revolver. Doesn't seem fair somehow. Too bad. You lose. No more of your face in my dreams. No more struggling to get away. Die now.

The man jerked, but kept his feet as the bullet hit him squarely in the chest. Jim fired again and again, the body soaking up the bullets, Good God, is this a dream again, will he never drop, why isn't he falling, you've got to die, you've got to die!

Slowly crumpling now, sliding down the tree which had propped him up, life leaving his eyes forever. He picked up the revolver where the man had dropped it. The shiny chrome had worn away in years of hard use, but the inscription was still clear.

Presented to Captain James Mosely, December 1962.

He started the long walk back.

"YOU okay?" Al asked as he was loaded on the stretcher.

"Very much so. Looks like your war is over too."

"Could be," said Al. He grimaced in pain. "These assholes won't give me any morphine either. What does a guy have to do to get some good drugs around here? You gave that crazy Mexican some," he said accusingly.

The corpsman, who had been taking Al's blood pressure, said to Jim, "Looks good. Don't see how a bullet that keyholed like that and went all the way through could have missed all the major blood vessels, but it did. Course, he has a lot more belly than most, so it had more room."

"Fuckin' comedians everywhere," groaned Al. "You plannin' on playin' Vegas next?"

"How is Billy?" Jim asked.

"He'll make it. Lost a lot of blood, and his arm isn't going to be much good, but he'll make it."

They loaded Al on the ambulance. "See you in Benning," he was saying as they closed the door.

Yeah, he thought, I guess you will.

CHAPTER 18

THE tall thin captain sat in the waiting area at San Francisco International Airport, staring at nothing at all. People came and went, some of them glancing at the rows of ribbons pinned to his chest, the jaunty green beret tipped over his forehead. Others pointedly ignored him. Still others scowled, angry to see one of the baby-killing warmongers sitting so brazenly here in the open.

Dennis Fulbright was one of the latter. A full-time student at Berkeley for over six years now, he felt no shame at using his parents' meager funds to stay out of a war which he felt to be immoral, illegal and downright dangerous to your health. He'd changed majors a number of times, was now working on physical education. It suited him. His body was of the makeup to respond well to the hours of weight training, increasing the girth of biceps and chest by several inches each. He was young enough that the nights of debauchery with the free-loving girls and the drugs in the Haight didn't have much effect on him. The few fights he had been in with people generally much smaller and weaker than he convinced him that he was invincible.

He approached the pig, thinking that it would be amusing to roust him. Inflated his chest, tensed his back, making the deltoid muscles atop his shoulders form a V. He fondly liked to think it made him look like a cobra. Stood directly in front of the man, who continued to stare straight ahead.

"Hey," he husked from deep in his chest, deepening his voice to mask the fact that it was still, to him, annoyingly and unexplainably high. "Green Beret!"

Still no reaction from the man. He wondered if he was drunk. So much the better. "Big, badass Green Beret," he tried again. "You ain't shit. Supposed to know a hundred and one ways to kill a guy. Bullshit! Baby killer, warmonger, murderer! A hundred and one ways to kill a man, my ass!''

Slowly the man looked up at him, his eyes focusing at last. Stared him directly in the face. There was something there, something in those eyes that chilled him to the bone. Ghosts, perhaps, the souls of hundreds, thousands, staring at him from the light blue eyes, sucking him in, beckoning him to join them.

The man stood up, smiled slightly, finally spoke. ''Pick a number, motherfucker,'' he said.

He turned away quickly, moving through the crowd and hoping that no one he knew had seen him. Resolving that if that bitch he was seeing from the sociology class gave him any more crap tonight, he was going to beat the shit out of her.

Behind him the captain sat back down, resumed his vacant-eyed stare. Hours yet before the flight to Atlanta. He'd debated going and seeing Lisa, decided that it would have been too painful for them both. Thought about going to the airport bar, decided that he couldn't be bothered. So he sat in the hard plastic seat and let the world move around him.

It gave him time to think. To try and decide what he was going to do now. It was a novel feeling. He had never expected to live this long. Now it looked as if, barring accidents, he had a lot longer to go. Was astonished to realize how much he had depended on the war to keep him from having to make decisions. Now that war was no longer available to him, never would be. He would never be going back. He was suffused with a strange sense of loss.

What you gonna do now, Jimmy boy? he reflected, somewhat amused in spite of himself. What are you going to do with the rest of your life?